AMELIA'S ECHOES

H S SKINNER

For all my friends and family, and anyone who's ever survived a hurricane—
real or manmade.
Surviving a storm, whether it's emotional trauma or something wicked nature
throws at us, takes immense courage and fortitude.
Surviving it with grace, an overwhelming willingness to help others, and an
unshakeable belief in the ultimate goodness of our fellow man is what makes
us wonderful human beings.
We have all that in spades.

PROLOGUE

*D*oc Mason stood in the doorway of the hospital room—a room filled to overflowing with flowers. Thought of the waiting room he'd just left—a room just as full of people as this room was of blooms—people as well as blooms of every color and description. Only one person—a most important person—was missing to complete the circle of close family and friends—Jeff.

Doc's eyes met Del's and he eavesdropped shamelessly as she spoke to her grandson.

"Charlie Bear, Jeff just called. He's on his way."

Charlie didn't even take his eyes off the still form in front of him. "Thanks, Grandy. Did you hear that, Jennilee? Jeff will be here soon."

Doc's gaze focused on the couple inside, one in the bed and one beside it—Charlie and Jennilee. Impossible to think of one without the other, they were close, closer than any humans he'd ever seen, had been since they were born. He should know—he'd been there when they were born twenty years ago, had watched them grow, and he definitely did not want to be anywhere around when either left this world. Neither would make it without the other.

It sounded so cliché to say that, but for Charlie and Jennilee it was true.

1

Charlie and Jennilee had finally reached their goal—they were married, they owned the house of their dreams, they were well on their way to having everything they'd ever wanted, and now this. Sometimes, life sucked.

Charlie sat in the same spot he'd been in for the last couple of days. Beside Jennilee's bed, her hand in his, crooning softly, constantly. Doc shifted a bit nearer so he could catch Charlie's fervent whispers.

"Come on, Jennilee-love. Come back to me. Hear me. Hear me calling to you. You have to come back. Don't leave me here all alone. Come on, Jennilee-baby. Don't let them win. We've beaten them before, we can do it again."

Charlie's pleas nearly broke Doc's heart. After all they'd been through, it just wasn't fair. If anyone deserved better it was the physically and emotionally battered angel lying in the bed and her stalwart defender.

"Open those ocean eyes of yours and look at me." Charlie commanded. Pleaded. Cajoled. "What color are they today, Jennilee? Gray and stormy? Green and peaceful? The color I like best—a happy blue-green with just a hint of gray? Come on, Jennilee-honey. Wake up, and I'll brush your hair. Want me to sing to you some more? I can send Grandy for my guitar. I'll…light your way." Charlie's voice broke, just a smidge and he bent his head over their clasped hands.

How many times had Doc seen them just like this? Hand in hand, oblivious to the rest of the world. Charlie brushing Jennilee's spun-gold hair, singing to her, doing his utmost to protect her from the bad things in life. Jennilee grounding Charlie, giving him her total and unconditional love, both of them completing the other.

Doc cleared his throat softly. Charlie's head came up and he swiveled the least bit.

Doc urged, "Let Del or Sadie or Angel or…someone else sit with her for awhile, Charlie. Get some rest. It won't do Jennilee any good if you make yourself sick tending her." Doc knew the offer was futile even as he made it.

"I'm not leaving her. In fact, I've just decided. I'm taking her home. There's nothing else you can do for her here."

"Taking her…"

Charlie was right. There was nothing else the doctors or the hospital could do for her. Other than bruises, Jennilee just looked like she was sleeping. A sleeping princess under an evil spell—one that prevented her from waking. A kiss wasn't going to do it—Charlie had already tried numerous times. If any prince could, it was Charlie. Charlie, with his white blonde hair and dark chocolate eyes, eyes that saw only Jennilee. Charlie of the true heart with all the valor and courage, the chivalry, of a knight of old.

Even though Doc knew Charlie was talking about the antebellum mansion and grounds he and Jennilee had spent the better part of ten years lovingly restoring, he got an instant flashback to years earlier. When Charlie or Jennilee'd said *home* in that tone of voice, they'd meant Grandy's house.

Another flashback, and Doc knew exactly what part of *home* they craved. Like looking at a picture, he could clearly see the two of them as children. Charlie and Jennilee, ensconced in Grandy's handed-down-for-generations rocking chair, Jennilee in Charlie's lap, curled in a ball. Charlie, arms tight around her, rocking and singing to her in his wonderful baritone.

The rocking chair cure had worked time after time before, maybe it held one more miracle—for that's what it would take to bring Jennilee out of this and save both of them—a miracle.

That, and Jeff.

CHAPTER 1

 uly 1984

JEFF RIVENBARK DROPPED the bag containing his workout clothes and tossed his wallet and keys into the irregularly shaped bowl beside the front door. An exquisite abstract bowl carved out of a cypress stump by his best friend Charlie. A bowl that sat on an equally exquisite hall table their mutual friend and Charlie's business partner, Mose, had crafted.

Grinned as he always did at the picture sitting beside the bowl. Himself and Charlie, Jennilee sandwiched in the middle. His best friends in the whole world, they'd been still in high school when that picture'd been taken, the fall of their senior year.

Just after a football game—a hotly contested one in which Charlie'd scored the deciding touchdown in the final few seconds. Snagging the pass with his magic hands, Charlie'd ducked and dodged and run flat out most of the length of the field to score, Jeff running interference and guarding him from attack the whole way.

The win meant they were going to state playoffs. They'd celebrated on the field, after, jubilant. After the game ending whistle, with the crowd pouring out of the stands onto the field like sugar from a broken bag. All those people, and Jennilee'd homed in on Charlie like a carrier pigeon going back to its base.

Jeff and Charlie had still been pounding each other on the back, doing an exuberant victory dance with the full moon glowing like a spotlight behind them when Jennilee made her way to them. Charlie caught her up, spun them both in dizzy circles, kissed her soundly. Jeff snagged an ecstatic Jennilee from Charlie's arms to claim his hug. Charlie claimed her back, the three of them laughing and completely carefree for the moment.

They'd been standing like that, a study in happiness, arms around each other, when Mr. Matt snapped the picture. Owner/editor of their hometown paper and their good friend, he'd made sure they all got copies—in color. The same picture had made the front page of the Ridgerunner and the first page of the sports section in the Raleigh News and Observer.

Jeff and Charlie in their sweaty, grass-and-dirt stained uniforms, helmets dangling from their free hands, huge grins on both their faces. Jennilee proudly wearing Charlie's letterman jacket, Charlie's class ring very much in evidence, hanging around Jennilee's neck on a gold chain.

A study in contrasts as well. Jeff, with his nut brown hair and hazel eyes, Charlie with his white blond hair and dark chocolate eyes—the two of them stalwart defenders, bracketing Jennilee who looked, as always, like a fairy-tale princess, even in jeans and a sweater. Jennilee of the golden hair and ocean eyes.

As close to a brother and sister as Jeff would ever have, all three only children, all three had grown up in the same small southern town. Their lives had diverged after high school, but they kept in close contact.

Shaking his head at the memories, Jeff paged through the accumulation of mail that'd built up since he'd last checked his mail box. Junk, junk, and more junk. Wait! Jeff grinned as he got to the bottom of the stack.

A letter, more likely a card, and probably hand made at that. Not from Charlie or Mose—their talents lay with wood. From Jennilee—no longer merely Charlie's girlfriend or even his fiancée—now his wife. The amount of talent the three of them possessed was staggering, but Jennilee was unbelievable all by herself. Being around them was a humbling experience.

Jeff laughed out loud. He didn't have to open the card to know what it said.

Get your butt home—we miss you!

Best man in their storybook wedding a scant two months ago, Jeff hadn't been home since. Shook his head again. Jennilee was politely insistent, and once she pulled you within her range, it was like a planet holding onto its moon. She adored family, and like any good shepherd, couldn't stand to have her charges scattered. Liked them all right where she could keep her eyes and hands on them. Where she could keep them safe and well fed.

The thought of Jennilee's cooking making his mouth water, Jeff carefully opened the envelope and tugged the card out. A few well-placed strokes of blue and gold with splashes of melon and salmon depicted a beautiful watercolor of the view off Charlie and Jennilee's front porch, a watercolor done by Jennilee. The Newport River at daybreak, the sun just coming up, turning the sky and the water misty gold.

Jeff could practically hear the gulls and shorebirds, smell the salt tang, could almost feel the gentle morning breeze on his face. Charlie's and Jennilee's boat bobbed softly on its tether, coolers and fishing poles and lifejackets on the dock and waiting, everything looking so realistic he could almost reach out and touch it.

Jennilee pulled no punches! Snickering, Jeff flipped the card open. There, in Jennilee's graceful and distinctive script, five words.

WE'RE BACK, *and you promised.*

LIKE THAT FEIST dog of hers—once Jennilee got ahold of something, you could hang it up. And just like Jewel with a treat or a bone, she hung on. Just like Jewel after a squirrel or a rabbit, Jennilee could be unbelievably tenacious.

Yes, Jeff had promised to visit after they got back from their honeymoon. He hadn't given any specific time, but that wouldn't hinder Jennilee. The sooner, the better, as far as she was concerned. As much as he regarded them as his siblings, he knew they thought of him the same way.

Jennilee'd written right after they got back from their honeymoon, a long, detailed letter. She'd invited him then, but he hadn't wanted to intrude. That thought made him snort out loud, rudely and inelegantly, and laugh at the same time.

Any time you were around the two of them, you felt like you were intruding. Jeff couldn't remember a time when Charlie and Jennilee weren't so wrapped up in each other the rest of the world could have fallen away and they wouldn't have noticed.

They deserved all the happiness they could glean. Charlie and Jennilee weren't just only children, they were pretty much orphans to boot. Oh, Charlie's dad was still living, but he'd been an alcoholic for a lot of Charlie's growing up years, and Charlie'd been raised by his grandma.

Jennilee hadn't been nearly so fortunate. Charlie's mom had merely disappeared when he was four. Jennilee's mom had been brutally murdered a few months later, and Jennilee'd been raised by her sadistic aunt.

Which brought Jeff full circle. The reason he was here, spending more time with cadavers than real, live people, studying hard so he could become part of the FBI's forensic team, was because he'd been instrumental in finding Charlie's mom. Thirteen years after she disappeared, Jeff had been using his dad's metal detector, looking for Civil War relics. Instead, he'd found a set of keys, which led to the gruesome discovery of Iris Meyers' body.

Her head had been bashed in, she'd been tossed into the trunk of her car like a bag of trash, and car and all buried in an abandoned field. That smacked of not just murder, but a cold, calculating killer.

Killers—hard to believe a single person would have gone to those lengths to hide the body.

A burning desire to catch the culprits, still at large, fueled Jeff's passion for his profession. Somewhere in that trunk was a clue to Iris' murderer, and Jeff intended to find it. He could give Charlie and his dad that, at least, since he'd been the one who literally opened that particular can of worms.

Reprimanded himself silently. Enough dark humor! Most people didn't appreciate it, and he wouldn't hurt Charlie for the world. Or Jennilee. If he didn't go now, she'd just keep asking. Every time Jeff made an excuse, Jennilee'd just smile and say okay, and he'd feel like a heel for letting her down.

"Give it up, Jeff. You know you're going." His voice rang startlingly loud in the quiet of his apartment.

What was there to hold him here? School was out for the summer, he had vacation time coming from work, and his boss had been hounding Jeff to take some time off. Besides, he needed a break. Needed to talk to someone who hadn't been murdered, someone who would actually talk back and move their lips when they did it.

"You are losing it, Jeffro. It's not bad enough you talk to dead people, you talk to yourself, and that's not much better."

Dropping the junk mail in the trash can, Jeff used a magnet to stick Jennilee's latest card on the frig to join its mates. Called work, and headed for his bedroom to pack.

Opening his closet, the first thing that caught his eye was the suit he'd worn to Charlie and Jennilee's wedding. The suit Jennilee'd sewn for him. The suit that fit him better than any suit he'd ever owned.

Jennilee hadn't just made his suit, she'd made Charlie's, and Tony's. And her dress, and both bridesmaids' dresses, the miniature suit their ring bearer wore and the dresses of the flower girls as well. Jeff had almost laughed out loud at the look on Charlie's face when he saw Jennilee in her wedding dress for the first time. Talk about shock and awe! 'Course, it was hard to laugh with your jaw hitting the ground.

Throwing jeans and T shirts, shorts and socks and underwear and his toiletries into a duffle, Jeff thought about one of the bridesmaids in particular. Rachel was married, but not Angel. Charlie'd told Jeff he'd met a great family during his stay at college, one that adopted him and Jennilee, and that Jeff really needed to meet Angel—one of the daughters.

Charlie'd said something, repeatedly, about Jeff asking Angel out, but their plans had never meshed. If he'd been in Chinquapin Ridge, Angel'd been in Raleigh. If she'd been with Charlie and Jennilee, he'd been elsewhere. They'd been introduced that one time at Grandy's—everyone had been there for dinner.

Jeff had shown up late and left early, and an introduction was all they'd had time for. He'd seen her brother Tony several times with Charlie and Jennilee, but he and Angel hadn't actually spent any time together until just before the wedding, at rehearsals. She'd ended up catching the bouquet, he'd caught the garter.

Everyone knew what that meant.

Perish the thought. He was *not* ready to settle down.

Securing his apartment, Jeff settled his duffle and pointed his Harley south. Visions of a dark haired angel—ha, ha—filled his head as he wondered if Angel would be at Charlie and Jennilee's.

Only one way to find out.

CHAPTER 2

*C*harlie and Jennilee both lifted their heads at Jewel's single sharp bark.

"Hear somebody comin', girl?"

Answering Jennilee with a series of yippy barks, Jewel ran to the door and danced impatiently.

"Somebody she knows." Charlie and Jennilee shared a grin.

Charlie and Jennilee put away their respective tools and cleaned up their spaces. Whoever was coming to visit took precedence over woodworking and stained glass.

It might be Grandy, Charlie's grandma that had practically raised them both, or Mose, their business partner and collaborator. It could be Tim and Rachel and the kids—their foreman and his family—and also their dear friends. A bunch of other people might be coming down the long driveway, but those were the most likely prospects.

Looking out the wide windows of their loft workspace, waiting to see who appeared, Jennilee nestled snugly against Charlie. Her back to his front, his arms securely around her. Shiver after shiver ran through her as Charlie's lips teased up and down her neck and over the sensitive spot just behind her ear while they waited.

When the Harley broke around the last curve Jennilee let out a delighted squeal. "Jeff! He finally decided to pay us a visit!"

Charlie didn't squeal, no matter how much he felt like doing so. They hadn't seen Jeff since their wedding, and they had a lot of catching up to do.

Waiting till Jeff parked his bike before letting Jewel out, Charlie and Jennilee followed the ecstatic dog down the stairs of the loft of the old boat shed they used for a studio and out to the parking area.

Busy fending off Jewel, still astride his bike, Jeff's arms were full of wriggling white and black and brown furball as he tried to get his helmet off at the same time. Laughing, trying to keep his balance under her ferocious assault, Jewel had her muzzle as far under his helmet as she could get it and was giving him kisses on every inch of skin she could.

Since her tongue was like a lizard's and at least as long as her body, she had quite a reach.

Charlie and Jennilee burst into laughter at Jeff's words. "Down, Jewel. Give me a minute and I'll take the helmet off. No! Not my eyebrows. Not my eyebrows!"

Finally getting Jewel out of his face long enough to undo the fasteners and drag his helmet off, looking at Charlie and Jennilee, Jeff returned their wide grins. "You two think this is funny, don't you? How 'bout I hold you down and let Jewel…"

Jennilee laughed outright, Charlie smirked, "That's what you get when you stay away for so long. She misses you. If you'd come home more often…"

"Yeah, yeah, yeah." Jeff swung off his bike. Clasping forearms with Charlie, they caught each other in a tight hug, pounded each other's backs.

Letting go of Charlie, Jeff put his hands on Jennilee's shoulders and looked her up and down. "Well, well, Mrs. Meyers. I have to say marriage agrees with you." To his delight, Jennilee blushed prettily.

"Hey, that's a married woman you're ogling!"

"Did you hear that, Jennilee? He's going all caveman on you. You can't even hug an old friend?" With that, Jeff pulled Jennilee into a bear hug, smugly daring Charlie to object.

"Keep that up and you'll be eating beanie-weenies the whole time you're here." Charlie's pseudo threat had exactly the effect he intended and they all burst into laughter while Jewel spun in excited circles and barked madly.

"Jennilee, did you hear that? He's threatening me. Again. What are you gonna do about it?"

"Me? I'm not cooking beanie-weenies. You're on your own."

"Jennilee, I'm shocked. You know you don't cook beanie-weenies, you eat them out of the can. Cold."

"Not me! You can have my share! I'm having a steak and a baked potato for supper."

Laughing and carrying on, the three of them headed to the house, arms around each other, Jennilee sandwiched in the middle.

"Don't you two ever work? You on permanent vacation or something? It's practically the middle of the day and you're just..." Going up the front steps and crossing the wide porch as in tandem as a team of Clydesdales, Charlie swung the door open. Jeff choked, momentarily speechless. "Holy cow! You guys have been busy!"

Their house, mansion really, had been livable when they'd had the wedding here. Not completely finished or furnished, but well on the way. What they'd done since was nothing short of remarkable, and that was just what Jeff could see.

The vast higher-than-two-story foyer with its graceful twin arcs of stairs now boasted framed pictures of Charlie and Jennilee and their multitude of family and friends all up and down both sets. Straight ahead, looking like a beaded fringe, some kind of viny plant in a long planter hung down from the center rail. A jungle-worthy Jade plant sitting smack dab in the center of the foyer made a stunning centerpiece. Not tall enough that it blocked the view of the front door from the wide hall beneath the center railing, but tall enough to command attention.

A huge chandelier shimmered rainbows over the whole thing, and it wasn't even turned on, merely reflecting sunlight from the domed skylight Charlie'd installed two-plus stories up.

"Wow. Just wow!" Jeff whistled in appreciation.

"Wait till you see the rest of the house!" Jennilee's eyes lit, sparkled like the crystal above them. "Let's go put your stuff in your room and we'll give you a tour."

"My room? Like every time I come here I have my own room and no one else uses it? Even when I'm not here?"

"Absolutely."

Jeff noted some of the changes as they walked up the stairs and down one of the seemingly endless halls. Charlie and Jennilee had taken over the entire northeast end of the house on the second floor for their own use, and his room was just down the hall from their suite.

Stopping in front of a closed door, Jennilee took a deep breath, held it before letting it escape in a rush. "If you don't like it, just say so. Or if you want to change something…"

"Open the door, Jennilee. I'll love it. Whatever you did, I'll love it. I promise."

"*We* did. Both of us, and Mose." Jennilee swallowed, and turned the knob.

Pointedly keeping his eyes on Jennilee's, Jeff scrupulously avoided looking at Charlie, knowing the fury Jeff was tamping down for Jennilee's sake was smoldering in Charlie's eyes. Damn Jennilee's aunt for making her feel worthless! Nothing Jennilee ever did was less than spectacular, but a lifetime of put-downs and insults had left their mark. No one else would even have caught Jennilee's slight hesitations, but Jeff and Charlie knew Jennilee too well.

Opening the door, Jennilee stepped to one side. Jeff could do nothing but stare for a long moment. His duffle hit the floor with a thud and he took a step forward as his eyes took in the details.

A huge bed dominated the room, covered in a brightly colored quilt. A beautiful quilt he was sure Jennilee'd pieced and quilted. The matching dresser and tall-boy that completed the set were either expensive antiques or more likely, something Mose had crafted. Either way, they were exquisite. Jeff never could tell the difference between Mose's creations and fine antiques—his stuff was that good. Jennilee'd said Mose helped, so no doubt the stuff was his.

Looking around some more, he noted a desk, done in the same style, and an adjoining door he was sure led to a private bathroom. Heavy drapes framed the French doors that opened out onto the second story porch. Pulled to the sides now, closing them would ensure he could keep the room dark in the morning, just like he liked, though he doubted he'd get to try that theory out.

Some of Jennilee's stained glass crafted into an intricate starburst pattern made the fanlight over the French doors glow like a cathedral window.

A big braided rug beside the bed splashed a brilliant spot of contrast against the polished hardwood floors. Another braided rug, smaller, resided on the floor beneath an oversized leather recliner, one with a good reading lamp on a pole right behind it.

The walls were painted in a shade Jeff immediately decided was his new favorite color, the trim in white.

The whole room gleamed, radiant with light and with love.

When he could tear his eyes off the beauty before him, he sought Jennilee. "Will you decorate my house?"

Jennilee blinked. "You don't have a house."

"When I get one."

Jennilee gave a half laugh. "What about your wife? What if she doesn't like it?"

"Then she won't be my wife."

Jennilee's laughter pealed out. "You're going to choose your wife based on whether she likes my taste in decorating?"

"Decorating, cooking…" Stalking Jennilee, Jeff backed her right up against Charlie, caught her around the waist and lifted her up for a smacking kiss on the cheek.

"Whoa, whoa, whoa. You can hug my wife, but I draw the line at kissing. Go find your own wife." Pretending to protest, Charlie's eyes shone with gratitude as they met Jeff's over Jennilee's head. Few people understood just how deep Jennilee's wounds were.

"No wonder you two don't have time to work. You've spent all your time on my room. This is really my room? I can't believe you did this for me."

Jennilee beamed at him. "We hope you use it—lots."

Charlie wrapped his arms around Jennilee from behind. "Seconded."

"Unpack your stuff. I'm going to go see if that last load of laundry is done yet." Charlie loosened his hold so Jennilee could stand on tiptoe and brush a kiss across Jeff's cheek. She turned and tilted her face up to Charlie. He framed her face with his hands and grinned at Jeff.

Jeff groaned. "Don't even get started on that. I'll never get fed."

Jennilee laughed, a laugh cut short as Charlie did it anyway. Finally letting her come up for air, he gave her a gentle shove in the direction of the door. "Be there in a few, Jennilee-love."

"Take your time, guys." Jennilee headed out, Jewel on her heels.

Retrieving his duffle from the hall, Jeff set about exploring his room in more detail. "Charlie, I can't believe you guys did this for me. This is..."

"Thank Jennilee. I just followed her lead. Jeff, man, what you just did for her..."

"If she could see anybody but you, I'd have snagged her a long time ago."

Grinning conspiratorially at each other, the two of them started making plans for Jeff's stay.

"That card Jennilee sent was like danglin' bloody meat in front of a hungry piranha. When we goin' fishing?"

"Everything's ready—we're just waiting for you."

"Time's the tide makin'?"

"Mid-morning. We'll go early tomorrow morning."

"Don't change your schedule on account of me."

"Don't have much of one."

The two friends grinned at each other again. Jeff might tease Charlie and Jennilee about not working, but the two of them worked like dogs, had since they were little. Charlie and Jennilee'd never seemed like children—they'd been more like miniature adults trapped in children's bodies.

Adroitly employing what Jeff had long ago termed Charlie's Midas touch, the two of them were probably millionaires by now—multi-millionaires—and they deserved every penny of it. That's why they were living in this huge old mansion, one they'd found the summer they were ten while they were out riding their bikes. They'd spent countless hours of their childhood wresting the gardens back from the jungle it'd become, once again making it a showplace.

Started doing the same to the house—two stories, rectangular, with full wrap around porches on both floors—when they bought it on their eighteenth birthdays. Probably didn't owe a dime on it, either.

Jeff shook his head ruefully. "You two are something else, you know that?"

"It's for her, Jeff. Everything I do is for Jennilee."

"Yeah, I know. Hey, I saw your motel comin' in. Y'all expandin' already?" It was funny—Jeff could hide his accent and speech patterns, become a verbal chameleon for the most part, but let him come home and in a few moments he'd picked up the slower local rhythms and started dropping the consonants off the ends of his words again.

Charlie's eyes lit. "Oh, yeah. Tim did, and does, a fantastic job of managing everything. He's a wizard with the construction crews, and the motel has really taken off. We can't keep up with the demand for rooms. I think we're going to do more efficiencies, too. Maybe a real string of apartments."

"Tim and his family still livin' in The Judge's house?"

"Yep. That's one of the perks of the job. What were we gonna do with it? Jennilee won't ever step foot inside it again, refuses to even acknowledge it's there."

"I can pretty much guess what you'd like to do with it."

Charlie made a rude sound. "If it was up to me? Yeah. I'd raze it in a heartbeat, then burn the pile until there was nothing left and scatter the ashes. Salt the ground, too. Turn the whole place into a paved parking lot, pay someone to scatter french fries out there everyday for the gulls."

"Tell me how you really feel. Don't hold back."

Shared laughter filled the room and unspoken words hung in the air. Jennilee would never step foot in The Judge's house again because that's where she'd been raised. Treated like a slave. Worse. And by the very people who should've been taking care of her.

Right next door to Grandy's, it wasn't like they could just avoid that part of town or anything. The Judge's house was there, a constant reminder. Tim and Rachel had four kids aged seven and under, and the house rang with their laughter. An improvement, a vast improvement, it would take a long time to exorcise all the demons.

"Enough about that! Jennilee can't wait to show you what we've done with the rest of the house. She only left us alone for a few minutes so we could do the whole male bonding thing."

"If we were any closer we'd be Siamese twins." Jeff snorted, and grinned. That was Jennilee, excellent little sheepdog that she was. She knew exactly when to stay right on their heels and when to back off. Grinning more, Jeff shared his mental observation with Charlie. "Jennilee's a sheepdog."

Instead of getting insulted, Charlie picked up instantly on Jeff's meaning. The two of them were still laughing when they caught up with Jennilee.

"I don't even want to know." Jennilee grinned over her shoulder and kept folding clothes.

"Jennilee. I'm…flabbergasted. I thought you made all yours and Charlie's clothes—poofed them into existence with your magic wand or something. Those look like store-bought."

"These are store-bought. I only make the special stuff. Don't wanna waste magic on mundane things. There—I'm done. Ready for your tour?"

Jeff could only shake his head in amazement as they walked around. With Mose's help, Charlie and Jennilee'd been buying up old houses since before they were teenagers, fixing them up and reselling them. They had the mechanics of remodeling and restoring down pat, and they'd put that knowledge to good use.

They'd turned their suite of rooms into an apartment. Huge bedroom and bathroom, kitchen, laundry room—one with a commercial front-load washer and dryer—living room, and several smaller rooms. Rooms that could be used for a nursery and extra bedrooms and bathrooms when they needed them for the kids they were eager to start having. A sewing room for Jennilee, neat shelves holding enough material to make outfits for the whole town in any color they wanted. Jeff'd bet a year's pay that any one of the sewing machines—plural— cost more than he made in a couple of months. Shoot, maybe a year.

That was just their end of the upstairs.

What they'd done with the rest of the house turned out to be just as unbelievable. Everything, everywhere in the house, bore the stamp of Charlie's and Jennilee's love for each other. What they hadn't done, Mose or Grandy or Miz Sadie—Mose's mom—had.

Saving the best for last, making the kitchen their final destination, Jeff let out a whoop when Jennilee ushered him in the door. Mostly finished by the time Charlie and Jennilee'd gotten married, it was the special touches they'd added since that made their kitchen stand out.

Jennilee loved to cook, and Jeff loved to eat her cooking. Always the heart of any home, this kitchen was as welcoming and loving as Jennilee herself, besides being a chef's delight.

Walls painted a bright Granny Smith apple green, the upper cabinets were white with glass fronts, a mixture of clear and stained glass. The lower cabinets were white, with flowers and herbs painted on them. Fresh herbs in decorative pots lined the windowsill over the sink. A huge island dominated the middle of the kitchen, barstools ranged around three sides, shiny copper-bottomed pots and pans hung overhead.

The appliances were all restaurant size and quality, and no expense had been spared. Not that Jeff cared as much about the appliances as he cared about the results Jennilee coaxed out of them. This just gave Jennilee a better starting point.

A scarred and well worn farmhouse table, antique, a good fifteen feet long and only two very wide planks across, held the place of pride in front of a bank of windows, a cobalt vase of zinnias and cosmos and Batchelor's buttons and daisies smack in the middle. Jeff was pretty sure the table was an antique because trees just didn't get to grow that big anymore, and the table had to be a good five feet across. Bright, seasonal placemats in front of each chair, golden wood glowing with polish lovingly applied on a regular basis, and the whole rested on another of Jennilee's braided rugs.

"So, what do you want for supper, Jeff?"

"I thought you said steaks and baked potatoes?"

"I'll fix you whatever you want. I was picking."

"That's fine by me."

"We've got plenty of time, then. Wanna go see the shop?" Jennilee snagged steaks out of the freezer, unwrapped the white paper covering them, set them on the counter to thaw. Just as quickly she sliced three big baking potatoes in half longways. Layered bacon bits and butter and thick slices of Vidalia onions in the middles and stacked the potatoes back together like she was building Dagwoods. Drizzling the outsides with olive oil and sprinkling them with sea salt, she wrapped them in foil and put them on the counter beside the steaks without missing a beat.

Jeff watched her deft movements and licked his lips. "Sure, you two. I can't wait to see what you're working on now."

"I'm still finishing up the stained glass fanlights for over all the French doors and Charlie... Jeff, you gotta see this to believe it. What he's working on now..."

Jeff and Charlie exchanged amused looks over Jennilee's head. A riot to listen to when she got wound up, and she was definitely that right now.

CHAPTER 3

*J*eff got his steak, and his fishing trip.

The steak and baked potato—like everything Jennilee cooked—tasted awesome, but then, Jeff hadn't expected anything less. Like an accomplished magician, Jennilee kept pulling things out of her hat.

Not just the steak and baked potato—not that they wouldn't have been enough all by themselves—but homemade mushroom gravy, fresh from the garden sliced tomatoes and corn on the cob and cukes in vinegar, homemade light rolls slathered in butter, and to top it all off—one of Jennilee's chocolate pies with a graham cracker crust, slathered with fresh made whipped cream.

Pretty much in heaven, Jeff adored Jennilee's cooking as much as she loved to feed him, and after supper, they'd stayed up late, talking and catching up. More pure heaven as far as Jeff was concerned.

And more still… Awakened at the crack of dawn by Jewel jumping on his bed, she nosed her face under Jeff's pillow and washed his face thoroughly. Turning his face the other way, Jeff burrowed deeper under his pillow.

It didn't help. Always eager to play and loving this new game, Jewel leaped over him and wriggled her nose under the other side of the pillow. Burying his face in the mattress, Jeff snugged the pillow tight down over his ears. That just egged Jewel on. She cold nosed his neck and then his side from waist to armpit.

"I give, I give!" Laughing, Jeff rolled over and tried to catch Jewel. Still on the bed, she went down in a play bow, wagging her tail ferociously and grinning in anticipation. Jeff made a couple half-hearted attempts to catch her before giving up and enticing Jewel to him.

"C'mere, girl. Belly rub? Wanna belly rub?" Ears pricking, Jewel fell for the magic words. Catching her and ruffling her ears, he pretended to fuss while Jewel wriggled like a tadpole. She ended up on her back, all four feet blissfully in the air while Jeff scratched her belly and talked nonsense to the little mutt. "Think you're so tough, don't you? Feisty little Feist, aren't you? You goin' fishin' with us this mornin'?"

A sharp bark and Jewel jumped off the bed. Running to the French doors she waited expectantly, ears pricked and tail wagging, one foot lifted.

"They sent you in here to get me up, didn't they?" Jeff snorted to himself. Never much of an early riser, he'd bet Charlie and Jennilee'd been up for a good while.

Dancing in yapping circles, Jewel ran back to the bed, ping-ponged off it still barking madly and ran back to the doors.

Jeff groused, "Alright, alright, I'm coming. Go tell 'em I'll be right there, but there better be some coffee involved. Go on, Lassie, go get Gramps."

Jewel barked again, nosed the French door open enough to slip through and disappeared.

"Well. There for a second, I was afraid you'd learned how to turn doorknobs." Jeff grinned at the space the little dog had just vacated. Charlie must've opened the French doors enough to let Jewel in, and Jewel was more than smart enough to open any door that was almost closed but not quite latched.

Flopping back on his pillows, mighty fine feather pillows on a mighty fine bed, Jeff considered staying right where he was—for all of about three seconds. Long enough to think about Jennilee's most recent card, plenty long enough to think about the boat waiting at the end of the dock and the fish in the river just begging to be caught.

Knew, too, Jewel's wake-up call was the only one he'd get. Confirmed night-owl to their early bird-itis, he'd overslept before when the three of them had something planned—which was a great part of why he hadn't bothered to close the drapes. Once was all the chance he'd get with those two. Charlie and Jennilee would leave him —in a heartbeat—then rub it in for days about how much they missed him—and how many fish they caught and how much fun they had.

Grinning, semi-dressed in cut-offs and an old faded *Journey* T shirt, Jeff followed Jewel's route out onto the porch. The enticing aroma of fresh coffee had him picking up a little speed. The sight of the food covered table on the porch outside Charlie and Jennilee's French doors set his mouth to watering.

Looking up at Jewel's welcoming whine, spotting Jeff, Jennilee smiled to rival the sun and poured him a mug of coffee. Handed it to him and laughed knowingly as he wrapped both hands around the thick white ceramic and took a long swallow.

Taking another delicious swig, eyes still closed in bliss, Jeff opened them, grinned at Jennilee and raised his cup. Her coffee was as good as everything else she fixed. Holding out his cup for a refill, he pulled out a chair.

Charlie goaded, "Don't get too comfortable, Jeffro. You ate enough last night to founder a horse, and if you want to get any fishing in, we gotta get a move on. Tide's risin'." Grinned and slipped an arm around Jennilee.

"Just because you're always up before the roosters isn't any reason for the rest of the civilized world to have to adhere to your schedule." Jeff gibed back as he contemplated his ready to be filled plate and the array of offerings.

"Ooh." Charlie let his mocking response draw out. "Three big words in the same sentence. College must be getting something through that hard head of yours." Charlie grinned wider. "Not too bad for an *almost* Valedictorian."

"Almost only because the two of you double teamed me. You'd've never gotten Valedictorian if Jennilee hadn't helped you...study."

Laughter rang out all around. "No pity, bud. Shoulda spent more time hitting the books than chasing girls."

"Tough job, but somebody's gotta do it." Jeff forked bacon, done to a turn, onto his plate.

"Yeah. Like they had to twist your arm."

"Hey. Hey! I never forced any of those girls to go out with me. I practically had to beat them off!" Spooned fresh cantaloupe, scooped into bite sized balls, out of a bowl.

Well used to their bantering, Jennilee shook her head and passed platters and bowls. Charlie and Jeff always carried on like this, had since they were little.

Tipping his chair back, Charlie propped his feet on the arm of another chair, sipped his coffee, teased Jeff and watched him eat. "Probably a good thing you don't live here. You're worse than a horde of starving termites in a lumberyard."

Appealing to Jennilee as he slid three eggs, sunny side up, and fried potatoes, then a couple pieces of country ham onto his rapidly filling plate, Jeff tried to figure out where to put a couple hot biscuits. "Jennilee, make him stop. He's ruining my appetite."

Jennilee huffed an exaggerated sigh. "Kiss and make up, boys. I'm ready to go fishing."

Charlie and Jeff looked at each other, made kissy lips. "Happy now, Mom?"

"Nope. I didn't get a kiss out of that."

Jeff groaned and focused his attention on his overflowing plate as Jennilee pursed her lips and held her face up to Charlie expectantly.

Despite Jeff's appetite and Charlie's teasing, they were out on the river while it was still slick, before the morning breeze fired up with the rising sun. It looked like Jennilee's card, all rosy gold, with real sound and sensory effects this time, far better than Jeff's remembered ones.

How many times had they done just this? The three of them, boat loaded with coolers and fishing gear, headed for…somewhere? Not Shackleford Banks, not Cape Lookout—not today. Today they were just going to hit some of their favorite fishing holes right here in Newport River, maybe run across the river to Haystacks. A bunch of marshy hummocks, wound through with cuts and creeks, it made for some awesome trout fishing.

Charlie and Jeff stood in the stern of the boat, Jennilee sat in the middle while Jewel perched on the tip of the bow cap and leaned into the wind pretending to be an old timey figurehead.

First stop—their favorite trout hole out near the Intracoastal Waterway. A natural and man-made stretch of connected waterways, you could go pretty much from Florida to Massachusetts without venturing out in the ocean. Numerous inlets connected the ICW with the Atlantic and made ocean travel possible if so desired. Used by commercial barges, snowbirds, and commercial and recreational boaters, the ICW provided safe passageway up and down the Atlantic coast.

No hits there, so they moved out to another spot in the Intracoastal, and from there worked their way up to the Core Creek Bridge. No hits for the guys but Jennilee was having a ball. Charlie'd fixed her up a bottom rig, and she was pulling in nibble fish two at a time.

The guys used curly tail grubs in different colors designed to entice the trout. The guys called them that—Jennilee mockingly called them what they were—plastic worms. Jennilee used bait shrimp on her bottom rig, consisting of two hooks on leaders about six inches apart, with a one ounce lead sinker at the bottom. When the sinker hit bottom, the two hooks floated out to the sides and waved their bait temptingly in the current.

Small fish weren't long in taking the bait. Mostly pinfish, with a few small croakers and hogfish thrown in. No keepers, but a lot of action. Jeff and Charlie were enjoying watching Jennilee. Watching her was almost more fun than actually catching fish themselves.

Sharing a grin at her enthusiasm, they watched her reel in two more, deftly take them off the hooks and toss them back overboard. Expertly re-baiting her hooks, Jennilee flipped her bail and cast her line back out. The water wasn't very deep, around twelve feet or so, and it didn't take long for her sinker to touch bottom. Feeling the bump as it hit, Jennilee immediately took a half crank on her reel and tipped her rod up to keep tension on it.

The rod instantly bent double and Jennilee crowed in delight. "This one's a keeper!"

Leaving their lines in the water, the guys kept a close eye on Jennilee's prospect.

Reeling slowly but steadily, occasionally pulling her rod up higher and reeling in the slack she created, they saw a flash close to the surface of the murky brownish-greenish water, and the fish dove back down. Jennilee kept at it, laughing exultantly as she brought a nice sized flounder into the boat.

Unhooking him, dropping him in the cooler with the ice, Jennilee shut the lid and taunted, "Guess y'all are eating PBJs."

Trying to look pitiful, Jeff poked out his bottom lip. "You'd eat that and make a guest eat peanut butter and jelly?"

Laughing, Jennilee re-baited her bottom hook. Her line hadn't stayed in the water long enough for all her bait to get gone. "You're not a guest, you're family, and you've got a line in the water same's I do."

"You're supposed to be feeding pinfish and leaving the real fishing to the experts."

"Well, Jeff, seein' as how I've got the only fish in the cooler, I guess that would make me the expert, now wouldn't it?" Jennilee smirked and cast her line back out.

Charlie drawled, "Now Jennilee-honey, if you're gonna be like that, I just might make you clean your own fish."

"Not a problem—as long as y'all are gonna fix the coleslaw, and the fried potatoes, and the spoonbread, and the baked beans, and…"

Faced with evidence of another of Jennilee's feasts, Jeff assured her fervently, "I'll clean all the fish you catch, Jennilee. Don't you worry about it."

Jennilee's rod tip twitched the least little bit. She started reeling, cocked an eyebrow at Jeff. "All of them?"

"The keepers, Jennilee. Just the keepers."

Jennilee laughed and Jewel barked her agreement.

Nothing more but pinfish showed up, so they pulled anchor and headed back down the Intracoastal—Innercoastal, as all the locals called it—to the port. Being one of the only two deep water ports—Wilmington being the other—in North Carolina, around the Morehead City port, where they were headed, was a great place to fish.

Tying up to the old railroad trestle, they fished some more. Charlie caught a couple hogfish, Jeff caught a trout and a big croaker, Jennilee caught three black bass and a puffer. The tide started boiling through on its way back in.

"Let's head back and hit Haystacks for a bit. Tide's runnin' too fast to fish here anymore." Reeling in, Charlie waited till the others got their lines in and started the motor.

While they were riding, Jennilee opened a smaller cooler. Jewel watched avidly. It didn't take long for Jennilee's actions and Jewel's fixed attention to catch Jeff's interest.

"Whatcha got there, Jennilee?"

Not bothering to ask if Jeff was hungry, Jennilee just grinned as she passed him a couple ham biscuits and a cold Mountain Dew, passed the same and a Pepsi to Charlie. Shared bites of her biscuit with Jewel.

Backtracking till they hit Haystacks, they let the boat drift some before they anchored in one of the many slews. Jennilee, tired of fishing, kicked back and watched the water and the sky. The guys continued to fish, reeling in a couple nice trout each. Jennilee listened to their competitive ribbing with a wide smile on her face and lots of eye-rolls in Jewel's direction.

Lazily watching the guys, Jennilee tied a loop in the excess anchor rope and dropped it over the side. Catching her movement, Charlie nudged Jeff, who picked up the long pole kept on board in case they needed to tie up or to pole the boat. Probing over the side in several places, reaching shoulder deep before he hit bottom, Jeff nodded and grinned.

Mostly only a couple feet deep here, even at high tide, they'd long ago discovered a hole right in this area. Somewhere between fifteen and eighteen feet deep and perfect for swimming without worrying about slicing yourself open on oysters. Also perfect for diving, if and when Jennilee felt so inclined.

No diving today. Without a word, Jennilee rolled off the bow and disappeared beneath the water with barely a splash. Jewel bailed right behind her mistress and the guys weren't long in following. Letting the tide carry them away from the boat and then swimming back the foursome cooled off in the green water.

Hooking a foot in the handy loop, the boys clambered back aboard while Jennilee continued to dive and roll and swim like a well contented dolphin. As if she'd called them—and maybe she had—a pod of the gregarious marine mammals appeared out of nowhere. Circling around Jennilee and Jewel, they blew and squeaked and chittered like they were having a real conversation with the human and the canine. Dove over and under Jennilee and Jewel and swarmed around the boat while the guys watched, utterly entranced.

Paddling and yipping excitedly, Jewel swam this way and that, communing with her watery brethren. One of the dolphins, as enraptured with Jewel as she was with them, whirled and twirled and spun around Jewel for the longest time, like the mutt was a long-lost pod member. At last came nose to nose with the muttley. A series of back and forth noises along with lots of head bobs on both parts and the dolphin sank under, then came up beneath Jewel. Balancing on the dolphin's head, Jewel rode up and up as the dolphin practically tail-walked out of the water and Jewel stepped right off onto the bow cap like she and her fishy friend had practiced this a million times.

Grabbing a proffered dorsal fin, a laughing Jennilee let the same dolphin tow her a ways down the canal. Letting go and swimming back, the whole pod followed Jennilee. Reenacting their little game of follow the leader over and over, the dolphins at last gave a series of chirrups and head nods and arching leaps before disappearing underwater.

Show over, Jennilee didn't need the loop, didn't hitch a ride on the dolphin elevator. She merely held up a hand and grabbed the one Charlie held down to her. Locking wrists, pulling her into the boat, Charlie grinned down at her and gave her a long, lingering kiss while Jeff clapped and whistled.

"Whew! I was starting to worry there for a bit. Thought maybe you were gonna grow a tail of your own and swim away with them."

"Way to go, mermaid!"

Making dolphin sounds while bobbing her head enthusiastically, Jennilee dropped into her seat and laughed and laughed. Wringing her hair out, she twisted it in a knot.

Fishing over and done with the advent of the dolphins, Charlie snorted, "Okay, folks. Since the show and the fishin' are over for the day, let's head in."

Jeff pulled up the anchor while Charlie started the motor. Putting the boat in gear, Charlie headed her home.

Stashing the anchor beneath the bow cap, Jeff made his way to the stern to stand beside Charlie.

Jeff didn't say anything.

Charlie didn't either, just opened the throttle wider.

Grinning like the Cheshire cat, Jennilee mentally ticked off seconds.

Raising his voice to be heard over the motor, Jeff opined, "This sure is a sweet boat, Charlie."

"Yep."

"Way better than your dad's old wooden skiff."

The three of them shared a grin at the memories that conjured. Long, lazy days of their childhood spent out here in the river, just the three of them. Clamming, fishing, crabbing, oystering, just boat riding. Learning invaluable lessons about life and relationships, lessons that couldn't be taught or bought.

"Yep."

"Way better than that Chris-craft you had."

More memories drifted between them, weaving tighter connections and strengthening already unbreakable bonds. Trips to Shackleford, to the Cape, indelible teenage memories of day trips and camping, of food and fellowship and fun.

"Yep."

Turning her back to the guys, Jennilee covered her mouth with her hand, trying not to laugh out loud.

"So, how long have you had her?"

Shrugging nonchalantly, Charlie turned the wheel one way and then the other, grinnin' as the boat responded like a dream. "A while. You really should come home more often. You wouldn't get so behind on...stuff."

"Come on, Charlie. Don't be so stingy." Jeff wheedled, trying to get what he wanted without being completely obvious.

"Stingy? What are you talking about? I take you to my best fishing holes, ride you around in this beautiful and fully customized Boston Whaler, complete with a stunning bikini clad woman…"

Jeff gave up. Charlie could tease him forever, or until they ended up back at the dock and he lost his chance. "Let me drive."

Jennilee had one hand over her mouth and one arm wrapped around her ribs.

Opening the throttle a little more, Charlie cupped a hand to his ear. "What? You wanna drive? My boat? I don't know… Been a long time since you were out here in the river. Things change. Shoals and channels move, people put up pound net stakes, stake off oyster gardens, lots of things can happen."

Voice going up a notch in aggravation, Jeff conceded. "Alright, Charlie! I give. I promise I'll come home more often. Now will you let me drive?"

"You want to drive her? All you had to do was say so."

Jennilee lost it, not even both hands over her mouth enough to contain her laughter.

Charlie and Jeff tussled good naturedly as Charlie eased the throttle back and prepared to give up the wheel. Jeff shoved, Charlie planted his feet and elbowed back, not quite ready to let Jeff off the hook.

"You're a pain in my ass, Charlie Brown. Always have been." Shouldering Charlie out of the way, settling one hand on the wheel and the other on the throttle, Jeff grinned in anticipation.

"Jeff! How can you say that? You know I'd do anything for you—what are best friends for?" Charlie tried for innocent and injured, but it wouldn't fly.

"Jennilee, I don't know how you can put up with this aggravatin' lug, but then again, you're as bad as he is."

Jennilee laughed harder, the sound ringing over the water like one of the bell buoys. Scooping up Jewel, she settled into her seat at the order she knew was coming.

"Hold on." Jeff opened her up and they flew across the water.

They didn't go straight home, instead ran back up the Innercoastal past the Core Creek bridge almost to Oriental. Jennilee sat back and enjoyed the ride, mentally shook her head. Boys and their toys!

When they finally made it back to their dock, Jennilee and Jewel headed for the house. The guys stayed dockside to set the boat to rights and clean the day's catch in an old soapstone sink, complete with lights and running water for just those reasons.

Charlie and Jeff cleaned the boat, cleaned the fish, used the fish heads and guts to bait a couple crab pots and dropped them over the side. As long as they were playing, they decided to throw the cast net and see if they couldn't come up with a few shrimp to add to their bounty.

Adequate himself, Jeff enjoyed watching Charlie, an expert with the cast net. A circle of net with weights spaced along the outside edge and a drawstring in the middle, not everyone could use it. It required a lot of strength and skill to hold it just right and collect all the loose edges before throwing the net. Done right, anchored in the right hand, collected a swath at a time with the left and thrown with the right in a discus thrower's letting-go motion, the net would flare open, settle over the water, and sink. The long drawstring doubled as a leash, looped around the thrower's right wrist.

When you pulled the drawstring, the weights came together, making a bag that trapped anything under the net when it sank. Charlie and Jeff took turns, bringing in a couple pounds of shrimp each, talking casually, catching up a little more.

Heading the shrimp, they threw the heads back into the river, put the shrimp in the cooler with the cleaned fish.

"So, how long?"

Flashing Jeff a wide grin in answer, white teeth in a tanned, handsome face, dark eyes alight, Charlie didn't pretend to not know what Jeff was talking about.

Jeff's eyes went wide. "No way."

"Yes way."

"You've got to be kidding."

Charlie shook his head, grinned wider.

Jeff made gagging noises. "This is the longest you two have been apart since you got married?"

"Yep."

Jeff shook his head. "Most people, much less most married people, can't stand that much closeness."

"We're not most people."

"Never have been."

They shared a look, and a grin, and then Charlie sobered. "I can't keep her in bed."

Jeff blinked, and fired back, "Sounds like a personal problem, Charlie Brown. I mean, it's been two months. The honeymoon's over." Charlie didn't shove Jeff off the dock, or lambast him verbally, letting Jeff know just how serious it was.

Looking in the direction of the house, Charlie looked back to Jeff. "I always knew... I mean, Jennilee gets a lot of stuff done. I've never seen anyone work like she does. I just never... She doesn't sleep, Jeff."

"What do you mean, she doesn't sleep?"

"She'll stay in bed if I ask her to, but even if I'm holding her, even if it's dark, I can feel the wheels turning in her head. Jennilee never shuts down, Jeff. If I don't make her stay in bed with me, she's up and doing something."

"Yeah, well, you're the ones who wanted that monstrosity." Jeff indicated the huge house with a tilt of his chin.

Charlie gave a rude snort. "You think I'd let her try to keep that place clean?" They shared another look, one that spoke volumes. Jennilee could and would, there was no doubt in either of their minds about that, even if she killed herself trying. She'd had loads of practice cleaning her aunt's house. And cooking. And everything else her aunt had dumped on Jennilee since she'd been a small child.

"You've got a housekeeper?"

"A housekeeper? We've got *staff*. And Suki's off limits to you."

"Suki?"

"Down, boy. Japanese, I think. Oriental, at any rate. She told us her real name, but Jennilee's the only one who can say it right, so we went with Suki."

"Off limits?"

"Yeah, you old hound dog. Off limits, in capital letters."

"Just because, unlike you, I haven't been in love with the same girl literally since I was born..."

"No, just because you'll chase anything in a skirt."

"Or out of it."

Another shared grin and without another word, they each took one handle of the cooler full of ice and supper. Each with a fistful of poles and tackle boxes, cooler between them, they made their way to the house. Leaving the cooler and their fishing gear in the mudroom, they washed up at the sink there and headed through to the kitchen.

As he knew they would, Charlie and Jennilee greeted each other like they'd been apart years instead of the forty-five minutes, hour tops, since they'd been in each other's company. Jeff didn't bother to try and stop them—that would only encourage them more. Didn't really care. It was nice to know his two best friends were so much in love, even if it could get embarrassing at times—like right now.

Jennilee had stuff laid out on the island for BLTs, and Jeff set about making himself several. He was halfway through his second and eyeballing his third by the time Charlie and Jennilee joined him.

Taking one look at what Jennilee had ready for lunch, Charlie raised molten eyes to hers. Grinned a slow, heated grin that had Jennilee reciprocating and Jeff shaking his head and fixing his gaze on his next sandwich.

He grumbled and took another bite. "Do y'all have to turn everything into a sexual innuendo?"

Charlie's melted dark chocolate eyes stayed on Jennilee's warm ocean eyes. "You're just jealous."

"You bet. Never considered BLTs to be an aphrodisiac before. Gonna let me in on the secret?"

"Nope." Charlie kept grinning and Jennilee watched, attention fixed, as he layered a BLT, mushed it, and offered the first bite to her. She accepted, eyes locked on Charlie's, chewed slowly. Watched unblinking as he took the next bite.

"Y'all are gonna have to turn up the AC or something."

Charlie kissed Jennilee, and agreed. "Or something."

CHAPTER 4

On the porch, Jeff kicked back in the hammock. Charlie and Jennilee snuggled on the glider, her head on his shoulder, his arm around her. Jewel flopped on the cool porch boards, already out. The humans were somnolent, nearly asleep when Jeff blurted, "Who is she?"

Total, knowing silence from Charlie and Jennilee.

"Come on, guys. I played a big part at your wedding, and believe me, I'd've noticed a beautiful woman like that. Especially one dressed to kill—if it was 1950." Opening his eyes, Jeff rolled to his side to face Charlie and Jennilee. "Well?"

Charlie cleared his throat. "I guess you saw the pictures, huh?"

"How could I not? You two have pictures of everyone plastered everywhere."

"Remember that day Jennilee disappeared and we couldn't find her?"

"That day she scared us all shitless?" Jeff cast an accusing glance at Jennilee. Miles away, *states* away, unable to get home in time to help, his heart still stopped every time he thought about *that day*.

"Yeah, that one."

"How could I forget that, but what does Jennilee disappearing have to do with that woman in your wedding pictures?"

Jennilee began, "Jeff, you know the heirloom plants we sell are called Amelia's Echoes, 'cause they're a gift from the past."

"Yeah, I know that. And?"

Charlie took over. "Amelia was the previous owner's wife."

"I know that, too."

Jennilee picked up. "You know she died and Mr. Clyde hasn't been back since."

"That's what you said."

Jennilee took a deep breath. "That woman in our wedding pictures? She's Amelia."

"Whoa. Backup. How could she be at your wedding, be in your pictures, if she's..." Jeff stared in disbelief.

Charlie and Jennilee nodded as one.

"She's a ghost?"

More nods.

Jeff blinked, let out a low whistle. He knew Charlie and Jennilee well enough to know when they were pulling his leg, and they weren't. "I bet Mr. Berto had a fit about those pictures."

Charlie and Jennilee laughed. Mr. Berto Marcellini, photographer extraordinaire, and a great friend, had done their wedding photographs.

"He was going to destroy them. He thought someone had been messing with his camera or something, especially since Amelia only showed up in a few of the pictures taken in the garden and the cemetery."

Jennilee smiled up at Charlie. "We convinced him to let us keep them."

"How do you invite a ghost to a wedding? Send an invitation through the United Spooks Post Office? And what does..." Jeff swallowed. "...Amelia have to do with Jennilee disappearing?"

"Amelia...kinda..."

"...watches out for me."

Jeff's eyebrows shot up. "A ghost. Watches out for you."

"That day... I came out here and fell asleep. I was so worried about all that mess with my aunt, terrified she was going to get everything Charlie and I'd worked so hard for, and I thought I was just dreaming." Jennilee looked to Charlie for help.

Jeff reminded her, "Half the county came out here and looked for you."

"She wasn't here."

"Make up your mind, Charlie. You said you found Jennilee here. Was she or wasn't she?"

"Then. Wasn't here when everyone else looked. Actually, she was, but she wasn't. I drove out here to see if her car was here, and if it wasn't, I had several other places to check. Her car was parked in its usual spot when I got here, but no Jennilee, no Jewel. Starting with the cemetery, I walked all over this place. Couldn't find either one of them."

"Bud, I think you've been out in the sun too long."

Jennilee muffled a laugh against Charlie's shoulder.

Charlie continued. "Dead quiet out here that day, I called and called—figured even if Jennilee wouldn't or couldn't answer, Jewel would. I walked all over the grounds, all over the porches, all over the inside of the house. I finally went back to the family cemetery...and there she was."

"What do you mean, *there she was*?" Jeff swung his confused gaze from Charlie to Jennilee and back to Charlie.

"I swear to ya, Jennilee was curled up beside Amelia's grave on a blanket of fresh flowers and Jewel was right there."

"Fresh flowers? In the middle of winter? Jennilee?"

Jennilee shrugged. "I can't explain it, Jeff. Amelia...let me know everything was going to work out."

"We haven't told anyone else about this." Tightening his arm around Jennilee, Charlie pulled her closer and pressed his lips to the top of her head.

Throwing his hands in the air theatrically, eyes to the heavens, Jeff intoned like he was auditioning for Julius Caesar, "Why not? Everyone has a resident ghost. Not only has one, but talks to it on a regular basis and performs magic tricks with said ghost, invites it to their wedding and takes pictures of it." Giving a snort, Jeff snarked, "I reckon for anyone who can converse with dolphins, a ghost isn't that far out of the realm of possibility." Jeff rolled his eyes, rolled onto his back, draped an arm over his face.

Charlie and Jennilee burst out laughing. Their combined laughter was the last sound for a good while as they all drifted into naps.

Later, climbing the stairs to take showers and change out of their fishy smelling clothes, Charlie and Jennilee went on ahead. Jeff stopped to look at the photographs artfully lining the wall beside the curving staircase. One of the staircases. The matching one across the foyer had just as many pictures displayed along its length. He'd look at them later.

Where he'd just glanced before, now Jeff stood and took in every detail of the woman's...of the ghost's...of Amelia's picture. Knockout gorgeous, wearing a smart pink skirt and jacket, tight waisted and wide shouldered with a wide brimmed hat cocked becomingly to one side, Amelia stood beside Jennilee, the two of them framed by a riot of flowers. Jeff remembered well the exact instant this picture had been taken, and he knew full well there hadn't been anyone except Jennilee in this shot.

Not anyone who could be seen by the naked eye, at any rate, but there she was. Amelia's sleek blond hair was rolled on the sides in a style made popular in the forties. Jeff didn't know what it was called, but he'd seen it on some of the older actresses, in black and white movies. Bettie Davis. Katherine Hepburn. Classy ladies.

Sky blue eyes and a peaches and cream complexion smiled back at him. All Amelia needed was a pair of wings and she'd make a perfect angel. Maybe she already was one. Lord knew, and so did everyone else, Jennilee needed all the angels she could scrounge.

Jeff found himself talking to the portrait. "Thanks, Miz Amelia, for everything you've done for Jennilee. Thanks a bunch. Charlie and I do what we can, but she needs all the help she can get." Starting to walk away, a thought hit him. What did he have to lose? He sure wasn't getting any farther than anyone else had with his investigation.

"Miz Amelia, if you've got any pull on the other side, I could use some help myself. I will find out who murdered Charlie's mom, and I'll bet everything I'll ever own the same persons who killed Charlie's mom murdered Jennilee's as well. I've made it my mission in life to put the culprits put away so they can't inflict this kind of lifelong pain on anyone else, but mostly so Jennilee, and Charlie, can get some closure."

Jeff didn't get an answer, hadn't really figured he would.

Stripping off his clothes once he reached his room, Jeff headed for his bathroom. Stopped and eyeballed the wrapped package on the bathroom counter, a package that hadn't been there before. Debated who'd left it there. If Charlie had, no telling what was in it up to and including a lifesize...*live* scorpion or a giant cockroach—one of those hissing ones—or a fake but totally realistic giant spider, but the joke would be at Jeff's expense. Jennilee he had no doubts about. Dead bodies and gore he could handle, no problem. Bugs...not so much. Not that he—candidate for sainthood that he was—would ever do anything like that to Charlie. Snickering and shaking his head Jeff started unwrapping, gazed in delighted awe at the enclosed object.

Jennilee. Definitely Jennilee.

Still shaking his head, opening cabinets and drawers, he might as well have left his toiletries home. Jennilee'd stocked his bathroom with all his favorite products. Soap, shampoo, razors, even his favorite aftershave.

Standing under the pounding spray, Jeff shook his head repeatedly and laughed to himself until the bathroom echoed with it. He'd known Jennilee had a lot of talents, but he sure hadn't known she could communicate with ghosts. Dolphins he'd sorta figured on, but a ghost?

Taking his time, sure that they would, Jeff headed for Charlie's and Jennilee's end of the house. The hall door stood open, silently inviting him in. Making himself at home in their living room, he waited impatiently. Found a rock station on their stereo and cranked it up. Wandered around looking at things.

Like the rest of the house, everything in here was chosen, not just with care, but with love. Like the rest of the house, everything in their living room reflected that love. Lingering at the open roll top desk, one he was sure Mose had crafted, Jeff let his eyes wander over the papers scattered there.

He had no sense of eavesdropping or snooping. If Charlie and

Jennilee had minded him seeing it, they wouldn't have left it out. Perused a gardening article perched right on top of a stack of papers.

Not because he had the slightest interest in growing anything or ever would, but because of the article itself—penned in Jennilee's gracefully distinctive script. Shook his head.

Coming out of his and Jennilee's bedroom first, wearing nothing but shorts and still toweling his hair, Charlie turned the stereo down to a less than ear splitting decibel.

Jeff smirked. "Hope I'm not interrupting anything."

Charlie grinned in response. "Like we'd let you."

Holding up the article, Jeff looked questioningly at Charlie, who nodded.

"She's been doing it for Mr. Matt for years."

"How come I never saw it before? I'd've noticed something in the local paper written by Jennilee."

"Not just the Ridgerunner, and she uses a pen name."

"Because of her aunt."

Charlie grimaced in agreement.

Time to change the subject. "Who all's comin' tonight?"

Charlie shrugged. "Whoever Jennilee called."

"I didn't think she was fixing all that food for just us. Not that I couldn't put a hurtin' on it."

Jennilee's laughter filled the room. "Jeff, you'd put a starving elephant to shame."

"Jennilee, an elephant would weep with gratitude if he could get ahold of one taste of your food." Putting the paper back, Jeff crossed the room. "How come you didn't let me know you wrote articles?"

Reddening a bit, Jennilee shrugged. "You don't garden."

Jeff stated proudly, "I've never grown anything, never will. I'll leave that entirely up to you and Charlie. While I may not know anything about gardening, I do know good writing when I see it. That's an excellent piece, Jennilee."

Jennilee blushed even more at Jeff's praise.

Hugging Jennilee, Jeff planted a kiss on top her wet head. Wrapping her arms around his waist, Jennilee sighed contentedly. "I guess we'll have to keep you, Jeff. You're really good for my ego."

"Charlie doesn't tell you..."

Giving Jeff a heartfelt squeeze, Jennilee laughed. "He tells me all the time how wonderful I am, but then he's prejudiced in my favor. It's just nice to hear it from an unbiased source."

"Prejudiced? Jennilee..."

Jennilee ended up sandwiched in a big, laughing, bear hug while both guys tickled her. Jewel danced around the trio, yapping her fool head off.

Sitting on the couch, Jeff watched, as he had countless times before while Charlie seated Jennilee on a low, padded stool in front of his chair. Toweled her hair gently until it was mostly dry, brushed it. Jeff had watched many a time as Charlie'd done just that and then proceeded to braid it in an elaborate crown. This day, Charlie left it down.

While Jeff had never had any desire to brush a woman's hair, Charlie loved doing it. Loved Jennilee's hair, period. Long, a waterfall of gold silk, it fell to the lower curve of her bottom. Charlie was constantly running his hand down the unbound length of Jennilee's hair, tangling his fingers in it, wrapping it around his hand—one more intimate thing that bound the couple together.

Memory drawn back further, to a time when Jennilee had inexplicably whacked her beautiful hair off, Jeff winced inwardly at the bad time that'd resulted... Only to find out later, years later, bully Butch had held her down and done the dirty deed and Jennilee had taken the blame so Charlie wouldn't go after Butch. Clenching his fists, Jeff looked at his friends—lost in their own world—and drew a deep breath. Let go of his fury. Over and done with.

Closing her eyes in bliss, Jennilee tipped her head back while the brush traced long strokes from the crown of her head to the ends of her hair. "Find everything in your bathroom ok?"

There wasn't any use in protesting, so Jeff gave in gracefully. "Sure did, Jennilee. Thanks a bunch. And thanks for that cool souvenir."

Opening her eyes, Jennilee smiled as Charlie snorted out a laugh. "Do you have any idea how many shops she dragged me through?" Charlie mimicked in an exaggerated Scarlett O'Hara falsetto, "We have to find the perfect gift for Jeff. Why, I'd just never forgive myself if we didn't bring him back something special from our honeymoon."

"You could've brought me a hot girl. Hey, speaking of hot girls, that housekeeper of yours—does she wear one of those sexy French maid's uniforms? You know, one of those miniscule black outfits with a tiny white apron and a frilly little cap? Those things really turn me on."

Shaking his head, Charlie kept his eyes glued to Jeff's.

"I know you said she was off limits, but maybe I could talk her into trying one on for me." Warming up, Jeff rubbed his hands together and elaborated on his fantasy. "High heels, too. Fishnet stockings."

Choking on a laugh, Jennilee focused her gaze on something behind Jeff while Charlie grinned wickedly and made a slicing motion across his throat with his finger.

Rising, Jeff turned and plastered a charming smile on his beet red face. Met the obsidian eyes of one of the most drop dead gorgeous women he'd ever seen. Charlie'd said Oriental but he hadn't gone into detail. Not just Oriental, but mixed race, and as was so often the case, the best of both worlds.

Tall and slender, her high cheekbones set off elfin features and tip tilted eyes fringed by long lashes, café au lait skin. Shoulder length hair that matched her eyes and framed her exquisite face, bangs that brushed her delicate brows. Red lips curved in a perfect bow—a bow that looked like it was ready to release an arrow.

Charlie was practically rolling on the floor, Jennilee was still snickering as she made unnecessary introductions. "Jeff, meet Suki. Yesterday was her day off, which is why you didn't meet her yesterday. Suki, this is Jeff, our friend we've told you so much about. By the way Jeff, Suki's eating with us."

Charlie stopped laughing long enough to choke out, "Was, if your atrocious manners didn't turn her stomach."

Jeff angled his upper body in a half bow toward the woman so clearly radiating icy disapproval. "My deepest apologies, Ma'am. I meant no disrespect to you. Any joking was directed entirely at Charlie, I assure you."

Suki said nothing, merely stared Jeff down, arms crossed and eyes glacial, fingers tapping out a marching rhythm on her bicep.

"Ma'am, might I ask you a question?" Not waiting for her answer Jeff plowed ahead. "You are so absolutely beautiful, why in the world are you here, keeping house for Ricky and Lucy? You should be a movie star, or a model."

"Shut up, Fred." Charlie and Jennilee chimed in together.

"You're digging deeper, man." Charlie sniggered, enjoying Jeff's discomfort—immensely.

Jennilee added her two cent's worth, followed by more input from Charlie. "Jeff, Suki doesn't need you to tell her she's beautiful."

"She sees her face in the mirror every day, man, and right now, she wouldn't believe you if you told her the sky was blue."

"I meant that in the nicest way, no sexual digs implied."

Ignoring Jeff and his outrageous antics, Suki told Jennilee, "I'm finished with what we had on the list for today. Anything I can do to help with supper?"

Jennilee and Suki moved into the apartment's kitchen, words filling the air like dust motes in a sunbeam. The hum of their animated conversation contrasted vividly with Jeff's heated accusations.

He looked first to Jewel, pretending to be half asleep in the corner of the couch. She pricked her ears and thumped her tail languidly, rolled her one visible eye at him. Chuffed silently. "You! You didn't have to bark and growl, but you could've at least looked toward the door or something. See if I rub your belly any more, you ungrateful wench."

Rounding on Charlie, Jeff picked up a pillow off the couch and threw it along with his words. That's why they were called throw pillows, wasn't it? "And you! You enjoyed every second of that! Watching me make a complete and total ass of myself!"

Catching the pillow and firing it back, Charlie made no effort to contain his mirth. "Ah, but Jeffro—you're so good at it."

A burst of laughter from the kitchen assured the guys Jennilee and Suki were discussing the very same thing.

The girls returned a few moments later to find Charlie and Jeff rolling around on the floor, grappling and tussling. Evenly matched, neither could get the upper hand. Suki watched avidly as Jennilee stopped them cold.

She didn't raise her voice, didn't threaten them with their lives if they destroyed her furniture, didn't reprimand them and tell them to take their immature antics outside. Jennilee merely set the tray on the coffee table and tinged a fork on the rim of a plate.

Jeff froze instantly and Charlie took advantage, immediately pinning him. No round-ending bell had ever stopped a match so effortlessly. Craning his neck, trying to see what treat Jennilee had now, Charlie blocked Jeff's view, refused to let him.

"Make nice, boys, or Suki and I won't share."

Charlie and Jeff weren't long in untangling themselves and heading her way. Charlie even held a hand out and helped Jeff to his feet.

Jeff almost drooled as he saw what the tray held. Jellyroll. Homemade jellyroll. Jennilee's homemade jellyroll, filled with her homemade black scuppernong jelly and dusted with powdered sugar. Big glasses of cold milk, so cold perspiration already dotted the outside of the glasses, little beads running down the sides.

Sitting on her stool in front of Charlie's chair, Jennilee started cutting thick slices. Charlie slid into his chair behind her and Jeff sat on the couch, while Suki took the other chair beside Charlie and Jennilee. Jeff watched as attentively as a starving hound as Jennilee put a slice on a saucer and handed it to Suki.

The next one was his. Cutting a third slice, Jennilee handed it to Charlie and leaned back between his knees. Jeff stopped with his fork halfway to his mouth.

"Jennilee, aren't you eating any?"

Jennilee threw back her head and laughed, missing the look that flew between Charlie and Jeff. "I only want a couple bites, and Charlie will share. I can't eat as much as you guys. If I did, I'd be as big as Miz Sadie in about three days."

Jeff snorted around a mouthful of jellyroll. Miz Sadie, Mose's mom, was beloved by them all—and rotund as an igloo. Polishing off his piece, taking a long drink of milk, Jeff held his plate back out to Jennilee.

She shook her head and obliged. "Did you even taste that?"

"Sure I did. If you get to be any better of a cook, I'm going to kidnap you."

"I've seen your *kitchen*, Jeff. As much as I love you, I'm not cooking in that...that..."

"Closet?" Charlie suggested. "Cubicle? Cubbyhole? Need I say more?"

Jeff sulked, "It's a kitchen. I've got a stove and a sink and a frig and everything."

"You can call it whatever you want. I'm not cooking there, not even for you."

Suki joined in the hearty laughter that followed Jennilee's fervent statement.

CHAPTER 5

Finished with their snack, they moved downstairs. People started showing up a little later. First came Tim and Rachel and the kids. The kids, except for baby Cassie, as soon as they greeted Charlie and Jennilee, immediately headed outside to the colorful playground equipment. Real metal playground equipment, and not merely swings and slides—Charlie had purchased the whole shebang when the local school put them up for sale. Tall metal A frame swing set, equally tall slide, merry-go-round and monkey bars and see-saws, all freshly painted and kept in top-notch condition.

Grandy and Mr. Donnie, Charlie's dad, popped in next, and Mose and his dad, Mr. Jubal, arrived last. Taking her turn cooking at Grandy's restaurant tonight, Miz Sadie wouldn't be able to make it.

All the adults gathered in the huge kitchen at the bar or the table, conversation and laughter flowing like water in a fast moving stream full of big rocks.

The guys eventually drifted outside to do guy things before Charlie and Jeff started cooking their portion.

Combining the cooled cornmeal mush portion with the eggs and butter she had creamed and ready in the mixing bowl to make spoonbread, Jennilee put it along side the baked beans, already in the oven, started frying the home fries. Got out the ingredients for tartar sauce and cocktail sauce, made a couple more gallons of sweet tea. Put ice in the glasses and stashed glass and all in the freezer.

The pots Charlie and Jeff had baited earlier yielded an impressive amount of blue crabs. They'd fry the fish and cook the shrimp and crabs outdoors near the oyster pit, since Charlie'd run a gas line to the pit and had burners set up there. A big iron skillet ready and waiting for the trout and croaker and black bass and Jennilee's flounder, the filleted fish were salted and ready to be breaded, merely waiting for the oil to heat.

Charlie set a pot of water on a burner for the crabs, and another smaller one for the shrimp. Neither would take long to cook once they hit the water.

Jennilee and the women draped checkered tablecloths over the series of picnic tables in the shade of a huge old live oak, put out all the trimmin's. Plates and silverware and napkins—plenty of napkins, and pads of newspaper for the delicious but extremely messy crabs. The chilled glasses would be put out at the very last minute.

Little Timmy and Elizabeth and Corey ran over to join the adults. Timmy, with all the pomposity of his six and a half year old gregarious self, ran backwards and led the way, keeping an eye on his younger sister and brother, declaring loudly to anyone who would listen that he was starving. Jewel dashed from group to group, her tail a constant blur.

Jennilee sat at the table and held baby Cassie while Rachel herded the rest of her troops indoors to wash up. Cooed to the baby—more toddler now, at fifteen months, gnawing happily on a peeled cucumber, and gazed contentedly at the riot of activity going on around her.

Off to one side, Mr. Jubal and Mr. Donnie played horseshoes. Tim sat in a lawn chair in the shade, cheering for both of them, gleefully calling ringers and misses. Charlie and Jeff were cooking and still ribbing each other, she didn't have to hear the words to know that. Grandy and Suki were toting stuff from the kitchen with Mose's help, Rachel trotting right behind them.

She would've been flabbergasted to know the hot topic of conversation in each little enclave was…her.

Jeff looked at Charlie as they tag-team traded already fried fish for just breaded fish in a well practiced move. "Jennilee still not eating much?"

"You know how she is as well as I do. I have to watch her like a hawk. Jennilee loves to cook and wants everyone else to eat till they pop, but she just takes a bite here and there, slips a lot of her food to Jewel when she thinks I'm not watchin'."

"Reckon a baby would help?"

Charlie grinned and nodded. "Oh, yeah."

"Nothing yet?"

"Not for lack of trying. Somethin' else she worries about."

"Like she needs somethin' else."

Sharing a look, they kept cooking—Jeff poured the boiling water off the shrimp and dumped them in a bowl of ice while Charlie checked the crabs.

Pitching his shoe, Jubal grinned at Donnie as he gained another point. "Our girl looks mighty fine holdin' that baby."

Taking his time, and his turn, Donnie agreed. "Sure does. I'm lookin' forward to bein' a grandpa as much as they're lookin' to be parents."

"Yeah, we keep lendin' em ours, but they still want a houseful." Tim shook his head ruefully and tried to look morose, couldn't pull it off as Timmy and Elizabeth ran toward the table followed by a screaming Corey.

"Wait! Wait fo' me!" Of course Timmy and Elizabeth didn't listen, just ran faster.

In the midst of the food-laden procession coming out of the house, carrying the hot pan of spoon bread on one huge palm and the baked beans on the other with a thick hotpad beneath each, Mose asked, "Suki, you makin' sure little missy ain't workin' too hard? Jennilee takes on too much, always has. You gotta watch her every second or..."

Instead of taking offense and snapping at Mose, Suki rolled her eyes and agreed with him. When she'd first started working here, she'd thought they were all crazy-protective over Jennilee. Now...

"Stop worrying, Mose. You know I do. Charlie and I hardly let her out of our sight, but she's a grown woman. Give her a little credit."

Grandy chimed in. "We do give her credit...for everything we know about."

Rachel laughed and added, "If you look up *overachiever* in the dictionary, Jennilee's picture is right there. Serious overachiever."

Mose grumbled and added, "Yeah, it's right there. It's also right there beside *worrywart, mother hen...*"

Nudging Jeff, Charlie pointed with his chin. Looking in the indicated direction, Jeff caught the look on Mose's face as he paced Suki. Jeff let out a low whistle. "So that's the way the wind blows. No wonder you warned me off Suki. Mose know yet?"

Charlie made a rude sound. "He knows. He's just pretending different. Suki knows too, but she won't say anything until Mose does."

Jeff shifted his gaze from Suki's exotic beauty back to Mose, looking like a statue of a giant rendered in anthracite. "Let me guess. Mose won't say anything because he considers Suki to be white."

"Yep. That's pretty much it."

"What does Suki say?"

"Not much, but Jennilee thinks Suki's half in love with the big softie. It wouldn't take much for her to fall all the way."

"Bet Jennilee loves that."

"Oh, yeah. You know how she feels about Mose. How we feel. To Jennilee, and me, he's mentor and big brother and favorite uncle and cousin all wrapped up in one."

"Guess Mose isn't really that much older than us, huh? He just seemed it when we were growing up."

Charlie snickered. "Funny how your perceptions change. People that seemed ancient when we were little really aren't that old. Mose always seemed so much older than us, but he's not—only about ten years."

"Can't you just see him with a couple rugrats of his own?" Sharing a grin, Charlie and Jeff finished off their cooking and started carrying stuff to the table.

Smiling as Charlie came closer, Jennilee held her face up for his kiss. "What are you and Jeff plotting now? And don't tell me nothing —I know you both too well."

Charlie kissed her, drew back a smidge. "Jennilee, would we...plot? Shame on you for even thinking such a thing." Charlie brushed a hand down Jennilee's cheek.

"Um-hmm."

"Plop. The word is plop. See?"

Deftly removing Cassie from Jennilee's arms, Charlie placed the baby gently in the highchair at the end of the table while Jeff plopped his butt on the bench beside Jennilee. Charlie plopped down on the other side of her.

"You two..." Jennilee was shaking her head and trying not to laugh. "You two are impossible."

"Yeah, but we love you." Charlie and Jeff both leaned in toward her at the same time, squishing Jennilee between them.

Everyone else seated, Grandy said the blessing, and they commenced to eatin'.

Jennilee watched in disbelief and everyone else watched avidly as Charlie and Jeff proceeded to plop some more. On Jennilee's plate. Every time they got their hands on a bowl or platter, one or the other plopped a big serving of whatever they held on Jennilee's plate before they served themselves even.

Knowing better than to protest, Jennilee just watched. Finally, when there was no more room on her plate, they quit. Everyone else kept filling their own plates and watching.

Jennilee let out a deep breath, and all motion ceased as she looked from Charlie to Jeff and back to her plate. No one wanted to miss what she had to say. "Hope y'all are hungry, cause I know you didn't dish this plate up for me."

Jeff sing-songed, "No dessert unless you clean your plate. Right, kids?"

Timmy's face was solemn as he intoned, "That's what mom always tell us, Jennilee."

Elizabeth looked sorrowful. "Bet you fixed a really good dessert, too."

Timmy and Elizabeth eyed Jennilee intently. Corey, not about to be left out, banged his spoon on his tray and chanted, "Eat, Jennilee. Eat." Banged his spoon again for emphasis and repeated, "Eat." Cassie giggled and cooed from her highchair at the other end of the table.

Jennilee shook her head. "No fair ganging up on me. I can't possibly eat all that. I can't even eat half of it."

Charlie coaxed, "Come on, Jennilee. I'll peel your shrimp for you."

Jennilee sighed. "Charlie, I know how to peel shrimp. If these hadn't been fresh caught and the shells as flimsy as wet tissue paper, I'd've peeled them before you boiled them."

Jeff noisily clacked the nutcrackers he held in one hand. "I got your crabs."

Total silence as Jeff's unintended double entendre sank in. The adults lost it and the kids giggled and laughed even though they didn't have the slightest clue what was so funny.

A toss up as to whose face turned redder—Jeff's or Jennilee's—when the mirth had subsided somewhat, Charlie bargained some more. "How 'bout this? For every bite you take, I'll give you a kiss."

Loud groans came from the rest of the table.

"For Pete's sake! Do I look undernourished to you?"

Charlie shook his head, his eyes fixed on Jennilee's. "Nope. Just under-kissed."

Cries of *no way* and *not possible* filled the air, Charlie and Jennilee oblivious to all of it.

All teasing aside, they got Jennilee to eat quite a bit.

Jeff, no urging needed, ate quite a bit himself. That, and absorbed the atmosphere.

Love. Pure love.

"ASK HER." Timmy elbowed Elizabeth, a tad harder than necessary in typical big brother fashion.

"Ow!" She shook her head. "You ask. I asked her last time."

"Ask me what, guys?" Knowing full well what they wanted, Jennilee looked from one to the other at their fierce whispers.

"Can we go swimming, and will you go with us?" Timmy asked

Jennilee, but turned his head to the side and stuck his tongue out at his sister.

"That depends on your manners, and you're asking the wrong person."

All the adults could do not to laugh, Timmy took a deep breath and made his apology and request and backed up his reasoning at the same time, all without pausing. "Sorry, 'Lizbeth —Mom, is it okay if Jennilee takes us swimming 'cause the tide's high enough and we got suits here and we did all our chores today and..."

Raising a hand, Rachel ignored the groans coming from her offspring at her words. "You know you have to wait half an hour, and while you're waiting, you'll have plenty of time to help clear the table."

Opening his mouth, a mutinous look flashing in his eyes, Timmy started to appeal to his dad.

"And if I hear one word, we're going straight home. After we help clean up."

Timmy sighed heavily. "Yes ma'am. Can we start clearing the table now?"

"When everyone's done eating and not before."

All eyes settled on Mose, fork halfway to his mouth, plate still covered by seconds and thirds and fourths.

Jennilee couldn't help it. She burst into laughter. "I think a good bit of your half hour will be over by the time Mose is finished."

Timmy looked hopefully at Mose.

Mose's white teeth flashed in his dark face. "I think right much of you, Timmy-boy, but I'm not rushing through this fine meal so you can go play at being a mudpuppy."

Timmy perked up. "What's a mudpuppy?"

Another burst of laughter from the adults, and everyone went back to talking while Mose explained to the wide-eyed kids about water-dogs and their habits.

Jennilee leaned across the table and put a hand over Tim's. "You okay? I noticed you didn't play horseshoes with Mr. Donnie and Mr. Jubal."

"Fine, Jennilee. No need to worry. I'm just tired—been climbing stairs all day, and you know I'm lousy at horseshoes."

"Are you sure? I can call Doc…"

Tim appealed to Charlie and Rachel. "Assure Jennilee I'm fine or she's going to have me in the hospital."

Charlie and Rachel shared a look, included Jennilee in it. Rachel grinned and twined her fingers with Tim's. "He's fine, Jennilee. No pain, no twinges, no nothing—thanks to you bullying him about therapy and such."

Memories swirled thick around them, as thick as the humid air. When Jennilee and Charlie met Rachel and Tim and the kids, Tim had been out of work with two broken legs and the whole family had been living in their station wagon. Jennilee spread her wing over them, tucked them under, and the rest was history.

"You'd tell us…"

"I'd tell you, Jennilee. The only time I even remember about my legs is when the weather's about to change, and I can tell you right now it's not going to rain any time soon."

"Climbing stairs?" Jeff stopped shoveling food long enough to ask.

"Yeah, on the new addition to the motel. Between building inspectors and keeping an eye on the crews…"

"You love every minute of it." Rachel threw her arms around Tim's shoulders and hugged him tight, brushed a kiss across the side of his face.

Accepting her buss, turning fully to her and kissing her full on the lips, Tim backed off enough for the others to hear. "Yes I do."

Charlie slung an arm around Jennilee and grinned. "So do we, 'cause when you do all the work, that means we get time to play."

A round of laughter, then another as Timmy asked hopefully, "Time to play? Has it been half an hour yet?"

Jennilee flashed the youngster a smile. "No, Timmy. More like five minutes. We'll swim, I promise. By the time Mose gets done and we get everything cleaned up and get our suits on…"

"And by the time I get your hair braided." Charlie pulled Jennilee close and brushed a kiss across the top of her head, tangled his hand in the long length of her unbound hair.

Elizabeth piped up, "Will you do mine, too, Charlie?"

"Sure, munchkin. C'mere and I'll do yours first."

"Just like Jennilee's."

"Just like, Elizabeth. Want me to do yours, too, Timmy?"

The adults all burst out laughing at the horrified look on Timmy's face. "Un uh, no way. How come you always braid Jennilee's hair anyways? Why doesn't she do it herself? Boys aren't s'posed to braid hair."

Jeff chortled. "I've been asking them those same questions for years, Timmy my boy. Don't worry—your hair is too short to braid. Even I know that."

While Charlie braided Elizabeth's hair, Jennilee moved on to her next victim. All she had to do was look in Mr. Jubal's direction.

Raising a hand and giving a low chuckle, he forestalled her. Normally as forthcoming as the beanpole he resembled, Mr. Jubal would willingly parcel out his words for Jennilee. "I'm fine, Jennilee. More than fine, and so is Sadie. I'm still working my way through your books. Just finished *Moby Dick*. That was some fish. I picked up the *Iliad* today. Might put that one back for later and choose another."

"Your books." Jennilee never missed a beat, and she wasn't arguing.

Charlie met Mose's eyes, grins and identical head shakes coming from both. "You might as well give up, Mr. Jubal. Jennilee ceded her grandfather's books to you a long time ago and she's not going to change her mind."

Jennilee's face lit. "Mr. Jubal, Charlie and I just bought a couple huge boxes of books—at that big estate sale on the other side of New Bern—to add to our library. We haven't even opened them yet. Would you like to go through them?"

"I surely would, Jennilee. I might just go do that while y'all go play fish."

"I'll be glad to show you where they are, Mr. Jubal. I'm not much of a fish either." Rising gracefully Suki began gathering empty platters and bowls. Glared at Mose and gave him a stern warning even as she made sure the ones still holding anything were well within his reach.

"Don't you dare hurry through the rest of your meal. Sit right there and take your time."

Lifting a loaded fork in salute, Mose kept right on eating.

Hair braided, table cleared, and suits on, Suki and Mr. Jubal headed for the boxes of books while the rest of the crowd hit the water.

As they'd done since they were little, Charlie practiced cannonballs off the dock just to see how much of a splash he could make while Jennilee swam underwater. She stayed under so long they'd've worried had it been anyone but her.

Long ago, Charlie had named Jennilee mermaid—his mermaid—and so it seemed. She could hold her breath longer than anyone they knew.

Timmy tried his best to copy Charlie, and Elizabeth practiced holding her breath so she could learn to swim like Jennilee. Grandy held baby Cassie for a bit, played with her and Cory in the shallows while the rest of the adults jumped into the deeper water at the end of the dock and swam and played.

Cautiously putting his feet down in the murky water, Jeff encountered only sand—no mucky mud. "Hey Charlie! How'd you manage this? Jennilee wave her wand or something?"

Oyster shells and nasty mud covered the bottom of the river for the most part, and you had to be extremely careful where you placed your feet.

Charlie laughed. "I have a couple loads of sand dumped here every so often. I don't like the mud."

"What's CAMA say about that?"

CAMA—Coastal Area Management Authority—the arm of the government responsible for permits that had anything to do with land use close to the water. In other words, you weren't supposed to build a dock, or fill wetlands, or dig ditches or disturb a single piece of marsh grass without their approval.

Charlie's wide grin flashed. "Don't know."

Jeff shook his head. "Better to ask forgiveness than permission?"

"Exactly!"

A standing joke among the locals—if they wanted something, the permits would automatically be denied. If a big developer came in and wanted to build condos or marinas or strip malls—well, money talked.

Jeff laughed and shrugged. Charlie had the money now, and if he wanted to butt heads with CAMA, more power to him.

Jeff felt like he'd stepped back in time to his own childhood, caught in a time warp maybe. They were all here and now, right there as adults, and yet he could so plainly see the children they'd been doing exactly these same things.

The crowd played Marco Polo and tag and chicken and other water games. Just like when they were little, punctuated with lots of laughing and carrying on and shoving people off the dock and coming up underwater behind or beside someone and scaring the daylights out of them.

Walking out on the dock, Suki had to stop and catch her breath at the sight that met her eyes. Mose, holding Cassie in the crook of one arm while he dangled Tommy and Elizabeth off the other. Laughing, he lifted and dropped his arm like a huge piston with the two children dangling from it like they weighed nothing. Cory had Mose from behind, arms around Mose's neck and clinging to his back like a monkey.

Charlie and Jennilee shared smug grins at the look on Suki's face.

"Y'all about done playing fish? 'Cause I got the marshmallows and graham crackers and Hershey bars all ready for you at the oyster pit." Suki's call had them all scrambling out of the water onto the dock and heading for shore.

Quick passes under the open shower at the end of the dock, and they were ready for s'mores.

Charlie and Jennilee the last to step under the shower head, everyone watched without seeming to, without meaning to. Standing close to Jennilee, Charlie casually loosened the splice that held her braids in a tight coronet, ran his fingers through her hair and fanned it out. Tipped her head back and rinsed the brackish river water out of the glorious mass.

Towels wrapped around them, they made all the s'mores they could eat, roasted a few marshmallows as well while Jennilee enlightened them about the evolution of marshmallows.

Kids and adults, they listened enthralled. Waiting on her perfectly tanned on the outside and ooey-gooey melted on the inside marshmallow to cool, Jennilee informed them, "Y'all know that pinkish lavender flower that bloomed last month, the one I showed y'all?"

Groans and shared eye-rolls all around, as the whole crowd ragged on Jennilee—as usual—about her penchant for pointing out weeds.

Ignoring them—as she always did—Jennilee enthused, "Marshmallows were originally made from the boiled roots of that plant. Guess what it's called? Marsh mallow, or Althaea officinalis. As far back as ancient Egypt, the Egyptians added the boiled concoction to honey and grain and made a kind of cake out of it. The Romans knew about it, used it mostly as medicine. The French are the ones who made a true candy out of marshmallows, but they had to be formed one at a time. In the early nineteenth century, a machine called an extruder was invented and marshmallows could be mass produced from man-made ingredients. That's how we got marshmallows as we know them, and why we're eating this delicious treat right now."

Swallowing the burnt-black marshmallow in his mouth, Jeff smacked his lips, and queried the crowd at large. "Y'all know what we called Jennilee when we were kids?" Head shakes all around. "Encyclopedia. If you wanted to know something, you didn't have to drag out the Funk and Wagnalls or Encyclopedia Brittanica. All you had to do was ask Jennilee. She knows more useless facts and trivia than anyone else I know. Right, Charlie?"

"Absolutely, Jeff." With a wicked grin, Charlie pulled Jennilee close. "For instance, if I wanted to know the history of, say...kissing..."

Loud groans from everyone followed by laughter.

"...all I'd have to do is ask Jennilee. Well, Jennilee?"

"Kissing. Hmm. Did you know that Cupid..."

The rest of her explanation got lost in their demonstration.

The adults sat and savored, replete, while the kids bounced and ran around like puppies until they were completely worn out and it was nearly full dark.

Rachel and Tim packed up their kids, Cassie and Cory already asleep, Timmy and Elizabeth well on the way.

Directing his comment to Charlie and Jennilee, Mose observed, "Looks like I need a ride. Seems Dad took off. You know he goes to bed with the chickens. 'Sides, he probably found more than one book in that stash you invited him to look through and he's on another world right now. Next thing I know, he'll be hounding me to build another bookshelf." Mose's amused rumble vibrated through the warm night air.

Before Donny and Grandy could volunteer, Suki's fluid tones chimed in. "Already taken care of, Mose. Mr. Jubal asked me to carry you to his house so you could pick up your truck."

Goodnights all around, slamming car doors, and everyone was gone except Charlie, Jennilee, and Jeff. They managed to hold in their laughter until Suki's vehicle was well away.

"Mr. Jubal sure is a wily old fox." Jennilee's voice was full of laughter.

"You got that right. More power to him." Charlie's was, too.

"What's on the menu for tomorrow?" Grinning into the dark, oh so content to be a part of this again, Jeff hadn't realized just how much he missed this...closeness. The camaraderie, the knowing you were accepted and loved no matter what. Family. Home.

"'Bout the same as today—nothing much." Charlie moved to one side of Jennilee and Jeff automatically took up his station on the other side as they started walking to the house.

Sandwiched between them, Jennilee said, "We have to go to town tomorrow morning and then we don't have anything we have to do until tomorrow evening."

"Yeah, tomorrow's our night to help out at Grandy's."

"That mean y'all are eatin' supper at the restaurant?"

Knowing laughter met Jeff's eager inquiry.

"Do you ever think about anything besides filling your stomach?" Reaching around Jennilee, Charlie cuffed Jeff affectionately on the back of his head.

"Well, yeah. Actually, I do."

Snickers from Charlie and Jennilee, and Jennilee choked out, "Blonde, brunette, or redhead."

"Hey! I resemble that remark!"

Their combined laughter wafted out over the yard and gardens, echoed off the forest at the edges of the yard, drifted out over the river.

NONE of them paid any attention to the sound of a boat motor purring, far out on the water. Practically everyone around here had a boat or skiff, and most people spent a great deal of time fishing or clamming or merely boating.

CHAPTER 6

"*H*ey! Where's my bike?" Jeff's indignant cry rang across the now sunny yard.

"You been here goin' on two days and you just now thought to wonder about your bike?" Charlie made tsking sounds and shook his head.

"Give, Charlie. What'd you do with it? I still owe a lot of money on that bike and..."

Not about to let Jeff off the hook so easy, Charlie managed a sorrowful look and a sympathetic tone as he told Jeff, "Manuel probably got it."

"Manuel?"

"Yeah, Manuel. A Mexican guy who hangs around here sometimes."

"Some...Mexican's got my bike?" Visions flashed through Jeff's head. Car thieves. Chop shops and stolen parts and border crossings in the dark of night. A lot of payments yet to be paid with no bike to show for it.

"Jeff. Calm down. Charlie's teasing." Jennilee laid a soothing hand on Jeff's arm.

"Yeah, man. Calm down." Charlie smirked at Jeff over Jennilee's head.

Jeff made a face back at him.

"Enough, you two."

"He started it."

"Your motorcycle is fine, Jeff. Manuel is our...foreman here. He runs things here the way Tim runs our construction crews and stuff."

"What do you think this is, Jeffro? The big bad city? That's what you get for moving so far away and living in a crime riddled neighborhood and..."

Glaring, trying not to laugh, Jeff knew better than to fall for Charlie's pranks. He could've left his bike parked right where it was with the keys in it for a hundred years and no one here would have touched it. Not like he'd been so easily conned into thinking.

"So where did this...Manuel put my bike?"

"In the garage with the other vehicles, Jeff. Rest easy. Manny can't stand to see a vehicle left outside. He's probably already washed and waxed it at least twice." Jennilee took off walking toward a building that just could be seen through the trees—a long, low many doored building that hadn't been there two months ago. Jeff trailed behind her while Jewel dashed ahead eagerly.

As soon as Jennilee's back was turned, Jeff punched Charlie in the arm, tussled, got him in a headlock and gave him a noogie.

Despite his awkward position, Charlie was laughing, laughing way too hard to put up much of a fight. "I *told* you, we have *staff*."

Giving them adequate time to scuffle and get it out of their systems, Jennilee remarked, "You're going to love our new ride, Jeff."

Momentarily forgetting about getting even with Charlie, Jeff wondered what kind of new vehicle they'd purchased to put in their new garage. Something hot. Something better than the '68 Ford pickup Charlie'd restored and driven all through high school, was still driving. Better than the used Crown Vic Mr. Donnie had given Jennilee for graduation.

Both passable, they weren't exactly what Jeff thought someone with Charlie's and Jennilee's money should be riding around in.

"A Jaguar. Tell me you got that hot little number we were drooling over a couple months ago at your bachelor party. Tell me, Charlie. Or maybe…a Ferrari. That red one we saw in *Car and Driver*." That's what Jeff would be driving if he had a tenth of the moolah the two of them had in their bank account.

His beloved Harley the first thing he spotted when they entered the garage, after assuring himself she was fine, Jeff let his eyes rove over the open stalls of the interior—fine, mighty fine—and then the other vehicles. The woodgrain-sided Jeep Wagoneer Suki drove, Charlie's truck, then Jennilee's Crown Vic and…

At the look on Jeff's face, Charlie crowed. "That's what you get for thinking, and that kind of thinking is why you'll never have any money in the bank!"

Not the cars of Jeff's dreams, but a Jeep Wrangler. Used, if he knew them, and he did.

Spiffy, and new looking, but Jeff would bet anything Charlie and his dad had repainted and re-upholstered it, probably dropped a new engine in as well.

Crossing the space until he stood toe to tire with the doorless and open top CJ-7, extra-wide tires, Jeff ran his hands over its glossy red paint like he would a woman in a silk negligee.

"At least you had the good sense to get a Laredo."

"Wanna drive her?" Charlie dangled the keys in a tempting jingle.

Jennilee had to laugh at the torn look on Jeff's face, and his words.

"Un uh. I know what happens when I drive you two around. You'll both crawl into the back seat and… Un uh. No way. I'll ride in the back."

Before he could get in, Jennilee and Jewel hopped in the back seat, settled comfortably. "We're not going far, Jeff. You can have shotgun."

"Wonders never cease. And don't think this lets you off the hook. You're enjoying this as much as he is." Still pretending to be aggravated, Jeff climbed in the passenger seat. "Just where are we going?"

Grinning in response, Charlie started the engine at the same time he hit the door opener. "Not far. Got somethin' we wanna show you."

Jeff rolled his eyes, a gesture he knew they both picked up on. Turning his head he looked to the side before letting a wide grin slide over his face. Yep, they were up to something alright.

Instead of heading down the driveway, Charlie pulled out of the garage and headed in the opposite direction, past the garage down a grass and dirt track bordering part of their extensive gardens.

Winding through the woods, they came out next to a huge, grassy field.

"Cows? You brought me out here to show me cows?" They were still up to something, but Jeff couldn't for the life of him figure out what.

"Not just cows, prime Angus beef. That steak you ate last night came from our herd."

"Is this like going to a fancy restaurant and picking out the lobster you want for supper?"

Leaning up between the seats, Jennilee rested an arm on both. "We didn't bring you out here to show you steak on the hoof."

Jeff's eyes roamed the sea of green. He still didn't see anything except grass and cows and a barn Charlie kept driving toward.

Only it wasn't a barn.

"Holy shit, you did it!"

Laughing, Jennilee had her arms around Charlie's neck from behind, her face close to his. Charlie was grinning like a possum. The barn that wasn't a barn was a...hangar. Inside...a Cessna 170, capable of carrying a pilot and three passengers.

"Jennilee got me flying lessons for my birthday a couple years ago."

"Yeah, I remember."

"We got the plane so we could..."

"Let me guess. You bought a plane so when Jennilee wants new fabric in a color she doesn't already have you can fly her to wherever and she can pick it out and still be home in time to cook supper."

Jennilee laughed harder, a sound both men relished.

"That too, but we really got it so..."

"...we can..."

"...go on..."

"...trips." Charlie and Jennilee finished together.

Well used to their fractured sentences and truncated speaking rhythm, Jeff just continued to stare.

"We were hoping…"

"…you'd…"

"…go with us."

"Where and when?"

"Bermuda, tomorrow." That from both of them.

"This plane won't make it to Bermuda."

"No, but it will make it to a major airport. Raleigh or Wilmington."

"Who's the fourth victim?"

A moment of silence, and then Jennilee chirped, "Angel. She's coming down this afternoon."

Jeff grinned and forgave them their tricks. Things were looking better and better.

After exploring the Cessna inside and out, he only had one question.

"This thing gonna take off like a Harrier?"

Charlie grinned and clapped Jeff on the back. "See that pasture out there? It does double duty—cows on it, it's a pasture." Waggled his eyebrows. "Cows off, it's a runway."

Sometime while he'd been poking his nose into every nook and cranny, Charlie'd braided Jennilee's hair into a tight coronet and she'd gotten back in the back seat. Sliding into the passenger seat, Jeff waited to see where they'd take him next.

Next proved to be a huge trailer park just outside of Morehead City, couple hundred trailers easy. Driving past it, Charlie parked the jeep in the shade at the edge of a field full of heavy equipment, all doing heavy equipment things. Turning in his seat, giving Jennilee a serious kiss, he stroked his hand down the side of her face. "We'll only be a minute, Jennilee-love."

Smiling like the Madonna, Jennilee made herself comfortable in the back seat, working on some of her ever-present embroidery while Charlie and Jeff got out and walked toward the equipment. Jewel curled up beside Jennilee.

"Y'all thinkin' about buyin' this trailer park?"

"Already did."

"Y'all own a *trailer park*?" Jeff did some quick mental calculations.

Couple hundred trailers at a couple hundred dollars a month, each, added up quick. Good for them.

"Mobile home estates. Mobile. Homes. Not trailers. Not trailer parks. That sounds like...white trash. And, yeah, we own a couple."

A couple? "So what are we doing here?"

"Promised Tim I'd meet him here."

Appearing as if Charlie'd conjured him, Tim and Charlie spoke some kind of carpenter/plumber/electrician/owner/foreman/construction type shorthand, accompanied by head shakes and nods and gestures. Lots of gestures. Both satisfied with the results, they went their separate ways.

On the way back to the jeep and Jennilee, Charlie remarked, "We're adding about fifty more units and replacing some that have gotten too old."

"Guess if I ever get back here for good, I won't have to look far for a place to stay."

Charlie made a noncommittal sound. Upon reaching the jeep, he leaned over the side, kissed Jennilee, and informed her, "Jeff thinks we're gonna let him rent a trailer from us."

Looking around Charlie, Jennilee beamed at Jeff. "He does, does he?"

The two lovebirds shared a look rife with serious messages.

Teasing him about something, Jeff didn't have a clue what. "Actually, I was hoping for something more along the lines of one of your apartments at Garner House."

Charlie and Jennilee shared another look. One of their teenage projects, Garner House had been—and still was—a very successful one. A beautiful old place, Mose had helped them restore it and divide it into gracious apartments. The first place they'd kept for their own, their first rental, one they still owned. Mose had claimed the guesthouse for himself and still lived there.

"Funny you should mention Garner House. That's where we're headed next." Flashing Jeff a blinding grin—one matched by Jennilee —Charlie hopped into the driver's seat.

Shaking his head, Jeff made himself comfortable in the passenger seat. They'd let him in on the secret when they were ready and not a moment before.

Making a pit stop at the Winn-Dixie Deli, they picked up the makings for a quick lunch. Lunchmeat, cheese, sub rolls, chips, stuff. Mission accomplished, they loaded the jeep and headed back to Chinquapin Ridge.

Long before they pulled up in the driveway, Jewel was standing, dancing impatiently on the seat. Even jumped between the seats to stand on Jeff's knees with her front feet planted on the dash and look out the windshield, whining expectantly the whole time.

"Where's Mose, girl? Are we almost there? Think he's gonna give you a good belly rub, don'cha?"

Catching himself, Jeff slanted a look at Charlie, didn't dare look at Jennilee.

Charlie kept looking straight ahead, not trying very hard to suppress a huge grin. "I didn't say a word."

"It's you two. You talk to this mutt like she's human, and now you've got me doing it."

"Not got you doing it…"

"…caught you doing it…"

"…again."

Laughter rang out and Jewel barked enthusiastically.

Hearing the sound of Charlie's and Jennilee's jeep with its distinctive wah-wah-wah off-road tires, Mose smiled to himself. He'd been in a fast downward spiral of depression, on the fast track to insanity, when the two of them had dragged him into their schemes.

He had the knowledge, they had the need.

Charlie and Jennilee had needed to make money so they could save money—piles of it so they could buy and restore the house of their dreams. He'd played a huge part in making their dreams come true.

He'd needed, too. Needed to feel like he had a purpose other than the killing machine he'd learned to be in Vietnam. An excellent soldier —too excellent—he'd been wounded, decorated, wounded, decorated —over and over. Not that he'd ever shown them to anyone here, but he had pret' near every medal the military handed out and then some.

A debilitating wound and an honorary discharge followed by the abrupt change from military to civilian life—especially the laid back time warp that was Chinquapin Ridge—had been too much. Mose saw enemies behind every bush, heard enemy gunfire in every sound, trusted no one. Couldn't eat, couldn't sleep, couldn't focus long enough to hold a real job.

He'd been slowly withering away, withdrawing farther and farther into his own nightmare delusions when Charlie and Jennilee had presented him with an option.

They needed to buy old houses and fix them up but they were too young—not even in their teens yet—for anyone to take seriously. Mose, already known far and wide as a wizard with wood and restoration, all they had to do was combine their resources.

Mose had the knowledge, and the age, and he took what they said as Gospel.

They'd formed a partnership, one that laid the foundations for the wealth the three of them had now. Using Mose's skills and know how, they'd bought house after house, redone them and resold them.

Both kids willing to work like dogs, they'd absorbed all the knowledge Mose dished out. Their restorations had earned a well deserved reputation, sold for top dollar. He couldn't be prouder of them if they were his own flesh and blood.

He'd helped them; they'd saved him.

Mose rubbed his leg, the one that had gotten him discharged. He still limped when he got over-tired, and it hurt occasionally. Neither limp nor pain was bothering him now.

Looking around his shop, one filled with top notch tools and works in progress, Mose shook his head. If he'd given them the means to make their dreams come true, they'd done the same for him. Given him more—a reason to live.

Mose's talent for working with wood was legendary. The furniture he created seemed more…conjured…than made by human hands. He could coax the inner beauty out of any piece of wood, turn a plain board into a work of art.

His creations and re-creations graced many a mansion and museum, but none were as fine as the ones he'd done for Charlie and Jennilee. He imbued every piece he did with love, the love of his craft and love of what he did, but none held more love than the ones he fashioned for not merely his best friends and business partners, but two of the people he thought the most of in the whole world.

Hearing Jewel's sharp bark amid laughter and joking from her humans, Mose's grin widened. They'd dragged Jeff along with them today, not that he'd expected anything less. Jeff had been as much a part of their growing up as Mose himself. Just as important, in a different way.

Charlie and Jennilee had worked side jobs and done chores for anyone that needed something done—anything to add to their stash and further their dreams. Jeff had spent more time just being a child. Mose might have helped them be adults, but Jeff grounded them, reminded them how to be young.

Never as goal oriented as Charlie and Jennilee when they were kids —but then, not many adults were as focused as those two—Jeff was certainly focused now. Had been ever since the life altering event of finding Charlie's mom.

Mose had every confidence that Jeff, having found the body hidden for so long, would also nail the murderers.

Jewel reached him first. Launched herself with the full expectation Mose would catch her, and he did. By the time the kids caught up to her, Jewel lay cradled like a baby in one of Mose's strong arms, belly up, getting the belly rub of her dreams. Mose's talented fingers knew all her hot spots.

"See! What'd I tell ya! I knew it!" Jeff made them all laugh with his observations.

Jewel turned her head to look at him upside down, blissfully happy.

Jeff's next words were directed at Jewel. "You're a traitorous wench, dog!"

Jewel continued to regard them indifferently, perfectly content where she was, all four feet in the air and a sublimely goofy look on her face.

"Alright girl. That's enough."

Letting out a heavy sigh at Mose's words, Jewel wriggled and twisted until she turned right side up. Making no move to get down, she instead draped herself comfortably over Mose's huge forearm and dropped her head on her paws.

"I'm not holdin you all day, pup. I got things to do."

Another sigh, and Jewel jumped down, disappeared out the shop door.

Jennilee laughed and shook her head. "She'll just head for Garner House, see if Josh and Will are there. If they are, she'll pull the same deprived routine on them."

"It's your fault, missy. You talk to that mutt like she's human, and you've got the rest of us doing it, too."

"What'd I say? Didn't I just say that?"

More laughter at Jeff's words, laughter the men loved to hear from Jennilee. They all sheltered her, insulated her, as best they could, but the shadows and the hurt ran deep.

"You at a stoppin' point, Mose? We brought lunch."

"Jennilee, are you trying to feed me till I pop? Seems like we just got done eatin' at your place last night."

"I'll take that as a yes. Mose, why don't you show Jeff what you've been working on and I'll go start."

"I'll carry the stuff for you, Jennilee."

Groans and eye-rolls from Mose and Jeff did nothing to deter the couple.

"None of that hanky-panky stuff in my kitchen, ya hear?"

Laughter from Charlie and Jennilee as they headed out the door, hand in hand, was his only answer.

Jeff observed wryly, "Those two are as predictable as that mutt. You always know what they'll be doing."

"You should try workin' with 'em sometime. They're like a couple toddlers—if it gets quiet, you know they're up to no good."

Almost to the guest house Mose had claimed for his own, Charlie and Jennilee heard Mose and Jeff laughing. Shared a quick grin and a longer kiss, no doubt in their minds exactly what the two were laughing about.

Jeff looked around, as always in awe of Mose's creations. "Hey, Mose. I just want to thank you again. The stuff in my room—wow. Just...wow."

"Glad you like it. I..." He shrugged. "...made what Jennilee said."

"I guess you've seen my room."

"Yeah."

"Nobody's ever..." Jeff trailed off, at a loss for words.

Mose finished softly. "...taken care of you quite the way Jennilee does."

"Yeah. It's like I told Charlie—Jennilee's a sheepdog. World class."

Mose and Jeff burst out laughing again. "You got that right. Left up to her, she'd have her whole flock right there, right where she could keep an eye on each and every one."

Enjoying a leisurely lunch, the foursome reminisced and caught up some more. In preparation for tomorrow's trip, Charlie and Jennilee left Jewel with Mose so she wouldn't be at the house by herself, even though Suki was there and Jewel wouldn't technically be alone. No qualms about leaving her with Mose, he'd spoil Jewel, and Jewel would lavish him with doggy affection.

Heading back to Charlie's and Jennilee's, sun beating down on them, wind in their hair, radio blasting, the three friends were happy as clams.

Driving down the long driveway, instead of going back to the house, Charlie cut off down a side road that led in the general direction of the hangar.

"What now? We gonna pick out supper? We just had steak last night."

Charlie reminded Jeff, "Patience is a virtue." Kept driving.

Jeff squirmed impatiently in his seat. "I've seen enough cows for one day."

"Don't you want to see more of the farm?" Charlie looked at Jennilee in the rearview. "I think we should show him some more of the farm."

She met his gaze and matched his grin. "I think you're right."

Jeff rolled his eyes, making sure Charlie and Jennilee saw him. Charlie kept driving.

"Just how much does *the farm* consist of?"

"Besides the original 650 acres?"

"Besides."

Charlie flashed Jennilee another lazy grin in the rearview. "500. On either side."

"And?"

"And that much across the paved road as well."

"Planning on owning the world?"

"Just my corner of it."

Jeff shook his head. They rode for a bit more, until they came out on the river shore. Charlie drove the jeep to the middle of a clear spot on a high bluff. High for around here anyway, actually only twenty or so feet above sea level. Graceful, ancient live oaks dripping with Spanish moss dotted the space here and there, and the scrub grass had been recently mowed.

Getting out, they walked around.

Jennilee waved a hand at the expanse as she and Charlie strolled to one side of Jeff, hand in hand. "You like this?"

"It's a beautiful spot, guys. Thinking of building something here?"

Charlie drawled, "That's up to you."

"What do you mean?" Jeff stopped and stared at them.

Jennilee leaned her head on Charlie's chest, just over his heart. He tucked her head under his chin and they wrapped their arms around each other, both of them focused intently on Jeff.

"It's yours…"

"…if you want it."

Jeff repeated himself. Slowly, head cocked. "What do you mean?"

"This lot…"

"…is yours…"

"…when you're ready…"

"…to come back here…"

"…and settle down."

"Mine?" Jeff's voice came out in a wobbly squeak.

"Yes, yours."

"Mine?"

Both of them nodded, grinning like possums.

Jeff swallowed, his heart in his throat. "Fine." Swallowed again, hard. Laid down the law. "I'll take the land, but you are not paying for the house."

"Jeffro, nobody said anything about paying for your house."

"Maybe not, but I know you two and I can see the wheels turning."

"How's this—you provide the plans and the dinero—we'll provide the materials and the construction crew."

"I don't know what to say, guys."

"Say yes, bonehead."

Jennilee held out a hand to Jeff. "Please say yes, Jeff. We know you won't want to stay at the main house with us forever, although you're always welcome and we're always glad to have you. This way, you'll be close but you'll still have your privacy and…"

Jeff took her hand. "Jennilee, you don't have to bribe me. I'm… stunned. Ecstatic."

"So does this mean we're gonna have a new neighbor?" Charlie quipped.

"I've got…things to do first. I'll be here as soon as I can."

Jennilee moved from Charlie's arms to Jeff's. They all knew what *things* he felt he had to do.

Holding Jennilee with his left arm tight around her, Jeff clasped forearms with Charlie.

To ease the emotions overwhelming them all, Jeff teased, "What happens if I decide to move?"

Without missing a beat, Charlie shot right back, "Then we'll repossess and give the house and land to someone we really care about."

Their shared laughter rang over the land and water, bounced off the live oaks. Settled into Jeff's heart like a healing balm.

CHAPTER 7

$\mathcal{T}$hey hadn't been back at the main house long when Angel showed up. The four of them ended up in the game room.

All Jeff could do was shake his head again. Charlie and Jennilee might have spent their childhood working their asses off instead of playing like normal kids, but damned if they weren't making up for it now.

A regulation size pool table, a trove of pinball machines, foosball table, air hockey table, a wide variety of video arcade games, an antique drink box filled with Pepsi and Mountain Dew—real glass bottle ones—the cream sodas Jennilee so adored, amid a plethora of other bottled drinks—and the crowning touch—a genuine Wurlitzer juke box.

Topped off with an immense jar full of quarters just begging to be utilized.

Jeff and Charlie quickly engaged in a pool duel, the girls egging them on. The sounds of balls being racked and broken and sunk were interspersed with trash talk and laughter and the smooth sounds of classic rock and oldies.

Charlie and Jeff shared more than one ecstatic grin when the girls weren't paying attention. No words were necessary—anything that made Jennilee laugh made them happy.

The girls drifted off to catch up on each other's lives and play a couple games of Ms. Pac, followed by a round or two of Joust. The boys, having tired of pool, waged war on the Galaga machine.

They ended up crowded round one of the vintage pinball machines, Charlie and the girls cheering Jeff's performance. Game over, high score secured, Jeff let out a whoop and danced in a circle, arms pumping, butt wagging. "Woohoo! Top that, Charlie Brown!"

"I will, but it's gonna have to wait. We gotta head for Grandy's. Y'all comin?"

"Are you kidding? I wouldn't miss a free meal at Grandy's for anything."

"Who said it's gonna be free?"

Jennilee and Angel shared a grin/eye-roll/head shake and headed for the door.

"What about you, Angel?" Nudging Charlie out of the way, Jeff jogged close to the girls, wormed between them, threw an arm around each.

"Me? My parents own a restaurant/catering business. I'll do anything at Grandy's restaurant Jennilee and Charlie want me to."

Jeff leered and asked, "Anything? How do you feel about French maid's outfits?"

Angel eyed him up and down. "Probably take some doing, but I'm sure we could find one to fit you."

A moment of dead silence, followed by uproarious laughter.

They took the jeep, guys in the front, girls in the back. Jeff wasn't sure what they were up to, but both Charlie and Jennilee had changed into clothes that looked like they came straight out of the fifties. Not Miz Amelia dressed to kill style, more teenager on a date style.

Jennilee, hair braided in a tight coronet, had on sandals and white capris and her madras plaid blouse was knotted in front, showing off a sliver of her trim belly. Charlie had on jeans, the cuffs rolled up, and a white T shirt and loafers, hair slicked back into a DA, a la James Dean.

Jeff had taken one look and just started shaking his head. Halfway to town, he was still shaking his head. There was no telling with these two.

Angel hadn't worn the outfit he'd requested, but she was still a knockout. A dark foil to Jennilee's rain of golden hair and ocean eyes, Angel's cloud of shoulder length inky curls and equally dark eyes were set off tonight by a sexy red top and white shorts.

Arriving at Grandy's restaurant, all Jeff could do was shake his head again. Next door to Charlie's and Jennilee's motel, both of them right on Highway 70, Del's Diner did a booming business. Five o'clock, and already the parking lot was full, the porch holding the spillover from the restaurant, people waiting their turn to get in.

Jeff surveyed the restaurant building. Like everything they did, the diner and motel bore Charlie's and Jennilee's distinct stamp. Neat and trim, but welcoming. Flowers everywhere, rocking chairs on the porch. A much bigger porch than he remembered. "Y'all add to Grandy's again?"

"Had to." Charlie drove around back, parked in a spot marked reserved and they got out.

As they drove past, Jennilee's knowing eye surveyed the hanging baskets and the flower boxes on the rails and the tubs of flowers in the parking lot. Satisfied with their condition, she took Charlie's hand and they went straight in the back door.

Greeted and were greeted by, not just Grandy, but Miz Sadie as well.

Accepting the hugs, Jeff stood back and let Miz Sadie look him up and down.

"My stars, boy. Jubal said you'd come home to visit. You's skinny as a rail. You need to come home more often and let me and Jennilee and Del fatten you up."

Jeff didn't dare look at Charlie and Jennilee, knowing just the smirks that would be on their faces. "Jennilee's been trying to fatten me up my whole life, Miz Sadie, just like you and Miz Del. She's done an excellent job the last couple of days, but I sure could go for some of y'all's...anything. Nobody where I live knows how to cook like you three."

"Hmmph." Pleased with Jeff's compliment, Sadie turned back to what she was doing, muttering all the while. "Young'uns move off, don't take no care of themselves. Nobody cooks anymore. Starve to death in a full pantry."

Charlie and Jennilee and Jeff shared wide grins and got out of Miz Sadie's way. Grinned too, because none of them had any intentions of letting Miz Sadie fatten them to her standards. Even Mose couldn't clean his plate when Miz Sadie dished up, and it remained a pure wonder how Mr. Jubal had stayed such a beanpole after being married to Miz Sadie for decades.

"How come y'all are both cookin' tonight? I thought you took turns?" Jeff snatched back a hand just in time as Miz Sadie thwarted his attempted thievery with a warning lift of her wooden spoon.

"Boy, you knows better'n that. You always was hardheaded."

Snickers from the peanut gallery had Jeff putting on a wounded look. "You just said…"

"Don't you be twistin' my words, Jeffrey Rivenbark! I said you needed to eat, not snitch my food a'fore it's ready."

"We're both cooking tonight because…" Grandy began, caught the slight head shakes and mischievous grins on Charlie's and Jennilee's faces, changed what she'd been about to say. "We run a…special on Thursdays, and it takes both of us to keep up."

Still clueless, Jeff asked, "Y'all are that busy on a weeknight? That's great."

Charlie headed for the door to the main room, tugging Jennilee with him. "Stay here and catch up, Jeff, and don't annoy my cooks or…"

"You said I had to help. That's all I was trying to do…help." Jeff's innocent words and expression were met with laughter all around.

Jennilee started, "We have to go…"

"…work. Some of us have to work, Jeffro. Don't hamper or hinder my cooks and maybe, just maybe, we'll let you have a cookie…if you behave."

Angel snickered as she added, "I notice they didn't tell you to clean your plate. Guess they don't have to worry about that."

More laughter. A well known fact, Grandy, by way of Jennilee, gave a cookie to all the little kids who came in and ate to their parents'

75

satisfaction. Almost as well known as the fact Jeff was a bottomless pit.

Charlie and Jennilee disappeared through the swinging door and Jeff settled in to see if he could wheedle samples while Angel watched his antics interestedly. Hand in hand, Charlie and Jennilee moved through the main room and the adjoining dining rooms, stopping to speak with long time customers here and there and greeting the new ones. Jennilee's eagle eye took in everything, noting what had been done, what needed to be.

As they moved through they also spoke with the waitstaff and busboys, the hostesses and the girls manning the cash register/dessert counter.

Jennilee stopped at the glassed dessert counter, checking and double checking the contents and display. All the fine desserts inside—cakes, pies, cookies, candies and confections—were handmade by Grandy and Miz Sadie. Charlie busied himself on the small bandstand, setting up, testing acoustics and instruments and such.

Picking up his guitar, Charlie began strolling around the restaurant, playing and singing. Jennilee, without stopping what she was doing, began singing too, her voice a sweet accompaniment. Jeff and Angel, drawn by the sounds, popped their heads out of the kitchen and were shown to their table—the front and center table Charlie and Jennilee reserved for their special guests.

Wandering, playing this and that and special requests as they were called out, Charlie and Jennilee were enjoying themselves immensely and it showed.

Chin in hand, Angel leaned closer to Jeff and remarked dreamily, "Have you ever seen them when they weren't like this?"

Jeff gave a rude snort. "Like what? Looking at each other like a couple moonstruck calves? They're always like this."

"It's nice, though. They're so much in love."

Jeff grinned. "It is nice. More than. I just like to tease them. They're special enough by themselves, but when you get the two of them together..."

"...they glow."

"Hey! Don't you start, too!"

"Start what?" Angel blinked innocently and grinned back.

"You know exactly what I'm talking about. The way they always finish each other's sentences. It's like…"

"…like they share the same brain?"

Jeff laughed, drawing a cheeky grin from across the room from Charlie and Jennilee, as if they'd heard his and Angel's conversation. "The same heart and soul, more like."

"Seems that way, doesn't it?"

"You don't know the half of it. When I said they were always like this, I meant it. As long as I can remember, they've been…a unit. You know, like some of those old couples you see that have been married seventy-five years and still call each other dear and sweetheart and mean it. The ones that get antsy if the other gets out of sight. That kind of close."

"Yeah, I know exactly what you mean. My Nonnie and Poppie are like that."

Jeff and Angel fell silent, lost in their own thoughts, interrupted now and then as Jeff rose to greet old friends.

Charlie stopped playing for a moment, long enough to give Jennilee a drink out of the glass one of the waitresses handed him and to take a long drink of water himself while Jennilee stopped and talked with one of her favorite pint-sized customers.

"Hey, Jennilee. How come you always have your hair up? I like it down, Jennilee."

Jennilee threw her head back and burst into laughter as she knelt so she'd be eye level with Ricky. Her ardent admirer since she'd bested one of the local bullies in front of him, right there by the dessert counter as a matter of fact, Ricky and Jennilee had a special relationship.

"Hey yourself. Charlie'd rather have it down, too, Ricky. I don't want your food in my hair, and trust me—you do not want my hair in your food."

Ricky looked to Charlie for support.

Charlie shook his head and grinned. "She's right, Ricky. On both counts. How 'bout if I promise to get her to let it down later for you? Will that work?"

Ricky considered, tipped his head to the side. "I s'pose. Can I have fried okra tonight?"

Jennilee laughed again. The night she'd taken down Butch had been the first time Ricky tried okra. It'd remained his favorite vegetable ever since, probably would be for life.

"Absolutely! Are you going to have meatloaf or fried chicken with that?"

No hesitation. "Fried chicken, please."

"Just tell Sarah. She's got your section tonight. I'll remind her to give you extra okra."

"Thanks, Jennilee." Ricky wrapped his arms tight around Jennilee's neck. Hugging him back, she winked over his head at his grinning parents.

Pulling back quickly in the way of small boys who've been affectionate enough in public, Ricky looked up at Charlie. "Charlie, will you play *Red Baron* for me?"

Charlie mock frowned. "You don't really want to hear about Snoopy and the Red Baron again, do you?"

"Please? Pretty please with sugar on top and mo-las-ses."

"Well, since you asked so politely..."

Charlie and Jennilee broke into song, and it was hard to tell who was grinning harder.

They played and sang for awhile longer and then took a break, sitting down with Jeff and Angel to catch their breath.

"You call that working?" Jeff took a bite of fried chicken and a long swallow of Miz Sadie's sweet tea, so dark it was almost black and nearly syrup, but oh-so-good.

Kicking back, Charlie rested one ankle on the opposite knee, slid an arm around Jennilee and let a wide grin take over his face. Waiting till Jennilee got a good drink, he took the glass he and Jennilee were sharing and drank thirstily. "Helping. I said we were helping tonight, not working."

"So what are we supposed to do?"

"You're doing it, man. Sit here and enjoy."

"And listen to you rib me all day tomorrow about doing nothing? No thanks. Give me something to do."

"You heard him, girls. He wants something to do. Volunteered, even."

Angel kept a straight face. "Lots of stuff needs doing in a restaurant, always."

Jennilee quipped, "Dishes. We have lots of dirty dishes."

Massaging Jennilee's neck, Charlie pulled her close for a kiss. "Trash needs to be taken out."

Jennilee kissed him back. "Windows washed."

"Floors mopped."

"Alright, you two! I'll sit here. I don't want to hear it tom…"

"Not a word, Jeffro."

"We promise."

Jeff looked disbelievingly from Charlie to Jennilee.

"You two are scaring me."

Charlie tapped one hand on the table, Jennilee matched him with one of hers and together they beat out a rhythm.

"…B…b…baby…"

"…you jest ain't seen nothin' yet."

Jeff groaned and covered his eyes with a hand. Looked to Angel. "See what I have to put up with? All the time. All. The. Time."

Heads turned as their laughter rang out.

Heads turned a bit later, especially Jeff's, when Charlie and Jennilee took the small stage.

Charlie had redone Jennilee's hair. Not completely down, Charlie'd wrapped it in a fist-sized coronet with a pony tail hanging from the middle and swinging to her every move, like Jeannie from *I Dream Of Jeannie*. Jennilee swayed to the music while Charlie played his guitar and both of them sang.

They did an awesome show, hits from the forties and fifties along with a lot of silly songs and Sha-Na-Na type stuff. Jeff's jaw almost hit the ground when Mose and Mr. Jubal joined them, Mose's deep bass and Mr. Jubal's fiddle playing melding perfectly with Charlie and Jennilee.

They finished with an instrumental duo by Charlie and Mr. Jubal that easily rivaled anything from Flatt and Scruggs.

Laughing and holding hands, the foursome took deep bows and stepped down to thunderous applause.

Out of his seat and to them in a matter of steps, Jeff caught Charlie in a one armed bear hug, pounded him on the back, quit pounding and held out that arm for Jennilee. Laughing and carrying on, the trio had a flashback to long ago. Another jubilant time, just like this.

"Y'all do this every Thursday? That was...awesome!"

"Glad you approve, Jeffro."

Jennilee, still breathless, beamed at the two of them.

"Grab Angel and let's get out of here before we end up playing all night."

Sharing grins, Jeff headed for Angel while Charlie and Jennilee said their goodnights and followed Mose and Mr. Jubal into the kitchen.

"No wonder y'all have so many waitresses and busboys here. I thought you were just trying to boost the local economy or something." Jeff caught up with them in the kitchen, all of them still on a high from the performance.

"We are boosting it. In our own little way."

Jeff crowed, "I'll say! Mose—I've never heard you sing in public before. And Mr. Jubal—it sure was good to hear you play again. You should be in a recording studio. Both of you."

Mose smiled a slow smile that started on one side of his face and worked its way to the other. "Wouldn't do that for anyone but Jennilee."

Mr. Jubal just grinned as he tucked his fiddle into its case.

"Thanks, y'all." Safe in the sanctity of the kitchen, Jennilee gave Mose and Mr. Jubal both a hug and a peck on the cheek. Lacing their fingers together, Charlie eased Jennilee toward the back door.

"Y'all headin' out?" Grandy paused her bustling for a moment.

"Got stuff to do tonight, Grandy. 'Sides, we're too hyped to sit still and if we stay here..."

"...we'll end up playing another set or two..."

"...and we'll never get out of here."

"Be careful, y'all. Love you."

"Love you too. Don't work too hard." With that, Charlie and Jennilee slipped out the back door, Jeff and Angel in tow. Instead of heading toward the jeep, they headed across the parking lot toward the motel.

"What now? Y'all are going to do another show at the motel?"

"Can. Hadn't planned on it."

That was all Jeff could wheedle out of Charlie until they reached the four story building. Using a pass key and going in a side door, Charlie made straight for the elevator, and not the public one. A private one that only went to the top floor.

Waiting till the elevator door closed, Jeff stated dryly, "I know I'm always tellin' y'all to get a room, but if you think we're gonna wait while you two..."

Angel elbowed him from one side and Jennilee got him from the other.

Jeff yelped. "Hey! No fair double teaming me!"

Charlie snorted a laugh. "Wuss. Shouldn't dish it out if you can't take it."

"Yeah. I thought you were such a big macho football hero." Angel added to the verbal harassment while Jennilee snickered.

"Charlie's the football hero. Charlie's the hero, period. Just ask Jennilee."

"He's my hero, for sure. Always has been."

"So what..." Jeff hushed as the door opened and they piled off the elevator into the lush suite facing them.

"Holy penthouse, Batman!"

"Owner's suite, Robin. Jennilee and I need a shower, and then we were thinking about heading to the Beach Tavern and shooting some pool. Or we can stay here and get in the pool. Whatever you guys want to do."

"Beach Tavern, definitely. That way I can kick your ass and have witnesses to prove it."

"You wish."

Jeff and Charlie scuffled good naturedly. "Y'all take more showers than anyone else I know."

"That's 'cause we work harder than anyone else you know."

"Get going so we can get going."

"Refreshments..."

"…if you want them."

Charlie and Jennilee disappeared into the bedroom.

Jeff didn't even wait till the door closed before moving. "Alright!"

Angel asked in total disbelief, "How can you possibly still be hungry? You ate a whole platter of fried chicken by yourself!"

Jeff grinned as he reached the bar. "Not hungry. Thirsty. They're talking about liquid refreshments. And it wasn't a whole platter."

"Pretty darn close."

Spying the ice bucket and inspecting the contents, Jeff crowed, "Natural Light for me, oh yeah. Guess the Bartles and James are for you." Twisting the top off a B&J, Jeff handed it to Angel, twisted the top off his beer and wandered around the suite. As usual, with everything they touched, it bore the distinctive stamp of Charlie and Jennilee.

Wagging her bottle, Angel couldn't resist teasing a little more. "You want a glass or you gonna…chug out of the bottle?"

Indicating her bottle with his own, Jeff riposted, "Speak for yourself, woman. I can…sip. They've really convinced you I'm a caveman, haven't they?"

"You do a pretty good job of that all by yourself."

Laughter and small talk till Charlie and Jennilee returned, not too much later, Jennilee's still wet hair in a single thick braid this time. They looked like any normal just out of their teens couple headed out for a night of fun.

Jeff made a rude noise in his head. *Normal? Those two? No way!* They might look normal, but they were so far above the pale it wasn't funny.

In the jeep once more, they headed for Atlantic Beach and one of their favorite teenage hangouts. They'd been frequenting the Beach Tavern since before they were old enough to drink, perfecting their pool shots.

Once inside, they waved to the regular bartender when she looked up, made their way to her in order to show Angel's ID. She scanned it, handed it back.

"Y'all want your usual, plus one?"

Nods and grins and the foursome headed for the pool room to

claim a table. Girls against boys, and Jennilee broke. Admiring the view when it was Angel's turn to shoot, Jeff feigned innocence when Charlie poked him with the business end of his pool cue. Trying to stifle a grin, Jennilee just looked ceiling-ward.

The waitress appeared with a plate of nachos, one Sprite in a glass, a pitcher of house draft, and two empty glasses. Jennilee automatically picked up the pitcher and poured both glasses full, expertly holding the pitcher sideways so the beer wouldn't foam.

Handing one to Angel and one to Jeff, she took a sip of Sprite and passed the glass to Charlie. Countless rounds of pool later, Jeff finished off the last pitcher and they headed out, Jeff grumbling.

"Y'all have an unfair advantage—what with having a pool table at your house and all."

Charlie ribbed back. "You won your share—you're just a sore loser."

"An El's shrimp burger would go a long way towards..."

"How can you even think about food?" Charlie and Jennilee burst into laughter at Angel's disbelieving question.

"He's a..."

"...bottomless pit."

"Besides..."

"...El's is closed."

More laughter as they all got in the jeep, guys in front again and girls in the back. Riding in silence and enjoying the beautiful night, instead of going straight home, Charlie drove down the beach road a little ways, pulled into the Oceanana Pier parking lot. Without a word, they all kicked their shoes off, got out and ambled toward the beach. This late, they had it to themselves. Quiet waves kissed the shore and retreated in a soft, soothing lullaby.

"I love the ocean!" Jennilee inhaled deeply and twirled in circles, arms outstretched, head thrown back.

Catching her and pulling her close, Charlie slipped the tie off the end of her braid, wove his fingers through her hair until it hung loose and free, the heavy miasma of cigarette smoke and stale beer already dispersing in the salt laden breeze. "Most mermaids do." Heads together, they moved even closer for a long, drugging kiss.

Jeff heaved a tolerant sigh. "Let's walk, Angel. They'll catch up." Meandering down the shore, away from the pier and the lights, they walked companionably close, just in the edge of the surf.

As predicted, catching up not too much later, Charlie asked, "Hey guys, wanna go..."

Jeff inserted, "...skinny dippin'? Alright!"

Angel stopped so fast Charlie and Jennilee almost ran her over. "Are you crazy? It's dark out here."

Jeff exclaimed, "Exactly! Skinny dippin' is way different than swimming with clothes on." Charlie and Jeff high-fived.

"Angel, don't let the two of them get to you. We're goin' swimmin'. You don't have to if you don't want to and you certainly don't have to skinny dip. You can wear your bra and underwear—it's just like wearing a bikini. That's what I'm doin'. The guys are keeping their boxers on. I, for one, have to get the smell of cigarette smoke off me."

Angel digested all that for a moment. "Y'all are really going swimming? Right now?"

In answer, dragging a somewhat reluctant Angel with them, the other three moved up into the dry sand and shucked their clothes. Dropping them in piles, they turned and ran for the water. Angel followed, a little slower. Charlie and Jennilee splashed out into the surf side by side, hand in hand. Jeff slowed and waited for Angel.

Taking her hand, he encouraged her, "Come on in, the water's fine."

"Yeah, but is it cold?"

"This time of year? Not hardly. It wasn't cold when we were wading, was it? Put your arms around my neck and I'll carry you."

"Your caveman side is showing. Again."

"I give you my word I won't throw you in."

Angel hollered in the general direction of Charlie and Jennilee. "Can I trust Jeff's word?"

Charlie and Jennilee's answer came ringing back, in stereo. "With your life!"

"Promise you won't *accidentally* drop me in, either."

"Angel! You act like I'm a..."

"...prankster? You bet. I'm warning you—I've got brothers. Lots of brothers."

"Are you threatening me?"

"Huh. I don't need my brothers to fight my fights. I can hold my own, thanks to them and their *pranks*. They taught me well. I know every dirty trick in the book and then some."

Jeff threw back his head and laughed. "I'll just bet you do. How's this? I give you my word not to get you wet in any way, shape, or form until you're ready."

Angel amended, still not quite trusting him or his motives. "Until I say so."

"Deal." Jeff twisted their clasped hands into a handshake. "How about a kiss to..."

"Don't push your luck, mister."

Charlie and Jennilee's voices, with the ocean making a muted background, started singing The Rolling Stones *Satisfaction*. Their laughter followed, rich and pure.

Ignoring their teasing antics, Jeff carried Angel out to where Charlie and Jennilee frolicked in the deeper water. Diving into the waves, attempting to bodysurf on waves far too lethargic for such action.

Angel finally got brave enough to give Jeff the ok. Arms wrapped tight around his neck, she let him immerse her feet and legs. As soon as her feet touched bottom, she jerked up and clung harder.

"What if I step on something?"

"The bottom is real sandy here, but if you're worried about it, just float. Don't put your feet on the bottom." Suiting actions to words, Jennilee flopped on her back like she was sprawled on her queen size bed at home.

Angel didn't loosen her hold any and Jeff asked, "Piggyback?"

"Yeah. I'm not quite as brave, or trusting, as y'all."

Shifting Angel to his back, Jeff tucked his arms under the backs of her thighs, just behind her knees.

"You guys do this a lot, don't you?"

"Used to. Not so much anymore."

"Not as much as we'd like, that's for sure." Charlie floated beside Jennilee, their fingertips touching.

"Hey, Angel. Wanna swim? Hold on to me and I'll do all the work."

"I can swim."

"You don't have to do anything. Just relax and enjoy."

"Why do those sound like chauvinistic, sexist comments?"

"Great minds think alike?"

Laughing so hard she lost her stability and sank, Jennilee rolled as she went under and swam off. Came back underwater and under Charlie. Goosed him and came up sputtering and laughing as he let out a yelp and floundered to his feet.

That led to a lot of squealing from the girls as Charlie retaliated by using the flat of his hand to splat water in Jennilee's direction. He inadvertently caught Angel in the crossfire, Jeff splatted back, and the war was on. In their dodging and ducking and shifting, aided and abetted by the gentle push and pull of the water, the foursome moved about quite a bit.

Focused on each other and their playing, in the space of a heartbeat everything changed. Everything they did, every movement, every breath, was outlined in luminescent silvery green. Each drop of water was visible, whether on their skin or in the air.

Angel squalled and tried to climb higher on Jeff's back. "Ok. Now y'all have totally freaked me out. What the hell is that?"

Jeff snorted, "Thought you said you swam?"

"In our pool, and trust me—none of us ever turned green and sparkly."

A glittery Jennilee stood up completely so that the upper third of her body was out of the water, lifted her arms and spun in a slow circle, trickling streams of liquid light from her hands and looking for all the world like the mermaid Charlie'd named her. The guys and Angel held their breath and watched, enthralled.

Jennilee laughed, and spoke breathlessly. "Ocean magic."

"Yeah, I understand that, but what kind?"

"Jennilee's mermaid magic." Charlie and Jennilee moved together, lips touching, making their own kind of magic.

Angel redirected her question to Jeff. "What is this stuff?"

"We call them phosphors."

"Which are?"

"Tiny phosphorescent sea creatures that give off light when they're disturbed."

"They don't bite, do they?"

"Some luminescent things can hurt you—jellyfish, for example—but not these. They're totally harmless. See?" Scooping up a handful of water, Jeff turned his hand sideways and they watched as it made a waterfall of light from his hand back to the ocean.

They swam, and made trails and whorls and swirls of light in the water. Even Angel. Jennilee made shallow dives, spun in the water, turned this way and that until Angel expected to see pods of dolphin and schools of fish and all manner of sea creatures answering Jennilee's exuberant call.

Jennilee moved out deeper and deeper until she was almost treading water, bouncing lightly to keep her head above with each slight swell that came by. Charlie stuck close, knowing what she wanted. A good foot taller, he had no problem keeping his feet on the bottom and his head above water. She put her hands on his shoulders, he cupped his hands. Pushing down on his shoulders, Jennilee lifted herself, put a foot in the cradle of his hands, and he launched her.

A graceful arch as Jennilee sailed up and backwards, shining as if she really had scales, legs together until it seemed she truly had one appendage instead of two, water cascading from her in glittering streams of light. Arms outstretched over her head, she disappeared beneath the water with hardly a sound and only a spreading ripple of phosphors to mark her entrance.

Completing her back flip under water, she circled right back up to Charlie and they repeated their exquisite water ballet over and over.

"Wanna try?" Jeff offered to toss Angel but he could no more have taken his eyes off Charlie and Jennilee than he could've stopped watching a high wire circus act at the peak of its performance.

Angel, equally entranced, whispered close to his ear, "No thanks. She makes it look so easy."

"Yeah, Jennilee's that way about everything."

Together they watched, lost complete track of time, didn't even notice it was getting lighter and lighter. Exploding over the horizon, a full moon turned everything it touched to silver, made a shining path across the water right to them.

Charlie tossed Jennilee one more time, and it seemed to the watching couple as if he threw her over the moon. Landing with her usual flair, she came up laughing, rose and locked her arms around Charlie's neck, kissed him long and deep.

Jeff and Angel could almost see her mermaid's tail undulating gently underwater, keeping her afloat in front of her human lover.

Jennilee still held close against him, Charlie called a halt. "Enough, guys. We're never gonna get up in the morning if we don't go and mermaid here will play all night if we let her."

Spell broken, they made their way back to shore, found their clothes. A happily tired foursome meandered back to the jeep, Jennilee tucked close under Charlie's arm, right against his heart. Jeff and Angel walked right beside them, shoulders and hands brushing occasionally.

Grabbing beach towels from the stash Charlie and Jennilee kept in the jeep, drying off, trading towel snaps and jokes before getting semidressed—shirts for the girls and shorts for the guys— and wrapping the towels around themselves, they loaded up.

They drove across the Atlantic Beach bridge and through Morehead City, practically a ghost town at this time of night. By the time they reached Chinquapin Ridge, they hadn't seen another vehicle in at least ten minutes and they were the only ones on the road as far as they could see in either direction.

"What do they do around here, roll up the streets when the sun goes down?" Used to Raleigh's night life, Angel shook her head in amazement.

Jeff leaned around his seat and grinned at her. "Pretty much."

The soft sounds of *Peaceful Easy Feeling* and *Let Your Love Flow* and *You're my Jamaica* and other beloved favorites pouring out of the radio were the only manmade sounds after that as they passed through Chinquapin Ridge and hit the long stretch on the way out to the house. The jeep's tires humming on the pavement, summer wind in their hair, and they were all filled with the kind of tired contentment that only comes from playing hard in good company.

The full moon making it nearly bright as day, Charlie killed the lights. Magical, driving in the blue-white solitude with only the moonlight to guide them, they could plainly hear the night creatures singing their own golden oldies in the ditches alongside the road, frogs and crickets and such.

The night-song followed them down the long driveway, right to the garage and then to the house.

CHAPTER 8

*T*he next day passed in another blur of happiness. Charlie piloted his small plane and passengers to Raleigh Durham International where they caught the small, private Learjet—pilot included—that was waiting for them.

Theirs for the day only, not theirs. Jeff asked.

Mouth hanging open, head shaking. "Tell me that's not yours, Charlie Brown."

Charlie gazed thoughtfully at the Lear as they crossed the tarmac. "Not yet. I can't justify the expense. Yet."

A short hop to Bermuda and they spent the day playing tourist. Catching their return flight late in the day, Charlie flew them home in time to watch the sun go down on their little slice of Paradise.

Saturday was every bit as great even though they did nothing near as exciting. Just normal everyday small town fun. They slept a little late, at least Jeff and Angel did, woke to another of Jennilee's spectacular breakfasts.

Hot from the oven homemade cinnamon rolls covered in sweet icing. Fresh squeezed orange juice. Custom omelets, with a vast array of fillings to choose from. Bacon and sausage. And of course, Jennilee's most excellent coffee.

Breakfast over, they moved en mass to Charlie's and Jennilee's workshop for a bit. Jeff and Angel watched as Jennilee deftly packaged and wrapped some of her one of a kind kaleidoscopes and some of Charlie's intricately lifelike carvings.

Jeff watched over Jennilee's shoulder as she addressed each package in her distinctively beautiful script. "Far out! You're sending those baubles to Ireland and the whittling to Bolivia?"

Jennilee answered absently. "Baubles are what Charlie keeps me knee deep in and whittling is what Mr. Franks does to innocent sticks while he's sitting on the bench in front of the post office."

"Yeah, yeah, yeah. Your stuff's way better than that, but still... Ireland? Bolivia? That's awesome."

"Baubles?" Charlie's tone and his stalking movements sent Jeff scooting out of the way with a huge grin on his face.

"Baubles? I'll have you know..." Spinning the office chair Jennilee was seated in, Charlie pinned Jennilee and kissed her, long and deep. Coming up for air, forehead to forehead, he informed Jennilee, "The macaroni and plastic bead bracelets your boyfriend Ricky is always giving you are *baubles*. What I give you, on the other hand..."

Jennilee laughed, totally carefree. "Jealous? Of a little kid?"

Jeff teased, "You've given her plenty of baubles in your day, Charlie Brown. Every ring you found in a box of Cracker Jacks or was spit out of a gumball machine..."

Angel quipped, "And she's still got every single one. I've seen them in her jewelry box."

Jennilee grinned. "I treasure each and everyone. Baubles or no."

"Maybe I should carve you another jewelry box—one for baubles and one for..."

Jennilee instigated the kiss this time. Murmured against his lips, "Don't you dare! They're all equally precious to me."

Her statement might have rung false coming from anyone else, but the trio surrounding her knew it to be true. They'd all seen her wear Ricky's heartfelt gifts and Charlie's priceless jewels with equal aplomb, sometimes side by side.

Seen her wear the necklace of double wooden hearts Charlie'd carved for her out of a naturally shaped hardwood burl right alongside gems that could easily have graced a queen's jewelry casks.

Her engagement ring and wedding ring were prime examples. Charlie'd commissioned both to his exacting specifications. Gold, white gold, aquamarines and diamonds, they suited Jennilee to a T, and she never took them off.

Today was no exception—around one slender wrist she had on Charlie's ID bracelet, the silver one—real silver and not chrome plated —he'd given her while they were still in high school, around her neck the heart shapes. The dangly earrings she wore—they were another story altogether. Charlie'd purchased them for her yesterday in a little jewelry shop on the waterfront in Bermuda.

Mermaids, cunningly wrought of silver with mother-of pearl accents, each with a bright sapphire for an eye, emerald chips making their tails flash and wink.

Jeff snorted, "I'm just surprised she doesn't still have the strings of every single candy necklace Charlie bought her when we were kids."

A round of laughter, and Jennilee said, "I have to draw the line somewhere. Besides, as I remember, you ate more than your share of the candy off my necklaces."

"Y'all shared those, too? My brothers and sisters and I..."

A meaningful look between the other three and Jeff grinned, "We shared pretty much everything. Candy cigarettes, sodas in wax bottles, sodas in glass bottles, you name it."

While the girls were laughing, reminiscing about simple childhood pleasures, Jeff shot a look at Charlie, one he caught. They hadn't shared every single thing, but then, Jennilee'd been downright close-mouthed about the horrors that went on at her aunt's.

Charlie—especially Charlie—and Jeff had known some, guessed at more, but even their worst imaginings hadn't come close. For one thing, Jennilee'd been ashamed to tell them of all the *chores* her aunt had dumped on her young shoulders or the way her aunt and her cousin treated her. And those horrors didn't even include Jennilee's uncle. Going along with everything his wife said, he was the one who physically punished Jennilee on her aunt's say-so.

Those memories had Charlie and Jeff unconsciously moving closer to Jennilee.

"Hey, guys. Back off. You're steaming up my tail." Putting both hands against Jeff's chest, Angel shoved. Pretending to stagger back, he rubbed circles over his chest where Angel's hands had touched him.

"Easy, easy. Be gentle with me. I'm delicate."

Angel snorted, "Delicate, my ass."

"And a very nice ass it is, too."

"Jeffrey Rivenbark... If I so much as catch you looking..."

Jeff grinned cheekily. "So it's okay if you don't catch me?" Ducked just in time as Angel tossed one of the shop rags at his head.

Charlie and Jennilee shared knowing smiles, eyes alight.

Riding into town in the jeep, as carefree as they'd been the day before, they swung by Mose's and picked up an ecstatic Jewel. Watched as Jennilee gave Mose a hug, nearly made him blush when she gave him a souvenir from their trip to Bermuda.

Cradling the small piece of wood in his huge hands like it was a fine porcelain figurine and he was terrified of dropping it, Mose chided, "Jennilee...you gotta stop giving me stuff. I'm not a spoilt little kid who thinks he's supposed to get something every time someone goes to town."

Jennilee's laughter rang and echoed around Mose's shop. "I wouldn't buy you something if you thought you should have it. *I* thought you should have it—that's why you got something—and I didn't *buy* you anything. It's just a piece of driftwood I found on the beach."

"Jennilee..."

Openly laughing at the big man's discomfort, Charlie advised, "Give up, Mose. You know how she is."

"Yeah, Mose." Jeff sided with Charlie, tickled not to be on the receiving end of their affection for once. Waiting until Charlie and Jennilee drifted off with Angel so Angel could ooh and ahh over the works in progress, he sympathized with Mose. "You should see what they brought me back from their honeymoon."

Mose rolled his eyes. "I can only imagine."

Jeff nudged him. "What'd they bring you?"

"Who says they brought me anything?"

"Mose. This is me—Jeff—you're talking to."

"I know who I'm talkin' to. 'S that what they brought you?" Cutting his eyes at Angel, Mose laughed and laughed.

They left Mose, still chortling at Jeff's unresolved curiosity and his own sense of humor. Stopped by Grandy's for a bit and gave her the trinket they'd brought her. Pretended to be besieged as Tim and Rachel's kids spotted their vehicle and came flying around the privet hedge to see them. Gave the kids their trinkets and spent some time playing with them before heading into town proper.

Charlie dropped the girls and the packages off at the post office. "Jeff and I have to run by dad's garage. We'll be back at the pharmacy before y'all get there." With a kiss to Jennilee and a wave to both girls and a soft yip from Jewel, the guys began to back out of their parking space.

Glancing around the sparsely filled parking lot, looking across the street and down a couple of buildings to the pharmacy, Angel observed, "Wow. Your post office must be really slow if the guys have time to go to Mr. Donny's garage and get back to the pharmacy before us."

Jeff's laughter rang out and Jennilee stuck her tongue out at him. "I can tell you've never been to the post office with Jennilee."

"What's he talking about, Jennilee?" Angel found out, and quickly.

While Jennilee was standing in line, she spoke to everyone already there as well as everyone who came in. Answered endless questions about what was she mailing and where was the stuff going this time and gardening and cooking and recipes and what was the lunch special at Del's Diner today and what was in the goodie case. Inquired about everyone's families, answered the same inquiries about her and Charlie and Grandy and Jeff.

It took them awhile, but they finally got out of the main office and back into the lobby where the PO boxes were. Checking her box, chatting with a few more people as they came in, Jennilee eased her way to the front door. Got all the way out before she got waylaid again, this time by someone who hadn't been there when they went inside.

"Hey, Jennilee."

Jennilee smiled and shifted the mail to a more comfortable hold. "Mornin' Mr. Franks."

Angel was hard pressed not to laugh as she took in the scene. An older gentleman sat on the bench, stick in one hand, knife in the other, shaving the stick into a pile of tinder with each slow, methodical pass of the knife.

Chatting with him for a few moments, Jennilee got as far as the flowerbed surrounding the flag pole at the end of the building. She'd just run satisfied eyes over it, and turned to Angel to say something when Mrs. Spence cornered her.

With no greeting or small talk, the older, matronly woman launched into a diatribe. "Jennilee, you and Charlie have to do something about..."

Half-listening to Jennilee's soothing tones, Angel let her eyes wander, wondered if they'd make it to the pharmacy before supper time.

They did, eventually.

Pushing open the door and stepping into the dim and blessedly cool interior of the old, tin tray high-ceilinged building—complete with dark wood floors that smelled of old wax and creaked with every step—Angel countered Jeff's laughter, added hers to it. "Jennilee, I swear. Do you know every single soul in town and their life history?"

Jeff crowed, "Told you."

Jennilee defended and deflected. "Yeah, well, you've been here a bunch of times, but now you've been properly introduced to the lot of them and they know your name as well, Angel. If they find out how big your family is..."

More laughter from all of them, including the pharmacist and the clerk and joined by several of Charlie and Jennilee's local friends as they entered the store in time to catch the exchange.

"Hey, Angel! Good to see you again. Heard you were in town, Jeff. Charlie and Jennilee, shame on you for hogging him." Waves and handshakes and hugs and back slaps of greeting all around, joking and carrying on.

As word got out the seemingly magic way it does in a small town, like a wildfire sparking and taking off, more and more of their old gang showed up, pouring through the door in trickles and fits.

Charlie threw out an invite. "Why don't y'all all come over to our place tonight? It's been awhile. Call the rest of the gang, whoever's not here, and we'll...do what we always do." Slipping an arm around Jennilee as she grinned, Charlie pulled her close for a kiss.

"Gag! Don't y'all ever get tired of..." Jeff grinned. Waving a hand like he was Lawrence Welk, everyone chimed in.

"Get a room!"

Shaking her head, Angel remarked dryly. "Y'all say that like you've said it a time or two before."

"A time or two?"

Another round of laughter and the whole crowd settled on the barstools ringing the grill and counter, started calling out lunch orders to a ready and waiting Jennilee. Moving behind the counter, she started frying up hamburgers and hotdogs and french fries and onion rings and making milkshakes.

She'd just finished serving everything when Charlie started singing his version of an old favorite Tom T. Hall song, just loud enough to reach the crowd surrounding him and Jennilee. *"Hello, Mrs. Rogers, you self-righteous biddy. We don't need your loud mouth, misinformin' the town."*

Jennilee stiffened and her face tautened.

All heads swung to the door as the bells jangled.

Jennilee came around the counter as the door pushed open, and Charlie put his arm around her, gave her a squeeze.

Total silence reigned for a long, intense moment as the two factions stared at each other—the crowd of silenced for the moment kids and a prune-faced old bat with a bouffant hairdo and cat eye glasses trading equally disgusted glares. Jewel's low growl vibrated from beneath Charlie's bar stool.

Bertha Rogers lost no time lighting into them. "Look at the crowd of you! Sitting around and stuffing your faces! Loafers and do-nothings, all of you. I see they've dragged you back into their midst, Jeffrey Rivenbark. Your momma will be so ashamed."

Jeff bristled around a mouthful of cheeseburger he was trying to choke down but Jennilee beat him to the punch.

"Bertha. Can we do something for you?"

"You! What are you doing here, and what's that vicious mutt of yours doing in a place of business? There are laws, you know. I need Mr. Timmons there to fill a prescription for me, not that it's any of your business. Just because you hoodwinked Mr. Gillikin into feeling sorry for you and he used to let you work here, you act like you own the place. Hmmph." Bertha sniffed loudly and turned up her nose.

Shifting Jennilee so she was in the vee of his legs, her back against his chest, Charlie pulled her close, wrapped both arms securely around her waist and pressed a kiss to the top of her head. Said in a deceptively mild tone, "Actually, Bertha, we do. Own it. From now on, if you want any prescriptions filled, you best go to Morehead or Havelock."

"You can't…"

"Mr. Timmons, Marcy?"

"Yessir," came from both of them at the same time.

His voice still softly polite, Charlie informed the pharmacist and the clerk behind the register, "Bertha won't be doing business with us anymore. See that her prescriptions are transferred to the pharmacy of her choosing. Now."

Bertha's mouth opened and shut, opened and shut. Her face went from crimson to plum to puce, an interesting color combo—if you were a planter full of flowers. Glaring at each of them in turn, she glared hardest at Jennilee and her dog, peeking out from between Charlie's and Jennilee's legs. Spinning on her heel, she yanked the door open, stomped out and slammed the door behind her.

Her theatrics would've gone over much better if her everything-but-the-kitchen-sink purse hadn't gotten caught in the—eight foot tall, very heavy wood framed with ornamental glass inserts—door and nearly snatched her off her feet.

The crowd managed to hold their laughter until Bertha reopened the door, freed her purse and slammed the door again, bells jangling madly.

Ben started making the distinctive dun-da-dun-da-dun-da-dun-da-dun-da sound of the Wicked Witch riding off on her broomstick and made them laugh harder. Choked out, "Good thing she doesn't have a bicycle with a basket, Jewel, or you'd be in trouble!"

"Charlie, I swear, if you were President of the United States, that woman would tell you that you needed to get a job." Robbie held his sides and chortled.

"Yeah, Jennilee. You too. If you were—I don't know—Queen of the World—she'd find fault." Sally, Robbie's cousin and Ben's girlfriend, added her two cents.

"She's been finding fault ever since we made her mad about something we were researching in grade school." Jennilee's smile didn't reach her eyes.

Swallowing the wad of burger in his mouth, Jeff licked his lips, slurped a drink of his milkshake. "I never could figure out how someone who hates kids so much got to be head librarian in a small town chock-a-block full of kids."

Angel, the only outsider, remarked astutely, "It's the perfect job for her." When everyone looked at her in disbelief, she continued. "Where else could she throw her authority around and tell everyone to sit down and shut up—and get paid to do it?"

Slow smiles changed to grins as the crowd erupted into gales of laughter at Angel's spot-on observation.

A bit later, Charlie let go of Jennilee long enough for her, with Angel's willing help, to clean up the grill area, kept his eyes glued to her as Jennilee moved to the other side of the store.

Using the store phone, Jennilee called Suki and let her know they'd need supper and party supplies, in quantity, anything they didn't already have on hand. Jewel stayed right on Jennilee's heels until Jennilee was back in Charlie's arms, then retreated beneath the barstool again and laid her head on her paws.

Someone at the far end of the counter suggested, " Hey, guys! Why don't we go to Minnesott?"

Angel queried Jeff as the rest of the crowd clamored excitedly. "Minnesota? What's in Minnesota?"

Jeff grinned hugely. "Minne*sott*, not Minnesota. Local beach on the Neuse river. It's up toward Havelock, off the Minnesott Ferry Road and not many people go there. It's actually Pine Cliff State Park, but everyone around here calls it Minnesott Beach, not to be confused with the town of the same name across the river. It's beautiful."

An hour or so later, Angel had to concede Jeff was right. Huge old trees on high ridges bordered the edge of the wide, shallow river, a river dotted all along the shore with equally huge Cypress trees. Picnic tables overlooking the river, a nice walking trail or two looping through the woods. Peace and quiet—at least until the whole gang showed up, and then the air was filled with shouts and laughter.

Having made a pit stop at Grandy's instead of going all the way back out to their house, both couples, courtesy of Charlie and Jennilee, were decked out in swim wear, complete with towels. Jewel had been left at Grandy's in care of Tim and Rachel's kids to visit for awhile.

Coolers appeared and couples disappeared, to wander the trails or the beach. Charlie and Jennilee and Jeff and Angel headed for the water. Too shallow to really swim in, perfect for wading and splashing.

Angel cocked a brow at Jeff and he snorted a laugh. "I'm not giving you a piggyback ride, not here. The water's not much more than knee deep all the way out to the channel—see out there where the water changes color?—and the bottom is fairly sandy. About the only thing you have to worry about stepping on here is a Cypress knee. Stay away from the trees and you should be in the clear."

"Shallow, huh? Your knees or my knees?"

Giving a shout of laughter, Jeff snatched Angel up in a bear hug, spun her around.

They played in the brackish water, had mad digging contests using their hands for clam-rakes to see who could find the most freshwater clams—inedible by their standards but fun to find. Ended up back on the beach, walking right in the thin verge where water met land.

The girls picked up small shells and bits of curiously shaped driftwood, the guys walked farther up on the sand, keeping an eye out for turkey tracks. Once nearly extinct in this area, the wild turkeys were making a comeback here. Judging from the tracks they found, there was quite a large population.

Making their way back to the main picnic area, Charlie, Jennilee, and Jeff watched with barely concealed amusement as Angel slipped her sandals on. They all preferred to remain barefoot even as they headed down the woods trails.

Angel mused, "This area seems fairly hilly for around here."

Jennilee gave a half-laugh. "Remains of ancient sand dunes, and yeah, all these hills and coves and creeks made a perfect place for moonshiners. Just ask the guys."

Charlie offered, "When it cools off, if we have a dry fall and you want to, we can come back and walk more of the Neusiok Trail, knee boots included. It goes quite a ways through here, some of it through swamp, and there are remnants of old stills everywhere. Jeff and I did quite a bit of exploring in our younger days. Found all kinds of interesting stuff."

Knowing how Jennilee was always collecting bits and pieces, Angel asked, "What'd you find, Jennilee?"

"A headstone."

"What'd it say?"

"No markings, just a big rock."

"Then how do you know it was a headstone?"

"Because there aren't any rocks around here. This one had obviously been hauled some distance, and it was the wrong shape and size to be a doorstep or a hearthstone. A grave marker is the only thing it could be."

"You have a strange fascination with graves. You're always putting flowers on the ones at your house."

Jeff's laughter rang through the trees as he walked backward in front of the others. "You don't know the half of it." When Charlie and Jennilee both shot him a look, he only told Angel innocently, "They've been helping keep up Oak Grove Cemetery since they were little. Voluntarily." Shaking his head, Jeff turned and leaped over a small stream. Pinwheeling his arms, he twisted and faced them once again as he pretended to lose his balance.

"At least they were doing something constructive with their time." The immediate sizzle of tension, there and gone between her friends like a zap of static electricity—no, more like an unexpected bolt of lightning from a clear blue sky—had Angel apologizing. "Look, I don't know what I said or whose toes I stepped on, but I'm sorry."

Jennilee kept hold of Charlie's hand and they leapt gracefully across the creek together, waited for Angel to catch up. Jennilee tossed over her shoulder, "No harm, and that's a common enough saying. Don't worry about it."

"Yeah, it's not your fault you didn't grow up with us and don't know every single one of our dirty little secrets." Jeff teased, but his eyes were haunted as they met Jennilee's, and then Charlie's. Apologetic as they swept Angel's face, he held out a hand to help her across.

Finishing their walk, they ended up where they'd started only to find an impromptu football game being played out madly on the beach. At least Angel assumed that's what it was. There was a football involved, anyway.

Letting out identical whoops of glee, Charlie and Jeff sprinted off to join the melee. Jennilee and Angel sat on a silvered driftwood log with the other girls and watched and cheered.

Angel managed to get out around her nearly constant laughter at the guys' antics, "I don't think I've ever seen a game of football played quite like this. What are the rules?"

"Probably not, and I'm not sure there are any. It's something the guys made up when we were little and there weren't enough players for real teams. They've been playing it ever since."

"It looks more like pictures of one of those primitive tribal games you see in National Geographic. You know, the ones where a bunch of half naked savages are riding shaggy little mostly wild horses bareback with their feet nearly dragging the ground and they're all chasing a goat head or something equally disgusting."

"Pigskin, Angel. They're chasing a pigskin. I'll be sure and tell the guys about your apt description of their *game*." Jennilee's laughter rang out, joined by the rest of the girls'.

Charlie was the last one to retain possession of the ball, dodging and dashing headlong amongst the herd from one side to the other. According to that and some other obscure—to the girls—rules, that seemed to have meant that he won. Won what, they weren't sure, but they joined in the hooting and hollering.

Digging through the ice in their cooler, Jennilee had a Pepsi and a Mountain Dew open and waiting when the guys reached them. Handed one to Charlie and one to Jeff.

"Jennilee, you give Women's Lib a bad name."

"Bite your tongue, Sarah. We like being waited on hand and foot." Blowing a kiss in Jennilee's direction, Jeff winked at Angel, chugged half his Mountain Dew.

"Well, she makes the rest of us look bad." Sarah pretended to pout.

Sarah's boyfriend Sam put his arm around her and teased, "Maybe you should take lessons. I am really thirsty."

"Not on your life! You want a drink, you know how to open a cooler." She pointed. "And ours is right over there."

"Spoilsport!"

As more than a few beers appeared and were consumed, Charlie did his best Mr. Clean impersonation, pointedly eyeballing the ones drinking. Watching as keys exchanged hands, Charlie was finally satisfied enough to relax.

Leaning close, under cover of the renewed laughter and chatter, Angel asked, "What was all that about?"

Jeff snickered. "The state mandated don't drink and drive rules have nothing on Charlie, and this crowd all knows and respects them."

"Rules?"

"You can drink at one of these get togethers if you want. Charlie has no problem with that as long as you keep it under control, but you damn sure better give your keys to someone sober. Charlie doesn't mess around with this shit."

"Go on."

Jeff sniggered. "Piss him off and the two of them will leave, and you won't get invited to the next shindig or three they throw. Step too far over the line just once, and you'll never be welcome again. Not only that, Charlie absolutely will not argue with a drunk. The "a" word's not even in his vocabulary. Either you hand over the keys, or he'll disable your vehicle until he decides you've gotten the point."

"No mercy."

Sobering, Jeff shook his head in agreement. "He's got plenty of good reasons."

Not too much later, pulling Jennilee a little closer, Charlie lifted a hand. "We're headin' to the house. Y'all come when you're ready." Charlie picked up his end of their cooler, Jeff took the other.

CHAPTER 9

"*T*acos? We're havin' tacos tonight?"

Jewel barked excitedly at Jeff's interested tone.

Jennilee didn't look up from the immense skillet full of hamburger she was busily browning but Charlie and Angel could still see the smile curving her cheeks. "Yes, Jeff. Would you rather we…"

"No! Hell no! I love…"

Charlie fired a couple ripe maters in Jeff's direction, maters Jeff deftly snatched out of the air. "Good. Then you won't mind helping get everything ready."

"Jennilee…"

"If you're gonna whine, pretty boy, you don't get any food." Charlie grinned slyly and smirked.

Jeff snorted, "Look who's talking, *Prince Charming*, and I wasn't whining. I just can't believe Jennilee is gonna let me use one of her precious knives."

"She keeps dull ones just for people like you." Drawing up like he was on the mound, Charlie winged a couple more maters across the island at Jeff. "They're in that drawer to your left."

Angel watched as Jeff began expertly juggling the tomatoes, even as Charlie drilled more his way, merely incorporating them into the spinning mass. "Jeff's not allowed to use your sharp knives, Jennilee? How come?"

Without missing a beat, keeping his eyes on the rapidly increasing as well as revolving maters, Jeff pretended to sulk. "Just because, once —*once*—a hundred years ago, I..."

Charlie broke in sadly, like he was announcing a death in the family. "Jeff scraped the sharp side of one of Jennilee's good knives down a cutting board."

Angel started laughing. "And she let you live?"

Jennilee made a face. "Y'all are so funny. Just because I respect a good sharp knife—I am not that bad about my knives."

Rounding on Jennilee, Angel quipped, "Oh, yes, you are." Laughed and watched the maters fly faster and faster until they became a whirling blur.

Eyes on the spinning discs, Jeff snarked, "It's not like Scrooge McDuck there can't buy you all the new ones you want."

"That's not the point, Jeff—you abused one of my *favorite* knives."

"Yeah, Huey. One of her babies." Charlie slipped his arms around Jennilee and squeezed, nuzzled his face into her hair and angled toward her lips.

"Cut it out, you two." Admonishing without taking his eyes off what he was doing, Jeff switched his throwing pattern so the maters were going behind his back before shooting back up over his shoulder, never slowing their rhythm.

Angel offered, "If you'll stop before you turn those tomatoes into paste, I'll cut them up for you." Waited a beat and then taunted, "Jennilee lets me use her good knives."

"Figures." Slowing down, catching each tomato as it stopped revolving, Jeff lined them up on the counter. "I'll do something else. Ooh, Jennilee—let me spice the meat!"

"Not on your life! The rest of us want to be able to eat some of this. You can spice yours up any way you like—later."

"Fine, then. Eat your old bland hamburger. I want some heat in mine." Grabbing the cheese grater and the block of cheese, Jeff set to.

Between the four of them they had all the ingredients ready in just a short while. Leaving the meat simmering, Jennilee disappeared into the huge walk-in pantry for a moment. Came back out with a jar in her hand. Passed the jar to Jeff with no explanation.

"You need this opened, Jennilee?"

Jennilee grinned. "Do what you want with it. It's yours."

Taking a good look at the colorful contents of the jar, Jeff let out a whoop of delight. "Hot peppers! Alright!"

"It's a salsa mix, Jeff. We made it for you from peppers we grew. Jalapenos, habaneros, some chili peppers, and... They're sliced so..."

Swallowing his bitter resentment of Jennilee's damnable so-called family, Jeff kept his grin in place for Jennilee's sake. Always, *always*, Jennilee offered him gifts like they'd be thrown back in her face. Not intentionally, and not because she doubted him or his reaction, but because deep inside, she was still that little girl who could do nothing right, was incapable of pleasing her surrogate family no matter how hard she tried.

Catching her in a big bear hug, Jeff pulled her close, pressed his lips to her bright gold hair. "Jennilee, I feel like Mose. You're always giving me gifts for no reason."

Jennilee hugged him back. "We love you. Both you and Mose. That's a perfectly good reason."

"Well, you don't have to worry about me not taking your gifts. I can't wait to try this."

Completely unaware of her slight hesitation earlier, Jennilee wasn't aware Jeff had picked up on it, and her laughter chimed out. "You just make sure that stays on your plate. I don't want anything to do with it. You should've seen us..."

Losing the thread of her words for a moment, Jeff's eyes met Charlie's over Jennilee's head. Charlie's eyes blazed with the same righteous indignation lighting up Jeff.

"...outside. We both coughed and sneezed for hours. Right, Charlie?"

Blinking at her call, Charlie's animosity was gone, just that quick, but then, he'd had plenty of time to learn to conceal his inner thoughts from Jennilee. "We sure did, Jeffro. You better enjoy that batch, bro, 'cause I don't know if I can stand to go another round with those hot peppers."

"Batch?"

"Yeah. There's a couple more jars of that stuff. Surprised it hasn't melted the rings off the jars. Actually, I'm surprised it didn't melt the spoon we stirred with, the pan it was cooked in, *and* the top of the stove."

Jeff smacked his lips. "Should be just about right."

Angel, silent witness to the currents flowing around and having a pretty good idea what this time was all about, had them all laughing at her declaration. "If so much as one drop of that comes anywhere near me—so help me, Jeff, I'll..."

Both men smiled at her, fully aware of and grateful for her levity.

Jeff huffed and shot a fierce look at Charlie. "Well, Angel, now that you've declared war, I'm the likely culprit in case *someone* decides to implicate me."

Waggling his eyebrows, Charlie grinned evilly at Jeff.

Jennilee's laughter filled the spacious kitchen as she danced from Jeff's arms to Charlie's and Jewel yipped a high-pitched accompaniment.

Later, with a bunch of people crowded around the huge table and more seated at the island, the jokes and ribbing flew fast and furious and the vast quantities of tacos and fixin's disappeared with almost equal rapidity. Jeff conned a few of the guys into trying a bite of his special sauce on their tacos.

Bites followed by a lot of coughing and choking and swearing, a lot of wheezing and red faces and teary eyes, and resulted in more than one drink being guzzled. Jeff munched contentedly, smiling all the while.

Only remnants left of the food, the crowd moved on to other things. By popular demand, they ended up this time, not in the game room but the music room.

Picking up one of his beloved guitars, Charlie began playing, Jennilee singing. They harmonized beautifully as they ran through *Killing Me Softly With His Song, Travelin' Man, You Are The Sunshine Of My Life,* and a few other mellow songs before cranking it up a couple notches. Started with a grinning nod in Jeff's direction and a rousing rendition of *Hot Rod Lincoln*, followed it with *Hurt So Good. You're So Vain. Jack and Diane. Only The Good Die Young. Life's Been Good.*

Some of the crowd sang along, some danced. Jeff claimed Angel for a series of dances, until both were breathless. Moving out of the flow of dancers, stepping to the side of the room, Jeff pulled Angel with him.

"I really love that about them, the way they're always so happy, the way they always wind up singing, and they always know the perfect songs for any occasion." Standing close to Jeff, Angel let her eyes wander over the crowd before coming to rest on Charlie and Jennilee.

Jeff's eyes were on Angel. Didn't have to follow her gaze to know she was looking at Charlie and Jennilee. "They see in music."

"What?" Angel turned to Jeff.

"Everything they do, they gravitate toward music, because they…" Jeff waved a hand, floundering as he attempted to explain. "…see in music. The way other people see in colors."

Angel grinned and agreed. "I never thought about it that way, but you're right."

"I keep telling them they should go pro, but do they listen? No."

"Guess you haven't seen this." Angel gestured to a framed citation on the wall, well camouflaged amongst a hodgepodge of the framed photos and mementos Charlie and Jennilee loved to plaster on at least one wall in every room.

Moving closer so he could read it, Jeff clenched his jaw to keep his mouth from dropping open and staying there as he caught a glimpse of what Angel was showing him. "Holy guacamole! They did it!" Tracing his fingers reverently over the glass, Jeff took his time reading the whole award.

Angel beamed like a proud sibling. "Pretty cool, huh? Not that either one of them would ever say a word about it. I saw it last time I was here."

"I know this song! I…love it! I…should have known…it was theirs —even though someone else sang it. It's been one of my favorite songs for the last couple of years!" Shaking his head, Jeff read the elegant gold lettering of the award again, read some of it out loud. "Best country song of the year, music and lyrics by Charlie and Jennilee Meyers."

"Yep."

"Hey! Didn't that go gold about a week after it came out?"

"Yep, and then platinum the following week."

"Hot damn!" Grinning like a possum, Jeff held out a hand and gave a half bow. "Another dance, m'lady?"

Laughing into the darkness, Jeff sobered, laughed again. He and Angel'd come out on the huge porch to cool off in the breeze flowing off the river, and because they'd both had enough of the company inside for a bit.

"What's so funny?"

Turning to face her, Jeff leaned nonchalantly on the porch post behind him. He could clearly see Angel's outline in the light spilling out through the French doors. "I was just thinking about that comment Sarah made earlier."

Angel didn't miss a beat. "About Jennilee making the rest of the girls look bad?"

"Yeah. Hard for most of them to understand. They think she's... brainwashed...or something. *Brain-dead...*to *want* to wait on Charlie, and me, to the extent she does."

"Browbeaten."

"Yeah. Have you ever seen another woman so..."

"...exuberant about life? About simply making others happy?"

"Exactly!"

"My mom. She has that same look of...utter contentment. Especially when she's got dinner going for forty or fifty of us and the house is full to bursting and you can't hear yourself think for the jokes and teasing and babies."

Jeff grinned and shook his head. "Women's libbers can holler all they want about equality, but as far as I can tell, all they've done is demean themselves. Cheapened their worth."

Angel chuckled and remarked wryly, "I should take that for the sexist comment it sounds like, except I happen to agree with you."

Jeff gazed into the lighted room, the occupants clearly visible. "Jennilee has no idea the immense power she wields. Charlie knows, says all the time that every thing he does is for Jennilee, but I don't think too many people take him seriously. She literally doesn't care, because her world revolves around him, but he's built this…kingdom…for her. She'd be perfectly happy to live in a grass hut and cook over a fire, as long as what she did made Charlie happy. He'd buy her the moon and transport the Taj Mahal there if she wanted, but she doesn't."

"It's like their music—everything one does perfectly complements what the other does."

"You got that right. Every single thing she does is geared toward making him happy and every thing he does, he does to make her happy. I believe that's the way it's supposed to be when two people love each other."

Angel threw a look over her shoulder into the room full of people. "It doesn't always work that way, but it works for them."

"Tell me about it. Given her early life, you'd think Jennilee would have servants to wait on her hand and foot so she didn't actually have to lift a finger, and she does, to some extent. Charlie knows Jennilee—knows she'd be absolutely miserable having to live like that, so he lets her cook and sew and do whatever else she wants, within reason."

"That's why he whisked her out of the kitchen so quick—so she wouldn't spend the rest of the evening cleaning up."

"Pretty much. Suki will take care of it. That's what she's here for."

"You're just full of chauvinistic comments tonight, aren't you?"

"You know that's not what I meant."

Angel's laughter rang out. "I know. I was just teasing. I know exactly what you meant."

Both of them were silent for a bit, and then Jeff spoke. "You do know they're pushing us together, hoping?"

Angel snorted. "I'd have to be blind, deaf, and dumb not to realize that."

"Nothing to get offended about. They just want everyone else to be as happy as they are."

"I'm not offended, not really. Jennilee means well."

"But you're not ready for the whole white picket fence thing."

"Yeah, well. I've never met anyone I could get that serious about."

"Me either."

Without either one intending to, they moved closer and closer together until they were almost touching.

Giving a token protest, Angel splayed her hands lightly against his hard chest. "Besides, I've got school, and work. I'm not ready to settle yet."

Jeff seconded it even as his arms encircled her. "Same here."

Shifting at the same time, they closed the miniscule gap remaining between them. Jeff bent his head just as Angel tilted hers up. Their lips met, did a little exploring, a little tasting, and both liked what they found. More than liked. Went back for seconds, then thirds.

When they reluctantly came up for air, Jeff had one hand tangled in Angel's curls, the other cupping her delectable ass, pressing her close to him. Angel had both arms around Jeff's neck, one hand curled around his nape and the fingers of the other hand clenched in his short hair.

"Jennilee's never wrong—about anything." Jeff was breathing hard.

Angel was breathing every bit as hard as he was. "Is that so?"

"Maybe we should...try that again. Just to make sure."

Angel's reply was lost as their lips met again.

They broke this time, and Angel tucked her head into the hollow of his shoulder. He dropped his head over hers, nuzzled his chin against the top of her head. She murmured, "I caught Jennilee's bouquet and you caught her garter."

"You've been thinking about that too?"

"Not so much thinking about it. It's just kinda been there, in the back of my mind."

"Mine too."

"You know what they say..."

"I always thought that was just an old wives' tale."

"Me too."

Standing that way for a while longer, both sighed at the same time, laughed together.

"Guess we should go back inside and mingle before they come looking for us."

"Yeah."

Neither one moved, content.

"Know what Charlie told me yesterday? No, I think it was the day before. Shoot, I can't remember when 'cause I'm on their time now."

"What, they have their own time zone?"

"More like a time warp. Everything cruises along on SCJ time when you're with them."

Angel laughed and supplied, "Standard Charlie Jennilee time."

"Exactly! Anyway, we were cleaning fish while Jennilee went in the house. Forty-five minutes, hour tops, and he told me that's the longest they'd been apart since they got married."

"I can believe that about them. It's marvelous they...can be that way. They even shower together."

"You noticed too?"

"How could I not? They disappear at the same time and they both come back soaking wet at the same time."

"Hmmm. I don't know about being together *all* the time, but I could probably go for joint showers."

Angel quipped, "Somehow I can't see you being all too worried about wasting water."

Jeff did his best Groucho Marx imitation, waggling his eyebrows and miming a cigar. "When I'm in the shower with a beautiful woman, wasting water is the least of my concerns."

Angel shoved at him half-heartedly, trying not to laugh, as he pulled her closer and they dove into another kiss.

"Charlie's never gonna let me live this down." Jeff staggered, then righted himself as they broke apart after this last kiss, one that was even better than the ones before.

Angel stumbled as well, gave a half laugh as Jeff caught her arms and steadied her. "Live what down?"

"That they were right about us all along."

They slipped back inside, not that anyone but Charlie and Jennilee had even noticed their absence. Immediately spotting them, noting their flushed and tell-tale faces, Charlie and Jennilee finished the number they were doing and broke into *You Are The Woman*, followed it with *Fooled Around and Fell In Love*.

Finishing that, Charlie told the crowd, "That's it for tonight, folks."

Amid the usual moans and groans and pleas for just one more, Mike spoke up. "Hey, guys! Rocky Horror's playing the late show in Morehead!"

That was all it took. The crowd agreed to go and dispersed to gather supplies.

Watching as the whole gang pulled a Poof! like a magician had waved his wand, Angel looked at Jeff. "Okay, I give. Rocky Horror?"

Jennilee, Charlie, and Jeff stared at her in amazement.

"What? Is that secret code for another one of y'all's whacked games or something?"

Jennilee choked out, "You really don't know what it is?"

Angel shook her head.

Charlie and Jeff exchanged a gleeful look and rubbed their hands together.

Jeff slung an arm around Angel's shoulder and informed her, "You are going to love this. It's an...interactive movie."

"Interactive?"

"Yeah. The audience...participates."

Angel parroted, "The audience participates?" Shook her head until her curls bounced as the other three laughed.

CHAPTER 10

$\mathcal{L}$aughing right along with them a couple hours later as they headed home, still picking rice out of her hair, Angel gasped, "Y'all have got to stop. Stop making me laugh. My ribs hurt, and my face feels like it's been broken and glued back together."

"Told you you'd like it." Jeff threw his declaration over his shoulder, his grin a slash of white against the darkness.

"How many times have you guys seen Rocky Horror?"

A moment of silent communion, and then Jeff answered for himself and Charlie and Jennilee. "Somewhere around twenty-five or so."

Wrapping one arm tight around her ribs, Angel bracketed her thumb and fingers firmly over her aching cheekbones and tried to stifle her laugh. "I can't believe I've missed that all these years!"

"Yeah, you got a long way to go to catch up!" Jennilee giggled and bumped shoulders with Angel.

Quiet after that, nothing but the hum of the tires and the wind going by and night noises in general breaking the silence. Charlie drove the jeep into their garage, parked and turned it off, and still none of them said anything, content with the night and each other.

It wasn't pitch black dark, but it was dark enough to see the vast expanse of the stars clearly, and to see where they were headed, the porch light drawing them in like a beacon. Almost back to the house, a loud *cak-cak-cak* sound split the air. The others didn't pay the noise any mind, but Angel jumped and clutched Jeff's hand tighter. "What the hell was that?"

Charlie answered lazily before Jeff had a chance to. "Huh? Oh, that. A marsh-hen."

Stopping dead in her tracks, Angel tried to yank her hand out of Jeff's, fully prepared to run like hell. "A Martian?"

Jennilee's laughter chimed out, echoed by Charlie and Jeff as she explained. "Not a *Martian*, a *marsh-hen*. It's a member of the rail family, a bird that lives in the marsh. The guys like to hunt them and some people eat them, but when you cook them, it smells like you're cooking a big ol' pot of marsh mud. I'll pass."

"Y'all are just weird. You know that, don'cha, just plain weird."

"Maybe, but even weird people gotta sleep sometime. Jennilee and I are headed upstairs. Y'all can do what you want, but we've been asked to sing at Miz Sadie's church in the morning."

"It *is* morning, in case you hadn't noticed, Charlie Brown."

"Later in the morning. What would be the point of singing right now? There's nobody awake to hear us. 'Cept you, and we already sang to you tonight."

Jennilee, tucked close to Charlie, under his arm and right up against his heart, offered, "Y'all are welcome to come."

Feeling Jeff stiffen, Angel had time to wonder why he didn't want to go to Miz Sadie's church. It wasn't prejudice, 'cause he treated Mose just like Jennilee and Charlie did—an important and beloved member of the family.

"Nah. Thanks for the invite. Another time. Gotta go do the obligatory family thing."

"Sorry, bro."

Jennilee offered consolingly, "She'd have found out sooner or later, even if Bertha Bigmouth hadn't started wagging her hinged-in-the-middle tongue."

"Yeah, well, time for a dose of alternate reality. Besides y'all's, that is."

Climbing the outside steps to the same beat, the couples crossed the wide porch still in step. Charlie got the door and the guys held back and let the girls go through. Putting a hand on Jeff's shoulder, Charlie squeezed, Jeff nodded stiffly.

Once inside, Jennilee turned to Jeff and wrapped her arms around his waist, buried her face against his chest. Took a deep breath and leaned back. "We're always here for you."

A strained smile lit Jeff's face and he tightened his arms. "Don't I know it. You've always been there for me. I really appreciate everything you do, guys. Everything you've always done." Nuzzling his cheek against the top of her head, he gave her a gentle nudge in Charlie's direction. "Tell Miz Sadie...I'm sorry."

"Will do. Night, guys." Arms around each other, Charlie and Jennilee vanished up the wide staircase.

Jeff drifted to the other side of the wide foyer, as he'd promised himself earlier, to check out the set of pictures ranged along the steps.

Angel shrugged and tagged along. Jeff would talk to her about what was bothering him, or not. She didn't say anything, just watched him looking at the framed pictures. She'd already taken her time and looked at all these, but they were just pictures to her, not the vivid memories they represented to Jeff.

Deciding she'd let Jeff tell her in his own good time why he was so reluctant to go see his family, Angel stopped in front of a picture—one of many such—of Jennilee, flanked by Jeff and Charlie. "Y'all did a good job keeping Jennilee occupied today so she wouldn't dwell on what happened at the pharmacy."

"You noticed, huh?"

"How could I not? The two of you haven't left her alone or let her be still all day."

"We try not to ever let Jennilee be alone, especially outside this house. This...sanctuary." Jeff got quiet, stayed quiet for so long Angel thought he'd forgotten her. Softly, still lost in his own thoughts, Jeff told Angel, "Bertha's been Jennilee's enemy from way back. Besides being the town librarian, Bertha is the mother of Jennilee's aunt's best friend."

All of which Angel already knew, but it still took a moment to decipher that convoluted statement. "So... Jennilee's aunt poured her poison in her best friend's ear, and she passed it along to Bertha—her mother."

"That's it in a nutshell." Moving up a couple steps, Jeff traced his fingertips over the glass of a prominent photo. "I have a copy of this same picture on the table by my front door."

"Looking at these, and watching you guys together—you must've been friends since you were little."

Jeff looked down at Angel and smiled. "Yeah. Those two are the closest thing I'll ever have to a brother and sister."

"That's what Jennilee says about you." Angel shook her head in amazement. "I don't think I've met more than a couple of people in my life who were only children until I met you three."

Jeff barked a laugh. Short and quickly cut off, but a laugh neverthe-less. "Jennilee confides in you quite a bit, doesn't she?"

"You say that like it's a big deal."

"It is to Jennilee, and therefore to me and Charlie."

"What about all the girls that were around today?"

"Jennilee's friends with them but…not close."

"Because of her aunt?"

Jeff's face twisted with anger. "Mostly. Jennilee's aunt is a patholog-ical liar, and right many people here still think Jennilee's the guilty party. A lot of kids weren't allowed to play with her or have anything to do with her. Weren't even supposed to talk to her."

"She's afraid of getting the ones that did in even more trouble."

Jeff pursed his lips and nodded. "That's Jennilee. Always trying to protect others, no matter what it costs her personally."

"Doesn't look like she could run you off."

Jeff threw back his head, eyes squeezed shut. "Jennilee couldn't beat me off with a stick."

Angel guessed shrewdly, "And that's part of the problem." At Jeff's startled look, she finished, "With your family."

"That obvious, huh?"

"Don't get all defensive with me. I'm on your side."

"I'm always defensive when it comes to Jennilee."

"So is Charlie, and Jennilee's the same way about the two of you."

"How'd you like to come with me tomorrow?"

"See for myself?"

Jeff held out a hand. "If you want to. No hard feelings if you don't. Hell, I don't want to go. I'd much rather go to Miz Sadie's church." His eyes lit and he rubbed his belly. "The singing's out of this world and the food is better."

"You and your stomach!" Taking his hand, they headed up the stairs, down the hall. Almost to their rooms, Angel asked, "Do you know what the pattern's called on the quilt Jennilee made for you?"

Jeff shook his head. "I should, but I don't pay as much attention to stuff like that as some people. I just know it's beautiful, and every stitch was sewn with love."

"I didn't know much about quilts until I started hanging around Jennilee. The one she made for me is called Sunshine and Shadow. She said it matched our opposite-ends-of-the-spectrum coloring, and because you hardly ever see one without the other, and because they're such intricately entwined parts of each other." Angel indicated a door. "This is my stop."

Coming to a halt in front of Angel's door, practically across the hall from his own, still holding hands, they turned to each other, drifted into a kiss. Jeff broke it off, rested his forehead against Angel's. "I'm not gonna even ask to come in." Leaned back enough to see Angel's face. "Not because it's Charlie's and Jennilee's house and it wouldn't be proper. They'd probably shoot off fireworks and make it a national holiday if they found us in bed together. And not because I don't want to, but because this is shaping up to be way more than a one night stand."

Stretching up and brushing a kiss across his lips, Angel dropped back down. "I feel the same way."

Jeff hauled her back up for another kiss, whispered close to her lips. "About 8:30, then?"

"Why so early?"

"Because..." Another long kiss. "That way I can catch them before church, which starts at 10:00. I won't have to stay long, and Mom wouldn't even dream of missing a service. That's just another opportunity to pray for her lost lamb."

"You don't seem very lost to me."

That earned her another kiss and a fierce hug. "I know why Jennilee loves you so much." Reaching behind Angel, Jeff opened her door and flipped the light on, stealing a glance at Angel's quilt and thinking how apt her description was. "Go on, before I change my mind."

"Ditto, to both." Laughing softly, Angel trailed a hand down his chest, and took a step backward. "Mariner's Compass."

"Huh?"

"That's the name of your quilt. Jennilee said she made it for you because it was layers and layers of an intricate pattern which creates a beautiful whole, and so you'd not only know where your home was, but so you'd always make your way home when you finished your journeying."

Jeff stood there a long while after the door closed, looking down the hall toward Charlie's and Jennilee's end of the house. Still laughing softly to himself when he entered his own room, still chuckling when he ran his hand lovingly over the quilt—*Mariner's Compass*—Jennilee'd pieced and quilted for him.

Looked from that to the stained glass over his French doors, done in the same pattern, quarter-size. And the matching design painted on the blades of the ceiling fan.

Leave it to Jennilee—she never did anything halfway.

Laughing out loud, he stripped and nothing but netted his dirty clothes into the hamper.

Reverently folding the beautiful quilt to the end of the bed, he crawled between the cool sheets. Drifted off, still smiling.

CHAPTER 11

Charlie and Jennilee were up and waiting when Jeff and Angel joined them the next morning. Again, the breakfast table was on the porch and again, it was loaded.

Homemade waffles this morning. Bacon, sausage, coffee, juice. Fresh blueberries and strawberries, chocolate chips, whipped cream, syrup.

"Didn't figure y'all'd be up this early." Grinning, Charlie saluted Jeff and Angel with his coffee cup.

"Then why'd you let Jennilee make so much food?" Grinning back, Jeff held a chair for Angel, seated himself.

"I knew you'd be up." With her usual painstaking attention to detail where people she loved were concerned, Jennilee smiled and poured a glass of juice for Angel, a mug of coffee for Jeff. Put an already buttered waffle on Angel's plate and a stack of the same on Jeff's.

Jeff drowned his in a lake of syrup, Angel covered hers with berries and whipped cream, added a scattering of chocolate chips. "Y'all eatin' at Miz Sadie's church after the sing?" Jeff didn't wait for a reply before forking a huge bite into his mouth.

Charlie shrugged. "Probably not. Depends on what y'all are doing...after."

"You want something else? Eggs, or..." Asking somewhat desperately, Jennilee rose half out of her seat as she made the offer.

Putting a hand over hers, Jeff pinned hers gently to the table. Swallowed the bite in his mouth—a cartoon character gulp—hard and noisy. "Sit, Jennilee. I'm fine. And I'll be fine. I'm an adult now, remember?"

Easing back into her chair, Jennilee stared unseeingly at the table and at the same time reached unerringly for Charlie's hand.

Shooting a look at Charlie, Jeff laid his free hand palm up on the table, waited. "Guess what?"

Angel laced her fingers through Jeff's.

Jennilee looked up, first at Jeff, then Angel, at their joined hands and a relieved smile lit her face. "You're going with him?"

"Y'all are starting to scare me. Is Jeff's mom an ogre or something?"

"Actually, she loves her son very much." Charlie squeezed, brought his and Jennilee's joined hands to his lips.

Jeff grumbled and sighed, "Too much."

Using their joined hands, Charlie tugged Jennilee closer until she sat more on his lap than in her chair. "Take the jeep if you want. We're takin' the Crown Vic today."

Jeff grinned at Charlie. "Will do. Angel'd love my bike, but I only have one helmet."

"The Harley's yours?" Angel's eager tone had them all laughing.

"You didn't think Mr. Tightwad there would spring for a new vehicle, did you?" Jeff aimed his fork in Charlie's direction before swooping back down for another load.

"I saw the bike when I put my Honda in the garage, but I didn't give it much thought." Angel shrugged. "They're always adding to their collection...s."

"Old stuff, not new. Charlie's had that old blue Ford pick-em-up truck since before he had his permit."

"And just how many vehicles have you been through in the same time period, Jeffro?"

"Can I help it if I like shiny things? New shiny things?"

"Fast things. You forgot fast." Tucked close against Charlie, Jennilee's smile shone genuine now, no shadows.

"Yeah, well. That too."

"Not so fast the way you put'em in the ditch or blew the motors, Jeffro."

"Why do you think I kept you for my best friend, Charlie Brown?"

"I know why—my dad's got a garage and all the right tools. And a tow truck."

Jennilee and Angel shared a look and burst out laughing.

OPENING the garage's walk-in door, Jeff ran a loving eye over his bike, gave it a pat, headed for the jeep. The Crown Vic was already gone, Charlie and Jennilee wanting to check the acoustics and such and visit a little before church started.

Hand in hand, Jeff and Angel made their way down the open stalls. Stopping when they reached the jeep, Jeff whistled softly.

Angel peered around him into the backseat. "What is that?"

"Jennilee's way of making me feel better." Grinning hugely at her, Jeff helped her in. "Other than that, it's one fine piece of equipment."

"Yeah, but what's it do?"

Jeff hopped into the driver's seat before answering. Gripping the steering wheel, he stared at nothing for a long moment. Turned to Angel. "You know what I do, how come I'm trying to get on with the FBI, and why?"

"Yeah. Jennilee told me you found a set of keys and that led to finding where Charlie's mom was buried, and that led to your interest in forensic science."

"Yeah, well that fine piece of equipment is a top of the line metal detector, which is how I found the keys, 'cept I was using my dad's old one. How'd you like to do some detecting?"

"Wind down, after?"

"You bet."

Almost to the main road, traveling leisurely down the long driveway between twin banks of riotously colorful flowers in full bloom, Angel asked, "How come y'all make such a big deal of visiting your parents if they're not that bad? I mean, Jennilee's all upset about it and…"

Jeff pulled out on the road. "Coming from a big family like yours, I don't reckon you'd have any idea. Growing up, the three of us being only kids, we gravitated toward each other, banded together. Made our own surrogate siblings. Of the three, I've got the most normal family. Grandy raised Charlie, and other than Grandy, Jennilee pretty much raised herself." Jeff fell silent for a bit, lost in his own thoughts.

Angel shook her head and mused, "I can't even begin to imagine being an only child. My family is so huge, and that's not even counting the aunts and uncles and cousins."

"I can't imagine that. Being an only means all the attention, good or bad, is focused on you. Jennilee got the worst end of that deal, all the way around. I've got no right to complain about something as normal as going to see my folks. Particularly when they'll be ecstatic to see me."

"I don't suppose it would've helped if we'd picked some of Jennilee's flowers for your mom. Women always love to get flowers."

Taking his eyes off the road, Jeff goggled at Angel. "Some of Jennilee's flowers? Are you crazy? Mom would take one look, know exactly where they came from, and burst into tears."

"She hates Jennilee that much?" Angel's temper started a slow burn.

"Mom? She doesn't hate anybody." Jeff sighed. "That sounds stupid, doesn't it? I mean, it's obvious mom has an intense dislike of Jennilee."

"Your mom doesn't like Jennilee but she doesn't hate her?"

"Mom's never met Jennilee. She…refuses. She just hates what Jennilee represents, if that makes more sense. No parents, a widespread—even though it's totally skewed—reputation for being incorrigible, definitely not someone you want your kid hanging around because she might drag your kid into trouble with her."

A light clicked on. "Jennilee's intensely loyal to you, and you return that feeling. Your mom's just jealous."

"Pretty much, except she couches it in nicer terms."

"I can promise you one thing. If what's between us is serious, you better be prepared for lots of siblings, 'cause mine *and* my mom and my dad will adore you, no jealousy involved. And your mom will be nice to Jennilee or she won't be welcome at our house."

"That's two things, and you're already planning our wedding?"

Angel blushed to the roots of her hair. "No, I am *not* planning our wedding! I'm just saying."

"I agree." Leaning toward Angel, Jeff palmed the back of her head, pulled her close and stole a quick kiss.

Angel sank into the kiss for a moment before giving Jeff a shove and admonishing him sternly. "Eyes on the road, hands on the wheel!"

Jeff complied, but flashed her an outrageous little boy grin. "Aye, aye, Capt'n!"

"Tell me how come half this crazy town thinks Jennilee is a cross between the Virgin Mary and a fairy godmother, and the other half thinks she's the firstborn spawn of Satan."

Jeff's infectious laughter boomed out. "I guess it takes an outsider to see the disparity so clearly, but you nailed it. The half that knows her knows the truth, and the other half doesn't want to. They'd rather believe the worst."

"Jennilee doesn't deserve that, not at all."

"Don't I know it. You're preachin' to the choir here."

"What did you do to try and change your mom's mind? And what about your dad?"

Staring at the road, Jeff blew out a breath, relieved Angel hadn't had to ask—because she knew he'd tried to sway his mom, just not how. "We're a very civilized family. We don't raise our voices to one another, and my folks don't believe in physical punishment. Dad? He just goes along with everything mom says because he doesn't want her upset."

Angel reached out and laid her hand on Jeff's thigh. Dropping one of his over it, he squeezed before continuing.

"Mom grounded me for a month one time—usually it was just a week—because she found out I was playing with Jennilee. Again."

Sensing more, Angel asked, "What happened when your month was up?"

"I didn't whine or fuss or beg. I just got up from the supper table every night and went to my room, just like I'd been doing the whole month. That went on for another three weeks, with mom encouraging me—begging me—every day to go out and play."

"As long as it wasn't with Charlie and Jennilee."

"Just Jennilee. Dad thinks the world of Charlie."

"But they're inseparable."

"Tell me about it. The only times they weren't together were when Jennilee had chores to do, or she'd been grounded."

"So what happened?"

"I stayed at the house, mostly in my room, refused to talk unless my parents asked a direct question. I did my homework and my chores, went to church, did everything a good little boy is supposed to do. Except play."

"Your mom caved?"

"In her own way. She cried so much, dad finally told me to go on, and if mom asked, just tell her I'd been with Charlie."

"She was so happy to have her little boy playing again she just ignored why?"

"Pretty much. Mom's good at ignoring what she doesn't want to acknowledge. After that, any time Jennilee's name came up, mom just burst into tears, which I ignored."

Both quiet for the rest of the drive, Jeff pulled up in the driveway of a neat little house.

In a neighborhood of obsessively neat houses, it stood out like a sore thumb.

House, yard, everything—immaculate.

Eerily so, right down to the knife-edged, ruler straight and blemish-free concrete sidewalk beside the ruthlessly trimmed and shaped hedges. To the postage stamp sized front yard with its American flag draped picture perfectly on its pole, the pole in the exact center of a perfectly round circle of white stone. A colorful flag which made a perfect foil to the blindingly white siding and inky black shutters of the perfectly symmetrical boxy little house, like a child's drawing. The equally white front door was flanked on one side by one exactly centered window, a tad on the smallish side, like a one-eyed monster with a squint. Blinds *and* curtains. Two fire-engine red geraniums in flawlessly matched planters sat at the bottom of the steps, one on each side, looking like mirror images of each other, right down to the size and number of leaves and blooms.

Angel stared. "Maybe I'll just sit in the car."

"Kind of scary, huh?"

"Like something out of a horror movie."

"Yeah, that's what I think, too."

"Good, 'cause I gotta tell you, if that's your idea of what a happy home should look like..."

"Nah. I know what I want when I build. Doesn't have to be a huge place, but I want lots of big windows and a wraparound porch. Lots of rockers and hammocks. Big kitchen. Comfortable furniture. Jennilee to wave her magic wand and do her thing with the flowerbeds and everything else."

Taking her eyes off the terrifyingly perfect—and impossibly impersonal—house, Angel focused them on the wonderfully warm man sitting beside her. "How old were you when you pulled your little stubborn stunt?"

Jeff snorted a laugh. "Seven. I give you fair warning—once I set my mind on something, I always get what I want."

Quirking a brow at that, Angel took a deep breath. "That's why Jennilee gets so upset—'cause you got in lots of trouble over her."

"Jennilee inspires that kind of loyalty. I knew she was special, even then, and well worth fighting for."

Something else clicked. "That's why you all tensed up when I made the 'do something constructive with your time' comment. Your mom must've said that to you—about Jennilee—over and over."

"Yep. And over and over and... The people in this town who don't like Jennilee... They never seem to see all the good stuff she does, and Jennilee's never been one to blow her own horn."

"Humph. Jennilee knew that you playing with her caused a lot of dissension between you and your parents."

"Yeah. Jennilee's all about family. You know that. It's the only thing Jennilee and I've ever fought about." About to swoop in for another kiss, Jeff froze as his eyes flicked past Angel. "Make up your mind, 'cause we've been spotted. I just saw the living room curtain twitch."

Angel gave a mock shudder. "I'm afraid if you go in alone, you'll never come back out."

"Feel that way myself, sometimes." Getting out and rounding the hood, Jeff held a hand out to Angel.

Taking his hand, Angel hopped out of the jeep. Kept hold of it as they walked up the sidewalk together. The door opened before they reached the bottom of the steps, like a great white getting ready to swallow its prey.

HOT, tired, and hungry, Jeff and Angel headed down Charlie's and Jennilee's long driveway.

"Hot damn! We timed that right. We're about half an hour behind them!"

Angel looked at Jeff questioningly. "Do I even want to know how you know that?"

Jeff waggled the fingers of one hand. "Maybe I'm magic."

"You wish."

"Yeah, that could come in handy sometimes. See that dust hanging in the air? Somebody went down the driveway ahead of us and not too long ago. Odds are, it's them. And I'm starving."

"You always assume Jennilee's going to feed you."

"No assumption about it. She's the one that's magic, and I like to eat as much as she likes to feed me. She'll have something ready."

"How do you know they didn't stay and eat?"

"The same way I know the sun comes up in the east."

"It's a pure wonder you don't weigh five hundred pounds."

"Metabolism. Can't help it. Miz Del always says I'd eat the legs off the table if there wasn't enough food on it. She's probably right."

"I take it you ate at Miz Del's a lot when you were growing up."

Resting a hand on his tummy as if to hold in memories of food that had passed its way, Jeff agreed, "Every chance I got. Usually ate there and at home. Jennilee knew and didn't care, and I just never told mom. Ate at Miz Sadie's every chance I got, too."

"Sort of like the neighborhood dog who cadges treats at everyone's house."

"I'll remember that."

"Ooh, I'm scared."

Pulling up in the drive, Jeff parked beneath one of the huge old wind-sculpted live oaks.

"Aren't you going to put the jeep back where you got it?"

Jeff grinned. "Nope."

"You and Charlie razz each other as much as possible, don't you?"

"What are best friends for?"

Angel hopped out this time before Jeff could help her. "Just keep that in mind when you meet my brothers."

Jeff was at her side in a few long strides. "They like to torment you, huh?"

"You could say that."

Jeff's head came up and swiveled toward the house. Angel watched him sniff-sniff-sniffing like a hound hot on the trail. Grabbing Angel's hand and pulling her along, he began alternating sniffs with listing food like he was reading the special of the day off a menu board.

"Fried chicken. Potato salad. Deviled eggs. Green beans. Light rolls. Lemon meringue pie."

Angel pulled back on their joined hands. "Slow down, and light rolls?"

"Yeast rolls. Jennilee's homemade. Can't you smell them?"

"You can smell all that from here?"

"I smell fried chicken and light rolls, and I know what she fixes with them."

"You're practically drooling."

"You got that right!"

Bypassing the front door, Jeff headed around the house on the porch. Burst through the French doors into the kitchen, an ear to ear grin covering his face. He'd been dead on about the food. Jewel barked once, a happy welcome home yip, but she didn't give up her vantage point on the window seat.

Jennilee looked up at their entrance, a matching smile lighting her face. "Perfect timing! I knew you'd show up. Food's almost done. You've just got time to wash up." Taking the last piece of chicken out of the cast iron skillet and laying it on a paper towel covered platter, Jennilee handed the platter to Charlie.

"There's not as much dirt on our hands as there is flour on you." Catching Jennilee up in a big bear hug, Jeff set her on her feet and used one hand to wipe the flour off her cheek. "You got a big ol' flour hand-print on your butt, too."

Jennilee's laughter filled the kitchen. "Don't I always?"

"Don't even, Jeffro. C'mere, Jennilee. I'll take care of that for you."

Jeff muttered as he headed toward the sink. "You, Charlie Brown, just want an excuse to put your hands on your wife's butt."

"It's there, and that's reason enough." Snagging the dishtowel Jennilee habitually carried slung over one shoulder while she cooked, Charlie brushed the flour off, stole a kiss, and copped a feel all at the same time.

Walking past, Jeff flicked the water off his hands at Charlie. Turning his body so Jennilee was out of the line of fire, Charlie retaliated by snapping the towel at Jeff. Paying their antics no mind, Jennilee moved serenely around Charlie and started pouring drinks.

"Ready, guys."

Seating themselves, they bowed their heads as Charlie said grace. "Lord, Bless the food before us, the friends beside us, the love between us."

Amens chorused out and they began passing platters and bowls.

Angel commented, "That's a really nice blessing, Charlie."

"Thank Jennilee. She read it somewhere, and we really liked it."

"How'd the sing go?" Jeff didn't pause in filling his plate.

"Great. Everybody said to tell you hi." Jennilee passed him the basket of rolls.

"Sorry I missed it." Taking the basket, he handed the potato salad across the table to her.

"How'd your...excursion go?"

Angel burst out laughing at Jennilee's question. "Y'all had me scared half to death thinking Jeff's mom was a female Attila the Hun or something."

"Yeah, all four feet ten inches and ninety pounds of her." Charlie shook his head. "She's a true Southern lady from the top of her perfectly coiffed head to the bottoms of her perfectly shod and amazingly tiny feet."

"Does she ever take her pearls off?" Taking a bite of chicken, Angel closed her eyes as the succulent taste hit her tongue.

"I think she sleeps with them on." Jeff paused, with a chicken leg halfway to his mouth and a light roll slathered in butter in his other hand. "Actually, I'm not sure she sleeps. I've never seen her with a hair out of place, or wearing anything except her color co-ordinated and perfectly tailored outfits."

Angel chewed, swallowed. "She was very happy to see Jeff, and she only dropped oblique hints about a hundred times."

Jennilee tensed, and Jeff laughed. "No tears, Jennilee. She did mention, however—and seconded—that Bertha thought I needed to get a real job and grow up."

Angel informed them with a smirk, "I told her Jeff was fantastic at what he did and he'd grown up very nicely."

"You did?" Jennilee perked up.

"Not only that, I told her Jeff and I are an item now—and that you're my best friend. If she wants to be invited to...anything...she's going to have to be nice to you or she won't be. Invited."

Jennilee and Charlie shared matching grins.

"Wow!"

"You really..."

"...told her..."

"...that?"

"I did. I was every bit as sugarcoated as she is, but I told her in no uncertain terms, and I meant every word. And she didn't cry when I told her because I changed the subject so fast she didn't have time."

Jennilee ducked her head but not before they saw the quick sheen of tears. Charlie clasped her hand, squeezed.

Jeff broke in, "You should've heard Angel singing my praises. Mom was so tickled she forgot all about being upset."

Charlie heckled Jeff, giving Jennilee a moment to compose herself. "Told you you shoulda come around sooner, Jeffro. We've been tryin' to get you and Angel together for a couple years now."

Blinking fiercely, Jennilee beat back the tears. Squeezed Charlie's hand. "Anybody want more tea?"

"Sit still, Jennilee. We're fine. Let me tell you the rest of our tale. You know what we did afterward—and by the way, Jennilee—that detector is swee-eet! We went out to—you know the spot—where I've found old coins and stuff other times, down by the old barge landing. I thought that site had been tapped out, but with this new equipment... It's way more sensitive."

Angel shook her head. "Jeff told me that little canal angling off the river and through the piece of swamp bottom there used to be the main way things got transported in to town. Hard to believe."

Smiling, Jennilee dug into her trove of information. "The trees in the swamp have grown immensely and the river's silted in a lot. The canal itself hasn't been cleaned out in...decades. Maybe since the turn of the century. There's a provision in the original town charter stating each local able bodied man had to donate so many hours a year to helping keep that channel navigable. It's also why the little crosswise piece of road that doesn't really go anywhere is Main Street, and the next one over is Market. When the wharf was operating, it was the center of town and everything spread out from there."

"Thank you for the history lesson, Encyclopedia. No keys this time, but look at what we did find." Jeff gestured to Angel, who pulled something out of her pocket, unwrapped it from Jeff's handkerchief.

Handing it across the table to Jennilee, Angel said, "It looks really old, but I have no clue what it is. Jeff said he didn't either. Any idea?"

Taking the object, Jennilee cradled it in her palm, picked gently at the crusted-on dirt. Stared intently, turned it this way and that. "I think you've really got something this time, Jeff. More than mere coins and buttons, cool as they are. No way for me to accurately date this, but it looks to be a penannular, or ring brooch, commonly used in centuries past to hold a cloak on, or a shawl. Penannular means almost a circle. See here, where the ends are bigger and it's not quite closed all the way? There's not a piece missing, it's supposed to look like this. This pin here is attached to the ring part and would have moved freely around the ring between the ends. The loose pin would have been inserted through a fold of the fabric, then the pin would've been brought through from front to back and the ring turned under the sharp edge of the pin to keep it on. Doesn't sound like it would keep a cloak from coming off, but the Celts used them for over six centuries. They can be made of precious or semiprecious metals and can be embellished with gems or stones or left plain. Brooches like this were often elaborately engraved with symbols, for protection or to show allegiances or beliefs. This one looks to be pewter but it could be silver because there's no rust, just oxidation and dirt from being in the ground for so long. At any rate, it's a rare find and whoever lost it probably grieved for a long time."

Getting a dreamy look on her face, Jennilee speculated. "Could've come over as a family heirloom from the Old Country with an emigrant or it could have been a gift from a sailor to his lady-love, or a gift from a lady to her love going off to war. No telling, but it's fun to imagine."

The other three stared at her so intently Jennilee squirmed uncomfortably. "What?"

Leaning close and kissing her thoroughly, Charlie drew back a hair's breadth. "You should've been a professor, Jennilee-love."

"Yeah, Jennilee. I'd've enjoyed taking your history classes."

Angel finally found her voice. "You make history come so alive, Jennilee."

Jennilee blushed as she handed the brooch back to Angel.

Angel took the piece reverently. "How do you know so much, anyway? You never cease to amaze me."

"Brain lint. Every thing she reads, sees, or hears sticks to her brain like lint. Always has." Jeff made his contribution and kept eating.

"The detector thingie said it's silver." Angel wasn't nearly as excited by the food as she was by her first treasure find.

Jennilee's face lit. "Then you really have something. It's old, and that would have been wonderful enough, but it could be worth quite a lot, depending on the quality of the metal."

"Jeff showed me how to…"

Charlie snorted, "I'll just bet he did."

Ignoring him just like she'd ignored Jeff's mom, Angel kept talking. "...use the detector and it started pinging like crazy. He even let me use that little—what did you call it, Jeff? Mattock?—thingy to dig this up. I'd never seen one of those either. That's a cool little gadget, with the flat scoop of metal on one side and the forked tines on the other."

Jennilee smiled. "I found that when we were cleaning out the back room of the hardware store. God only knows how long it'd been there, gathering dust, but it looked to be the perfect thing for Jeff's adventures. You know, a real mattock is quite a lot bigger and..."

"Enough history lessons for one day, Jennilee! Eat, or you're going to dry up and blow away with the next breeze." Snagging the chicken platter, Jeff helped himself to another piece, deftly slid a piece onto Jennilee's plate at the same time.

Passing the piece of chicken just as adroitly from her plate to Charlie's, Jennilee proclaimed, "Oh, no you don't. Y'all are not loading my plate like you did the other day. I eat all I want and I am not about to become the circus fat lady just to make y'all happy."

"Jennilee-baby, you always make me happy." Leaning close, Charlie held the chicken with one hand and tried to coerce her with a kiss.

Jennilee turned her head but they could all hear the laughter in her voice. "Cut it out! You are not sweet talking me into eating until I hurt. I've got stuff to do."

Focusing on something besides filling his belly for a moment, Jeff cocked his head. "Y'all bought the hardware store, too?"

Angel looked from one to the other. "Bought? She didn't say anything about..."

Jeff snorted rudely. "Why else would they be cleaning out the back room?"

Charlie gave a lazy grin. "Maybe we were just bored, Jeffro."

Licking the chicken remnants off his fingers, Jeff wiped his fingers with his napkin. "Humph. Y'all never get bored. So when and why?"

"Last year, and 'cause we wanted to."

"Yeah, right. I know you two, and you've always got ulterior motives. Probably bought it so you could get discounts on nails and sundry."

"Why not? We use enough of that kind of stuff."

Jeff patted Angel on the back as she choked. "You own the drug store and the hardware store? Why don't y'all just buy an island somewhere and build your own town?"

Jeff quit patting, began rubbing circles. "Why would they want to do that when they've got an already established one right here?"

"What..." Angel floundered, momentarily at a loss for words. "What...else are the two of you planning on buying?"

Jeff answered Angel before Charlie had a chance to. "Let's see... They've owned the laundromat since they were teenagers, and the car wash and..."

Angel stared. Charlie shrugged and said, "They were good investments. Both require a minimum of work, since neither one has a permanent attendant, and they pretty much take care of themselves, except for cleaning and repairs."

"Who's cleaning and repairing?" Raising a brow, helping himself to another deviled egg, Jeff popped it into his mouth.

"We hire teenagers who actually want to work to do the cleaning, and the repairs? Do most of them ourselves."

"Great, Charlie Brown. Guess I know who to call when my washer..."

"You do your laundry at the community wash center in your apartment complex so don't even, Jeffro."

"At least he *says* he does it." Angel didn't miss a beat as she dropped her bomb.

Jeff grabbed her in a pretend headlock. "Hey! Whose side are you on here?"

Laughing and breaking free of his light hold, Angel reminded him, "Brothers, remember? Lots of brothers. That was automatic. Can't help it." Angel dissolved into more laughter.

"I was gonna ask you if you wanted to go treasure hunting some more, but if you're gonna be that way Angel..."

"More? Where?"

Jennilee and Charlie looked at each other, then at Jeff. He nodded.

Angel looked at each one in turn. "Alright you three. Spill it. I'm getting pretty good at reading your minds, but I don't have a clue on this one."

Jennilee smiled and told Angel, "The lot where Jeff's gonna build his house when he's ready to move back home."

Charlie grinned and twirled a lock of Jennilee's hair around his fingers. "Soon's we get cleaned up here, we'll head out."

"I thought..." Jeff looked around the kitchen. "Where's Suki? We could go sooner if she..."

Charlie grinned wider. "We could and she would...but Suki stayed after the sing. Miz Sadie asked her to eat with the family."

All four shared matching grins.

CHAPTER 12

*J*ewel jumped out and bounded around as soon as Charlie turned the jeep off and gave her the okay. Getting a couple tri-fold lounge chairs out of the back of the jeep, Charlie ratcheted them open in the shade of one of the huge live oaks. Jennilee grabbed beach towels and draped one over each, tucked the end of the towels into the narrow plastic webbing strips. Charlie set the cooler beside her chair and made sure his chair and Jennilee's were as close as they could get.

Angel held the mattock and watched. Jeff already had the metal detector out, headphones looped around his neck, trying to decide where to start. Angel switched her gaze from Jeff back to Charlie and Jennilee. "I thought we were goin' to…"

"You and Jeff. We're gonna sit right here and watch." Taking Jennilee's hand, Charlie seated her, then himself. "If y'all get tired of digging, just point Jewel at the right spot and tell her to get the mouse. She'll dig to China."

"China, huh?" With that, Angel headed in Jeff's direction. Coming up beside him, she asked, "This is where you're gonna build that dream house of yours?"

"Yeah. You like it?"

"Love it. I can see the house, right there, on that rise, framed by those huge old live oaks. You'll want your bedroom on the second floor and on the water side so you'll have an awesome view."

"That also means we'll be on the side where the sun comes up."

"We? Now who's jumping the gun?" Angel grinned up at Jeff and they drifted closer together, into a kiss.

Pulling back a smidge, Jeff rested his forehead against hers. "It's them. They're contagious."

Turning their heads together, they looked at the couple relaxing in the shade. "Not a bad thing to catch."

"Nah. Wanna go first?"

"I think I will. I'm feeling lucky, and just so you know, I'm a morning person."

Jeff groaned as he surrendered the metal detector. "Not another one."

Relaxing on their beach chairs, holding hands and lazily playing footsie, Charlie and Jennilee watched the other couple. Bringing Jennilee's hand to his lips, Charlie asked, "Think they'll find anything?"

"They already found something."

"With the metal detector."

Jennilee burst out laughing. "Of course they will. You know as well as I do most travel used to be by water, and this is a perfect spot for landing and…having a picnic or…something."

Charlie's deep laugh rolled out, sounding of promises to be kept later, when they were alone. "Or something."

It wasn't long before Angel gave a triumphant crow and pulled the headphones off. "It's pinging! I found something!"

A coin, a metal bottle cap, and two metal buttons later, Jeff and Angel collapsed on a blanket Jennilee'd spread in the shade for them. "Soda or beer, Jeff?" Jennilee waited expectantly, cooler open.

"A good cold beer is hard to beat on a hot day."

"Beer it is." Lifting a bottle out of its icy bed, Jennilee handed it to him. "Angel?"

"Soda's fine. Pepsi, if you've got it."

"Sure enough."

Waiting till Jennilee settled comfortably once more, Charlie handed back the cream soda they were sharing.

Taking a sip of his beer, Jeff sighed in pleasure. Flicked the switch on the metal detector and idly waved it just off the edge of the blanket. They all clearly heard the pinging sound, even with the headphones lying between Jeff and Angel.

Handing the detector to Angel, Jeff twisted, reached over with the mattock and began scratching at the earth. Jewel, done chasing critters and insects for the now, watched him for a moment, head cocked. Leaping up in the air and pouncing, both front feet together, she began digging furiously.

"Hey, muttley, what do you think you're doing? Go dig your own hole!" Jeff pushed the little dog aside, laughing at her antics. Jewel circled around him and began digging in the same spot.

"Get the mouse, Jewel! Get the mouse!" Charlie egged Jewel on, not that she needed any encouragement. Dirt flew and Jewel began making frantic whining noises.

"Mouse? Why does that set her off?" Angel moved closer to Jennilee, wanting to be well out of the line of fire.

"She's a Feist. Their mission in life is to chase and catch little squealy things. When she was just a pup, we saw her playing with something she'd caught, thought it was a mouse and told her how good she was to catch one. She'd dug up a mole but by the time we realized what it was we'd already told her mouse. Now, any little squealy thing is a mouse to her."

"But there's no little squealy thing in that hole."

"We know that and so does she, but there *might* be, and besides, she loves to dig and she's not allowed to dig in the yard proper."

Paws pistoning madly, Jewel suddenly changed tactics and began ripping at the roots with her teeth. Abandoning that, she began digging again, rooting her nose in the deepening hole.

"How deep is China, anyway?" Angel laughed from the safety of Jennilee's side.

"She's nowhere near China. I've seen her dig until nothing shows but the tip of her tail."

A tail which was wagging ferociously right now. Giving a sharp bark, Jewel came up with something in her mouth. Jeff reached to take it from her and she danced away, circled around him and arrowed straight to Angel.

Jennilee said, "Take it, Angel. Whatever it is, she thinks it belongs to you."

"As long as it's not squealing." She started to hold her hand out.

Straight-faced, Jennilee said, "Oh, don't worry. She always kills whatever she catches before she brings it to us."

Jerking her hand back, Angel held it out again when the other three howled with laughter. Delicately placing what she was holding in Angel's open palm, Jewel backed up a tad and waited expectantly, ears pricked and tail wagging.

"She's got something but I can't tell if it's just an old acorn or..." Angel gently brushed at the dirt covering whatever Jewel had given her.

"Detector said..."

"Shh. Let me look." Turning the object this way and that, Angel dipped her hand in the cooler and got a little water, cupped it in her palm and swished the article around. "It looks like..." Angel sucked in a breath. "Wowsers. I think it's gold. Good dog, Jewel. Good dog!"

Amidst a rapid fire set of barks, Jewel turned acrobatic circles, her front feet setting down in the exact spot her back feet had occupied a scant second before.

All of them leaning closer to see, Jennilee was the first to say anything. "Cool! Silver and gold in the same day! That's got to mean something good."

Charlie rolled his eyes and snickered. "It just means now she'll be as gung-ho about detecting as he is."

Angel continued to expose the item. Jeff watched her movements as intently as Jewel watched when one of her humans had food. Forgetting the other couple, Angel and Jeff had their heads close together.

"Looks like..."

"...an old locket."

Their eyes met and they leaned into each other.

"Yep. She's been bitten, and good. Or should I say, smitten?" Slipping an arm around Jennilee, Charlie grinned like a possum.

Jeff muttered, "Ignore them," and moved closer until his and Angel's lips touched.

Charlie laughed and pulled Jennilee into his lap. When Jeff and Angel ended their kiss, they looked at the other couple. Charlie and Jennilee were deep into their own kiss, so Jeff and Angel went back for seconds.

Charlie snuggled Jennilee and waited. The next time Jeff and Angel came up for air, he suggested, "That stuff you found needs to be professionally cleaned. We know a guy, if you're interested."

"What? You mean you can't do it or Jennilee can't wave her wand and... Never mind. I'm just teasing, and I agree."

"Ready when you are."

It only took a moment to load their things back in the jeep, and they headed out again.

DROPPING off the items to be cleaned, they chatted with the man who was going to do the cleaning, looked at some of his finds for awhile.

Leaving, Jeff asked, "If Angel's gonna be one of us, don't you think we should give her a tour, let her in on our secrets?"

Narrating, Jeff played tour guide as Charlie drove a leisurely route around Chinquapin Ridge.

Waving a hand at the stop sign in front of them, Jeff told Angel, "That looks like an ordinary stop sign. See the identical one on the other side of the tracks? Those are invaluable markers."

Angel looked from one stop sign to the other. Looked at the perfectly straight roads bordering the railroad track on either side and ending about a block and a half away. "Y'all drag raced here? In the middle of town? Are you crazy?"

"Crazy? No. Bored and growing up in a small town. And the middle of town is one street over."

"What about the local law enforcement?"

Throwing a laughing look over his shoulder, Jeff pinned Jennilee with his hazel eyes. "Chief Mac? Jennilee's had him wrapped around her little finger since…"

"Jeffrey Rivenbark! You better cut out that lying right now!" Jennilee laughed as she refuted, "I do not have the Chief wrapped around my finger! Y'all were just sneaky enough you always knew who was on duty and where they were."

"Y'all? Don't even." Snorting a laugh, Jeff twisted farther so he could see Angel. "And you? Didn't you just complain the other night about them rolling up the streets around here? It was way worse five years ago. We'd run one or two heats and disappear. Even if someone heard us and called it in, by the time the cops got here we were long gone, scattered like leaves in the wind."

Angel asked skeptically, "You're telling me you never got caught?"

"Came close once or twice, and I blame that solely on my mechanic." Jeff jerked a thumb in Charlie's direction.

"And all you got was a warning and a reprimand?"

"Not a…reprimand. More like…a stern talking to, with hints of dire consequences if the perpetrators were caught along with dire warning stories of the old days." Jeff's voice changed register, sounding like an old fart. "When I was just a laddie, and we got caught pulling pranks, they made us spend weekends painting the street names on those concrete pylons. Or picking up trash. Or shooting rats at the town dump."

Changed back to his normal tone and snickered, "Chief Mac had his suspicions, but he could never prove anything."

Jennilee laughed at the smug cockiness in Jeff's tone. "Chief Mac knew. He knows this town like the back of his hand, knows exactly who has the fast cars and something to prove."

Grinning, Charlie met Jennilee's eyes in the rearview. "Only because he did the exact same thing when he was our age. Souped up his cars with loud engines and louder mufflers that annoyed the heck out of the older folks. Drove too fast, probably drag raced right here. I have all ideas he painted his share of those pylons."

"Radio blasting." Jeff and Charlie high fived, and Jeff bumped the radio up a notch.

Driving on at a properly sedate pace, they passed other childhood landmarks.

"See that, Angel? We spent a lot of time climbing to the top of that fire tower and helping whoever was keeping watch at the time. There's a big compass set in a table set in the floor to help pinpoint the smoke. You can see the world from up there. It's like flying."

"Y'all climbed up to the top of that?" Angel craned her neck and looked at the tall metal structure, nothing more than a skeletal A-frame and zigzag steps with a glassed-in observatory perched at the tip top, a captain's walk all the way around. "It must be...ten stories."

"Yeah, right around a hundred and twenty feet, if I remember correctly. Used to be, if the hatch was locked, you could spider underneath the platform and then monkey over the rail and open it from inside the observatory."

Angle swatted him upside the head. "Are you crazy?"

Jeff shrugged. "What? They padlocked it after they caught us doing that, and nobody uses the fire tower any more anyway."

Rolling along, Jeff pointed at the ball field. "We played a lot of games here, and Jennilee did a lot of cheering. Busted a lot of windshields with our home-runs till the parents learned to park somewhere else."

Next to it, the park with its playground, basketball and tennis courts, and community center.

"We spent a lot of time here, and they used to have the Halloween haunted house in the building there." Jeff asked rhetorically, "Remember that year they used peeled grapes for eyeballs and cold, cooked spaghetti noodles for intestines and made you stick your hands in it—in the dark?"

Charlie laughed. "Scared the crap out of us."

"Didn't stop us from going through...how many times?"

A bit further and, "We swam here at the fresh pond a lot while we were all still riding bikes. After we got our licenses, not so much. It must be spring fed, because that water is always cold." Elbowing Charlie, Jeff crowed, "Remember that time we were skinny dipping and the crowd showed up for a congregational baptizin'? We hid in the reeds till we like to froze to death!"

Just visible through the trees, Jeff indicated the water tower.

Watching it come into view, Angel exclaimed, "Don't tell me y'all climbed that on a regular basis." Angel looked from the squat flying saucer on spindly legs to Jennilee.

Charlie and Jeff exchanged a speaking glance, then Charlie locked eyes with Jennilee in the rearview, gave his wife a lazy grin that spoke volumes.

Jeff spoke. "Just Charlie, and just once." Pointed. "Look, right there. I can't believe you've never seen that."

Following Jeff's finger with her eyes, Angel started laughing.

Jeff bragged, "I was lookout. Took slowpoke here a solid two hours to do that."

Angel read aloud the over-large words painted on the water tower, inside a huge heart shape. "Charlie loves Jennilee."

Charlie defended, "I just wanted to make sure I didn't misspell anything."

Jeff snorted. "More like that's how long whatever coating you put on it took to dry. That's what you wanted to make sure of. How many times have they painted over that since you left for college and nothing will stick to it? I suppose they could sandblast it off, but everyone around here gets such a kick out of it they'd never do that."

"I'd just paint it again, and they know it."

"Not like everyone in town doesn't know how much you love Jennilee."

"Never hurts to remind them."

Driving a little farther, Charlie pulled into Oak Grove cemetery, parked in the shade, cut the motor. This stop needed no narrative. "Y'all can come or stay, whatever. Won't take us long."

Already in accord, with no need to consult Angel, Jeff assented for both of them. "We'll come."

Charlie helped Jennilee out, Jeff assisted Angel. Moving to the back of the jeep, opening a cooler and carefully lifting out two bouquets of fresh-cut flowers, Jennilee handed one to Charlie. Hand in hand, flowers cradled in their free arms, they headed across the cemetery, Jeff and Angel flanking them.

Charlie placed the flowers he carried on his mom's grave, Jennilee did the same on her mother's. The bright splash of multi-colored zinnias and cosmos and roses and baby's breath made a striking contrast to the heat-frizzled grass and the side by side gray headstones.

"Dad's been here today." Charlie indicated the remains of a recently wilted iris bloom on top of his mom's headstone, Iris' favorite and one the local florist kept in stock year round just for Mr. Donnie. Jennilee wrapped her arms around Charlie, squeezed. Putting his arms around Jennilee and squeezing back, Charlie sought and found Jeff's eyes. "He still grieves, but not like he did, thanks to you, Jeff."

Hazel bored into dark chocolate. "I will find them, Charlie Brown."

"Counting on it, Jeffro." A quick forearm clasp reaffirmed their vows.

Next stop, the pharmacy, for a round of malted milkshakes. A short drive from there and down a side street, Charlie pulled into the gravel parking lot of what used to be the moving company.

The sign on the front of the building proudly and elegantly stated, CJM Enterprises.

"In-town office, Charlie Brown?"

"Yep. We don't allow just everyone to come out to the house. Besides, this way, the crews can meet here in the mornings and we can keep supplies here and stuff."

"How come you didn't just meet Tim here the other day?"

"Morning, Jeffro. I said *morning*. That was *not* morning. He'd already been at work for...hours."

"Not my fault y'all don't need sleep."

Charlie prodded, "Ah, remind me who went to bed first last night?"

"Can I help it if I do my best work at night? Right, Angel?"

Angel laughed and tossed her curls. "That was not like it he made it sound. We were right behind y'all and we each slept in our own beds."

"I meant detecting. De-tec-ting. That's all I meant."

"Sure, Jeff." Ribbing and heckling came from all around as they got out and headed inside. Jeff took it good naturedly.

Unlocking the door, Charlie hit the lights and held the door open for the girls. "Feel free to wander for a moment. I gotta lay my hands on some paperwork and then we can go."

Jeff looked at Angel, rolled his eyes. She grinned and shrugged. Like everything Charlie and Jennilee did, this place was classy, but in a completely useful way. Spacious and yet no wasted space, lush plants in the big front window, pleasing colors throughout, a big desk that was obviously not Mose's work. Heavy, solid wood with a leather top, Jeff recognized it as one of the Base cast-offs from years ago.

Moving over to the window in the interior door that separated the office from the warehouse space, Jeff looked through, whistled. "Wowsers, Charlie. When'd you get those toys?"

Charlie didn't even look up from his seat at the desk. "No. Absolutely not."

"But... Charlie."

"No, Jeff. You are not wrecking any of my heavy equipment. Tell him, Jennilee."

Jeff turned puppy dog eyes on Jennilee.

"You heard him, Jeff." Jennilee waited a beat. "But a ride on your bike might suffice as a bribe."

Jeff sagged in defeat. "Charlie's already ridden my bike."

Another beat. "I haven't."

The guys looked at each other, then at Jennilee, who burst out laughing.

"You want a ride on my bike? Any time, Jennilee. Any time. And you don't even have to return the favor." Jeff was grinning ear to ear.

"Not so fast, Jeffro." Charlie sounded serious but his eyes were glittering with mirth.

They were still laughing and ribbing each other when they pulled up at Grandy's.

"Five. Four. Three." Charlie didn't get to finish his countdown before Timmy came streaking around the privet hedge separating the two big, old, identical on the outside houses. Waiting for permission to launch, Jewel bailed over the side and headed for Timmy at a dead run.

Boy and dog met in a boisterous dance of greeting.

144

The foursome got out of the vehicle, grinning at the sight. Timmy ran around the jeep straight to Charlie. Catching Timmy up, Charlie swung him high overhead. Timmy's high pitched laughter rang out, accompanied by Jewel's even higher pitched barking.

Questions poured from Timmy like water over a dam.

Jennilee attempted to answer, but Timmy was too excited to listen. Charlie slung him over one broad shoulder, face down, and spun in circles. Grabbing Jennilee's hands Charlie drew her into their dance. Added to Timmy's squealing laughter and Jewel's rapid fire barking was another high pitched voice.

"Me, too! Me, too!" Elizabeth, never far behind her older brother.

Jeff caught her up and copied Charlie with Timmy. Grabbing Angel's hands, the whole noisy bunch whirled and spun like children's tops right up the walkway and onto the porch.

A smiling Grandy stepped out the back door to see what the commotion was all about, not that she didn't have a pretty good idea anyway. "Guess this means y'all are staying for supper too. Already invited the neighbors." Before they could ask, she told them, "Chicken salad sandwiches and chips."

A noisy round of appreciation and a virtual stampede followed.

The seats around Grandy's big kitchen table rapidly filled up as the crowd already there was joined by Tim and Rachel and their other two kids. Mr. Donnie dropped by and was instantly drawn into the mix.

Leaning against a counter, Charlie stole a kiss every time Jennilee, busy helping Grandy, came within range of his arms and lips.

In a blink, the table was covered with platters sporting chicken salad sandwiches, saucers of big ol' dill pickles sliced lengthwise, bowls of chips, big glasses of ice tea and a huge plate of brownies right in the center.

The blessing was said, the honor falling to Timmy, since he'd set the table. Doing the standard God is great, Amen barely made it out of his mouth before his hands were wrapped around the sandwich he'd earmarked and he had it halfway to his mouth.

The rest of the crowd, a beat behind, opened their eyes and burst into laughter as Timmy and Jeff got caught in identical poses.

"You act like you're terminally starved, Jeff." Slower to lift her sandwich, once Angel got a taste, she treated her sandwich like Jeff's kisses. Swallowed and told Grandy, "Miz Del, this is the best chicken salad sandwich I've ever tasted."

"Thank Jennilee. It's her recipe, and she finished this batch. I just started it."

Everyone's gaze switched to Jennilee. "I can write it down for you if you want."

"It won't taste the same." Angel sighed and took another bite.

Grinning, Charlie tangled his fingers in Jennilee's hair, gently tugged her close and brushed a kiss across her temple. "Jennilee adds an extra sprinkling of love to everything she fixes. I've seen her. See that silver can on the back of the stove? She's got one just like it at our house."

"And all this time I thought it was bacon grease like everyone else keeps in their can." Jeff snorted a laugh and took another bite.

"She's got one of those, too." Charlie brushed another kiss, this time across Jennilee's lips.

Meal over and kitchen cleaned up, they all drifted outside. Adults to the porch, kids to the yard. Charlie softly strummed one of his beloved guitars while the rest lazed comfortably.

Timmy disappeared and reappeared a few moments later, ball glove and baseball in hand. Looking hopefully to Charlie, he grimaced at the guitar and locked eyes with Jeff. "Will somebody play catch with me? Dad says I wore him out already."

Charlie and Jeff shared a look. "We don't have enough for teams, but...catch, sure. We're game."

Dancing from foot to foot excitedly, Timmy repeatedly smacked his ball into his glove.

Charlie retrieved his and Jennilee's gloves from the cubbies in the mudroom along with a couple bats and extra balls. Carrying the equipment out to the playing field in Grandy's side yard, they threw a few balls back and forth, warming up.

Jeff hit a few, Charlie hit a few. The girls and Timmy took turns catching the pop flies and grounders before switching places with the guys.

Not even five minutes later, Grandy's yard teemed with young-sters, boys and girls. Charlie and Jeff grinned and exchanged high-fives, Jennilee and Angel just rolled their eyes. Looked like Timmy was going to get to play some real ball. Nothing pulled a gang of kids out of thin air quicker than the sound of a bat hitting a ball on a sultry Sunday afternoon.

Sides were quickly chosen, Timmy captaining one team and a boy named Josh taking the other. Charlie and Jennilee insisted on being picked as a unit and Jeff and Angel did the same so the teams were more even.

Playing until the street lights came on, the kids faded into the twilight by ones and twos, laughter and teasing shrieks marking their passage home. Hot, sweaty, and gloriously tired, Charlie and Jennilee, Jeff and Angel, and Timmy and Elizabeth gathered their equipment and made their slow way to Grandy's.

While they'd been playing ball, Tim and Rachel and Grandy had been making ice cream. Homemade, peach, and oh so good. Swal-lowing a mouthful of the ice-cold confection, Charlie casually mentioned, "The Kinston Blue Jays are playing an exhibition game tomorrow evening."

Jeff and Timmy perked up instantly.

"You got tickets, Charlie Brown?"

"Season." Charlie directed a look at Tim, who immediately started shaking his head regretfully.

"Can't, Charlie, I've got too much…"

"It'll be there."

Grandy started laughing. "You might as well give in, Tim. You know you want to go." Rachel's turn to start shaking her head and making excuses, Grandy shook her own right back. "I'll keep the babies. You young folk go and have a good time."

"I'm not a baby! Am I?" Elizabeth sounded ready to cry, fearing she'd be lumped in with her younger brother and sister and left behind.

Timmy's eyes lit and he opened his mouth. His parents' admonish-ments hit him before he had a chance to gloat.

"One word, young man…"

"…and you'll be staying with Grandy."

Jeff groaned. "They've corrupted you two as well."

Everyone laughed at his observation.

CHAPTER 13

$\mathcal{B}$ack in town the next morning, the guys went their way and left the girls to theirs. Strolling, taking their time, Angel followed Jennilee from store to store willingly, both of them laughing and carrying on. They'd already been to the pharmacy and the post office, checked out the newest shipment of clothes at the boutique, shoes at the shoe store, and made several other stops only to end up at the Red and White.

Angel got the distinct impression most of the smaller stores were here because of Jennilee's and Charlie's influences and backing. They didn't look like the typical small town barely-hanging-on Mom and Pop stores. No dusty items on cramped aisles, no been-there-so-long goods they were sun and time faded. Most of the owners looked to be young, and not in a handed down for generations, struggling to survive way. More of a just purchased, determined to make a go of it way.

Making a few purchases of her own, Angel watched as Jennilee picked out her purchases in each place, had the items placed on her tab and arranged for Suki to pick up her things and Angel's. Once at the grocery store, Angel watched silently as Jennilee snagged an empty cart from the parking lot and pushed it back inside.

"Why did you... There're plenty of carts already inside."

Heads turned as Jennilee's laughter silvered the air, rang down the aisles. "Because Mr. Ralph just bought them and I appreciate that. They're ever so much better than the old carts."

Digesting that for a moment, Angel changed tack. "Why don't you have the stuff delivered?"

Jennilee shrugged. "Don't want all those...people at my home. It's just...better for everyone this way."

Shopping and yakking non-stop as they always did, Angel pondered all the people who'd been there recently. It wasn't people in general Jennilee didn't want in her home, in her sacred space, it was strange, uninvited people Jennilee didn't want there. Shrugging, Angel couldn't find fault with that line of reasoning. Especially given Jennilee's background.

Charlie and Jeff caught up with the girls not too much later. Giving Jennilee a hug, Charlie pulled her close for a long kiss, kept his arm around her.

Jeff kissed Angel and sought her hand, wove his fingers through hers. Placing a six pack of Natural Light in the cart, he looked up innocently and said, "What? I'm down to a couple bottles left in the frig, and I'll pay for this."

"Yeah, yeah, yeah. That's what you always say." Charlie bumped shoulders with Jeff. Jennilee just grinned.

"I can't believe you already polished off all those beers in *your* frig." Jennilee made her comment solemnly, eyes twinkling.

"Y'all act like I'm an alkie or something. I only drink when I'm here —'cause I've got a built-in designated driver." Making a face at Charlie, Jeff turned his attention back to Jennilee. "All what beers? I've only had a couple, not even a six pack." The rest of her words sunk in. "My frig? What frig?"

"The one in your room, goofy." Angel couldn't hold back her laughter any longer.

"There's a frig? In my room?"

"We go to all the trouble of trying to make our guests as comfortable as possible, and knot-head here doesn't even notice." Charlie tsked loudly and tried to look sorrowful.

Scrunching up her face, trying not to laugh, Jennilee couldn't hold it in. Heads turned and smiles broke out on the other customers' faces at the sound of Jennilee's merriment.

Charlie paid for their purchases, all except Jeff's beer, and the four-some headed for the jeep.

Angel remarked, "I can't believe y'all don't have an account here. You've got one everywhere else."

"We've got one here. Suki makes our main grocery runs, but if we stop in and get a few things, we usually pay when we pick up. And you don't think I'd pay for Jeffro's beer? Especially when he said, and I have witnesses, that he'd buy his own." Grinning around Jennilee as he directed his comments to Angel, Charlie smirked at Jeff.

A leisurely drive back out to their home, a few rounds in the game room, burgers and home-fries for lunch. More communing with each other on the porch, in the hammock and on the glider.

Another trip to town, this time to get Rachel and Tim and the kids and head out for the ball game. Just as they passed the city limits sign, Charlie hit the brakes, brought the jeep to a sliding, screeching halt. Floored it as he backed up a few feet, floored it again as he drove forward, stomped the brakes again. He and Jeff peered out the sides of the open jeep as something made a loud popping sound.

Jeff, voice full of satisfaction, called out, "Got him!"

Angel, in the back seat, feet braced and clinging to Jeff's seat with both hands, looked at Jennilee. Unfazed by the guys' peculiar behavior, seeming to take it for granted, she wasn't even holding onto anything. "Dare I ask what y'all are doing?"

"Rattlesnake." Jeff again, in the same satisfied tone.

"All that...just to kill a snake?"

"Rattlesnake, and if he was farther out I'd've left him alone. This close to town... No way." Charlie shook his head. "I know snakes are good to have around for rodent control and stuff, but...no way I'm taking a chance that rattler is going to cross a little kid, or some little old lady out weeding her garden."

"I'm not sticking up for the snake—I loathe the nasty things. Just... kind of bizarre, the way you killed it."

Charlie and Jeff shared a look, and the girls didn't have to see them roll their eyes to know they shared one of those, too.

Jeff suggested, "We could've gotten out and whacked its head off with a machete."

Charlie added, "Or beat it to death with a shovel."

"Or hacked it to death with a hoe."

"Or blown it to bits with a shotgun."

"Or..." Charlie and Jeff high-fived at the endless possibilities.

Jeff sounded glum. "None of which we currently have in our possession."

Charlie attempted to cheer him up. "Although, we do have a tire iron."

Making gagging sounds, Angel protested, "Alright already! I get the point! Just...do y'all have to be so gruesome?"

Jennilee shuddered, and Angel thought they were on the same wavelength—for just an instant. "The human phobia of snakes is deeply ingrained, from the Biblical connotations of the serpent being the one who led Eve astray right on down through the ages to our fear of being bitten and dying a slow, excruciatingly painful death. That extreme phobia inspires instant loathing and a single-minded desire to eliminate the culprit in any way possible. In past times, it was considered an act of conscience for any adult male to kill any poisonous snake they came across in order to protect the women and children, and of course, themselves. In other words, the only good snake is a dead snake."

Angel took a good look at her best friend's suddenly pasty face. "Jennilee—you're scared of snakes!"

Jennilee shuddered again as Charlie put the jeep in gear and started driving. "You got that right. Not just scared—terrified. Have been for a long while." Jennilee's left hand slipped along side the seat and Charlie's right was right there to meet it. Lacing their fingers, he pressed their joined hands against the side of his ribs, next to his heart. Squeezed, held tight until Jennilee withdrew, afraid if she continued to cling, he'd sense more than just normal human fear of snakes. Maybe read her mind as he was so adept at doing.

She didn't dare tell them the whole of it—that their arch childhood nemesis had caught her alone, without Charlie or even Jeff to protect her. Butch had hounded her, chased her down, trapped her in a tiny old shed, one that had once been an outhouse. Shaking a wriggling burlap sack tied to the end of a long stick, he'd gleefully informed her it was full of irate copperheads and rattlesnakes. Tugging the string that held the bag tied shut, he upended the sack and dumped the contents just inside the door. Slammed and then braced the door shut.

For once, Butch hadn't lied. Jennilee'd gotten a good look at the snakes before the light was stolen from her, and they were definitely copperheads and rattlers.

The poisonous snakes and the unrelenting darkness, coupled with her abhorrence of closed in places, had almost pushed Jennilee over the edge. Only the thought of Charlie's distress at finding her body had grounded her, kept her sane enough to think her way out. All the while, Butch's hyena-like laughter taunted her from outside and the rattlers buzzed their discontent inside.

The one-holer was pitch dark and utterly empty save for Jennilee and her slithery companions and whatever spiders and insects and rodents inhabited this forgotten space.

Reaching her arms out frantically, first to the sides and all around and then over her head, Jennilee felt for anything that might aid her. Nothing. Already against the back wall, she could touch both side walls with her arms, didn't even have to stretch to reach them.

Turning sideways and trying not to think about the enraged snakes that even now were homing in on her, Jennilee braced her feet against one side wall, her back against the other, and began to crab her way up the rough-cut boards. Bit back a scream as her face and head came in contact with a spiderweb. Waved her arms and tried to get it off.

Calm down, Jennilee, and think! A little ol' spider is the least of your worries right now.

Crabbing upward like a mountain climber in a rock chimney until her head bumped the tin ceiling, Jennilee backed down a little and just held her position.

THINK, Jennilee! You've successfully used this ploy in hide and seek more than once. People don't look up and snakes can't climb, not straight up. The snakes won't be able to find you, just like nobody ever found you when you were playing hide and seek. They can't get to you. Butch will get tired of his games and leave soon. Don't scream, don't give him the satisfaction.

Reaching over her head one more time, Jennilee carefully felt the boards behind her and the tin over her head. Now that her eyes were adjusting a little, she could see dim outlines. Couldn't see the pitch black hole that was the floor, couldn't tell where the snakes were.

Pushing against the tin—here, there, everywhere she could reach, finding a loose spot, she felt her heart leap with hope.

Calm! You have to stay calm until Butch gets tired and leaves.

Butch walked around the outside of her prison, banging on the walls, shouting taunts. Laughing. The rattlers inside responded to every thump and bang with their own maracas.

Gritting her teeth, Jennilee tried to remember what was the longest she'd ever pretended to be Spiderman. Tried to relax and conserve her energy.

It got quiet, too quiet. Jennilee froze, barely breathed. Good thing. The taunts and the hateful laughter started up again.

"What do you think of my presents, Jennilee? Getting cozy with any of them yet? You like snakes, don't you? You must. You're always hanging out with that snake Charlie. He can't help you this time."

More demented laughter. "I think, just to make this game a little more interesting, I'm going to go home and get some gasoline. I'll tell everyone I saw a nest of copperheads in here and all I was trying to do was get rid of them. I'll be all sorry and upset when they find your charred body. How was I supposed to know you picked today to hide in a snake infested shack?"

Giving him a few more moments, just to make sure he was really gone, Jennilee made herself count—one Mississippi, two Mississippi— all the way to a thousand. Then did it again. She had to make sure he was far enough gone, but not so far he actually had time to get his hands on some gas. Pinpointing the loose piece of tin, she worked her fingers under it, pushed up as hard as she could.

Old, the outhouse turned shed had been built to last. A tiny bit of blessed daylight rewarded Jennilee's efforts, spurred her on. She pushed harder and more nails pulled out of the rafter the tin was nailed to, or maybe the nails pulled through the rusted tin. Jennilee didn't care which.

She kept working at it and the miniscule opening slowly got larger and larger. Too slowly. A noise from outside her prison had her heart pounding out fear in double time.

Don't panic! Butch hasn't had time to get home and back. Use that adrenalin to your advantage!

She pushed harder, beginning to despair as the tin and wood refused to part. She'd never get out of here before Butch came back. Legs shaking with the strain of holding her body weight in place, Jennilee's resolve was wavering.

She shoved again, tears streaming down her face. Couldn't keep in the sobs. The tin gave way with a loud screech, gave way so fast Jennilee almost lost her precarious perch. Clutching the exposed rafter with both hands, Jennilee clung like a monkey, pulled up until the weight was off her trembling legs. Held there, for just a moment, caught her breath.

Turned, hand over hand, until her dangling feet were in line with the small opening. Swinging her feet up, she hooked her heels on the top of the board. Pulling with her heels, she got her legs far enough out she could hook her knees, then wormed the rest of her body up and partway through the tight opening.

Before she could flip and turn stomach down, let herself down easy, the top board gave way and she fell in a windmill of churning arms and legs, landed hard on her back on the sweet green grass. Landed so hard she knocked the wind out of herself. Sprawled there for endless moments, writhing, trying to get her breath back. Clawing her way to her knees, she started crawling while she was still seeing spots.

A soft touch on her arm made Jennilee jerk away, drew a harsh gasp and brought her crashing back to the present. "Jennilee? Where'd you go? You alright? Charlie, something's wrong." Angel's worried tones had the jeep slowing immediately, almost as fast as they'd stopped for the snake, had Charlie's gaze riveted on the rear view.

"Jennilee?"

Forcing a laugh, Jennilee soothed him. "Nothing, Charlie. I'm fine. I was just having a flashback of the squamate kind."

Jeff snorted out a laugh. "Okay, Encyclopedia. I'm guessing that means snake. Why can't you just say snake, or even reptile?"

Tension dispelled with Jeff's teasing query, Jennilee smiled and drew a deep breath. Placed a hand on Charlie's shoulder and one on Angel's knee. "I'm fine, really guys, but can we talk about something else?"

"How come Charlie knows so many facts, but you know all the trivia? By the way, Angel, don't ever play Trivial Pursuit with Jennilee unless you wanna get your...butt handed to you. Everyone thought Charlie was the brain when we were younger, 'cause he spouted smart sounding stuff all the time and Jennilee hardly said boo to anyone. You've heard that saying, 'Behind every good man is a brilliant woman?' Well, it's certainly true in this case."

Charlie punched Jeff's arm. Jeff just laughed. "Keep your eyes on the road and your hands on the wheel, Charlie Brown."

Making a quick stop at the cemetery, they placed fresh bouquets of daisies and yellow roses on their mothers' graves, disposed of the older, wilted bouquets.

Having just gotten started down the road again, a couple blocks later Angel watched with quiet interest as Charlie and Jeff snatched their ball caps off their heads like twin marionettes attached to the same strings. In a smooth continuation of the same move, Charlie hit the light switch and pulled off on the side of the road.

She looked at Jennilee, who sat with head bowed, hands clasped loosely in her lap.

They stayed that way until the oncoming funeral procession was well past.

"Who was that? Friend of y'all's?"

Jennilee shrugged and said softly, "I have no idea."

"All that for someone you don't know?"

"It was somebody's loved one."

"Wow. I've never seen that done before."

"Small southern town show of respect. Don't imagine you have, not living in Raleigh."

"Well, it was very nice."

Charlie turned the lights off and pulled back on the road. "They must've been going to River's Edge or Maggie Hopewell. There weren't any funeral tents set up at Oak Grove."

"I say again...y'all seem...*obsessed* with cemeteries."

Jennilee laughed. "I guess it would seem that way to you, Angel. We don't put flowers on our moms' graves *every* day."

"Just the days we come to town." Charlie added and flashed Jennilee a grin in the rearview.

Jennilee said wistfully, "We never really knew our moms. It's our way of saying, *We haven't forgotten you. We miss you. We wish things had turned out different.*"

Angel absorbed that for a moment, couldn't imagine growing up without her mom. "You visit that one in your side yard almost every day."

Jennilee met and held Charlie's reflected gaze, smiled beatifically. "Yeah, we do."

Angel heaved a sigh and reached for Jennilee's hand, squeezed gently. "Someday you'll tell me why."

"Someday."

CHAPTER 14

*C*harlie didn't even get to start his countdown today. Standing sentinel at the end of the hedgerow between the houses, dancing impatiently from foot to foot, Timmy already had his ball cap on his head, ball glove on his hand. Spotting them as soon as they pulled into Grandy's drive, he started turning cartwheels and bouncing like Tigger.

Timmy started rattling off things before the sound of the jeep's engine faded. "Dad's got the van all gassed up and Mom's got the cooler packed and I called it so I get to sit beside you and..."

Jeff shot Charlie a look. Charlie grinned and shrugged. "His van."

"Fine. I see how you are. You'll let Tim drive with Jennilee in the car, but not me."

"I let you drive. You're the one who turned down an opportunity to drive this very vehicle just the other day."

"Yeah, but..."

"No buts. I offered, you declined."

"That was because you two would've climbed in the back seat and..."

"What makes you think we're not going to do just that today?"

"Get a grip on your...hormones, Charlie Brown. There are gonna be little kids in that van."

Helping Jennilee out of the jeep, Charlie slung an arm around her shoulders and pulled her close. Grinned. "Nothing they haven't seen before."

Jeff said, in his very best Daffy Duck voice, "You're despicable."

Laughing outright, Charlie glanced pointedly at Angel. "You've got your own girl now. Leave us alone."

Jeff grinned at Angel and proffered a hand. "Come, m'lady. We're switching coaches. No need to be assaulted and offended by...odious riffraff." Tucking Angel close against his side, Jeff stuck his nose in the air.

Timmy's head swung back and forth like the pendulum on a Grandfather clock as Charlie and Jeff continued to spar.

"Say what you want about me, but watch who you're calling riffraff. There's a lady present." Charlie shot Jeff a mock glare.

"*Odious* riffraff."

"Don't make me have to call for squirt guns at dawn."

Coming around the side of their van, arms full, Rachel ordered in her best she-who-is-to-be-obeyed tone. "Cool it, both of you, or I'll make you stay home with the babies. I am not listening to that bickering all the way to Kinston."

Charlie and Jeff made faces and rolled their eyes in identical *whatever* impertinence, like they were a couple of teenagers being reprimanded. Timmy watched the whole thing, his eyes as big as saucers. Hissed in a panic, "Behave, y'all. Don't think she won't do it, and you're gonna hate staying home with the babies and missing the game."

The quartet burst into laughter and Rachel turned her back, pretending to busy herself loading the van so Timmy wouldn't see the laughter she was trying her best to hide.

"So speaks the voice of experience. Guess we better behave, Jeffro."

Charlie and Jennilee kept all of them entertained all the way to Grainger stadium. Singing nonsense songs, playing games, making up jokes and riddles. Once there, on their way to their seats—primo, right behind home plate—Timmy lasted all of about three minutes before beginning his campaign for food and souvenirs.

"Didn't you have enough to eat on the way here? How many sandwiches did you swallow whole? And I don't believe there's more than a couple chocolate chip cookies left, and no brownies at all." Planting her hands on her hips, regarding her oldest son with fond exasperation, Rachel spared a glance for an equally guilty Jeff.

Timmy sidled closer to his partner in crime. "Jeff's hungry, too. Aren't you, Jeff?"

"Yeah, buddy. Always. Let's go. As long as it's okay with your folks."

Tim reached for his wallet. Charlie shook his head. "My trip, my treat."

Tim sighed, shared a tired side-eye with Rachel. "We'll hold the seats down, then. I've climbed enough stairs already today. I'm gonna sit while I can."

Rachel sat, blew out a breath, twined her fingers with his. "Second."

Clasping Elizabeth's hand, Jennilee stopped Elizabeth's protest before the little girl even got her mouth open. "We'll be back before the game starts."

Tim and Rachel looked at each other. Rachel leaned closer to Tim with a heartfelt sigh. He put his arm around her, she flattened her palm against his chest and they both settled deeper into their seats. Snuggling into his embrace, she let her eyes drift shut. "We'll be right here when you get back."

Timmy made a face and groaned.

Jeff looked down sympathetically. "We're surrounded, bud."

Timmy grimaced. "Yeah. Lovebirds everywhere."

"Um, hey, *lovebird*. Remember me?" Tipping her head, Angel stood with one hip cocked, hand firmly planted.

"Uh, Timmy. I have to abandon you. Angel's mighty sweet. Too good to pass up."

Charlie ruffled Timmy's hair as the boy's face fell. "You'll understand, one day. Come on. I'll buy you a hotdog."

Angst forgotten, Timmy enthused, "Ooh! Can I have two? And a slushie and…"

His name, just his name, from his mom and dad at the same time. "Timmy…"

Timmy's shoulders drooped, for just an instant, then he cast a sly, sideways glance at Jeff, then Charlie.

Charlie winked. "C'mon, squirt."

Timmy's grin split his face as he took Charlie's hand.

Without opening her eyes, Rachel informed them, "Fine, Charlie, but if he pukes in the van going home, you're cleaning it up."

Timmy's confidential and too-loud whisper was plain to all as the group separated, had all of them snickering. "Mom's got eyes in the back of her head. You can't get away with nothin'. Not with her."

Charlie grinned down at the tow headed little scamp. "Knowing you, Dennis, that's probably a good thing."

Timmy shot Charlie a confused look. "I'm not Dennis." Pointed a finger at his own chest. "I'm Timmy."

"Huh. All you need is a friend named Margaret and a slingshot in your back pocket."

"Margaret's a girl name. I don't need no stinkin' girl for a friend." Refocusing on the last part, Timmy asked hopefully, "Slingshot? Will you get me a slingshot, Charlie? I really want one."

"Definite no on that, and I don't even have to ask your mom."

Crowding close, Jeff broke in. "Hey, Charlie! Remember that time we…"

"Yeah. I remember. I remember gettin' our…behinds whupped. That's why I'm not getting him one."

Jeff sounded sulky. "Spoilsport."

"Yeah…I'm Mr. Spoilsport. I'll remember that when you have kids. Don't be surprised when your kids all get slingshots for Christmas. And pea shooters. And BB guns. And cherry poppers. And pocket knives. And…"

"Alright, already. I get the point."

Charlie shook his head and tsked loudly. "You've got your hands full, Angel."

"Is that so? Way I heard it, you're the instigator."

"Is that what you heard? I can't believe Jeff... Tell her, Jennilee."

Jennilee opened her mouth.

Wagging a finger, Angel said, "Don't even. There's no telling what lengths you'd go to for Charlie, what lies you'd tell."

Jennilee declared staunchly, "There's nothing I wouldn't do for Charlie."

"And Jennilee doesn't lie. Ever." Pulling her close and pressing a kiss on top her head, Charlie leaned back and gave her a stern look. "She just...prevaricates."

Angel quipped, "Omission is still a sin, Jennilee."

"Self preservation, Angel. Guys can't handle the real truth." Jennilee was openly laughing at Charlie, and Jeff. "On the other hand, I could tell you stories on both these guys that would make your hair curl."

"My hair's already curly enough, thank you."

"She won't, though. Can't...not without implicating herself." Jeff grinned around Angel at Jennilee. "She looks like Little Miss Innocent, but..."

"You got in trouble when you were little, Jennilee?" Elizabeth asked, eyes wide. Timmy was staring at her just as intently.

Dark memories pulsed through Jennilee's ocean eyes, like a big hungry shark circling a bloodied swimmer, but she blinked and smiled. Tipped her head at Charlie and then Jeff. "These two were always getting into scrapes and dragging me along."

Jeff snorted, "Guilt by association, ha. Don't believe a word of it. She was right there in the thick of things."

"Because I knew the two of you would always look out for me, protect me." Jennilee blew Jeff a kiss and gave Charlie a real one.

Charlie gave her a snappy salute and a two step shuffle, his serious eyes belying his playful actions. "Always, my love."

"Ooh, there's the hotdog stand. And they've got cotton candy and... Look at the ball caps! Can I get a miniature bat? And a pennant and..."

Charlie let go Timmy's hand as the boy tugged like a balloon on a windy day. "Stay where we can see you. We'll be there in a minute."

Timmy took off.

Pulling on Jennilee's hand to get her attention, Elizabeth pointed. "Jennilee, I have to go."

"You heard her, guys. Potty break. We'll be back as quick as we can."

"I'll be right here. Joey, go chase down Dennis before he gets in too much trouble." Crossing his arms, Charlie leaned up against the wall outside the door to the women's bathroom.

Angel opted to go with the girls.

As promised, they came back as quick as they could.

Angel was still moaning and groaning as they came out the door. "I don't know why public places don't make bigger bathrooms for women. There's never a line at the men's room door."

Jennilee bumped shoulders with Angel. "Chill out, Angel. Women always have the children with them so it takes us longer. The men will go find something to do while they wait. Or, in Charlie's case, hold up a wall and wait right here."

Charlie grinned and tucked Jennilee under his arm. "I've been keeping an eye on those two while I waited. Good thing Timmy doesn't have any money, and Jeff knows better than to give in to him."

Jeff spied them coming, walked backwards in their direction so he could still keep a watchful eye on Timmy. Joining him, Charlie's group rippled to one side like water moving around a boulder, made room for him at one end of their line and they all headed for Timmy.

Timmy turned to see how close they were, his eyes alight like Charlie Bucket when he caught his first glimpse of Oompa Loompa Land. "They've got...pretzels." He hollered the first, breathed the last like he was describing Willy Wonka's magical inventory. Waved his hands and shaped an immense, imaginary pretzel shape. "Those huge soft ones with the big salt crystals on them."

Laughing at his theatrics, they walked closer.

A jolt shuddered through Jennilee, alerting Charlie, vibrated across Elizabeth through Angel to Jeff. Instantly pushing both women and the child to the fore, the guys spun and stepped shoulder to shoulder to present a solid wall at their backs.

All three females and everyone close by heard the meaty thud of two fists connecting with flesh. Solid blows, so close together as to be nearly simultaneous. By the time the girls recovered their balance and turned, Charlie had some jerk pinned, the side of his face smashed against the wall, arm twisted up between his shoulder blades. Jeff had Charlie's back, fists clenched, raised and ready, facing out into the crowd.

Blood gushed from the jerk's nose, obviously broken. Charlie didn't slack up his grip in the least, in fact bore down harder when the guy's scruffy buddies started making loud excuses. Used the palm on the jerk's head to grind the jerk's face harder into the wall, wrenched harder on his arm.

"Let up, man. It was just a joke."

"Yeah, a dare."

"He didn't mean nothin' by it."

Charlie looked over his shoulder past Jeff, his slow, deadly glare taking in, memorizing, each of the wannabe toughs.

They backed off, hands raised.

Charlie turned his attention back to the young man he held pinned. "Do you see that beautiful blonde over there? The one you were getting your jollies groping?" Waited till the young man nodded as much as he was able.

"That's my wife, cretin. You are going to apologize to her, and then you and your cronies are going to leave this place."

Struggling futilely, the idiot moaned, "But we just got here. We paid good money for our tickets, same's everyone else."

"Everyone else didn't harm my wife."

Whining now, "I didn't hurt her."

Charlie clamped down.

The whine escalated into a girly scream. "Ow. Owwwww. You're hurting me."

Leaning closer, pinning the jerk's body with his own, Charlie kept a tight grip on the arm between them. Fished one-handed in the jerk's back pocket, pulled out his wallet, flipped it open, read his driver's license. "Well, Bradley Owen Foster the Third of 156 High Creek Court. Says here you just turned seventeen. Keep pulling stupid stunts like that and you won't make it to eighteen." Thumbing the license out of its clear sleeve, Charlie returned the wallet to the pocket.

"You can't do this! Can't do anything to me. I'm a minor! My dad's a lawyer!"

"A lawyer? Is that so? Good for him. I'm sure he knows all about the law, then. All about assaulting a woman. Wonder what your parents would think of your asinine behavior? Not to mention the sleazeball trio you're hanging with. Better go straight home and tell 'em exactly what happened, 'cause I damn sure intend to."

"Okay, okay. I give. Just don't tell my parents."

"Fat chance. March your ass over there, and it better be sincere." Charlie shoved harder, wrenched a little more, before letting go and stepping back.

The jerk slumped and using the wall for support, rolled on his good shoulder to face Charlie, cradling his abused arm. Both eyes already swelling, a decided lump on his jaw, he opened his mouth to voice another protest. One murderous glare from Charlie had him snapping his mouth shut.

"Hey, you lunatic. You can't do this. We'll call the cops."

Turning his head and looking over his shoulder once more at the jerk's ally, Charlie said pleasantly, with an absurdly chilling smile, "Call them. I'll have you all arrested. It would be my pleasure."

Instant squalls came from all three of the jerk's cronies. Squalls overridden by Charlie's coldly authoritative voice. "You...scumbags seem to think it's a joke to lay hands on innocent women in public. All of you are going to apologize to my wife, and then leave."

The guilty party mumbled through his blood clogged nose, "C'mon guys. Do as he says."

One of the idiots, dumber and more belligerent than the others, protested, "He can't make us apologize, and he damn sure can't make us leave."

Flexing his muscles, just a little, Charlie smiled wider, a wolf who'd given his last warning snarl and was on the verge of attacking.

"Just do as he says." Something in the jerk's tone finally got through to his friends.

Charlie's grin became, if possible, more cold and deadly, his tone more pleasant and all the more frightening for it. "That's right, *boys*. Do as I say, and no one else will get hurt. Then do yourselves and the rest of the world a favor and learn some manners before you venture out in public again."

When none of them took him seriously enough to move, Charlie barked, "NOW!"

Charlie on one side and Jeff on the other, they paced the staggering, bleeding jerk back to Jennilee. Spun and flanked her like a couple presidential bodyguards who'd just spotted a threat.

The one who'd dared touch Jennilee stopped in front of her, didn't raise his eyes above her knees. "I'm...sorry."

Charlie cleared his throat, a sound more growl than cough.

Shooting a terrified look at Charlie, the jerk scrutinized Jennilee's waist. "Very sorry, ma'am." Flicked another nervous glance at a stone-faced Charlie, back to Jennilee. Swallowed. Met her eyes this time. "Truly sorry I touched you inappropriately. You have my word it won't happen again. Ma'am."

Charlie gave a terse millimeter of a nod.

Jerk slithered out of the way like a smidge of grease dropped in a hot iron skillet sliding to the outside.

Shuffling by, the others gave their grudging apologies as they made their way to a nearby exit.

The whole altercation, from first blow to last apology, had taken less than two minutes.

Watching them through the turnstiles and out of sight, Charlie didn't even blink. Taking a deep breath, he hauled a ghost-white pale Jennilee up against himself. "It's okay, Jennilee-baby. You're fine. I'm fine. They're gone."

Jennilee nodded jerkily. Her rigid posture said different and so did her shadowed eyes. She buried her face against Charlie's chest and fought to breathe.

"Jennilee. Jennilee?" Angel touched her friend's shoulder, concern evident. "Charlie, is she..."

Charlie shook his head, indicated the kids with his eyes. "She'll be okay. Give her a minute."

Jeff nodded at Angel when she looked to him, dropped his gaze to the two wide-eyed kids. Timmy about to burst and Elizabeth about to burst into tears. Did his best to distract them before the chatter and tears broke free. "Hey, can we eat now?"

As distractions went, it should've been a great one. It didn't work very well, or for very long.

Timmy blinked, torn between food and commentary. "Wowsers, Charlie. I thought mom was tough on us about apologizing. I hope I don't ever do anything I have to tell you sorry for."

Taking out his wallet, Charlie tossed it to Jeff who immediately herded Timmy closer toward the concession stand.

A couple hiccuping heaves of breath and big, fat tears spilled over and started running a river down Elizabeth's cheeks. Angel comforted the girl when Jennilee, totally out of character for her, didn't appear to notice.

A few minutes later, clutching his hotdog in one hand, drink in the other, Timmy took a breath and erupted. "Charlie, you and Jeff were great! I saw that guy come up behind Jennilee and I saw her face get real white and then... You both hit him and then you took him out while Jeff guarded your back. You should've beat him up some more. I don't know what he did, but he deserved it."

Everyone looked at Charlie. He smiled for the kids, but it never reached his eyes. Both arms around Jennilee, his hands stayed in constant motion, rubbing her arms and back comfortingly, tangling in her hair. He'd only stopped his ceaseless motions long enough to get his wallet out and pass it to Jeff.

Charlie tipped his head and Jeff corralled Timmy again in a jiff. "Come on, Timmy. Let's go get you a bat and a hat." Taking two steps on their way to go stand in line to get their souvenirs, Timmy instantly got all their attention when he stopped so fast Jeff almost fell over him.

"Uh oh." Timmy's eyes went huge again as he spotted a security guard headed purposefully in their direction, being spurred on by a well dressed, middle aged woman. "Charlie." Squeezing his hotdog so hard ketchup and relish oozed out and plopped on the floor, he pointed with his drink. "She looks like a rich Bertha."

Elizabeth, having wound down to sniffles, started crying again in earnest. Angel picked her up and the little girl buried her face in Angel's shoulder, arms tight around Angel's neck.

The guard confronted Charlie when the irate woman pointed her finger and accused in an earsplitting shriek, "That's him! He's the one! I saw the whole thing!"

"Sir, this woman insists you started a fight, beat up some teenager." Charlie shook his head. "Nossir."

"He did, too! I saw him! See—there's blood all over the wall and the floor, right there."

Laying a cautioning hand on Timmy's shoulder, Jeff squeezed in warning as he felt the youngster tense and get ready to defend Charlie.

Meeting the guard's wary gray eyes, his own unshadowed, Charlie stated, "I instigated nothing, sir."

Tall, as tall as Charlie, with sandy brown hair and a direct, no nonsense gaze, the muscular guard judged Charlie's calm words and his protective posture, the woman he held so tightly against his chest. The other couple, hovering super-close, the distraught kids. His eyes agreed with Charlie, but he didn't even get his mouth open before the Bertha twin started squealing like a stuck pig.

"Liar! I saw it with my own eyes. Him, and that one there. Both of them attacked that poor boy for no reason, but he's the one who wouldn't let the boy go." The expertly made up, dripping with expensive jewelry woman was puffed up with self righteousness, shrill with indignation.

Keeping his cool, Charlie pulled Jennilee tighter into his embrace as he once more addressed the stadium security officer. "One of your *patrons* assaulted my wife. We had a...come-to-Jesus meetin'."

Looking at the close-knit group, obviously highly upset about something, then the outraged woman, the officer grimaced. "Ma'am, it seems you misunderstood what you saw."

"I know exactly what I saw! I want them thrown out of the stadium this instant! Do you have any idea who I am? I will make your life a holy hell if you don't do something, right now."

The guard obviously did know the woman, and well. He swallowed hard, sweating bullets, stuck between the proverbial rock and a hard place. Grinding his teeth so hard his jaw jutted to one side, trying to keep the peace, trying to placate the woman and not piss off an obviously in-the-right Charlie, he conceded, "Sir, would you mind stepping into the security offices for a moment, till we can clear this up?"

"No. There's nothing to clear up. We're going back to our seats to try and enjoy the game. We appreciate your concern."

"I'll have your job if you don't do something *this instant!* That poor boy probably needs to be hospitalized, and he should pay for it!" Stabbing her finger in Charlie's direction again, the woman got a little too close, a little too vocal.

Timmy bristled, Jeff took a step in the woman's direction, Angel moved closer to Jennilee, Elizabeth sobbed loudly. Jennilee twitched, started to lift her head. Charlie tightened his arms, splayed one hand across Jennilee's upper back, one across the back of her head, fingers tangled in her hair.

Flicking the woman a dismissing glance, completely ignoring her diatribe, Charlie told the guard smoothly, "I have his name and address, if you want them. I don't think you'll have to worry about him or his friends coming back and harassing anyone else."

"Your job is on the line! Do you hear me? Do something!" The woman repeatedly drilled her lethally long, perfectly manicured and polished nail into the guard's chest.

Taking a step back, plain good manners and upbringing dictating he not retaliate against a woman, the harassed guard looked around the woman to Charlie, started to say something.

An older, white haired man broke through and stepped out of the gathered crowd, breathing hard. "I don't know what that self righteous biddy thinks she saw, but I can tell you these two should be awarded a medal. That cocky..." Swallowing *son of a bitch* and *bastard* and a few other choice epithets, the man chose a more family appropriate description while he caught his breath. "...delinquent got just what he deserved. This lady here wasn't the first they assaulted. That crowd of hoodlums has been making their way around the stadium, taking turns. Picking out a victim and daring each other. I've been trying to catch up with them, at least keep an eye on them until I could let one of you guards know, but..." He indicated his cane. "I'm not as quick on my feet as I used to be."

Drawing herself up, hands on her hips, looking down her nose, the

Bertha clone sneered, "And how would you know what went on here?"

Thin as a reed, slightly bowed but standing strong, the older gentleman snorted a laugh at the woman's imperious question. "I may be crippled and slow, but there's nothing wrong with my eyes. This young man here did nothing except protect his woman. Too bad there aren't more like him and less like you."

The growing crowd burst into laughter and applause, the woman's face got redder and redder, visible even beneath her makeup.

"Do you have any idea who I am? I'll…"

"No, and I don't care. You're an idiot from the word go. Stop flappin' your yap and go back to your seat so the rest of us can enjoy the game in a modicum of peace."

The woman's mouth opened and closed, opened and closed. "You just wait till I tell my husband about you! All of you! He'll…"

Like a reed dancing and swaying in the wind, the older gentleman straightened, threw his head back and laughed in her face. "I survived the D-Day invasion and the rest of WWII and then Korea. The unfortunate and more than likely utterly browbeaten husband of one shrill, long nosed shrew doesn't scare me."

Stepping between them, visibly trying not to laugh, the guard interceded. "Thank you both for helping clear up this matter. Everybody head to your seats, please. The game's about to start."

A Mexican standoff for a breathless moment, then the woman tossed her head and harrumphed loudly.

Waiting until the woman left, stomping off in a huff, high heels clacking with every furious step, very unladylike imprecations filling the air around her, Charlie took his hands off Jennilee long enough to take his wallet back from Jeff and take out a business card.

Taking the pen the guard handed him, scribbling down on the back of his card the information he'd read and memorized off the kid's license, he handed both to the empathetic security guard. "My name's Charlie, and that's the perp's name and address." Thrusting his chin at the departing woman's backside, he said, "If she attempts to make life unbearable for you, contact me. Our info's on the flip side."

Shaking hands with the guard, Charlie turned to the older gentleman, held out his hand. Taking the arthritic one gently but firmly in his, he shook it as well. "Thank you, sir. Not just for your aid, but for your service. Is there anything we can do for you?"

"Not a thing, lad. It's nice to see there are a few true gentlemen left in the world. Does my heart good. Men like you and your buddy there and beautiful women like your wife are a big part of the reason we fought."

Jennilee shivered and looked up, some semblance of returning awareness flickering across her face as the shadows began to depart.

Smiling as his eyes met hers, the older gentleman bobbed his head. "Marty Robbins, like the singer, 'cept I can't carry a tune in a bucket. Pleased to meet you, ma'am."

It took Jennilee a moment to react, like a statue slowly coming to life. Smiling wanly, she captured his hand in both hers, held it with a butterfly touch. "Jennilee Meyers, and this is my husband, Charlie. You have my thanks as well. Would you like to sit with us? We're close by, right behind home plate."

Starting to refuse, Marty thought about his solitary seat between complete strangers halfway 'round the stadium, made the mistake of looking at the little boy and girl. Two faces, one hopeful and one teary, scrutinizing his every expression. Beamed. "I'd love to. If you can get another seat this late. I'm not about to reprimand someone else for their lack of manners and then steal a seat from someone who paid for it."

"Not a problem, sir." Charlie backed Jennilee. "We have a whole block of seats to ourselves. Never know how many friends will turn up."

"Charlie Meyers?" The security guard kept looking at Charlie like he knew him from somewhere and just couldn't make the connection. "Where do I know you from?"

Charlie shrugged. "State, maybe? I graduated this past spring."

"Ben Adair, and I didn't go to college. I went right into the work force, soon's I graduated from high school." Snapped his fingers as he looked back and forth from Charlie to Jeff, face lighting up like stadium lights. "Football! You—both of you—took state playoffs in '81! You're...Jeff Rivenbark. You two were unstoppable. Poetry in motion."

Emboldened by the admiration in Ben's tone, Timmy offered, "Charlie's got all kinds of trophies."

As if his words gave them permission to move, their little group came to life like a stuttering film getting past a rough spot. Jerky at first, then smoothing out.

Angel put Elizabeth down, Jeff put his arm around Angel, pulled her close for a quick kiss. Charlie held out a hand and Jennilee twined her fingers through his.

"We need to get the rest of our refreshments and souvenirs and get back to our seats." Jennilee, pretty much recovered now, sounded like her normal self. Mostly.

"I gotta get back to work. Nice meeting you folks. Sorry about the trouble." Giving them a wave and a friendly grin, Ben sauntered off, eyes peeled for any more troublemakers.

Jennilee asked, "Would you like something, Mr. Robbins?"

"Marty, and no thank you."

"Well, Mr. Marty, if you'll wait right here for us, we won't be a moment."

Charlie swung Elizabeth up on his hip. Jennilee produced a kleenex out of thin air and dried the tears, wiped Elizabeth's nose.

Jeff and Timmy got back in line, avidly discussing the pros and cons of various treats.

Sidling up to Jennilee, Angel rubbed her comfortingly on the back. "Come to Jesus?"

Jennilee laughed, and heads turned. Not her usual laugh, but still attention getting. "A hellfire-and-brimstone see-the-light-talkin'-to."

Walking back to their seats, loaded down with food and trinkets, the group flanked Jennilee, surrounded her. Cocooned her. Charlie and Elizabeth on one side, Timmy and Mr. Marty on the other, Jeff and Angel bringing up the rear.

Swiping Jeff's drink, Angel sucked hard on the straw, handed it back. Asked him quietly, "What was that all about? Not you guys, I understand that, even if I don't have a clue how you knew what was going on enough to react that fast, but Jennilee. She pushed us back behind herself and stood between me and the kids and you guys like she was the next line of defense."

Jeff took his time answering. "There was—still is—a horrible bully in our town. He made Jennilee's life pure hell while we were growing up, tormented her far more than we'll ever know. She stood up to him time after time, for herself and for those too small and weak to defend themselves. Paid dearly for every one of those defenses."

"Okay, I get the bully thing. That's not what I asked you."

Taking a deep breath, Jeff kept his eyes on the willowy blond in front of them. "Make no mistake about it—had one of those thugs gotten around us, Jennilee would have taken him down without thinking twice, before they even thought about getting close to y'all, or died trying. The only reason she didn't go around Charlie and me and on them is because she didn't want to distract Charlie and get him hurt, and going after those creeps would have left you and squirt without any protection."

Angel cast a disbelieving look from Jeff's serious face to Jennilee's slender back, Charlie's hand smack in the middle, fingers woven through her golden tresses.

"I know, I know. She doesn't look the type. Trust me, you don't want to make her mad, or arouse her protective instincts. She won't fight back until she gets pushed to the edge and beyond, but once she crosses that line..."

"Jennilee?"

"Yeah, Jennilee. Our sweet little berserker. As loving as she is, she can't stand to be touched against her will, or backed into a corner."

"I guess she's got good reason, huh?"

"You have no idea. On their sixteenth birthdays, I'm the one who had to tell Charlie about the rumors Bully Butch was spreading about Jennilee. He—we—slipped out, left their party, and hunted Butch down. Charlie ran Butch to ground in his own front yard, beat him into the dust, literally, but not before Butch got in a lot of taunting about the hell he'd put Jennilee through. Worst part is, what he confessed to is the tip of the iceberg. She can't abide a bully and her reactions are almost quicker than ours. That's a big part of why Charlie and I pushed you guys forward."

"Hmmm. I thought she was...upset about what those jerks did."

"Jennilee? She's more upset with herself because she doesn't like losing her temper and going off in public, and it was a close thing."

As if her ears were burning, Jennilee glanced over her shoulder, gave the whispering couple a smile.

Angel smiled back. "We'll talk about this more later." Leaning close and giving Jeff a swift peck on the cheek, Angel smiled up at him. "My brothers just might think you're worthy of dating me."

"Might, huh?"

CHAPTER 15

Strolling down Chinquapin Ridge's main street the next afternoon, side by side and hand in hand, Angel pointed with her chin. "There goes that girl."

"What girl?" Looking across the street in the direction she'd indicated, a wide smile broke across Jeff's face. "Michelle!"

"One of your friends you introduced me to at the diner the other night. I could tell there's a lot of history between you, just from the way you said her name."

"So how come you don't sound jealous?"

"Do you want me to?"

"No. You have no reason to be."

"She's a good friend to Jennilee, isn't she?"

"Yeah. We dated off and on through high school. Nothing serious for either of us, but she's one of the few girls who'd have anything to do with Jennilee. For that alone, she'll always have my undying affection."

"You dated because she'd go out with you guys, dare to be seen with the Scarlet Letter."

"Yeppers."

"Looks like she's headed for the pharmacy."

"Probably wants a milkshake. That old machine in there sounds like an earthquake in a ball bearing factory but it makes the best ones I've ever had. Want one?"

"Sounds good. Reckon Jennilee and Charlie will know where to look for us? We didn't say…"

Jeff snorted a laugh. "They'll head for the pharmacy as soon as they finish what they're doing, and they never have to look hard for me anyway."

"Just look for food, huh?"

Laughing, hooking an arm around Angel's neck and pulling her close, Jeff taunted, "Why, I oughtta…"

"Down, Moe."

"You do know they're my heroes?"

"Figured that. I deserve an extra large shake if I have to put up with you *and* the Three Stooges."

"I foresee lots of extra large shakes in your future."

"A wise guy, eh?"

"You love them too!"

"Never said I didn't."

Laughing and carrying on, still hand in hand, they stumbled their way inside the pharmacy. Letting their eyes get used to the darker interior, they located Michelle right where Jeff said she'd be. Seated at the grill counter on one of the tall chrome stools, eyes locked on the noisy milkshake machine.

Turning at the jangle of bells, Michelle's face lit. "Hiya, Jeff! And… Angel. Good to see you two again. Sorry I was in such a hurry the other night. I'd've loved to have stayed and watched Charlie's and Jennilee's performance."

Giving Michelle a swift, hard, one-armed hug, Jeff stepped back, seated Angel and then himself on the swivel top stools. "You should've made time. Their show was great, and they even got Mose and Mr. Jubal up on stage with them."

"Really?" Michelle's drawled observation had them all laughing. "I should have stayed. Haven't heard Mose sing or Mr. Jubal play in far too long."

"I bet. How're your studies coming?"

"'Bout the same as yours, I expect. Long and tedious, but it'll be worth it in the end. I'm only here now because summer classes got cancelled for a couple days."

Giving Angel a peck, Jeff told her proudly, "Michelle's gonna be a doctor."

"Wow. For such a small town, y'all sure have a lot of talent."

Throwing her head back, Michelle laughed. "Probably not really, it's just such a small place you know everyone and their accomplishments and failings. Not like a big city."

A few more of the old gang drifted in and settled themselves, keeping Marcy busy and the milkshake maker humming.

Charlie and Jennilee joined them and jests and laughter filled the old building, bouncing off the high ceilings and the oiled hardwood floor, the bells over the door ringing a merry accompaniment.

The sound of a vehicle outside, sans muffler, had them all looking toward the huge plate glass windows, rattling with the heavy sound.

Laying on the horn loudly and incessantly, the driver of the vehicle proclaimed his arrival.

The first one on his feet, Jeff crowed, "Holy cow, Stevie did it! He finally got that hunk of junk running!"

The guys moved en masse toward the door like a herd of hypnotized lemmings.

The girls sat still and shook their heads.

Angel quipped, "What is it with guys and old cars?"

Laughing heartily, backs to the door, none of them paid any attention when the bells jangled sweetly. Just figured it was one of the guys coming back in to reclaim his milkshake.

Around slurps of her shake, Michelle asked, "Anybody wanna go to the beach? Tomorrow's my last day here for awhile and I need my ocean fix."

Instant plans for a beach excursion exploded in the air until a voice made itself heard over the happy chatter.

"Jennilee. Excuse me, Jennilee?"

Spinning on her seat, Jennilee faced the newcomer. "I'm Jennilee. Can I help you with something?"

The brunette bombshell's face fell. "You don't remember me, do you? I...need to speak with you. Privately. I have something to tell you."

Antennae vibrating, Angel and Michelle, taking the guys' places and flanking Jennilee, shook their heads.

Needlessly.

Jennilee was already shaking hers. "Anything you have to say can be said right here in front of my friends."

The woman twisted her hands together nervously. "I can't believe you don't remember me. Charlie introduced us." Jennilee continued to stare blankly. The stranger rushed on desperately. "That day at State. When you came to visit him."

Jennilee shrugged dismissively. "I visited a lot, and women are always flocking around Charlie."

"I'm...Marlee. Surely you remember now?"

Shaking her head, Jennilee ordered, "Get to the point."

"I'm pregnant."

"I'd say congratulations but you don't look very happy about it, Melly."

"*Marlee!* I don't want...congratulations."

"What do you want?"

Giving the staring females a pitiful look from under her lashes, Marlee whispered, "It's so...embarrassing to have to say this to you."

"You need help? You don't want the baby? I'm sure we could help you find a good home..."

"I don't want it at all!"

Jennilee's reply should've been accompanied by puffs of frosty air. "If you're looking for money for an abortion, Marlene, forget it. We don't condone the murder of innocents."

Gritting her teeth, the woman ground out, "*Marlee!* My name is *Marlee!* Are you being this obtuse on purpose or are you really that stupid?"

Jennilee blinked and gave the woman a cold smile. "Say what you have to say and stop beating around the bush."

"I didn't want to shame you like this in public, but you give me no choice. I've followed you for days, and you're never alone."

Angel and Michelle simultaneously shifted closer in support.

Jennilee's eyes narrowed dangerously and she spat, "You... followed me?"

Digging herself deeper, the woman nodded.

Sliding off the barstool, Jennilee inquired frigidly, "Just how is it you think you're going to shame me, Molly?"

"The...baby... It's...Charlie's."

A heartbeat of total silence, and then uproarious laughter, led by Jennilee.

Someone in the crowd called out, "This is a joke, right? Somebody put you up to this?"

Face getting redder by the second, the woman wailed, "This isn't funny! My life is ruined!"

Sucking up a long taste of extra-chocolatey milkshake, Jennilee stared the woman down. Handed the shake without looking to Angel. Crossing her arms and her ankles, cocking her head, she rested negligently against the barstool behind her. "We're not laughing because you're pregnant, Mallory. We're laughing because you're stupid enough to try and pin the blame on Charlie."

"It's his! I swear it's his!"

More laughter, laughter which almost covered the jangling bells.

Jennilee shook her head, eyes never leaving the other woman's. "What happened, Melanie? You found out how much Charlie's worth and thought you'd claim a piece of it for yourself? Forget it. We don't cave to blackmailers. Never have, never will."

"It's his! I went to his room, that one he rented over the garage at the Marcellini's. That's where..."

More laughter, and Angel stepped in. "Don't even. Charlie's never had any woman up there without at least one chaperone *and* the door wide open, not the whole time he lived there. Not me, not my sisters, not my nieces or cousins, not even my mom and especially not Jennilee. *Ever.*"

"He was drunk. He..."

When the laughter died this time, Charlie's deep voice filled the void.

"Marlee. If you're going to throw stones, you need to find someone who doesn't live in a glass house. Or in this case, a fishbowl."

Whirling to face a thunderous looking Charlie, flanked by a great many of his male friends, all looking equally intimidating, Marlee stuttered and stammered. "What's that supposed to mean?"

"This whole town is one giant fishbowl. Everyone knows me. *Everyone.*"

"So?"

Deceptively relaxed, Jeff stated, "So everyone knows Charlie'd never cheat on Jennilee."

Allowing Jeff to take up the gauntlet, Charlie stared into Jennilee's eyes, unspoken messages filling the space between them.

"Maybe you all don't know him as well as you think! People go away to college, get away from home, they change. They get...wild."

Jeff shook his head. "Not Charlie."

"He was drunk! I swear he was drunk. He invited me up there to have a drink and things...got out of hand." Marlee looked around at the grim faces, each and every one shaking their heads and denying her words.

Jeff's eyes narrowed. "I don't think so. You really should have done your homework better."

"You people are insane! How can you be so sure? You weren't even there!"

Jeff shook his head slowly. "Didn't have to be there. I know what I know."

"Would you speak English? Stop talking in riddles!"

Enunciating clearly, speaking slowly like he was talking to someone of severely limited intelligence, Jeff enlightened her. "Charlie's dad was the town drunk for most of his growing up years."

"And?"

"When you grow up with the town drunk for a father, you do one of two things. You either follow in his footsteps, or you become a teetotaler."

"Oh, no. Charlie drinks. Just because you all think he's Mr. Wonderful..."

Skirting past the odious female, Jennilee sailed into Charlie's waiting arms and locked hers around his neck. Looking up at him, face radiant, Jennilee offered, "He is Mr. Wonderful. My Mr. Wonderful. All mine."

Returning her smile, Charlie tipped his head. Jennilee stretched up on tiptoe, their lips meeting, fusing.

"That's disgusting! How can you be like that after what I just told you? I'm pregnant, and the baby is his!"

Lost in each other, Charlie and Jennilee didn't even look up.

Rubbing his hands together, Jeff gloated. "Charlie's dad also owns a garage and a tow truck."

Giving Jeff a drop-dead look, Marlee sneered, "What does that have to do with me?"

"Partly it means that even if Mr. Donnie hadn't been such an alkie, Charlie's helped him clean up enough wrecks caused by drunks not to ever have any desire to touch alcohol. It also means that if you don't haul ass out of town and keep going, that same tow truck, courtesy of me, is gonna disappear your car. Permanently."

Moving to Jeff's side, slipping tight against him when he lifted his arm and encircled her, Angel informed him with a toss of her curls, "She's been following Jennilee."

"Say what?"

Angel narrowed her eyes. "I'm thinking... Restraining order. Oughtta be easy enough to get."

"Libel."

"Stalking."

"Harassment."

"Blackmail."

"Forget the restraining order, we're talking serious jail time."

Marlee pointed at Charlie. "He drinks! I saw him at the grocery store, buying beer."

Jeff laughed, not a nice sound. "You suck as much at being a detective as you do a liar. Charlie's never bought a beer in his life."

"I saw him!"

"You saw me buying a six pack. *Me.* And I drank every single one of those six."

Joining her friends, standing in front of Jeff with her arms crossed and the drop-dead glare on her face directed at Marlee, Michelle scoffed, "You're from a big city. Otherwise, you'd know how tight small town friends are. We know each of our friends' failings, but we also know each other's strengths. Charlie and Jennilee are each other's strength, and they'd never betray each other. You're a fool to think they would." Reaching out, she clasped the hand Jennilee reached out to her, stretched her other up to cover Jeff's when he placed his hand on her shoulder.

Faced with such a unified front, Marlee steamed hopelessly. "You won't get away with this! I'll get even. You can't do this to me! I'll see you in court!"

Meeting Marlee's threats with yet another round of laughter at her expense, the crowd flowed around her like a puddle of mercury. Joining together again at the counter, the crowd reclaimed their unfinished shakes amid a babble of conversation.

Enjoying the last of her double chocolate, ignoring the intruder, Michelle inquired, "We still on for the beach?"

A chorus of ayes answered. Shakes finished, surging around the unwelcome visitor—standing statue still and stewing—once more, the whole gang beelined for the door. Marlee's next threat froze them, for a heartbeat.

"I'll kill myself."

Slurping noisily, chasing what was left of his shake with his straw to get the very last drop, Jeff needled, "First time in your life you've been told no? Didn't get what you want?"

Stamping her foot, hands waving about like a demented octopus, Marlee declared, "I cannot believe how cold-hearted you are! The whole lot of you! Damn you to..."

The bells jangled again.

Holding Jennilee tight against himself, Charlie exclaimed, "Chief Mac! Doc! I'm sure glad you showed up. I was just about to call you both."

Instantly picking up on the tension, Mac asked, "Somethin' wrong, Charlie?"

"Not with us, nossir. This young woman here seems to be having a mental breakdown of some sort. She's the one who needs help, and right away."

Red-faced, Marlee screamed, "There's nothing wrong with me! I..."

While Chief Mac and Doc looked askance at the foaming-at-the-mouth stranger, Charlie inserted smoothly, "This is Marlee... I've forgotten her last name. We had some classes together at State. She burst in here awhile ago and..."

"Classes together? We had more than that!" Pointing her finger at Charlie, she screeched, "He got me pregnant and he refuses to take any responsibility!"

At the totally disbelieving looks Chief Mac and Doc shot her, she shrilled, "Charlie raped me! He got me drunk and he raped me." Went from screeching to sobbing in the space of a heartbeat.

No one there was moved by either.

Charlie met the Chief's eyes squarely. "Chief Mac, Marlee's clearly delusional. She needs help."

"We'll take care of it, son." Doc held out a hand to Marlee.

Marlee shrieked, "What? I'm not going anywhere with you! I haven't done anything! He's the guilty one!"

Charlie offered, "I'll call Tony Marcellini. He may remember Marlee's last name so we can at least get in touch with her folks."

"Give me Tony's number and I'll do it, Charlie." Pulling a notebook and pen out of his shirt pocket, Chief Mac waited expectantly.

Charlie rattled off the numbers.

"Stop talking around me like I'm not here! You can't do this to me! I'm being railroaded!"

Michelle informed Mac and Doc, "Marlee's been throwing out insane accusations since she got here, and she told us she's been following Jennilee for days."

Pinning Marlee with steely eyes, Mac repeated in a frigid tone, "Following?"

Jeff added forcefully, "Not to mention, libel, harassment, stalking."

Angel smiled coldly at Marlee. "You forgot blackmail...and Marlee threatened to kill herself when Charlie and Jennilee wouldn't cave to her demands."

"I did no such thing! I came here looking for help and all I get is grief!"

Jeff stared Marlee down. "Chief Mac, there's a whole room full of witnesses if you need to take our statements."

"I know where to find you if I need you." Mac's knowing gaze once-overed Jennilee, settled on Charlie.

Meeting Mac's look, Charlie tipped his head toward the door in a barely perceptible motion.

Mac nodded.

Jeff and Angel stayed close to the couple on one side, Michelle on the other as they headed to the door. The others filled the intervening space.

"You bunch of freaks! What is wrong with you people? I tell you I was raped and now I'm pregnant and all you do is laugh? You believe Charlie *because he told you so*? What kind of bullshit is that?"

Gathering Jennilee even closer, Charlie pulled the heavy old door open and escorted her out.

When the door shut behind them, they could still hear Marlee's tirade.

Until Stevie started his vintage Grand Torino and gunned the motor.

AT THE BEACH, Jennilee paced back and forth in the edge of the surf all by her lonesome, head down like she was searching for the perfect shell.

"Charlie, is she…"

Eyes locked on Jennilee, Charlie shook his head, cutting off the rest of whatever Angel'd been about to ask.

"She'll be fine. Just gonna take her awhile. She'll be fine. The ocean soothes her." Charlie swallowed hard and repeated his mantra like a devout monk chanting and ticking off beads on his rosary. "She'll be fine."

Pressing her face into Jeff's hard chest as Charlie wandered off in Jennilee's direction, Angel murmured, "How come Charlie's not comforting Jennilee like he usually does? Neither of them even seemed that put out about that horrible woman's nasty accusations. Why is she so upset now?"

Tucking Angel close, rubbing his hands up and down her back and tangling them in her curls, Jeff soothed. "Besides that whole thing about not getting out of control in public?"

"What are you talking about? Jennilee didn't lose it. Not at all. If that'd been me, I'd've scratched that lying bitch's eyes out."

"You'd defend me like that? In public?"

Angel snorted. "You bet your sexy little ass I'd defend my man. Anywhere. Unconditionally." At Jeff's shocked look, Angel continued smoothly, "Except I'd have to agree about the drinking part, 'cause I've seen you…"

Giving a shout of laughter, Jeff wrapped his arms around her waist and spun them both, plastering his lips to hers. Heads still together, he whispered his thanks. Sighed. "Jennilee's not upset about what Mattel said. She's grieving for the baby. If there is one."

"Oh, yeah. I should've caught that one."

"And Charlie? He is no doubt going to go hot and heavy with his lawyer as soon as he gets home and gets his hands on a phone. Scratch that. I'll eat my Harley with a fork and no salt if he didn't already do it while we were at Grandy's changing and grabbing towels. Melon-head'll end up regretting she ever tangled with him. If she doesn't end up in a psych ward."

"Wow."

Jeff growled. "Yeah. You don't screw with Jennilee and not come out of it unscathed."

Stroking a hand down Jeff's chest, Angel teased, "Down, boy."

Jeff flashed a quick grin that came nowhere near his eyes. "I'm as stoked as Charlie. He's just in a position to do more about it."

"I don't know about that. You're trying to—*going to*—find their mom's murderers, and that will more than balance any tipped scales you have in your head."

Jeff opened his mouth but nothing came out.

"Why do you keep looking so flabbergasted?"

Shutting his mouth with an audible snap, Jeff answered, "You say the nicest things."

"Huh?"

"Did you mean it when you said you'd believe me? If another woman told you I got her pregnant?"

Angel smirked. "You have quite a reputation with the ladies, don't you."

Jeff shrugged, unrepentant. "I've...had a lot of girlfriends."

"You ever cheat on any of them? Get any of them pregnant and walk away?"

"No. Hell no."

Angel snuggled closer. "You are a good man, Jeff. A most honorable one."

"With you and Jennilee as my champions..."

A long kiss later, holding hands, they headed in Jennilee's direction. Planted next to Jennilee's now stationary form, arms crossed and wide-spread feet firmly braced, Charlie looked like the statue of a fierce warrior from times past. One guarding a beloved queen.

All of them watched as Jennilee crouched down. Cupping a double handful of ocean water she rose gracefully, arms extended, letting the water trickle from her cupped hands back to the ocean like a sacred offering. Long golden tresses covering her back and wrapping around her hips, concealing her swimming suit, skin gleaming like honey-toned silk, Jennilee looked every inch a pagan goddess worshipping the ocean.

Jeff heaved a silent sigh of relief, one Angel echoed, as Jennilee's hand reached out and touched Charlie's. Enfolding her much smaller one, he drew her close.

They all stood quietly for a bit, side by side, ankle deep in the surge and retreat.

Face tilted up, eyes half closed, Jennilee inhaled deeply through her nose, seemingly scenting the wind. Opening her eyes wide, staring blindly out at the vast expanse of blue-green, Jennilee murmured in a straight-from-the-oracle-at-the-temple tone, "Storm coming."

Charlie moved his big body noon-shadow close, eyes locked on his beloved. "Hurricane?"

Jennilee nodded. "Bad one."

Sharing a look, Jeff and Angel looked up at the cloudless blue sky, down at the ripples of waves sloshing at their feet, out across the barely there incoming waves.

None of them doubted her. Not in the least.

Shaking off her fey mood like a muddy dog coming out of a swamp, Jennilee spun into Charlie's embrace. Leaning up to kiss him, arms around his neck, she bubbled, "I want to go somewhere fun. Busch Gardens. Or Carowinds. King's Dominion. Six Flags. Disney. All of the above."

Charlie didn't blink. "Tomorrow soon enough?"

"Yes, and I want..."

"All of them?"

Jennilee's laughter rang out.

Arms solidly around her slender form, a grinning Charlie looked to Jeff and Angel. "Better pack your bags, guys. I'll call Tim and Rachel as soon as we get home. Looks like we're goin' roller coastering."

CHAPTER 16

a few days spent doing just that and it was back to the humdrum of everyday.

Although, roller coastering seemed an apt description for Jennilee's entire life.

Having stopped at Grandy's, both to assure her they were back and pick up Jewel as well as drop off Rachel and the kids, Charlie looked up when Tim stepped through the kitchen door. Meeting Charlie's gaze, Tim flicked a glance at Jennilee, talking animatedly to Grandy.

Radar pinging, Charlie shot a look at Jeff only to see the same ready wariness on Jeff's face.

Charlie scooted his chair back from the table. "Be right back, ladies."

Tipping her face up for the requisite kiss, Jennilee turned back to Grandy. "Grandy, you should have seen... You have to go with us next time. This was so spur of the moment... Next time we'll plan our trip better and give you more warning so you can find someone to take over for you at the Diner."

Angel and Rachel chorused their agreement, with Grandy laughingly agreeing.

Their females' bright chatter fading, the guys stepped out on the back porch.

"Spill, Tim."

Holding out a stack of envelopes, grim faced, Tim said, "You need to see this." While Charlie flipped through the envelopes, Tim continued. "Thanks for taking Rachel and the kids. They had a ball."

Charlie's stare locked on Tim.

Tim shrugged. "Don't know how long those have been in the mailbox. You know I never check it. The kids have too much fun doing it, and Rach always lets them take turns. Elizabeth just handed these to me. Thank God she isn't reading much yet."

Passing the stack to Jeff, Charlie moved to the porch rail and stared unseeing out at the backyard and further, to the river.

Reading the addresses, to and from, Jeff felt his gut clench. "This can't be good. These are all addressed to Ms. Jenny Lee, address next door, and they all look to be credit card statements. How long have y'all had a PO box now? Ten, twelve years?"

Holding onto the rail so hard his knuckles were white, Charlie gritted out, "I should never have let Jennilee sway me to drop it. I should've had that bitch thrown in jail. No more mercy. I'm done, and so is she."

She didn't have to be named, the way the devil didn't have to be specified when you mentioned evil.

Celie. Jennilee's aunt.

Scanning the stack with its Visa and MasterCard and Am Ex and expensive department store logos in the top left corners, Jeff curled his lip. "No tellin' how much damage she's already done."

"At least it won't take long to find her and have her arrested." Turning to meet their stares, Charlie smiled. The way he'd smiled at the baseball stadium the other night. At the hoodlums.

Jeff's answering smile was just as deadly. "You've had her followed? All this time?"

"You bet your ass I have. Should've put her under the jail when I had the chance." Eyeing both the other males like a general surveying troops, Charlie ordered, "Not a word. Do you hear me? Not a word to Jennilee."

Snapping a cocky salute, Tim shook his head. "My lips are sealed,

Boss."

"Have the post office hold your mail for awhile, Tim."

"Not a problem. I'll tell Rachel. We don't want that stuff coming through, anymore than you do."

Jeff remarked, "She must've gone on a spree, to have all these come in at once like this."

Charlie vowed grimly, "It'll be her last one."

Jennilee appeared at the door. "Charlie? Somethin' wrong?"

Switching gears in a blink and giving her a genuine smile, Charlie stepped closer, enfolding her in his strong arms. Kissed the top of her head. "Work related, and nothing you need to worry about, Jennilee-love."

"Okay. Grandy wants us to stay for supper. You too, guys."

Jeff smacked his lips. "Sounds great."

Tim nodded acceptance.

Smiling like the cat that got the cream, Jennilee informed them smugly, "I already called Mose and Suki and Miz Sadie and Mr. Jubal. And Doc and Chief Mac and Mr. Tom."

Jeff cheered. "Woohoo! Sounds like a party!"

Sharing a look with Jeff, Charlie said, "Perfect. I need to talk to all of them anyway."

"Coconut cake?"

At Jennilee's offer, Jeff started salivating like someone'd rung a bell. "Can we eat dessert first?"

Jennilee laughed. "As long as the kids don't catch you. How'm I gonna explain the missing piece, though?"

Jeff rubbed his hands together. "Taste testing? Sampling? A big rat?"

Charlie jibed, "Yeah, a two legged one."

REPLETE, Jeff leaned back on Grandy's couch and laced his hands over his rounded belly. Gave a satisfied sigh. "Jennilee, I don't know what I'm going to miss more—you or your cooking."

Jennilee's face fell. "Already? Seems like you just got here."

"I know. Seems that way to me, too. Duty calls."

"Tomorrow?"

"Yeah, early."

Pressing her face against Charlie's hard chest for a moment, Jennilee lifted her head. "Have a safe trip back, and come home when you can."

Sharing a heated glance with Angel, Jeff drawled, "Angel and I already talked about it. We'll be back weekend after next. And I'm bringing an extra helmet."

Jennilee's face lit. "Thanks for the heads-up. We'll see what kind of plans we can come up with."

Jeff grinned lazily at her enthusiasm. "Be hard to top what we've done this last week or so."

Jennilee sighed and snuggled Charlie. "I love it so, when we can all get together."

Tight against Jeff, Angel smiled and covered a yawn. "Speaking of which, Jennilee, Momma wants you and Charlie to come to Raleigh next week. Some big shindig at the restaurant."

Charlie grinned. "Mr. Berto been takin' pictures again?"

Angel tossed her head. "Always, but that's not what this is about." Holding up both hands at their inquiring looks, Angel shrugged. "Momma just said to tell you, and make sure you showed. And Grandy. Jeff?"

Jeff's eyes widened. "Meet and greet, huh?"

"They're gonna love you. Tell him, Jennilee."

"How could anyone not love Jeff?"

Drawn like a moth by the sounds of talking and laughter coming from the living room, Mac looked around the doorway. Saw just what he thought he'd see. Charlie and Jennilee bug-in-a-rugged in Grandy's old rocking chair, Jeff sprawled on the couch, a girl by his side. A permanent one this time, if he was a betting man.

"Charlie? Hate to break up your confab. You said you need to speak with me, and I gotta get goin' here shortly."

"Yessir." Unfolding himself from the rocker and reseating Jennilee in one smooth move, Charlie dropped a kiss on her lips. "Be right back, Jennilee-sweet." Shot a look at Jeff.

Picking up on it immediately, Jeff launched into a tale about one of his escapades. "Did I ever tell you girls about..."

While Jennilee and Angel listened raptly to Jeff's outrageous tale, Charlie and Chief Mac slipped out and down the hall to the room Charlie'd used as his office for years.

Mr. Tom and Mose joined them. With Mose standing sentry in front of the closed door, Charlie sat at his desk in his big leather chair and pulled them into the loop. Details shared, Charlie leaned forward, forearms on his desk, hard eyes sweeping the men one by one.

"Mr. Talton, the same PI we used last time, is on top of this. I want this ended. Done. Finished. No more Get Out of Jail Free cards for that conniving bitch. See to it."

Leaned back in his chair and wove his fingers together. Tapped his thumbs impatiently.

Total silence for a breath. "Which bitch, Charlie?" Mac's query set them laughing.

"Yeah. You sound like one of those mob guys from the movies." Mose's white teeth flashed in his dark face as he leaned against the door.

Lacing his fingers behind his head, leaning his head against the back of his chair and staring at the ceiling, Charlie blew out a deep breath. "Good thing I don't have access to thugs like that. Especially in this situation. Seems like there's always someone who wants to hurt Jennilee. I'm fed up with it."

Tom advised, "Keep your cool, Charlie. This will...all get taken care of. Legally."

"Why? Why can't they just leave her alone? Jennilee would never hurt a fly, and all her life, all she's known is people trying to hurt her in one way or another. It's like she's a...pain magnet or something."

Mac shrugged. "I don't have any easy answer to that, Charlie. Don't think there is one. It just...is."

Mose spoke up, slowly, marshaling his thoughts, his deep voice resonating. "Jennilee's...good. In its purest form, like an angel. Through and through, she's nothing but love wrapped in human skin. Just like she pulls us in with her love, evil is attracted to her vicinity, to try and destroy that goodness."

Charlie heard Jeff's response to that in his head, as clearly as if Jeff was in this room and not down the hall keeping the girls distracted. *So, what? We need Holy water and silver crosses? An exorcism? Garlic necklaces, anyone?*

Charlie told the other men, "Yeah. I've told her the same thing myself. It's just...hard. Not to do anything. Just like the other day. Jennilee never doubted me, not for an instant, but she shouldn't have had to deal with that in the first place. And then to find out that... worthless piece of trash...has been following Jennilee... I need to take some Navy SEAL training or something. I thought I was doing a fairly good job of protecting her. Evidently not. Not if some psycho bitch can get that close and I didn't even notice."

The rest of the men shared a glance and started shaking their heads.

Mac gave it his best shot. "Charlie, we don't want to hear that from you. Tourist season is in full swing. Nobody pays any mind to strangers in town. You take better care of Jennilee than anyone else possibly could. What else could you have done, except hire body-guards, and wouldn't that give Jennilee fits. She'd never stand for it."

Tom prodded, "Remember how miserable it made her? When all of us were watching out for her and she couldn't go anywhere without an escort and at least one of us popping up to boot?"

Charlie growled, "She still doesn't go anywhere by herself. I won't al..."

Guffaws this time from the peanut gallery drowned out Charlie's words.

Mac spoke for all of them, and Jennilee, his measured words full of wisdom. "Trust me, son. Women don't like to hear the *allow* word. Especially when it concerns themselves coupled with don't *and* it's coming from the man in their lives."

Mose added in a dry tone, "Not sure if you noticed, but Jennilee's quite capable of taking care of herself."

Charlie shot his friend and partner a fulminating glare. "That's not the point now, is it?"

Taking no offense, Mose advised sagely, "All you can do, all any of us can do, is what we can. That, and make sure the good we surround

Jennilee with far outweighs the bad trying to infiltrate. Kinda like Vietnam. Only we're gonna win this war, hands down."

Charlie stated grimly, "We'll win. If I have to buy a solar system and spaceship us all to an uncharted planet."

Mose crossed his tree trunk arms and lifted a brow. "Well now, Captain Kirk. Better make sure this new planet of yours has plenty of plants or our girl's gonna be mighty unhappy."

Tom settled a hand lightly over his full belly. "Yeah, and something to cook."

More chuckles as they tried to draw Charlie out of his downward spiral of self deprecation and rage.

Mose reiterated quietly what they all knew to be true. "Charlie. You hardly ever get more than a handsbreadth away from Jennilee. Besides that, she's more than proficient in hand to hand, not to mention her deadly aim with a gun."

Charlie looked from Mose to Mac, his eyes lingering on each of their faces. "And I thank you both for the teaching."

Mose asked, knowing the answer. "She still carry a pocketknife?"

"Never leaves home without it, and it's as sharp as any of her favorite kitchen knives. Handguns in all the vehicles."

Mac heaved a sigh. "Well, there you have it. Jennilee's as safe as we can make her."

"Not enough. It's not enough."

Mose shared a glance with Mac and Tom. Shrugged.

CHARLIE SAT in his office after the others left, brooding. Thinking about ex SEALS/Rangers/ Green Berets for hire as hulking bodyguards, and blueprints for Fort Knox, weighing Jennilee's wrath against her safety. And his own sanity.

Sticking his head around the doorjamb, Jeff gave a low whistle. "Ruh roh. You're thinking about doing something that's gonna land you in the doghouse for a long, long time, Shaggy. I've seen that look on your face too many times. Better deep six that line of thought right now."

Shooting his best friend a drop-dead glare, Charlie snarled, "What am I supposed to do, Jeff? That's the woman I love more than life, and any slight or threat against her is one against me. It's my responsibility to take care of her. I'm in a position now to do something about stuff like that, not like when we were kids."

Coming in and closing the door, Jeff made himself comfortable, leaning a hip on Charlie's massive desk. Snagging a couple disparate items off its surface, Jeff started juggling.

Keeping his eyes on the items and off Charlie, Jeff voiced his thoughts. "Jennilee may be gathering, but so are you. Everywhere you go, someone you meet ends up loving her as much as we do and feeling just as protective. The ball game the other evening—that looked to be a disaster with two total strangers attacking her, and boom! Right there, two unknown champions sprang to her defense, and how much you wanna bet those two will reappear and bring reinforcements?"

When Charlie said nothing, Jeff kept juggling, kept plugging. "So far, the good's far outweighing the bad. She's always had you and me. When she who shall not be named lobbed a horrible attack and drove Jennilee to Raleigh and your arms, she met Tony, and his whole family. For every person who wishes Jennilee ill, she draws in ten times that many who love her unconditionally."

No response had Jeff naming names. "Grandy. Mac and Doc and Tom. Mose and Mr. Jubal and Miz Sadie. Mr. Cyrus. Mr. Donnie. Will and Josh. Tony and Angel. Mr. and Mrs. Marcellini. Mr. Berto and Albert Lee. Ben and Marty."

Listening to Jeff drone on and on, Charlie thought about what Jeff wasn't saying. In every single person he named and instance he was obliquely referring to, someone intending Jennilee harm had been bested and she'd gained not only friends, but in some cases, family.

"I know what you're saying. I just don't see any good coming of this latest...fiasco."

"Something will show its face, you'll see. Or someone. It always does."

Jeff's parting words rang in Charlie's head long after the last roar of Jeff's Harley faded.

CHAPTER 17

*T*he next day, sitting behind his big desk—*Charlie Meyers, President* name plate prominently displayed front and center on an otherwise entirely bare surface—glaring at one of the two males on the other side, they rang louder. As if someone had not merely tugged on the bell rope but was swinging from it, putting their whole body weight into each pull.

Bradley Owen Foster the Third.

Bad thing.

Mr. Foster the Second.

Good thing.

Having been given a ringside pass to the show about to commence, Tim stood off to one side, arms crossed, watching.

Standing up, walking to the window in the shop door, Charlie stared out at the big equipment housed there. Thought about what he and the boy's father had just discussed, and all its ramifications. Discussed while the boy remained outside in the father's air conditioned Mercedes. Now that the boy had been called in...

Swinging around, Charlie strode across the floor and stopped in front of the teenager slouching insolently as only teenagers can in one of the guest chairs. "Well, Bradley Owen Foster. Your father seems to think you owe my wife and myself more than an apology."

"Brad." The single syllable was muttered belligerently, without looking up or making eye contact. Braver now, with his father here to back him up, Bradley Owen Foster dared far more than he had when he'd almost wet himself at the stadium.

Or maybe the lesson learned had been short-lived.

"Bradley. Owen. Foster. Do you know why women in the South give their children three names?" Not waiting for an answer, Charlie continued, his voice low. "It's so the kids know when they're really, really in trouble. See, one name is what you're called...to dinner, during hellos and goodbyes, that sort of thing. Two names, well, you're on somebody's short list. All three names, that's when you know you're in deep shit." Taking his time, Charlie enunciated clearly, "Bradley Owen Foster."

All false bravado, Brad sneered, "What? If you're trying to scare me, it won't work. If you hit me again, Dad'll press charges. Won't you, Dad?"

Mr. Foster cleared his throat. "Mr. Meyers and I have reached an agreement and this is the way it's going to be, Brad. You will work for Mr. Meyers for the rest of the summer. Without pay."

"Wait! That's not fair! No way am I..."

"You will live with Mr. Tyndall there, his foreman. You will report to work each morning with Mr. Tyndall. You will do whatever Mr. Tyndall tells you to do, without complaint, or you will be shipped out."

Brad looked up, finally, at Charlie, a triumphant gleam in his still raccooned eyes.

Charlie smiled.

Brad quailed.

His father added, "Shipped *out* is not the same as shipped *home*. If you are shipped out, you will be spending the next year or two of your life at a military academy of my choosing. You will graduate, with honors. After graduation, you will either enlist in the service or you will be disinherited."

"You can't make me!"

Sharing a grim look with Charlie, Mr. Foster looked back to his son. "Oh, but I can."

Lunging to his feet, Brad pointed at Charlie. "He can't make me do anything. He's got no authority over me!"

Mr. Foster leaned back in his chair, all lawyerly sincerity in his three piece custom made silk suit. Crossing one knee over the other, locking his fingers around his topmost knee, he told his son, "His *authority* is in my briefcase right now. Your admission papers are already filled out and signed, as well as the tuition check. You choose, son. As your father and as a lawyer, I advise you to choose wisely. This is your last chance, son. If you fail to satisfy Mr. Meyers and Mr. Tyndall, there *will be no going home.* You will go directly to the academy."

Eyes bouncing back and forth between Charlie and his dad, Bradley dropped back into his seat and protested vehemently. "How can you do this to me? I'm your only son! You act like it's the end of the world. I didn't even do anything that bad."

"As my son, you are a direct reflection on me, and your mother. Neither of us likes what we're seeing."

"It was a prank!"

"Son, a prank is a joke that makes everyone laugh and harms no one. What you did can in no way be construed as a joke, and it caused a great deal of harm. And unfortunately, this isn't the only thing you've done. I'm sure your decision will be the right one." Rising, settling his elegant suit back in place, Mr. Foster picked up his briefcase and nodded to Charlie. "Unless I hear from Mr. Meyers that you are ready to attend the academy, I will pick you up the day before school starts."

"Wait! You can't be serious! You can't leave me here with…them."

Reality began to truly sink in as Mr. Foster's hand wrapped around the doorknob.

"Dad! Dad? Where're you going? You can't… At least make him give me back my driver's license!"

Pausing, without looking over his shoulder, Mr. Foster answered. "I'm going home. I can. And I have your license. Whether you get it back or not depends on you."

"How'm I supposed to drive? To go anywhere? What about my car?"

Opening the door, Mr. Foster exited and closed it behind himself with a quiet click that heralded all the devastation of a bomb about to go off. Brad glared out the big picture window as his father got in his Mercedes and left.

"Get changed, boy. You're makin' me late...er."

Throwing...the foreman a drop-dead look over his shoulder, Brad repeated in a much less than civil tone, "Changed?"

Giving the boy's pristine Izod button down dress shirt, his spotless, perfectly creased Saddlebred shorts and spiffy Sperrys a slow once-over, Tim drawled, "Unless you're plannin' on workin' in those fancy duds you're wearin'. Get. Changed."

"What am I supposed to..."

Pointing to a pile of non-descript work clothes in the corner, Tim jerked his head. "Employee bathroom's through the shop door and to your left. Three minutes and I'm outta here."

Brad sneered at Charlie, "Thought you were the boss. You gonna let him talk to me that way?"

Charlie smiled again. Rolled his shoulders and flexed his hands into fists. Held his smile, held Brad's gaze until the boy dropped his and stumbled to his feet. Still scrambling to regain his mental equilibrium as Tim vanished through the shop door, the boy followed, dragging his heels.

Deliberately ignoring the work clothes.

Charlie watched, via the window, as BOF bypassed the bathroom and trudged sullenly across the concrete to Tim's truck.

Turned and eyed the left behind apparel.

Grinned.

THE NEXT WEEK, Jeff's words rang again.

Rang loud and clear as Charlie looked around at all the smiling faces gathered at the Marcellini's restaurant. Closed to the public for this event, the space was none the less filled, tables crowded.

Filled with friends and family, a laughing, chattering, happy crowd, the love palpable.

Slow gaze drifting over the assembled crowd, Charlie looked at the couples, young or old, married or dating, so obviously in love. At the children of all ages, the next generation of love.

Friends and family. Friends who'd become family, expanding and adding to the circle created and nurtured by familial love.

Circles. All of life was a circle, filled with overlapping circles.

Raindrops stippling a still pond.

A giant Double Wedding Ring quilt pattern on a planetary scale.

Dropping into the empty seat beside Charlie, Jeff jibed, "Why so maudlin?"

"Didn't know you knew that word, bro."

"Got it off a slip of paper in a fortune cookie. As in, don't be."

"It's just...this. All of it." Charlie waved a hand to encompass the crowded room.

Jeff agreed softly. "Yeah. I know what you mean."

Meeting Jeff's steady gaze, Charlie admitted, "Been thinkin' about what you said. You nailed it."

"Oh?"

"I met Marlee and Tony at State. Marlee's a shit, through and through, but kinda because of her, Jennilee met Tony and the rest of the Marcellinis. They've practically adopted her."

"Both of you, Charlie Brown. Told you, anything that tries to harm Jennilee boomerangs back with good things. In spades."

Charlie mused, "Because of the Marcellinis, Jennilee acquired a best friend and found her dad. And you got a girlfriend who just happens to be that very same best friend, thus filling in the pieces of one circle and interlocking with another. And another, and yet another."

A sappy look on his handsome face, Jeff locked his eyes on Angel. "Yeah.

"Guess her brothers think you're good enough to date their sister."

Drawing the back of his hand across his forehead, Jeff mimed flinging sweat drops. "Touch and go there for a bit, Charlie Brown. Thought all six were gonna chew me up and spit me out. Or at the very least, take me out and beat the crap outta me."

"No worries, mate. I'd'a had your back." Charlie snorted a laugh. "Besides, I already put in a good word for you, and Jennilee hasn't stopped rhapsodizing about your boundless charms."

A very pleased look plastering itself on his face, Jeff tested the water. "How's that whole thing with psycho bitch going?"

Laughing out loud at that, Charlie shook his head. "More circles. Because I lived in the Marcellini's over-garage apartment and there's always a bunch of people around, I've got scads of witnesses ready and willing to prove Marlee's lying. And, turns out Mr. Tom knows Bradley Owen Foster the second's father. Went to law school together. Not only that, Mr. Foster senior knows Marlee's family, as in go-to-the-same-country-club kinda way. Marlee's had problems before this. Marlee's lawyer is negotiating for clemency with one of my new lawyers. Won't do her any good."

"*One* of your new lawyers?"

"Yeah. Got a whole team now, not just Mr. Tom. She's goin' down like the Titanic."

Jeff almost cheered. "Atta boy, Charlie Brown. How's our problem child coming along?"

Charlie smirked. "Tim's introduced Bradley Owen Foster the third to hard labor. He's been digging six foot footers all week. In beach sand. That and hauling lumber and blocks and sheet rock and shingles and…"

"Now that I would pay to see."

"Not only that, BOF is staying with Tim."

"At the Judge's?"

"Yeah." Charlie practically purred.

"Woo doggie. Love to be a fly on that wall."

"Tim informed BOF he had two choices: He could bunk with Timmy, bottom bunk, of course, since Timmy's claim to the top is firmly staked, or he could have the small room in the attic."

"Jennilee's old room?"

"Yeah. No air conditioning and a window that's nailed shut, not enough room to swing a cat? You know what BOF said to that."

Empathizing with Charlie's unspoken fury, Jeff shook his head. "Timmy and I get along pretty darn good, but I don't know about bunkin' with the squirt. GI Joes and Matchbox cars and Legos and marbles everywhere. And questions. Lord, but that youngun can ask a question."

Charlie smiled evilly. "That's not the half of it. Timmy's every bit as much Jennilee's champion as we are."

"Givin' our boy hell, is he?"

"Don't think I'd be gettin' much shut eye if I was in the same room with Dennis. 'Course, poor baby's so exhausted…"

"And if he just happens to wake up with a wad of SuperBubble in his hair…"

Charlie smirked again. "He did."

"Or his shoelaces accidentally super glued together…"

"They were."

"Or slugs and frogs in his short-sheeted bed…"

"That too."

Sharing a look, Jeff and Charlie high fived.

Eyes on the girls, coming closer but still too far away to hear the guys' conversation, Jeff asked, "And the other?"

"Mr. Talton's on it like white on rice, but I'm thinkin' we should let Timmy be in charge of retaliation."

Jeff laughed out loud at that, was still laughing when the girls joined them.

Rising, both greeted their girls with a passionate kiss.

Fitting her curvy body to Charlie's, Jennilee asked, "What's so funny?"

Charlie shook his head. "Catchin' Jeff up on Timmy's latest exploits."

Rolling her eyes, Jennilee laughed. "Never mind. I don't need to know. Don't even want to."

CHAPTER 18

*J*eff and Angel showed, as promised.

Arriving at Charlie and Jennilee's Thursday afternoon within a few moments of each other, they crossed the yard and the porch hand in hand.

Opening the front door to greet them, Charlie and Jennilee caught the other couple lip-locked, bags dumped unceremoniously on the porch and waiting like well-heeled pooches.

Curling his lip in an ear-splitting whistle, Charlie clapped loudly and enthusiastically. A grinning Jennilee waited until the couple broke apart before throwing herself at Jeff.

Catching her one-armed, the other still around Angel, Jeff grinned at Charlie. "That land offer's lookin' better and better."

Eyes alight, Jennilee pulled back enough to frame his face with her hands. "You've got a lead?"

Giving her another squeeze, Jeff locked gazes with Charlie. Nodded. "Not much of one, and I didn't want to say anything when I was here last 'cause it wasn't definite."

Shooting an amused look at Charlie, Jennilee exclaimed, "We don't need the details or the fancy terminology. Just tell us in plain English."

"DNA. New test. One hair. Oh, and a partial fingerprint."

Charlie egged, "Use your words, Jeffro. Come on, you can do it."

Jeff launched instantly and passionately into an incomprehensible spate of forensic terminology.

Laughing fit to bust, the whole crowd stumbled across the threshold.

"So, what's on tap for this weekend?" Jeff looked from Jennilee to Charlie expectantly.

Jennilee's face lit even more. "Mr. Jubal and Mose are cookin' a pig at their place. Singin' after. Miz Sadie said it's to make up for not gettin' to feed you when you were home a couple weeks ago."

"Hot damn! What time?"

"Tomorrow afternoon. Till then, you're all ours."

Clapping Jeff on the back hard enough to fell a lesser man, Charlie enthused, "Up for some flounderin' tonight?"

"Walking the shoreline or polin' the skiff?"

"Skiff. Figured we'd take the girls, down around Harkers Island. Maybe out toward the Cape."

"Floundering? At night?" Sounding dubious, Angel looked to Jennilee for confirmation. And clarification.

Grinning, Jennilee clarified, hands twisting and turning and miming. "Lights on the boat. You stand on the bow and pole along real slow and look for flounder. They camouflage themselves by flattening into the sand and changing skin tone to match the bottom. Did you know flounder are born like normal fish with one eye on each side of their head and then one eye migrates to the other side so both eyes are on the same side?"

"You're joking, right?"

Shaking her head, Jennilee crossed her finger in the air over her heart. "Instead of being upright like other fish, flounder are flat. Look kinda like a magic carpet when they swim." Holding her hand out like she was getting ready to shake someone's, then turning it perpendicular to the floor like she was measuring an invisible child's height, Jennilee demonstrated while she was talking.

"So... What? You call them and they just jump in the boat?"

Shaking her head again, Jennilee started laughing. "You gig them." At Angel's blank look, Jennilee elaborated. "Poseidon's trident thingy?

You use a smaller version of one of those and you sorta spear down and pin the flounder to the bottom. When you're sure you've gigged him good and tight, you flip him into the boat and start looking for another bed."

Angel raised a brow. "Okay." Drawled out her opinion, heavy on the sarcasm. "We're going spear fishing for camouflaged, not to mention sleeping, Picasso fish."

Jennilee laughed. "You'll love it. It's so peaceful out on the water at night."

Wrapping an arm around Angel's shoulders, Jeff gloated, "Not to mention tasty. Jennilee, are you gonna bake…"

"Jeff, you know if you want baked flounder, all you have to do is ask. We can have it for lunch tomorrow."

"With lots of potatoes and onions and bacon?"

"Don't I always?"

"Speaking of feedin' me, thanks for the care package." Rubbing his belly, Jeff smiled at Jennilee.

Looking from one to the other, Angel rolled her eyes. "Care package?"

"Got it the day after I got home. Chocolate chip cookies, peanut-butter brownies, a couple jars of my special hot sauce, a little of this and a little of that."

Angel rolled her eyes again and groaned. "And you probably ate it all in one sitting."

"Thought about it, but… Nope." He thought about other things that had been in the package. The latest issue of Southern Living, no doubt included by Charlie, one of Jennilee's articles prominently featured. A loaf of Jennilee's sourdough bread and a jar of her jelly. Homemade venison jerky, extra hot.

A picture of Angel and himself in an ordinary frame. A picture which now resided, not on the exquisite table by his front door, but on the scarred and worn secondhand end table that doubled as his nightstand.

He hadn't even noticed Jennilee taking the picture, but she was like that. Mr. Berto's shots were awesomely professional, had won all kinds of awards, but Jeff much preferred Jennilee's casual ones. While they might not have the panache Mr. Berto's boasted, Jennilee's were...real.

Real snapshots of real people doing real things.

Not that Mr. Berto's weren't real, and they certainly weren't staged.

Jennilee just had a knack for capturing people she loved.

Jeff laughed out loud.

When the others looked at him questioningly, he shrugged. "Arguing with myself about the definition of real."

Angel quipped, "What, now you're the Velveteen Rabbit?"

Jeff replied, all serious. "Well, he was loved into existence and became real because of that love."

Jennilee paraphrased softly, "Real isn't how you are made...it's a thing that happens to you." Meeting Jeff's eyes, Jennilee smiled. Leaning up to brush a kiss across his cheek, she whispered, "Glad you like it."

Giving Jennilee a quick, hard hug, Jeff stepped back and flashed a grin, not questioning how Jennilee knew exactly what he'd been thinking.

She just...knew. Just like she'd known to put that pic in a plain frame, so as not to take anything away from the actual photo. The plain frame...emphasized Jeff and Angel, heads close together, lost in each other, radiant smiles on both their faces.

"We're eatin' before we go, right." Jeff grinned expectantly at Jennilee.

A beat of silence, followed by laughter from all of them.

Melting into Charlie's embrace, Jennilee nodded. "Steaks with all the trimmin's."

Jeff slanted a mischievous grin in Angel's direction. "You don't need to go to culinary school to learn how to be a chef. You could just take lessons from Jennilee."

Angel sighed in agreement. "My teachers at college are great, but they're not Jennilee."

Hugging her close, Charlie bragged, "No one cooks like my Jennilee, for sure and for certain."

Jennilee's laughter silvered the air, melodious as wind chimes.

"Angel, I can teach you what I know but I can't give you a fancy-schmancy piece of paper for graduating."

Angel's turn to hug Jennilee, she did. Stepping back, smile lighting her face, she shook her head. "My professors might have the paper along with the ability to confer a degree, but you've got the God-given talent, Jennilee. That can't be taught. It's like love—either it's there or it isn't."

Jennilee smiled radiantly. "It all starts with wanting to make the ones you love feel good. Everything after that's easy-peasy."

Inserting himself back into the conversation, still contemplating *steaks and all the trimmin's*, Jeff practically sat up and begged. "Chocolate pie?"

Jennilee returned Jeff's grin. "Better. Mayonnaise cake."

At Jeff's whoop of delight and the reverent look on his face, Angel sighed. "Okay. I give. Spill."

Throwing her head back, Jennilee laughed some more. "I think this recipe originated during the depression, or maybe during WWII when they had a substitute for everything because of war shortages. Mayo's nothing but eggs and oil, so you substitute mayo for them in this chocolate cake recipe."

Jeff licked his lips. "It's indescribably delicious."

Angel snorted a laugh. "You sound like a commercial."

"Wait till you taste it."

Couple hours later, Angel had to agree with Jeff's assessment. Eyeballing the moist, tasty cake, Angel debated.

Laughing knowingly, Jennilee cut Angel another piece.

"I want the recipe."

Sliding the saucer across the table, Jennilee nodded. "Already wrote it down for you."

Angel heaved a rueful sigh and made a moue of disappointment. "It'll be just like your chicken salad. You gave me the ingredients, and I do exactly what you say, but it never tastes the same."

Leaving the house around dusky dark, they all crammed into the front seat of Charlie's truck and drove to Harkers Island to unload the flat-bottomed aluminum skiff.

Angel had to agree again.

Being out on the water at night was like swimming in the dark. She'd been out on the boat plenty of times before, just like she'd swum lots in the pool at home. During the day.

Being out here at night was like their swimming expedition the night Charlie'd tossed Jennilee over the moon.

The same, and yet not.

Magical.

The inches-deep water was mirror-smooth, the only sounds the quiet *splish* the gig poles made as they slipped into the water and steadily propelled the boat along and the soft slap-slap of water as the boat moved across it.

An immense blanket of stars shimmering overhead in a black velvet sky cocooned them, limiting their world to the boat and each other and what was revealed by the circumference of their light.

Jennilee and Angel stood on the wide bow cap. Twin lights, fastened to either side of the bow and pointed down into the water lit up the bottom like spotlights. All manner of sea creatures were revealed. Blue crabs scuttling for cover, pincers waving. Myriad little fish and sometimes big ones. Conchs snailing their slow way across the sandy bottom. Once-empty banded tulip shells, confiscated and inhabited by hermit crabs. Scallops slamming their distinctive brick-red and white shells shut and jet-propelling themselves away from the human intruders. Shrimp curling their tails and darting backwards. Stray shells and periwinkles and grass lumps and clumps of oysters covered in mossy green growths dotted the sand.

"Angel, right there."

The guys, poling from just behind the girls, held the boat steady while Angel scoured the bottom. Looking where Jennilee pointed, Angel saw only rippled patterns in the sand.

"Keep looking."

"Don't know what I'm looking for."

Jennilee giggled. "The outline of a fish. Think…fish platter."

Angel stared, trying harder. Gasped as what she was searching for suddenly popped into view like someone had outlined it with a black marker. "I see it! I do! Now what do I do?"

Handing over the gig she held ready and waiting, Jennilee coached, "Hold the gig tight and don't let go. Use it like a spear and aim for the head, right behind the eyes. Right there, a couple inches back from the point of the snout. The flounder's gonna flop around and stir up the water, so wait till it calms and make sure you gigged it good before you try to get it in the boat."

Doing as Jennilee said, stabbing downward, Angel almost lost her balance as events unfolded in the correct sequence.

Squealing in triumph as she struck gold, or in this case...fish, Jeff had the cooler open and waiting when Angel lifted her trophy and swung around with it on the end of her gig. The flounder slid off like it was greased, like Angel was a pro at this.

Jennilee gigged the next one. Gigged it so hard she had to pull it off the barbs on the end of the tines. After stepping down off the bow cap and dropping her catch in the cooler, Jennilee crouched and reached over the side to rinse the blood and fish slime off her hands.

As soon as she touched the water, Jennilee snatched her hands back.

Charlie picked up on it instantly. "Jennilee-honey, what's wrong? Jellyfish sting ya?"

Shaking her head, Jennilee finished rinsing her hands. "Nothing. I'm fine. It's nothing."

None of them believed her.

Giving up her primo spot on the bow cap without a word, confirming their suspicions that something was definitely wrong, Jennilee moved to the back of the boat. Charlie stayed right with her.

Shrugging, Jeff moved up beside Angel.

Charlie put his arms around Jennilee and tugged her close.

Taking over poling duties, Jeff moved the skiff along as he and Angel politely ignored Jennilee's silent meltdown.

Poling and gigging, they went quite aways down the shoreline.

"*What* is *that?* Jennilee?" Angel's loud squeal got all their attention.

Coming to stand just behind her best friend and leaning out over the bow so she could see, spotting the flattened helmet looking creature, Jennilee enthused in a nearly normal tone, "*That* is a horseshoe crab. Horseshoe crabs are living fossils, leftovers from the dinosaurs. The only true blue-bloods on the planet, they actually have blue blood. It's copper based, so when it hits the air, it turns blue. See that long spike of a tail? That's used to flip them back over if they get turned upside down."

"Are they poisonous?"

Kneeling down, reaching into the water with none of her earlier trepidation, Jennilee deftly scooped up the scary looking creature. "Kinda the stuff of nightmares, but they're totally harmless." Turning it over and showing Angel the underside, all churning legs and gills, Jennilee carefully righted the horseshoe crab and gently returned it to the water.

As they watched it swim off, Jennilee continued her spiel. "Horseshoe crabs are invaluable to medical science and even though they look like crustaceans, they're more closely related to spiders and scorpions."

Before everyone resumed their spots and they got back to the pleasurable business at hand, Angel drawled softly, "Now that you've expounded on the joys of being a freaky-ass sea creature... Are you gonna tell us what had you trippin' out awhile ago?"

Breathing hard, swallowing repeatedly, Jennilee played statue. Shivered. Pressing close behind her, Charlie rubbed his hands up and down her goose-bumped arms.

Reaching out to a frozen Jennilee, Angel fisted her hand instead. "Never mind, Jennilee. It's just..." Angel threw Jeff a pleading look.

Jeff finished. "...we worry about you."

Charlie snickered. The snicker quickly turned into a full out laugh.

Waiting until he could be heard, Jeff retorted dryly, "Oh, yeah. We've definitely been around the two of you too long."

Choking on a half-laugh, Jennilee returned fully to them like her spirit had been meteored back into her body. Sobering again just as fast, Jennilee said, "You have to leave. Both of you."

Angel stared, mouth open.

Putting a comforting hand on Angel's lower back, Jeff asked, "How much time we got?"

Jennilee sighed heavily. Shook her head as she replied in a strained tone, "You should leave before the sing tomorrow night."

Hands on her hips, Angel demanded an answer. "*What* are you two talking about? Why can't we stay for the sing? Are we breakin' some taboo or something?"

Jeff's two-word answer had Jennilee nodding like a bobble-head. "Hurricane. Imminent."

Angel spluttered, "But you said that...days and days ago."

Rubbing some more, Charlie pulled Jennilee back into the cradle of his strong arms. "How soon, Jennilee-sweet?"

Her tone growing more strained, she informed them, "Gonna start gettin' bad tomorrow night. Saturday..." Shaking her head, she trailed off.

Angel looked from one to the other. "The weatherman on the news didn't say anything..."

The guys burst into laughter.

Charlie shook his head and scoffed, "Yeah, right. No way the weatherman's gonna forecast a hurricane for the weekend. Not at the beach. Not and interrupt the flow of the almighty tourist dollars."

Jeff added, "Yeah. All you're gonna get out of him is the standard summer forecast for here: Hot, hazy, and humid with a chance of afternoon thunder-boomers."

At Angel's disbelieving splutter, Jeff asked, "Who're you gonna believe? The weatherman, with all his degrees and diplomas and fancy equipment... Swept out an arm in a courtly gesture. "Or our very own Jennilee, mermaid extraordinaire."

"I've said it before, and I'll say it again... Y'all. Are. Crazy."

"Comes with the territory, *dahling*." Wrapping his arm around Angel, Jeff brushed a kiss across her curls.

Charlie met Jeff's gaze, and messages flashed across the dark. "I think we've about tapped this shoreline out. What say we head to the hook of the Cape for awhile?"

Angel protested, "But... If there's... There's a hurricane coming! Shouldn't we...be doing something?"

Jeff answered for all of them. "We are doing something."

Charlie shrugged philosophically. "Nothing we can do until daylight tomorrow. Might as well enjoy the night."

CHAPTER 19

*F*riday dawned, already hot, hazy, and humid by the time the sun rose, a malevolent red sphere mercilessly eyeballing the world, a baleful eye worthy of Mordor.

So hot the ever-chorusing, heat loving cicadas trailed off around 7:30, falling totally silent by 8:00.

By 10:00 it was worse, and steadily worsening.

No slightest breeze, not the merest breath of air stirred anywhere.

An oppressive blanket of heat shimmered the air and sucked the life out of every living thing.

Trees stood wilted, branches drooping and leaves motionless, stalwart soldiers, captured and defeated by the brutal heat.

The slick cam water in the river glared a gunmetal gray, ruthlessly burnished by the sun-bronzed sky.

In stark contrast to the apprehensive stillness of the water and the sky and the vegetation, animate things bustled purposefully.

Utterly silent songbirds mobbed the feeder like it was the last airport in the world and they were almost-out-of-fuel planes. Hummingbirds zinged this way and that, not even fighting over who got to belly-up to the glass bottles full of life-giving nectar. Bees and butterflies coated the flowers in a never-ending stream.

The humans fit right in with the manic activity.

Boats were pulled out of the water, loose items such as lawn chairs and porch furniture stored and secured. The dock was dismantled in sections, stacked and chained down on a trailer, and stored inside the boathouse.

All the shutters were checked, ready to be fastened closed. Plywood was secured over each French door, and all the windows in the workshop. All the hanging baskets were taken down, all the planters taken off the porch rails, the whole colorful mess carted by the truckload to the workshop to be hung from the rafters and placed on the benches of the bottom floor.

Lending a willing hand clearing the porches, Angel watched as Manuel filled the vehicles with gas one by one at the on-site pump, then got busy with the riding mower, flying back and forth across the vast yard.

Marveling at the frenetic pace and sort of seemingly useless chores, Angel asked, "Jennilee? I understand about gassing up the vehicles, but how come Manuel's so worried about the grass?"

Not even looking up from what she was doing, Jennilee replied, "Need it as short as possible. Anything...displaced by the rising water... You need to be able to see...things. Snakes and such. Besides, with all this heat and the rainfall we're bound to get, the grass is gonna grow like crazy. Short makes for easier clean up of limbs and debris, and gives fireants and mosquitoes less place to hide after. We'll be too busy with cleanup to worry about mowing for a bit."

Suki returned from town, Wagoneer loaded to the gills. Pulling up close to the porch and the kitchen entrance, Charlie and Jeff unloaded and carried stuff in while Jennilee and Angel and Suki got busy putting stuff away.

Emptying one of a forest of paper sacks, Suki told them, "Shelves are already looking bare. Other people are gettin' antsy, too. Whole town looks like a fireant nest somebody poked a stick into."

Jennilee agreed placidly, "They'll be mostly empty by this afternoon, bare by this evening."

Looking massively confused, Angel asked, "But... How do people know?"

Charlie plopped another box on the island counter. "Long before people had weathermen, they had to pay attention to their surroundings. Some still do. And some, like Jennilee..." Charlie leaned close and stole a kiss. "Some...just know."

Angel pressed, "How? How do they know? I mean, this is just like any other miserably hot summer day to me. There aren't even any clouds in the sky. What makes this any different? Not that I doubt you, Jennilee."

"Kinda just a...feeling that something's not right, that...weather's comin'. The critters are all gorging like they do before a cold spell, and the river's level full."

Angel blinked at Jennilee. "Level full?"

That drew a laugh from Jennilee and Suki and the guys. Jennilee explained, "Look at the marsh along the river's edge. Ever fill a glass too full, and it didn't overflow? Just kinda swelled, bubble-like across the top of the glass? Then, all of a sudden, one more drop and... That's the way the marsh and the river are looking. Too full, and ready to spill over, but not quite there yet. The old folks call it level full."

Jeff added, "It's an optical illusion, got somethin' to do with the air pressure."

Knocking shoulders with Jeff, Charlie jibed, "Not that Jeffro here saw it, but... Red sky this mornin', too."

Angel rolled her eyes. "Red...sky? Have we moved to Mars or something?"

The other four looked at each other and chimed in unison, "Red in the morning, sailors take warning. Red sky at night, sailor's delight."

"*Where* do y'all come up with this stuff?"

When the laughter died down, Angel asked another question, "What's with all the extra supplies? Y'all have enough here already to..."

Charlie and Jennilee exchanged telling looks.

Eyes wide, voice thready, Angel protested, "You're staying? Here? But... You...can't stay here. You're right on the river. At least in town... you're a little farther from the water. And this house is...old."

Jennilee smiled up at Charlie, that special private smile that excluded everyone else. "That it is. This house is old, and well-built.

It's survived Hazel, and Donna, and Camille, and the unnamed storm in…'33 and a lot of other 'canes."

"But… You can't. Stay. You all need to go…somewhere. Raleigh. Or…Paris. Or Rome. Tokyo."

"Angel. Relax. We'll be fine, and there's nowhere I'd rather be."

Somewhat desperately, Angel threw out, "The Blue Ridge is gorgeous this time of year."

Jennilee replied serenely, "Actually, it's way better in the spring and fall. We'll go, and you're welcome to go with us.

Angel sat down heavily. "I thought y'all were…just gettin' everything ready before you left."

Charlie shrugged. "We've always stayed."

Jeff contributed, "Harder to get back in once you're out."

Jennilee assured, "We know how to do this, Angel."

"But… What if…everything gets blown away? What if…there's a storm surge and everything gets flooded?"

Jennilee calmly continued unpacking. "Then it will."

"That's why…all the bleach and bottled water and…"

Slipping an arm around Angel's shoulders, comforting her, Jeff quipped, "Yeah, normal people just buy milk and bread and tp. Or alcoholic beverages and munchies for their hurricane parties."

Leaning into his strength, wrapping her arms around his waist, Angel asked, "Why milk and bread and toilet paper?"

Looks were traded among the other four, and then all eyes focused on Angel. All four shrugged at the same time.

Jennilee tried to explain. "It's the same way if we get more than two flakes of snow. Milk…I've never figured that one out, unless it's because there might not be any for awhile after a 'cane, depending on how bad the roads get flooded and you can always use it for cereal. During a snow it's for making cocoa and snow cream. Except I prefer condensed milk. Makes the snow cream richer."

Angel guessed, "Bread's for making sandwiches, and tp, well that's self-explanatory."

"Pretty much. Most people buy ice, but we've got an ice machine here, and generators and plenty of gas so we don't need to buy any ice."

"Sounds like y'all are planning on settling in for the long haul."

Charlie and Jeff shared a look, and Jeff answered. "We've all been through this before, baby. Power's gonna go out. Only question is, for how long. Might just flicker, might be out for hours, or days. Might be out for weeks. All depends."

Jennilee reached out and touched Angel's arm. "We know the drill, Angel. Bathtubs and washing machines and big containers get filled with water. Even if it's not drinkable, it can be used to flush the toilets and such. We've got a good stockpile of batteries and flashlights and oil and oil lamps and candles. The stove and oven are gas, so even when the power's out, we can cook and we've got plenty of paper plates and plastic utensils and cups. We've got extra boots and rain-coats and plenty of tools for clean up. We've already got the outside of the house and grounds ready, and we'll get the laundry caught up and anything else, and then we'll...wait."

Wrapping his arms around Jennilee, Charlie grinned. "Know what the prettiest sight in the world is? Besides my beloved Jennilee?"

Angel shook her head.

"As soon as they can get out and about after the hurricane, a convoy of electric company trucks, headed our way. Those guys are great. I have the utmost respect and admiration for all of them. If it gets bad enough, the electric companies share linemen. Sometimes they travel incredible distances and we appreciate each and every one."

Slipping out of Charlie's arms and tackling another bag, Jennilee smiled. "You're worrying uselessly, Angel. You aren't going to be here anyway. We'll let you know how we fared as soon as we can. Phone lines will probably be down for awhile, so don't panic if you don't hear from us for a bit."

Scooping up an armful, Jennilee headed for the huge pantry. "Even if the lines don't go down, fireants will be looking for anywhere to get out of the water. They love to build their nests in those phone box pole thingies you see on the side of the road and sometimes it shorts the lines out. The only thing they love better is the concrete slab under a heating/ac unit. Those things are like ant condos for the rich and famous. Solid foundation, plenty of ventilation, and they can build upwards to their heart's content. Doesn't do much for the HVAC system when the power comes back on, though. That's why ours are on the roof."

"Besides that, the nasty little fuckers…" Jeff immediately turned beet red and swallowed, his upbringing instantly smacking him down for using impolite words with females present. "My apologies, ladies. The little…" Swallowing again, hard, like the four letter epithets he was choking back were whole pinfish going down the wrong way, Jeff changed direction. "They love to eat wiring. Or at least strip the plastic coating off the wires and then… It's a bad time."

Eyes sparkling at Jeff's discomfort and the overwhelming urge to agree with his sentiments, Charlie added, "Clog up the fan motors, too."

Coming back out of the pantry, arms full, Jennilee dumped what she was carrying on the island.

Angel frowned at her friend. "Jennilee, I thought you were putting stuff away."

Jennilee shot Angel a grin. "Different stuff. Now that we've done what we can to get ready for the hurricane, it's time to get stuff ready for Miz Sadie's and Mr. Jubal's pig pickin'."

Eyeing what she'd put on the counter, Jeff licked his lips. "'Nanner puddin'?"

Jennilee agreed with a teasing lilt. "Both kinds."

Angel sighed and shook her head. "I shouldn't do it, I know I shouldn't. I have to. There's more than one kind of banana pudding?"

Nudging the bananas in Jeff's direction, Jennilee nodded. "Charlie likes the old fashioned kind, made with homemade pudding and then baked with meringue on top. Some people like instant banana cream pudding topped with Cool Whip."

Switching her gaze from Jennilee to Jeff, Angel asked, "Which one do you like, Jeff?"

Getting ready to slice bananas with one of Jennilee's dull knives, Jeff looked up and grinned. "Both."

Angel groaned. "I should've known. What can I do to help?"

"Wanna put 'Nilla wafers in the bottom of the pans or make puddin'?"

Sighing again, Angel reached for the distinctive yellow boxes and a couple huge pans, some 9x13's older and bigger siblings. "I'll do the wafers. Wouldn't wanna ruin the pudding and disappoint everyone."

As Angel placed wafers and Jeff sliced bananas on top of them, Jennilee made both puddings and the meringue while Suki finished cooking the taters.

Jeff nudged Angel's arm. "Pay close attention, Angel mine. Baked flounder's one of my favorite dishes."

"Is there *anything* you won't eat?"

A moment of thoughtful silence, followed by meaningful glances exchanged with Charlie and Jennilee, and Jeff shook his head. "Come to think of it, I don't think there is. Haven't found it yet, at any rate."

Angel watched as Jennilee got out yet another big pan that matched the 'nanner puddin' pans and lined it with foil.

Scoring the dark side of two big flounders at one inch intervals, Jennilee placed them white side down on the greased foil and proceeded to fill the scores. Lemon juice first, then salt, then slices of onion, then strips of raw bacon.

Suki drained the already diced and cooked taters and poured them over and around the decorated fish and the foil was closed over the whole thing.

When the baked 'nanner puddin' came out of the oven a few minutes later, peaks and whorls of meringue perfectly browned, the fish went in.

What seemed like moments later Jennilee slid two four inch square CorningWare bowls and a spoon in front of Jeff, seated at the bar, attention fixed on the oven.

Digging in with gusto, Jeff offered the first bite to Angel.

Pulling her head back to look at the spoon, going cross-eyed in the process, Angel demanded, "When did you make these two, Jennilee? I didn't even see you..."

Slipping the spoonful of traditional 'nanner puddin' in her mouth, Jeff answered. "Jennilee always makes me my own bowls. One of each. Try them and see which one you like better."

Angel's *umm* was closely followed by her retort. Swallowing, she pointed her finger at Jeff. "You...are spoiled rotten."

Giving her a bite of the other and a cheeky grin, Jeff shrugged. "Yeah, so? Which one do you like better? 'Cause I'm good with you fixing either one."

Sliding both bowls out of Jeff's reach, silently admonishing him to wait till after he ate to finish his dessert, Angel accused, "Jennilee... you have absolutely ruined this man for me or anyone else!"

Dropping her arms around Jeff's neck from behind and hugging tight, leaning over his shoulder and giving Jeff a peck on the cheek, Jennilee laughed. "Ah, but look at the whole package. I may have spoiled him, but other than that he's a wonderful, intelligent, sexy, hardworking man with an unflagging appetite and a great sense of humor."

"Jennilee, you've got no call to be considering another man sexy." Peeling Jennilee off Jeff, Charlie pulled her close and locked his lips on hers as the others burst into laughter.

THE BAKED FLOUNDER was everything Jeff had promised and Jennilee'd delivered.

Savoring a few more bites, Angel scooped more taters on her plate. Speared some with her fork and mused, "I think I could eat just these potatoes and be perfectly happy."

Amused laughter from the others, and Jennilee told Angel, "We decided a long time ago we'd almost rather throw the flounder out and just eat the potatoes. The fish is good, but the potatoes are..."

"Divine."

"Inspired."

"Awesome."

Jennilee beamed, the supremely satisfied look of a cook who'd pleased the recipients of her efforts to no end.

"So, what time are we s'posed to be at Miz Sadie's?"

Angel chided, "Jeff, don't even tell us you're still hungry. Not after what you just put away."

Jeff looked Angel right in the eye. "Not right this minute, but I will be."

Angel groaned and Charlie and Jennilee laughed.

Charlie answered and Jennilee nodded her agreement. "They're plannin' on eatin' around 6:00. We'll probably go early and help set up tables and such."

"I'll be starving by then. We gonna go help Grandy get her place ready?"

"Yeah, and we gotta go check Garner House. Mose probably already recruited Josh and Will and the three of them did everything that needs doin', but we'll see if there's anything we can do to help and then head over to Grandy's."

Jennilee sighed, "I hate it, but y'all need to drive separate so you don't have to come back out here. You can just leave from the party."

Jeff pushed back from the table. "I gotta run by my mom and dad's anyway. Not that there's anything to clean up in their yard, but it's the thought that counts, right?"

Rising from her place at the table, Suki began clearing. "I'll bring the desserts when I come. Got some stuff to finish up here before I take off."

Getting up to help Suki, Jennilee missed the look that flashed between Jeff and Angel.

FEASTING DONE, vastly foreshortened sing rapidly coming to a close, people began piling into their vehicles and disappearing down Mr. Jubal's and Miz Sadie's long dirt driveway in a cloud of dust and taillights, each anxious to get home.

The trees, immobilized all day, were fighting to come back to life, struggling, moving one random branch at a time. A high branch here, a low branch there, like a sedated and shackled prisoner coming to and checking fingers and toes for response.

The heat, still oppressive, instead of being relieved in the least by the errant breeze trying to spring up was more akin to standing in front of a blast furnace and opening the door.

The high, wispy clouds that had scudded through earlier were being steadily chased away by thicker, angrier ones, frightened gazelles being hounded by lions.

Thin cirrus, fronted by patches of ominously towering cumulonimbus, with dirty little cotton-balls zooming past just above treetop level combined to make the sky look like an end of the world scenario.

Busy helping clean up, Jennilee kept throwing urgent glances at the lowering sky and urging Jeff and Angel to leave. "Head on, guys. Before it gets too bad and you can't."

Sharing a look, Jeff and Angel moved in for hugs.

Wrapping his arms around Jennilee, Charlie watched her as she watched their best friends leaving with a mixture of relief and resignation on her expressive face.

The first sprinkles hit as Charlie turned into their drive, sparkling their windshield and pocking the dusty road. Getting their stuff out, the wind gusted up and the sprinkles turned into fat drops. About to make a run for the house, Jennilee halted at the sound of a vehicle.

Shaking her head adamantly as Jeff and Angel pulled up beside them in Angel's Toyota, Jennilee stabbed a finger emphatically back the way they'd come. Stepping out, Jeff held up his hands in the age old gesture of peace.

"Don't even start, Jennilee. There's nowhere we'd rather be than right here with you guys."

Looking at Angel, just getting out, Jennilee drew a deep breath. "You *have* to leave. You can't stay."

Angel shook her head at Jennilee's panicked tone. "What he said, Jennilee. If you guys are staying, so are we."

Looking up at Charlie, hand splayed on his chest, Jennilee implored, "Charlie, make them…"

"Give over, Jennilee-sweet."

"But, Charlie…"

"Honey, they're adults and they've made their choice."

Drawing Angel to his side, Jeff reminded, "I've been through as many hurricanes as you have, Jennilee."

A harder gust slapped them and the rain began to sting.

Giving in to the inevitable, Jennilee jerked her head toward the house.

Both couples holding hands, they made a run for the porch, knowing the rain was about to shift to heavier, wind-driven missiles that would hit with all the force of angry hornets.

Stampeding up the steps and falling through the front door en mass, the couples collapsed against each other, laughing fit to be tied.

Jennilee threw her arms around Jeff. "Oh, you crazy man! I don't want you here but there's nowhere else I'd rather you be."

Hugging her close, Jeff cocked a brow at Charlie. "Does she always make this much sense?"

Draping an arm around Angel, Charlie grinned. "Always."

Angel smirked at Jeff. "Makes perfect sense to me." Frowned. "More sense than parking all your vehicles out in the middle of the yard when there's a perfectly good garage going to waste."

Jeff snorted. Holding out an arm for Angel, Charlie did the same for Jennilee. Girls exchanged and back where they belonged, Jeff explained as they headed for the kitchen to dump the empty pans they'd brought back from the party. "All those tall, stately pine trees around the garage are great for shading the cars. During a hurricane, not so much. The cars are far safer outside."

"Okay. I'll buy that. But why nose to nose?"

Jennilee answered that. "Because, head-to, the grills and radiators are protected. Like the Banks ponies. They'll form a circle with the smaller, younger, more vulnerable members of the herd in the middle. The bigger horses, as much as they can, turn their rumps to a storm and ride it out. If those ponies can survive hurricanes that way, our cars should be able to do the same thing."

Angel pointed out the obvious. "Ponies aren't cars."

Jeff's rich laughter rolled out. "Same difference."

"Jeff!" A barrage of high pitched voices greeted his laughter.

Angel watched in disbelief as kids poured out of the kitchen and down the hall, coming at them like a human tidal wave, receding just as fast when Rachel's voice, along with several other women's, demanded they return and clean up their messes.

Hands on her hips, Angel attacked. "Jennilee! Weren't you just pitching a hissy because Jeff and I stayed? And here you're having a party!"

Pulling Angel close and pressing a kiss to the top of her head, Jeff corrected, "Hurricane party, darlin'."

"And the difference would be?"

"A party's just havin' a good time. A hurricane party's when you gather everyone you love in the safest place and ride it out."

Slapping her hand over her mouth to smother a laugh at Angel's dark glare and raised brow, Jennilee offered, "I butchered that one, didn't I? Believe me when I say I had your best interests at heart. I couldn't bear it if anything happened to either of you."

Crossing her arms, nose in the air, Angel sniffed huffily, "I see how you are. Trying to get rid of us."

"Only because I love you beyond reason." Giving Angel a quick, fierce hug, Jennilee stepped into Jeff's arms, the strange tone from earlier, the same one from their floundering expedition, returning full force. "You shouldn't be here. You should've left when I told you. It's gonna get bad."

Charlie closed in as Jeff hugged Jennilee tight, both going on alert. Sharing a look with Charlie, pulling back so he could see Jennilee's face, Jeff quizzed gently, "What's gonna get bad, baby? The storm or something else?"

Eyes focused on something they couldn't see, Jennilee repeated in the same off tone, "It's gonna get bad."

Tearing out of the kitchen and barreling down the hall, Cory crashed into Jennilee's legs, knocking her back a step. "Jennilee!"

Bending down to the toddler, scooping him up, a grinning Jennilee raised the baby high in the air. "Where are you heading in such a hurry, little monkey?"

Blinking at her abrupt return to her normal tone, the others shared worried glances.

CHAPTER 20

"Charlie and Jennilee's house sure is different with all the shutters closed and the power out."

"Spooky, huh?" Arm draped around Angel as they wandered, Jeff waved his flashlight around and sighed. "I never figured out if it's the wind or the gloom, but, yeah. Turns everything into a...half-remembered nightmare."

"I'm just waiting for the monster in the closet to jump out."

"Better not let the kids hear you say that. We'll never get any of them to calm down."

Making a rude sound, Angel snorted, "Fat chance of that. Not with Jennilee giving them all—and just exactly how many are we supposed to be looking for?—flashlights and telling them to go hide."

Pulling Angel to a stop, tugging on her so they were face to face, Jeff shone the light on his face from below and waggled his eyebrows lecherously. "We could go...hide."

Leaning up and brushing a kiss across his lips, Angel retorted, "Thought we were supposed to be seeking."

Nibbling back, Jeff grinned. "Already found what I want."

"The kids, you dweeb."

"And now she's calling me pet names. Honey-pie, you shouldn't have."

A smothered giggle from behind a door had Jeff pouncing, dragging out a shrieking child. "Gotcha, you little twerp!"

Latching her arms around Jeff's neck, Elizabeth whispered, "There aren't really any monsters, are there? Timmy say they're real but..."

"Timmy's your big brother. He's s'posed to say things like that. It's his mission in life." Jerking his head at Angel, Jeff said, "Just ask Angel. She's got a bunch of brothers."

Looking around Jeff, Elizabeth stared at Angel, who nodded.

"Six of them, and they all love to torment me. I give as good as I get, though."

Face scrunching up, Elizabeth poked her bottom lip out. "I can't be mean to Timmy. Momma says."

Smirking somewhat evilly at Elizabeth, Angel disagreed. "I think you and I need to have a long talk, girlfriend."

Rolling his eyes, Jeff bounced Elizabeth theatrically on his hip. "Alright, squirt. We found you. Now you gotta help us find the rest of the tricycle motors."

Beaming, Elizabeth confided, "Daddy calls us curtain climbers and rug apes."

"Good call. What about crumb snatchers and ankle biters?"

"Yep. Is dweep kinda the same thing?"

Angel tried valiantly to smother her laughter as Jeff answered, "Dweeb, honey, and yes, it's the same. Angel calls me that 'cause she really likes me."

Sounding way too adult, Elizabeth batted her eyes. "Duh. We all know that."

An hour later, all children present and accounted for, some Angel knew and more she didn't, the whole crowd gathered in the immense library. The wind produced a constant moaning roar now, like a tornado stuck in place. Weird feeling, like being inside a reverse snow globe, all the swirling action outside and the frozen peace inside.

Snuggled on the loveseat against Jeff, Angel shook her head and whispered, "This is so scary, and Jennilee's turned it all into a game so the kids don't get frightened."

Looking around at the blanket forts and mattresses and sleeping bags everywhere, at the Coleman stove situated on the hearth and busily churning out s'mores for anybody who wanted one, Jeff nodded. "It gets better."

"What? Did they contract with Ringling Brothers?"

"More like Flatt and Scruggs. Just watch."

A particularly violent gust hit the house, rattling plywood and shutters, sideways rain drumming like heavy artillery fire against the side of the house and the boarded up windows, a ravenously battering beast who would go to any lengths to gain entrance.

The kids, all still wide awake, looked around fearfully. The adults tensed and looked worried.

Shivering, Angel curled closer to Jeff. "Sounds like a monster trying to get in."

Jeff pulled her closer. "Yup. I'll huff and I'll puff and…"

As if in response to his words, the immense house creaked and groaned. Things struck the siding, flying debris courtesy of the ever-rising wind. A massive concussion sounded, like a cannon had just been fired, loud enough the vibration was transmitted through the floor, probably one of the huge pines going down.

A ripple of unease ran through the kids and a few started sniffling. Before they could panic in earnest Jennilee diverted their attention.

Clapping her hands, Jennilee decreed, "Finish your s'mores and get a drink. Suki's got wet washcloths and you've all got your jammies on. Charlie and I have a special treat for you so make pit stops down the hall if you need to and get settled on your sleeping bags."

Picking up one of his beloved guitars, Charlie began strumming. Just like they did at the restaurant, Charlie and Jennilee put on a show with Grandy joining them this time instead of Mose and Jubal.

Half asleep herself, listening to the flowing notes, Angel murmured, "I had no idea Grandy could play piano like that. No wonder Jennilee and Charlie are so musically inclined."

Cuddling Angel, heels planted on the coffee table and ankles crossed, head lolled against the back of the couch, Jeff smiled. "I've spent many an evening just like this. 'Cept most of the time the lights were just dimmed and not hurricane lamps turned down low."

Looking around the cozy room, at the flickering light reflecting off the spines of countless books and anxious faces, Angel nuzzled her cheek against Jeff's shoulder. "I can't believe none of their talent rubbed off on you."

"Hey! I can play a radio with the best of them!"

Without missing a note Charlie and Jennilee both shot Jeff wide grins.

The trio played and sang deep into the night while the wind howled and screamed and beat against the house, searching for the tiniest foothold, seeking nothing less than total annihilation. The kids eventually passed out while the adults drowsed, rousing some with the more intense gusts.

Dozing, Angel woke and her eyes were immediately drawn to Jennilee. Jennilee's dulcet tones filled the room like gentle waves lapping at a moonlit tropical shore, Grandy's nimble fingers drew equally harmonious notes from the beautiful old piano. Snores and quiet breathing filled the minute spaces left by the rampaging wind.

Standing and stretching, Angel crossed to stand beside Jennilee. "How can you stay so calm? My insides feel like a bowl of jello in an earthquake."

Answering just as quietly, Jennilee gave her best friend a quick one-armed hug. "Worrying doesn't solve anything, doesn't change anything, and wastes time."

Blowing out a breath and rolling her eyes, Angel huffed, "Yeah, well, we can't all be Madonnas like you."

Jennilee's soft laughter filled the room. "I didn't say I didn't worry."

"Well, no one would ever know. You look cool as a cucumber."

"Humph. This cucumber is ready for a break. Wanna go walkabout with me?"

Eyeing her friend suspiciously, Angel asked, "Now you wanna leave? We're not really going to Australia or anything. Are we?"

Clapping a hand over her mouth to stifle her own laughter, Jennilee shook her head. "I've heard Australia has the most poisonous critters in the world. Not interested, even though it's awesomely beautiful.

Besides, it's too far from home. And, no, we're not going outside. Yet. We'll stay inside, I promise."

"Just can't stand to be away from Charlie, huh?"

"That too." Grabbing a couple big flashlights, handing one to Angel, Jennilee nodded to Grandy. "Be back in a few."

Sticking to Jennilee like Beggar's Lice to knee socks, Angel couldn't help but shiver. Without the soothing combination of Jennilee's voice, Charlie's guitar, and Grandy's piano running interference, the wind became the sole focus.

A very worrisome focus, as it shrieked and wailed with renewed vigor like an enraged and thwarted banshee.

As if whistling past a graveyard, Angel's words came out high-pitched and fast. "Now I know why people went crazy during the Dust Bowl era. How could you stand to listen to that for weeks and months? One night and I'm ready to pull my hair out!"

Jogging rapidly up the stairs, Jennilee never broke stride. "Yeah. It can get on your last nerve."

"Why are you in such a hurry and what would it take to get on your last nerve?"

"The guys are checkin' on…stuff. There was a really loud noise a few minutes ago. Must be bad or they'd've been back already. Let's go see if we can help with damage control."

Following some invisible trail down hallways and past closed doors like Charlie had left glowing psychic markers visible only to Jennilee, she led Angel straight to the guys.

Rolling her eyes, Angel drawled, "You have to teach me how to do that."

Eyes on her tall, handsome, blond-haired target, Jennilee absently asked, "What?"

"Teach me how to find Jeff like you can find Charlie."

Snickering, Jennilee shrugged. "It's a useful talent. Nothing I do on purpose. It's like…we're…magnetized."

"Charlie have the same talent?"

Charlie answered as a breath of fresher air, rife with salt and rain hit the girls. "Sometimes. It's not as reliable as Jennilee's."

Coming to stand beside their guys, Jennilee and Angel shone their flashlights over the damage.

The French doors leading to the porch bulged inward, glass shattered and hanging askew despite the plywood that had covered the exterior.

"What... What is that?"

Straining to see what had created the disaster, Angel took another step. Snagging her around the waist, Jeff stopped her in her tracks.

"Whoa, darlin'. Glass everywhere."

"Yeah, but..." Angel's eyes couldn't make sense of what she was seeing, especially in the spastic light from the flashlight beams.

"Looks like..."

"...a Bimini top..."

"...wrapped around an Adirondack chair..."

"...with a table umbrella for a sail."

Looking from Charlie to Jennilee to Jeff and back to Charlie, Angel stammered, "But...how? How could that stuff possibly get tangled up and picked up and thrown against your door? We're on the second floor, for crying out loud!"

Jennilee shrugged. "Seen weirder stuff after hurricanes."

Jeff added, "It's like when you pick up a conch shell all full of sand and smaller shells, packed inside so tight you can't get it out without breaking the conch and all you can think is how in the world could that possibly happen."

Jennilee sighed. "If that's the worst thing we have to clean up, we're way ahead of the game. And we haven't finished this room yet, so no furniture or anything to worry about."

Charlie hugged her. "At least it didn't get your stained glass. The rest of it can be replaced, no problem. Mose can do the woodwork and we've got glass to replace what was broken."

"Where'd you find enough old glass to do that?" Jeff sounded interested and at the same time like he was holding back laughter.

"Old glass? Why does it have to be old? Glass is glass." Angel looked as perplexed as she sounded, especially when the laughter Jeff had been holding in burst free.

Charlie and Jennilee made faces at him as he started explaining.

"Oh, no, sweetums. You can't use just any glass in a house this old and with owners who are such sticklers. You have to replace it with period pieces. They probably found a time traveling glassmaker and stashed him in the boathouse for just such an occasion."

Charlie snorted. "Or maybe we just found an old house slated for destruction and salvaged what we could."

"House, hell. You probably bought an abandoned country or something."

Shaking her head at their never-ending antics, Angel asked, "So how are you going to get that down? And what are you going to do about the rain coming in?"

"Nothing right now, and tarps. We've got plenty stashed on both floors. Come on, Angel. We'll go get a couple and some hammers and nails and let the guys move what they can of this."

By the time the girls got back with the supplies, Charlie and Jeff had most of the debris pushed out of the way and the doors partially back in place. They made quick work of closing the gaping maw with the tarp, since the plywood had been shattered by the flying debris.

Angel frowned. "Won't the wind just blow the tarp down?"

"Should be ok." Jennilee tilted her head to one side. "Wind's about to shift."

Hammer pausing in mid-swing, Charlie looked up. "Eye passin' over?"

Jennilee nodded.

"Eye? Eye of what? Newt?" Angel looked worriedly at Jeff when Jennilee and Charlie remained engrossed in their now silent communication.

"The eye is the center of the hurricane. Everything will calm down for a bit and then the wind will start up again from the opposite direction. A lot of times the backside of the hurricane is worse than the front."

"Worse? Worse than what we've already been through?"

Wrapping an arm around Angel, pressing his lips to her hair, Jeff consoled her. "It'll be worse but it probably won't last as long, and it'll be daylight soon. Hurricanes always seem worse in the dark. Hang in there, babe."

"Wanna go outside?" Charlie kept his eyes on Jennilee.

Angel goggled. "Outside? Are you crazy? Never mind. Rhetorical question. Can anyone play or is this an exclusive event?"

A few minutes later, standing outside in the curiously eerie calm amid the ringing silence, all traces of wind vanished, Angel marveled. "This seems so...weird now. Like all we've ever known is howling wind and this is...somehow wrong."

A murmured chorus of assent greeted her statement.

Venturing off the porch and out into the yard, they looked around at flashlight revealed damage. Branches everywhere, pinestraw in places pinestraw had no business being, leaves and bits of leaves plastered against the walls and shutters and plywood protected windows as if some nature obsessed decorator had redone the exterior with a chipper-shredder while they'd been huddled inside.

Jennilee exclaimed, "Turn your flashlights off and look up."

The others, especially Angel, gawked at the circle of brilliant stars revealed right above them in a flawlessly clear patch of sky.

Charlie threw out, "Half an hour?"

"Maybe. Doubt it." Jennilee shook her head. "Fifteen, twenty minutes, tops."

Taking her word as Gospel, the other three hastily got in gear. Guys taking the bottom floor of the porch, the girls took the top as they scouted for further damage. The wind was already gusting back up as they met where they'd started.

Standing on the porch, the rising wind teasing at their clothes and playing with their hair, comparing notes, enjoying the fresh air before they had to head back to the stifling heat inside, Jennilee reported first.

"Top floor's fine, just that one broken door. Don't know how that conglomeration of a wreck didn't ruin the porch rails and the roof."

Charlie added, "No major damage on this floor, at least nothing that can't be fixed with time and elbow grease.

Jeff snorted, "He neglected to tell you there's a skiff wedged on the front steps."

Jennilee and Angel looked at each other and burst out laughing.

Taking Charlie's hand, Jennilee clicked her light off. "A skiff? Do we know whose?"

Charlie shrugged. "An old wooden one. No numbers or name or anything."

A rushing locomotive sound high in the pines had them scooting back indoors just in time. The wind-driven rain struck the heavy doors like rat-shot from a too-close doublebarrel as the foursome moved deeper into the expansive foyer and back toward the library.

Jeff mused, "What did people say tornadoes sounded like before there were trains? And what did they eat before peanutbutter?"

Throwing a glance over her shoulder as if the noise behind them had taken form and was about to pounce, a wide-eyed Angel squeaked, "Tornado?"

Jennilee answered while the guys chuckled at Jeff's nonsense. "No. No tornado. Just the wind picking back up and the rain starting again. Did you know..."

Ignoring the concerted groan, Jennilee kept talking. "Peanutbutter was patented some time around 1885. It originally sold for something like six cents a pound, and was touted as a highly nutritious food source for people who couldn't chew. Peanutbutter..."

WATCHING JENNILEE STEADILY FORMING BISCUITS, Angel just shook her head. "Seriously? You're going to cook outside on the grill? In a hurricane?"

Smiling back at Angel, Jennilee kept pinching off bits of dough and rolling them between her floured palms. "What? The wind's all coming from the other direction, we've got fire extinguishers, and we have to use up some of this stuff before it goes bad. Besides, food always tastes better outside and the kids are gonna go nuts right here shortly. Better to get them outside and let them run around a bit while we can."

Angel muttered grumpily, "Never heard of anyone fixing biscuits on a grill."

Jennilee's laughter rang in the gloomy kitchen, dark except for the flickering circles of light provided by the hurricane lamps, their elegant curved glass chimneys and faceted bases making the kitchen seem like it had been caught out of time. "They come out awesome and they cook in about five minutes. Just have to remember to put them on the top shelf or the bottoms will burn."

Crossing her arms and making a face, Angel declared, "Hmmph. Thought you said that's why you had a gas stove. So you could cook in here if the power went out."

"Somebody didn't get enough sleep..." Jeff sing-songed cheerfully as he caught the last bit.

"No, I didn't. How can y'all be so...chipper? This early in the morning when you've been up all night listening to...that?" Exasperated, Angel flapped a hand toward the outside. Where the wind still raged, where the sideways sheets of rain beat against the house, despite the depth of the porches, with the eerie drumming sound only hurricanes could produce.

Catching her up in a bear hug, Jeff nuzzled. "Thought you said you were a morning person?"

"Thought you said you *weren't*?"

"Darlin', this ain't early morning, this is late night."

Unable to resist Jeff's teasing, Angel caved.

By the time she surfaced from his kiss, Charlie had joined them. Arms around Jennilee's waist from behind, he rested his chin on her shoulder and stole occasional nibbling kisses while he watched her deft hands shaping biscuits and placing them in neat rows on a cookie sheet.

"Grab those two skillets for me, please, Charlie. And, Jeff, you get the sausage and flour and oh, don't forget the spatula and the hot pads."

Angel awaited her orders, sure there would be some. Wiping her hands on a tea towel, Jennilee slung it over her shoulder and picked up the pan of biscuits. Starting after the guys, she grinned at Angel. "Would you grab the milk and butter and salt and pepper?"

Grinning back at Jennilee, she drawled, "You forgot the eggs."

"Sure did. You mind?"

Hands too full to carry lights, armed with their weapons of choice, their procession headed across the house to the leeward side. Working their way through gloomy rooms and heavily shadowed hallways like they were scoping out caves and grottos,

Angel followed along without comment until they ended up in the...

Angel giggled disbelievingly. "Ballroom? Y'all are gonna eat breakfast in the ballroom?"

A burst of laughter rang off the high ceilings of the huge room, still showing evidence of construction. Ladders, tarps, tools and various other obvious signs of work in progress were piled at one end of the spacious room.

Jennilee flashed Angel an over her shoulder grin. "Not actually in the ballroom. Unless you particularly want to. It's much cooler out here."

Stepping out on the porch, Angel looked around in amazement. Not just at Grandy and Suki, industriously sweeping the porch, but at the alien landscape. The tiny glimpses afforded by the flashlights hadn't done it justice. Where once Charlie and Jennilee's manicured yard and acres of lush flowerbeds had held sway, now a hellish landscape of broken branches, pinestraw, and unidentifiable flotsam and jetsam ruled.

The shrubs and flowers, partially stripped of leaves, the remaining leaves twisted and mangled, hung heavy with water, lashed by the ferocious wind and sculpted into strange parodies of themselves.

Most of the yard had become a small lake, making the stately pines, swaying and bending in a frenzied dance, look like storm tossed kelp.

The wind still roared in the tops of the pines as if a tornado had indeed come through and gotten stuck in place. The tops of some of them, wrung off and scattered here and there like giant-size confetti, acted as dams for the windblown debris, catching stuff and piling it even more. The rain continued to come down in sheets, sideways, upside down, every way but straight down.

And yet, her friends hadn't lied. Here on the porch, they might as well have been on another planet watching a film about natural disasters.

Soft gusts brushed by them, not relieving the sticky, humid heat in the least, merely moving it around like a bulldozer pushing thick mud. The rain didn't touch them, as if an invisible shower curtain protected them from the falling torrents.

Distracted by the awesome display of power and man's ultimate fragility, Angel almost missed Jennilee cooking on the grill. By the time Angel refocused, Jennilee was busily frying what looked to be a couple pounds of sausage in a lumber camp worthy iron skillet.

Sausage browned, Jennilee dumped multiple handfuls of flour into the skillet while Charlie cracked eggs into a huge bowl and Jeff whisked them with a fork like he'd become an industrial blender.

Stirring the flour into the cooked sausage until it resembled thick glue full of little brown lumps, Jennilee began adding milk and stirring non-stop. Giving the guys a nod, Jennilee divided her attention between the skillet full of sausage gravy and the second skillet, full now as well, as Jeff poured the eggs in.

Skillfully keeping both skillets going, stirring one way and then the other, deciding both were done, Jennilee nodded again and stepped back. Each wearing an oven mitt, Charlie grabbed one skillet and Jeff the other. Sliding the tray of biscuits onto the top shelf of the grill, Jennilee closed the half-barrel lid.

Angel blinked and rubbed her eyes, wondering if she'd dozed off while standing up. She sure hadn't seen anyone carry sawhorses out of the ballroom and balance a sheet of plywood on them, but the makeshift table was now covered with food and plates and silverware that had materialized just as magically.

As if an inaudible to her bell had rung somewhere in the depths of the huge house, sleepy-eyed kids started appearing, followed by sleep deprived adults, even more sleepy looking. Jennilee snagged one of the mitts and took the perfectly browned biscuits out of the grill. Setting them on the table, Jennilee unwrapped the end of a stick of butter, and rubbing it over each biscuit, let it melt a bit on top of each one. Grandy and Suki started dishing up plates.

Taking the plate Jeff held out to her, Angel stared at the bounty. Sausage gravy over a couple crumbled biscuits, scrambled eggs, fresh fruit. Raising her eyes to Jeff's, Angel let them drop back down to her filled plate, kept them there while Charlie blessed it.

Crowding her, Jeff snickered. "Don't worry. I'll finish whatever you can't."

One bite of the sausage gravy had Angel closing her eyes and savoring. Opening them, forking up another bite, she met Jennilee's laughing ocean eyes. "This is so delicious! I was kinda wondering, when you left all that grease in the skillet."

Jennilee winked and accepted the plate Charlie held out to her. "Gotta have a little grease to make good gravy."

Charlie and Jeff bracketed the girls, heaping plates in their hands.

Sweat popped out on Angel's brow. More sweat, in addition to what was already there. "Isn't it kind of hot to be eating this?"

Muffled, mouths full laughter answered Angel's innocent query.

"Yeah, but I don't want this sausage to spoil. It's also hearty and filling. We're gonna need all the calories we can down right here shortly, so eat up."

Angel eyed the trio suspiciously. "Need? What do you mean?"

Briefly detouring his fork on its way to its destination, Jeff waved the glob at the yard. "You're the one who wanted to stay. I tried to get you to leave, but, no…"

Charlie jibed, "We feed your sorry ass, bro. It's only fair you help with clean-up."

Slipping up behind the foursome, Timmy corrected, "Butt. Bottom. Rear end. You're not s'posed to say the other word. Better not let Mom catch you." He changed gears on a dime, holding his plate out and giving Jennilee puppy dog eyes. "Can I have more, please? I'm starving."

Hiding her smile, Jennilee took Grandy's just vacated place and dished him up another round.

Moving down the table to get another cup of juice, refilled plate in hand, Timmy half-turned. "Oh, and Jennilee, you've got a big ol' flour handprint on your…" Spotting his mom, Timmy waffled visibly before chickening out on pretending to be an adult and using the forbidden word. "…rear."

Corralling Jennilee, stealing one kiss, then two, Charlie handily disappeared the incriminating evidence with a few well placed swipes. Surfaced to see Tim and Bradley Owen Foster the Third coming out one of the French doors. Arms still around Jennilee, Charlie guided her to one of the upside-down five gallon buckets the crowd was using for seats.

Seating her, resting his forehead against Jennilee's for just a second, Charlie gave her another quick kiss. "Be right back, Jennilee-love."

Swinging around with military precision, Charlie glared at BOF like he was a captured enemy soldier. Not happy having the SOB here in the first place, Charlie had made his *wishes* explicitly, *abundantly* clear.

The evening before, Tim had escorted a goggling BOF through the house to Charlie's office, and a waiting Charlie. Had stood at attention just to the right of and slightly behind BOF as they both came to a halt a strictly proscribed distance in front of Charlie. Seated behind his immense desk, the gleaming top cleared, not even a speck of dust in sight, Charlie waited like a fat spider.

Or maybe a dragon.

Or a king of old, at the very least.

A not very pleased king.

A ruthless ruler who held the power of life or death over all in his kingdom.

One whose word was law.

One who had no qualms about laying down and carrying out said law.

BOF was not to so much as take a breath that Tim didn't approve first. Not to leave Tim's side, for any reason. Was not to have free rein in any sense of the word. If he was unable to understand those simple rules, Charlie could and would lock BOF in the small, unfinished room in the garage.

Unfinished as in no amenities. At all. No bed, no toilet, no air conditioning, no fan. Not even a window.

Starting to protest, his usual *that's not fair* spiel, BOF had taken one look at Charlie's fierce countenance and unforgiving eyes and kept his yap shut.

Wisely, he kept it shut now as well.

Snagging a plate, Charlie slapped a serving of scrambled eggs and a biscuit on it and dumped a ladle of gravy over the whole. Dropped it on the plywood in front of BOF with a thump that made the pile of silverware rattle. All without once taking his iced coffee eyes off BOF's.

Jabbed the ladle at a distant point of the porch.

Message received, loud and clear.

BOF might be here, but he wasn't welcome, wasn't part of the crowd.

And he wasn't forgiven.

Not even close.

While Suki nudged Charlie out of the way to serve Tim, Charlie kept his gaze fastened on the villain. Watching until he took his seat on the edge of the porch steps, Charlie turned back to Tim, eyes still on his target. Before Tim could join BOF, Charlie shook his head.

"Go sit with Rachel and the kids."

Tim blinked but didn't argue.

Eating and conversations picked back up where they'd left off.

Rejoining Jennilee and Angel and Jeff, planting himself firmly between his beloved and the not far enough away BOF, Charlie stood like a statue of Hercules, arms crossed and attention fixed like Jewel watching a rat hole.

In between shovels, Jeff grinned. "I love it when you go all He-man, bro." Patted his heart. "Gets me…right here."

"Bite me, She-Ra."

Grinning wider, Jeff kept shoveling.

CHAPTER 21

"*C*an we please? Mom said it was up to you."

Looking out at the flooded yard, at the trees swaying in the roaring wind, at the continually falling but not quite as hard rain, Jennilee considered. Looked back to the children.

"You have to promise…"

"We do, we do!" Hopeful voices chorused, hopeful faces beamed in anticipation.

Raised a hand for silence.

It fell, as fast as the liquid sunshine.

"Swimming suits on, towels at the ready."

Quivering like excited puppies, all heads nodded emphatically.

"Stay away from the trees and the debris. Watch out for fireants and snakes. Stay where we can see you."

Little bodies shifted, preparing for take off.

"Wait…"

Froze, prepared to beg, thinking Jennilee was about to change her mind.

"You have to put all the boards and stuff away when you're done."

Watching the stampede as the kids headed indoors, Angel shook her head.

239

Tipping her head, Jennilee smirked. "You're welcome to join them."

Angel didn't bother to dignify that with a response as she settled on one of the upturned buckets.

Stampeding back through, dropping towels on the porch before leaping over the steps, the kids squealed as the cool rain drenched them instantly. Splashing around in the yard-sized puddle, they chased each other, shrieking and screaming and blowing off steam.

Watching them running and playing, Angel rolled her eyes. "I can't believe you're allowing them to go out and play in this. Won't they get ringworm, playing in puddles like that?"

Jennilee and Rachel and burst out laughing.

Still laughing, casting a look at the ever lightening sky and the somewhat less than Niagara water falling, Jennilee asked, "Why not? The worst of it's over, and otherwise they'll drive us nuts shortly. They've been playing on the porch for hours. We've done Simon Says and checkers and cards and hopscotch and jacks and…"

Rachel agreed sagely. "Kids and puddles… They're magnetized to each other. Sooner or later they're gonna end up out there anyway. This way… We look like the good guys for allowing them to play instead of punishing them for sneaking out there or accidentally on purpose falling off the porch." Rolled her eyes. "I'm only surprised Timmy made it this long without "losing his balance.""

Jennilee stated, "We've been playing in puddles since we could walk. I have yet to get ringworm. Whaddya think, guys?"

Charlie and Jeff appeared, arms full, shaking their heads. "Nope, never got ringworm from playing in puddles. Been told that more times than I can count."

Tipping her face up for the requisite kiss, Jennilee admonished, "Play nice, boys."

Angel watched, jaw slack, as they joined the smaller children. "I should have known."

Watching Charlie and Jeff with stars in her eyes, Jennilee asked, "What? You didn't think the big kids were gonna miss this opportunity, now, did you?"

Making good use of the trove of squirt guns, filling them from the multitude of five gallon buckets they'd placed on the steps to catch rainwater for just such an eventuality, Charlie and Jeff waged mock battles with the army of whooping and hollering kids.

When they tired of that, Charlie and Jeff dragged out the skim boards.

Angel sat up, all sudden interest. "I thought those were for the beach."

Jennilee shrugged and enlightened her. "Edge of the surf. Lake-sized puddles. They work equally well in either one. Wanna try?"

"Heck yeah."

Jennilee grinned and picked up another Cheeto. "If you should happen to get ringworm, the pharmacy's well stocked with Tinactin."

TIRED AND STARVING, the well saturated crew regrouped on the porch in time for lunch. The sawhorse table was once more loaded down, this time with sandwich fixin's and chips.

Washing up in a bucket of clean water, the kids, big and little, milled around noisily with all the patience of a pack of starving hounds.

Jennilee, Rachel, Suki and Grandy assembly-lined the sandwich making and drink pouring, making sure everyone got served in record time, little kids first. Angel passed out the filled plates and helped the littler ones get seated.

Arriving back at the table in time to see Jennilee making more ham and cheese sandwiches, Angel watched in disbelief as Jennilee layered cheese and ham in a stack that would've made Dagwood swoon with pride, then proceeded to cover the lunchmeat with Ruffles before topping it off with bread and smushing the whole.

Shaking some Cheetos onto the plates beside the towering sandwiches, Jennilee handed the Dagwood with mustard to Charlie and the one with mayo to Jeff and busied herself fixing more.

Arms crossed, hip and head cocked, Angel stared until Jennilee looked up.

"What?"

"I know you did not just put chips *on* those sandwiches."

"Why not? That's the way we like them." Jennilee grinned and crunched a Cheeto.

Jeff sidled up beside Angel and offered her a bite. "Try it."

Shaking her head and turning up her cute little nose, Angel took the plate Jennilee was holding out. "Can I have some mayonnaise on the side, please?"

It was their turn to watch as Angel trilled, "Rrruffles have rrridges!" and dredged her chip through the glob of Duke's finest.

All motion stopped and Jeff pointed out, languidly waving his whole dill like a baton. "There's two or three tubs of chip dip on the table."

"You all put chips on your sandwiches and I'm the weird one? I don't think so." Angel crunched her chip and smacked her lips.

HELPING Charlie take down the plywood covering the French doors as the winds finally died down into fits and sputters, Jeff grunted and swore as he smashed his finger. For the third time. "So where's BOF? Wouldn't he be imminently more suited to this kind of slave labor?"

"Suck it up, whiner boy." Charlie flashed Jeff a crooked grin. "If you'd spend more time working out than sitting on your can, you wouldn't be in such bad shape."

"Yeah, yeah, yeah."

Shifting the heavy sheet, the guys turned it in a fluid, co-ordinated move and laid it flat on top of the stack already residing on the porch.

Tackling the next one, side by side, Jeff calculated. Slung his head in a quick move, flinging sweat drops.

Charlie squalled and jerked his own blond head. "Hey!"

"So?"

Charlie grinned evilly. "BOF is currently washing the lunch dishes. Just like he washed the breakfast dishes, just like he'll wash the supper dishes."

Jeff returned the grin. "Wondered why y'all weren't using paper plates and disposable cups."

"Now you know. When the little pissant is done with the dishes and the kitchen to Suki's satisfaction, Tim's gonna escort him out here. All this plywood's gotta be stacked in the boat shed for next time. Every. Single. Piece."

Jeff's grin widened and he snickered, mentally calculating the distance between house and shed, multiplying it by stairs and sheets of plywood. And knowing Charlie... Jeff swept his eyes slowly over the piece they'd just laid on the pile. Yep! There it was. A number, painted in the top corner, one Jeff never would've noticed if he hadn't been looking.

Oh yeah. Charlie had a rigid system for placing the plywood back where it belonged so it could be rapidly put in place over the correct windows next time it was needed.

Jeff snorted a laugh as he wondered how many times BOF would have to re-stack it all before he figured it out.

Charlie casually added to Jeff's unspoken question. "It goes overhead. On the beams in the small back room.

Sliding to the floor, legs splayed out in front of him, Jeff clutched his sweaty sides and laughed till he cried. "The small back room that's about the size of a Pullman bunk? Economy ticket?"

Charlie rubbed his hand together, eyes narrowed in anticipation. "Oh, yeah. He'll have to take it all down and move it back out in the main room. Can't do anything with it in the back."

"What about the train wreck on the second floor?"

Charlie slanted Jeff a smug look. "While we were playing squirt gun war and skim board champ with the kiddos, where do you think BOF was?"

PLYWOOD DOWN, windows and French doors open, it was still miserable inside, stifling even with the high ceilings and cross-draft.

Looking around at all the passed out children, Angel remarked, "Good thing you wore them out today. Don't think I'm up for another round of hide and seek."

Looking around, smiling fondly at the children sleeping in piles and drifts like exhausted puppies, Jennilee raised a brow. "Oh, yeah.

It's amazing. Without power, people revert almost instantly to going to bed when it gets dark and getting up at first light, circadian rhythms restored. They'll be stirring, and starving, in just a few hours."

Angel blinked and jerked. "Wait. Power. Didn't you guys say you had generators? Why are we sweltering in the dark? Again?"

Jennilee's laughter chimed out. "We did, and we do. No sense running the generators if the power's only gonna be off for a day or two. Besides, the kids think this is fun. Gives them good memories."

"More romantic, too. Gives us some good memories as well." Jeff sidled up behind Angel and wrapped his arms around her.

Laughing, Angel shrugged out of his hold. "Get off, you great sweaty ox."

Dropping his arms to his side, bowing his head and slumping in mock dejection, Jeff groused, "Guess this means the honeymoon's over."

Angel blew Jeff a kiss. "Cheer up, lover boy. We haven't even gotten properly started yet."

"Ooh, baby! Tell me more, tell me more!" Jeff batted his ridiculously long eyelashes coquettishly while Charlie snorted and Jennilee and Angel giggled.

A drowsy murmur came from one of the piles. "Knock it off, you guys."

The *guys* chorused, "Good night, Timmy!"

CHAPTER 22

*T*he next morning dawned fair and clear, as if the wind and rain had swept the sky clean. Not so the land.

The yard down along the river and halfway to the house was covered in detritus, as if the river, weary of man and his careless pollutions, had purposefully vomited back up upon the land all that had been dumped into her.

Jewel patrolled the edges, sniffing and nosing, jumping back in alarm repeatedly, barking ferociously at the multitudes of fiddler crabs like they were thieving marauders of the worst sort.

Besides all the storm wrack, and right along the leading edge of the debris field, marsh grass piled in slips and slubs coated everything several feet deep. Mixed in with the heavy reeds, every imaginable thing and some that weren't stuck out here and there like straggling survivors of a landslide.

Old crab-pots, faded lifejackets, pieces of net and broken lengths of docks, soda cans, beer cans, cooler lids, whole coolers, beach chairs, every conceivable thing and more lay strewn about as if wild animals had torn apart giant-sized trash bags and strewn the refuse everywhere.

Someone's picnic table standing on end rested side by side with an old chest freezer, also standing on end. Leaning against each other like drunken frat buddies, the two of them propping up a set of sliding glass doors still in their frame, impossibly intact.

Dawned fair, and clear, and *hot*. If the days prior had been miserable, this was pure misery. Air the consistency of pea soup made each breath seem as hard-won as if dragged in through a wet sponge, and there was little oxygen to be had.

The sun beat down on the Earth like a merciless hammer on an anvil of the gods, each stroke flattening and flinging sparks, throwing more heat, reshaping and reforming, melting everything it touched into an unrecognizable slag heap.

Standing on the edge of the storm wrack with the others, surveying the damage and peering cautiously at the fiddler crabs scuttling madly about, Angel shook her head at Jeff's low whistle.

"Incredible, Charlie Brown. I've never seen the water get this high in your yard. Even if the river was white-cappin' yest."

Charlie made a face. "Between the wind and the full moon, yeah. Hurricane couldn't have hit at a worse time, and the eye went right over us, so..."

Gesturing at all the oddball pieces of lumber and creosote poles, Angel ventured, "I wondered why you took your dock down. Now I know."

"Built it that way on purpose. Our dock is bolted together and cabled in sections so we can dismantle it and store it. Long as the poles are still there, it's not too much trouble to put it back up. Better than building a whole new one."

Jeff quipped cheerfully, "Looks like you'll be adding to yours."

"Like ours just the way it is." Charlie shot Jeff a speculative glance. "'Course, we could salvage all this stuff for yours."

Casting her eyes over the piles and heaps of debris buried in the marsh grass, Angel asked, "How are you going to separate the trash from the..."

"Treasure? That's half the fun darlin'."

"How can you possibly think digging through that stinking mess is fun?"

"Digging isn't. Finding is. And besides—correct me if I'm wrong, Charlie Brown—BOF is going to be doing most of the separating."

Jennilee, up to this point just standing quietly and staring, suddenly came to life. "I have to go check out the cemetery."

Sharing a concerned look, the other three stuck right with her as she trekked across the yard, skirting around the bigger piles, carefully stepping over smaller branches and following some invisible path Jewel nosed out.

In the lead, coming to an abrupt halt, Jennilee tilted her head and began talking to something. Sitting at heel and tilting her head the same way, Jewel gave one quick, joyful bark.

"Well, hello there! Glad to see you made it! I know, I know. The gardens are destroyed." Nodding like she was listening to something they couldn't hear, Jennilee promised, "As soon as we get back to the house. Go spread the word."

Sideways eyeballing Jeff and Charlie, neither of whom seemed surprised in the least, Angel craned left, then right, still couldn't see anything. Jerked back as some tiny creature buzzed past her.

"What'd ya jump for?"

Angel swatted at Jeff, laughter all over his smirking face. "I just got buzzed by Marvin Martian and you want to know why I jumped?"

"Yeah, well as long as he didn't bring any illudium Q-36, we're good."

Jennilee's laughter trilled across the yard. "You, Angel, are as fixated on martians as you keep accusing me of being about cemeteries."

"What am I supposed to think? Whatever that was was green, tiny, and fast moving."

"Stand still. He'll be back."

Suiting words to actions, Jennilee tipped her face up to the sun and cocked her head. "There. He's almost here."

A whirring sound and a flash of iridescent green had Angel goggling.

Not a martian, then, but a winged jewel.

A tiny hummingbird hovered inches in front of Jennilee's face, conferring silently, a feathered messenger.

Zipping around, he bobbed in front of Charlie, then Jeff. Elevatored up and down, then hovered in front of Angel longer, checking her out, long enough for her to get an up close and personal look.

"He's...beautiful." Angel kept her voice low, moved nothing but her lips.

Jennilee laughed again. "He likes you. He won't leave you alone now."

"How can you tell? How'd you get him to do that?"

"*I* didn't get him to do anything. They just know I usually fill the feeders and Charlie hangs them up. They're panicking because all the flowers are stripped. Hummers have to eat a lot and frequently because of their high metabolism."

"Kinda like you, Jeffro." Charlie smirked at Jeff.

Watching, better able to track the bird's movement now, Angel watched him zip back to the edge of the woods, a tiny black dot from this distance.

"They're such funny creatures. I love them so. We usually have thirty or forty hanging around. You should see their nests. They look like miniature hammocks with the ends tied together to make a sling. The eggs are incredibly tiny, about the size of peas."

Angel switched her gaze from the woods to Jennilee.

"You should hold one. It's like holding air. You can hardly feel them, have to look to make sure you're actually holding anything."

Angel's eyes, already wide, went huge. "They let you hold them?"

Jennilee threw back her head and laughed and laughed. "Not let me, no. Occasionally they get in the shop and get tangled in spider webs. They don't have a down gear once they get in a building, just keep bumping the ceiling. When they eventually get too wrapped in webs and too tired to fly, you can just pick them up. If you can get the spiderwebs off and get them to a feeder they'll be fine. You should hear them fuss! They'll fly off and sit in a nearby tree and chitter bad words, worse than when they're fighting over territorial rights at the feeders."

Charlie slung an arm around Jennilee and pressed a kiss to her temple. "Good thing they're not the size of Great Danes."

Jennilee mused, "They actually use spiderwebs and moss and dryer lint, pretty much anything soft, to make their nests. I've never figured out how they use the spiderwebs for nests when they get so tangled in the ones in the shop. Maybe they panic."

Reaching the cemetery, Jennilee surveyed the damage. Not bad, considering. Situated on a small rise, bracketed by huge live oaks, the ancient graves were well out of the water's reach. A lot of limbs and leaves and raking but nothing major.

Watching her wander, Jeff leaned close to Angel. "She'll do this herself. No way Charlie's letting BOF anywhere near this place."

Charlie stood sentry, knowing Jennilee was thanking Amelia, apologizing for not bringing any flowers.

Angel watched, knowing there was far more going on here than the others were letting on. Silent conversations rang in the heavy air with someone—or something—Angel couldn't see, any more than she'd been able to see the hummingbird at first. She sighed, content to wait.

Stopping in front of one of the graves, Jennilee bowed her head, reached out and laid a hand on the waist-high headstone.

A quick buzz, and there was their feathered friend again. Dipping and bobbing, flashing in the sunlight like an animated emerald and ruby brooch, the hummingbird settled on the very top of the arched marble, right next to Jennilee's hand. Her delighted laughter chimed out and mingled with its chirps and trills.

Jennilee's smile rivaled the sun.

Taking another route back to the house, walking along the edge of the woods this time and noting all the downed and hopelessly tangled trees, Jennilee picked up where she'd left off as if they'd never stopped at the cemetery, as if she'd never gone silent for half an hour.

Silent until they spotted a praying mantis.

Stopping, staring at the harmless looking insect sunning itself on a downed branch, Jennilee shivered. "Did you know praying mantis can catch and eat hummingbirds? I saw one do it once. Everybody's gotta eat but I've felt kinda hard-hearted about them ever since."

Charlie grinned. "Not hard-hearted enough to kill them, but she will pay the kids a quarter apiece for all the ones they relocate from the flowerbeds around the house and close to the feeders to somewhere out in the woods."

Angel gave Jennilee a quick one-armed hug and a brilliant smile. "Jennilee, defender of truth and beauty."

Jeff snorted. "She's even got Jewel trained to spot them. Next time you hear the dog barking like a maniac, watch the mutt and the kids. She spots, they transport, Jennilee pays."

Racing back from her explorations, coming to a sliding halt in front of the branch and its alien life form, Jewel proved Jeff's words true, barking ferociously, snapping and showing teeth.

Making them laugh, Angel observed, "Good thing it's not really a martian."

Jennilee shivered. "Rather have a martian. Those mean ol' things things are related to nasty cockroaches. The bugs themselves are bad enough. Guess it's God's idea of a joke to enable them to fly."

Completing their circuit and heading back to the house, the sound of a vehicle had them stopping and waiting as Manny drove out of the woods, the pinestraw covered driveway indiscernible from the yard.

Opening the door and jumping down out of the two-ton, mopping his face with a large red bandana, he crossed the yard to meet them.

"The garage is fine, no damage. I put all the vehicles back."

Charlie nodded. "Saw that. Thanks. Your place okay?"

Manny nodded. "Both driveways are clear. Had to cut up a few small trees but nothing major."

"Guess it's time to head out then."

Angel jerked to attention. "Head out? To where?"

Mind already a million miles away, Jennilee said, "You're welcome to stay here if you want, Angel. We gotta go check out the main road and if it's clear, get to town and make sure Grandy's house and all our friends fared okay."

Manny waved a hand at the vehicle he'd driven up in. "Figured that's what you'd want to do. Truck's all ready. Stuff's in the back along with extra gas cans."

"Thanks again, Manny. Stay here and do what you can. Tim's inside." Saying nothing about BOF, not in front of Jennilee, Charlie shared a long look with Manny. Waiting until he saw the acknowledgement flare in Manny's eyes, Charlie nodded.

CHAPTER 23

*A*ll of them already wearing jeans and heavy work boots and long sleeved shirts over T shirts, Charlie and Jeff handed the girls up.

"What kind of truck is this? I don't think I've ever seen one like it."

Jeff chuckled at Angel's question. "Leftover from WWII. Commonly called a Deuce and a Half, or a two-ton, or…"

Flipping switches, Charlie added, "They're heavy duty military surplus. Nearly indestructible and great for stuff like this. They can go anywhere."

Angel craned around but couldn't see anything. "So what stuff is in the back?"

"Chainsaws, axes, pitchforks, gloves, extra gas. Whatever Manny thought we might need."

"I didn't see him at the house last night. How come?"

"Manny? He stayed at his house, the foreman's place. Just down that road there." Charlie thrust his chin out.

Jeff advised, "Hold your ears."

Looking at him strangely, Angel did as he said.

Charlie pushed a button and the truck roared to life.

251

Cautiously taking his hands away from his ears, Jeff crowed, "You did it! How in the Sam Hill... A while ago I thought it was just quieter because it was all the way across the yard."

Grinning across the girls, Charlie put the Deuce in gear and only had to raise his voice a bit. "Couldn't stand all the noise, so I modified it."

Angel looked from Jeff to Charlie. "This is quiet?"

Jeff grinned hugely. "Relatively speaking. Normally you can't hear yourself think if this thing's running."

Holding Jewel in her lap, Jennilee smiled and lazily stroked Jewel from the crown of her little head to the base of her tail.

Swinging the huge truck around, Charlie headed them down the drive.

The devastation at the house had been bad enough, but Angel's first glimpse of the main road had her rethinking her definition of destruction.

Covered in pinestraw and leaves, it looked like the too-old banana version of the Yellow Brick Road. The deep ditches full to the brim with water, thickly scummed with leaves and pinestraw and branches, dotted colorfully with miscellaneous McDonalds bags and stray couch cushions and empty beer cans and discarded cigarette packs made the road nearly indistinguishable from the surrounding landscape. Only Charlie's intimate knowledge of the area kept them between the invisible white lines, and even that almost wasn't enough in the alien, war zone looking landscape.

He drove slowly, going over and around debris when he could, stopping the truck while he and Jeff got out and chainsawed fallen trees that blocked the hidden pavement.

On a run that normally took fifteen minutes tops, two hours into their excursion they were little more than half way to town. Rounding the curve that preceded the Mill Pond, Charlie slowed the massive vehicle to less than a crawl.

All of them goggled at what lay in front of them, exchanged uneasy glances with each other, and resumed staring in disbelief.

Stared at the huge Mill Pond, contained at this end only by a small earthen dam minimally wider than the two lane country road that ran across the top of the berm. Normally separated from the water by a bare row of scraggly, mismatched pines and sweet gums and water oaks and a scant couple feet of bank, the water, usually two to three feet below the top of the bank now lapped inches from the white line. The tree trunks poked out of water like jagged teeth and the scrim of myrkle bushes and immature pines and cypress and river birch and huckleberries filling in the empty spaces between them swayed like seaweed in the rising liquid.

The bridge over the narrow spillway, barely even noticed in everyday traffic, now looked a frail bulwark spanning the rampaging waters. Churning a violent sulfur yellow, frothing like a rabid creature, the roaring water beat against the bottom of the bridge like an angry troll too long confined.

Worming out of Jennilee's lap into Charlie's so she could peer out the open window, Jewel leapt from there to the back of the seat where she prowled back and forth cat-like, panting and whining anxiously.

Jeff swallowed. "How big's the Mill Pond?"

Charlie sounded just as strained. "Somewhere around a hundred and twenty five acres."

"That's a lot of water, Charlie Brown."

"Yeah. Yeah it is."

"If it comes over..."

"Yeah. If. If it comes over and backwashes into the swamp, creates a roll, right there along the low side..."

"It's gonna wash the the road out but good."

Five sets of eyes stared solemnly at the hundred yards of asphalt, give or take, between them and the next curve on the far side of the dam, as perfectly banked as any NASCAR track. The high side in this case holding back not legions of glory hungry fans but unimaginable quantities of insatiable water.

Putting the Deuce in gear, Charlie eased them forward.

Hunkering close to the back of Jennilee's head, shivering, Jewel fell silent as all of them glanced instinctively out at the vast expanse of water looming to their right as they snailed across.

Charlie gave a humorless chuckle. "At least there aren't any trees down right here."

"If the worst happens, and someone comes around either curve..." Jeff shook his head.

Charlie finished grimly, "They'll never find the car, much less the occupants. I'll send Collins back with some dynamite and sawhorses. He can put the sawhorses across this end with road closed signs and stay on the other end with the dynamite. If worse comes to worst, he can blow the spillway deeper. If that doesn't work..."

Exchanging dark grimaces over the girls' heads, Charlie and Jeff dropped their gazes to the girls' hands, tightly clasped.

Upon reaching the far curve, Jewel gave a sharp bark and all of the humans blew out breath they hadn't realized they'd been holding.

Another hour of slow going, chainsawing and with the help of the two ton, pushing/pulling logs off the road, and they were almost to town.

Stopped, staring at yet another small bridge, this one well and truly submerged, not even the tops of the guardrails showing under the fast flowing water, Charlie drummed his thumbs on the steering wheel. The huge truck idled noisily beneath them, front tires dipped in the lapping water like a determined swimmer confronting dangerous rapids.

"We gotta. *I gotta.* You guys can get out and stay here." Not looking at the other three in the cab, Charlie stared grimly, thoughts of Grandy's house and Mr. Jubal and Miz Sadie and the rising water behind them at the Mill Pond roiling in his head.

Covering one of his hands with one of hers, Jennilee whispered, "Whither thou goest..."

Turning to her, bringing her hand to his lips, Charlie let go Jennilee's hand and cupped her head. Leaning in for a demanding kiss, Charlie rested his forehead against hers.

Jeff chimed in, "Not even, bro. We've been across this bridge before when it was covered in water. In that damn pickup of yours. In an aluminum skiff for crying out loud."

Angel gasped, "In a skiff. In your *truck*, Charlie? Are you *crazy*? It's not just the bridge. There's gotta be two football field's length of water covering the road. And it curves right here. How can you even..."

Putting a hand on her best friend's thigh, Jennilee consoled, "One football field. We've done this before. It's not nearly as bad as it looks. Charlie's just spooked because of the Mill Pond. The water's not near as bad here. It's swamp on both sides so the water has to spread out." Indicating the well and truly marooned houses on Charlie's side with a wave of her hand, Jennilee informed, "These yards always flood during a heavy rain."

Panic only just suppressed, Angel shook her curls. "Yeah, but... Why didn't they build the bridge and the road higher? This is ridiculous."

Covering Jennilee's hand with his own and giving both girls a comforting squeeze, linking the five of them even more, Jeff added cheerfully, "D.O.T. graded it like this on purpose. The bridge is higher, has to be to get over the creek. But when the water spills over like this, if the road's high as well, the water will never go down. This way it can get past the bridge faster and it's more likely the bridge won't get washed out."

Some unspoken agreement reached, with barely a shared glance the guys both reached for their window crank, returned the triangle windows to their proper places with a snap.

Jennilee shivered, once, and Angel waited for the explanation, thinking wryly that was the same kind of unvoiced communication that flowed between herself and her siblings on a regular basis.

Didn't have to wait long.

Giving it some gas and manhandling the willful Deuce right down the middle of the invisible road, cantankerous old truck arguing with primeval force, Charlie set them in motion. The big truck obliged, pushing water out of its way like a cowcatcher clearing tracks of recalcitrant bovines. While the water purled off to both sides, it also rose higher, occasional waves splashing over the hood. The movement jostled a log and assorted attached debris, the reeds and branches giving way like a poorly constructed raft.

Drenched in sweat, miserable in the jeans they'd insisted she wear,

Angel squirmed uncomfortably and grumbled to herself. Why did they care if the truck, old as it was, got wet inside? Wouldn't it be a little better with the windows down? Not that there was much difference in the inside and outside temperatures, but at least their movement created a semblance of breeze, stirring the thick, muggy air in useless whorls and eddies.

A thump interrupted her internal monologue and Angel looked up in time to see an enormous black shape slither out of the assorted flotsam, onto and across the hood, straight to the windshield. Opening its mouth wide so they all got an up close and personal view of the white interior and vicious fangs, the cottonmouth writhed and struck, clearly blaming the occupants for its current predicament.

Angel let out a short scream, the guys instinctively flinched back, Jewel barked ferociously. Further encouraged by the show of fear, enraged by the proximity of prey and confounded by the invisible barrier, the irascible reptile struck again and again, lifting the front half of its body and throwing itself at the glass.

A strangled, nearly inaudible gasp from Jennilee and all of them switched their riveted attention to her.

White to the gills, cold and clammy, Jennilee stared with single-minded absorption at the blunt snout, now bleeding from its ferocious attack.

Pushing aside her own fear, Angel threw her arms around Jennilee and buried Jennilee's face against her shoulder, crooning to Jennilee like she would a child having a nightmare.

Adding to the surreal sense of being caught in a nightmare as Charlie tersely piloted the lumbering vehicle through the murky water, Jeff began quoting, as if by rote, punctuated by the thudding strikes.

"Agkistrodon piscivorus, otherwise known as water moccasin, cottonmouth, and a variety of other names, related to copperheads and rattlesnakes, is North America's only venomous water snake, fully capable of delivering painful and potentially deadly bites. Typically 24-48 inches long, they can get bigger, with the record standing somewhere around 72 inches. The species is plagued by an undeserved reputation of aggressiveness."

Jeff sucked in a breath that exploded vehemently as he pounded a fist on the dash. *"Fucker!* I told him he was wrong, but would he listen? No! It'd be worth capturing that SOB and wrapping it up and leaving it on his doorstep. Harmless my ass."

Lifting her head, Angel snorted a laugh. "Jeff? Are you okay? I can only hold one of you at a time and I've kinda got my hands full."

Giving a low growl that morphed into a deep guffaw, Jeff explained. "I had this teacher... Stupid idiot..."

"As opposed to smart idiots?"

"Do you want me to tell you this story or not? As I was saying, Wisconsin. Dumbass was from Wisconsin."

"Ah. So we have a stupid idiot dumbass. From Wisconsin. Go on."

Cupping Angel's chin, Jeff twisted her face to meet his and kissed her quiet.

"Some highbrow fancy-pants herpetologist from Wisconsin was teaching a class on swamp forensics. You know, like if a body was found in..." At Angel's indrawn breath, Jeff dropped that tack. "Never mind. He quoted what I just said to you. I stood up and asked him if he'd ever seen a real moccasin, much less a swamp."

Shaking his head and staring regretfully at the disgruntled snake, still attempting to pierce the glass with its fangs and rip it away piece by piece to get to the tasty humans inside, Jeff snorted. "He told me he didn't have to see a cottonmouth to know people were just scared of snakes in general and made up horror stories about encounters."

"Really? So how do you propose to entrap this vastly misunderstood specimen?"

"The snake or the instructor?"

Angel burst into laughter as Jeff looked around the cab as if a solution along with an impervious container would magically appear. Blinked as they shuddered to a halt, having reached the far side of the bridge *and* shallower water.

Releasing his two-handed, white-knuckled grip on the over-size steering wheel, Charlie turned to Jennilee and wrapped his arms around her, practically pulling her into his lap.

Giving up on his insane attack, the moccasin slithered off the hood and splashed silently into the water.

~

ABANDONING THE TWO-TON, switching their work boots out for knee boots, the foursome sloshed their way through nearly knee deep tannin stained water down Jubal's and Sadie's long, narrow driveway.

"Love me some Harkers Island tennis shoes." Holding one white boot out of the murky yellow water and twisting his foot consideringly, hesitating before stepping over a downed tree, Jeff eyed the boots like they were haute couture.

Holding Jennilee's hand, Charlie glared at the offending greenery looming into them from both sides, heavy with moisture and broken branches. "Gonna have to get Mose and the side-boy and whack this mess back."

Struggling to keep up, boots and humidity and too many clothes conspiring against her, Angel huffed, "Why do y'all always speak in a foreign language? Can't you just use normal words?"

A faint snicker from Jennilee, the first sound she'd made since they crossed the bridge, had the other three sharing relieved glances.

"A side-boy is a...tractor with a bush-hog that can be turned sideways so you don't have to use a chainsaw or loppers to trim growth like this. The boots are called Harkers Island tennis shoes 'cause a lot of people around here wear these all the time, no matter what they're doing. Just like *normal* people wear tennis shoes."

"Huh. Okay. So I guess leaving your truck in the middle of the road isn't going to be a problem then, 'cause *normal* people are still hunkered down in their homes waiting for someone to tell them it's okay to be out and about." Angel's dry comment had the other three laughing like loons.

Rounding the last bend, the four stopped so fast they had to hold onto each other to keep from toppling over. A glistening, churning, mahogany colored ball the size of a bushel basket floated down the deep ditch.

Angel balked like a mule. "What the hell is that revolting thing, 'cause this normal person is about two seconds from running back down the driveway screaming. It looks like...it's alive."

Jeff dropped an arm around Angel and Jennilee squeezed her hand.

Charlie made a disgusted sound. "It is alive. It's a ball of fireants. The queen is protected in the middle."

"Not for long."

All of them started and jerked their gazes across the wide yard to the shadowed porch.

Rocking, Mr. Jubal raised his pipe to them, waving smoke around like a shaman. "I was jes' sittin' here debating how I'm gonna light 'em up."

Raising a hand to the older gentleman, Charlie called, "Gas can still in the shed?"

"If it h'ain't floated away."

Keeping an eye on the floating mass, Angel trailed in Jennilee's wake as she sloshed them closer to the porch-turned-island while the guys headed around back.

"Everything okay, Mr. Jubal?"

Giving her a nod, opting for answering verbally, knowing she needed the reassurance, Jubal used his word quota for the month. "No trees on the house. Sadie's in the kitchen. Pigs are still in their pen. Yep. Jes' fine, Jennilee. Jes' fine. Y'all?"

"Same. Lot of clean-up but nothing we can't handle. You and Miz Sadie leave this mess to us. I mean it! I don't want to find out the two of you have been out here…"

"Jennilee! As I live and breathe! I thought I heard your sweet voice! What in the world you doin' here, child? And Angel too!" Flapping a dishtowel as if it could disperse the heat, Miz Sadie waddled out onto the porch, screen door slapping shut behind her.

Stepping up, hugging Miz Sadie, Jennilee answered, "Checking on friends and neighbors. Grandy's place is next in line. Need anything?"

Bracing her hands on ample hips, Miz Sadie cocked her head. "Nothing but some air conditioning. Gettin' spoiled in my old age. Sure glad we left the screen doors up. Would be miserable 'thout them."

Jennilee nodded and hugged Mr. Jubal, straightened as Charlie and Jeff came back with supplies.

"What are they…" Angel trailed off.

Jennilee plopped down on the top step like she was taking her place on the bleachers and the game was about to start. "Watch."

Preemptively knocking the dottle out of his pipe into the water, watching it hiss out of existence, Mr. Jubal made sure there wasn't the faintest spark of an ember left in the bowl. Placing the extinguished pipe on the metal table beside him, standing it upright on the bowl, upending his drinking glass over the whole, he made sure there was no faintest trace of fire anywhere close to them.

Having rigged some kind of sprayer, Charlie proceeded to coat the ball with gas.

Directing her question to no one in particular, Angel asked, "Isn't this dangerous?"

When no one replied, Angel dropped beside Jennilee, answered herself, and kept watching. "Why, yes. Yes it is. Extremely dangerous."

Squeezing Angel's knee, Jennilee told her, "The guys know what they're doing."

"I sure hope so."

Writhing ball thoroughly coated, Charlie slowly backed off to stand adjacent to Jeff, both stationed behind massive live oaks quite a distance from the seething ball and farther yet from the porch. Waiting while Charlie disappeared with the gas can and then returned, using the wide trunks for shelter, the two of them shared a look.

Charlie nodded, Jeff tossed something, and the world lit with a *whump*.

A trail of fire reached almost to Charlie, the fumes from the gas tracking his movements through the humid air, licking at the tree trunk between him and the carnage.

The ball burnt and twisted, the very surface of the water lighting and trembling with the intense heat and the skim of gas, crisping ants until there was nothing left but black scum on the water.

Waiting until the last flicker of a spark winked out, the guys gingerly headed to the porch, taking care to go way out of their way just in case.

Angel clapped as they approached. Slow, distinct claps that conveyed anything but approval. "That was really something, but was it really necessary? Or were you boys just being boys and playing with fire? You do know what they say about boys who play with fire?"

Charlie and Jeff high-fived. Jeff smirked, "Playing, but don't worry. I never wet the bed."

Charlie added, "Same as with that snake we killed. If those ants had been out somewhere... This close to Mr. Jubal and Miz Sadie..."

Jennilee agreed softly, "That many fireants are fully capable of killing a human. Or Mr. Jubal's pigs."

"How..." Angel sounded disbelieving, still not sure if that had been necessary or play.

Jennilee thrust with her chin. "That ball was headed toward the house. If they came in, got on Mr. Jubal or Miz Sadie before they realized what was happening, or if they attacked Miz Sadies's hens or Mr. Jubal's hogs..."

Throwing her hands in the air, Angel groused, "Snakes. Hurricanes. Fireants. What's next? The Loch Ness monster? Big Foot?"

Dropping beside her and leaning back on his elbows, Jeff quipped cheerfully, "No Nessie. Alligators maybe, but..."

Punching his bicep, still more than half mad at him for the ridiculous—and to her, utterly unjustified—chance they'd taken, Angel snarled, "Don't even."

Jeff just looked at her and blinked.

"Oh, he...heck. You're serious, aren't you." Drawing her feet up and wrapping her arms around her knees, hunching into herself, Angel peered around the yard turned swamp and the surrounding woods nervously. "You let me walk all the way down this driveway and you knew..."

"I didn't say there were any here, just that it was possible."

Smacking his arm again, Angel shook her head. "You are impossible."

Giving the glider a push with her foot, Miz Sadie moved back and forth and ruminated, "My Daddy lost his best sow, only sow, to a gator. Back in '40, '41 mebbe. He tracked that gator down and kilt it in the swamp. Cut that lizard open and got the hog back."

Angel stared, wide-eyed. "You're teasing, right?"

Miz Sadie slanted a placid look in Angel's direction. "Folks then couldn't afford to be squeamish. That was our meat for the winter and the hams Daddy sold paid for the yearly pair of shoes all us kids got and piglets for next year, since we lost the sow."

Holding his hand out to Jennilee, Charlie tugged her up. "Sorry to cut the party short but we gotta go check on Grandy. If the road's clear enough, we'll head across town and hit Garner House next."

"If it's not?" Miz Sadie's eyes gleamed with worry for her only chick, even if said chick was well over six feet tall and built like a brick house. And former special forces to boot.

Charlie assured her, "If it's not, it will be. Don't y'all worry about a thing here. I'll have a crew come out ASAP."

Sloshing their way back to the truck, they clambered back in.

Wrinkling her nose at the residual smell of gas, Angel elbowed Jeff. "What was that thing you threw?"

Jeff snickered. "Something I picked up from my buddies at the FBI."

Angel hadn't quite forgiven him for the scare yet. "And you just happened to have one in your pocket?"

Acting all innocent, Jeff quirked a brow. "You might be surprised at what all I carry in my pockets."

Angel rolled her eyes. "How'd you know to get behind the trees? As if what you did wasn't inherently dangerous enough, why did the gas follow Charlie?"

Leaning forward enough to see past Jennilee, Charlie answered Angel. "Humid like this, you really have to be careful. The fumes don't dissipate, they layer, like smoke on a still morning. Comes up out of the chimney and drifts back down then floats along the ground. Gas fumes do the same thing and you can get hurt bad in a hurry if you're not careful."

Jeff chimed in. "If we'd stood right beside it and lit a match, you'd be taking us to the hospital right now. Or the morgue."

Both girls shuddered. Angel melted closer to Jennilee. "No thanks. I still think you've lost your mind. Plural."

Jeff joked, "I knew you thought I was a whiz-bang, but I didn't know you thought I was as smart as two people."

Angel's elbow connected with his ribs in a hard jab, drawing an *oof* from Jeff. "Jennilee, I don't know how you've managed to keep your sanity all these years, dealing with both these brainless goofballs by yourself."

Jennilee's soft laughter filled the truck and spilled out the once more open windows. "They might be goofballs, but they're my goofballs."

CHAPTER 24

*B*attling their way over, under, around, and through, they made their slow way to Grandy's. Finding her house intact and relatively unscathed, they wended their way deeper into town, stopping at the shop.

Getting on the shop CB, knowing his crews would be monitoring theirs and waiting for orders, Charlie touched base with everyone he could reach.

While he was involved with his project, the rest of them took advantage of the facilities. Jennilee pulled waters and sodas out of the break room frig and passed them around.

Listening to the strange sounding call signs and nicknames and codes, Angel frowned. "Why doesn't the two-ton have a CB?"

Jennilee shared a look with Jeff and shrugged. "Never needed it before. It will after this. Besides, they have a limited range."

Shivering and rubbing her arms, Angel looked around the gloomy room, everything indistinct blobs like sheet covered furniture in an empty house. "I hate the plywood on the windows. It makes me claustrophobic."

Jennilee soothed, "Me too. It's coming off soon. Other things are more important."

"Like…food."

Throwing her head back in laughter, brushing Angel's arm in passing, Jennilee patted Jeff's. "Headed that way now."

Peering through the gloom at Jennilee's retreating form, Angel asked, "Where's she going? Jeff? What's she gonna do? Rustle up some grubs and ants with a side salad of mixed leaves and bark with dirty water dressing?"

Pulling Angel close for a lingering kiss, Jeff surfaced but kept his forehead pressed to Angel's. "Nah. Charlie keeps emergency supplies here in case…"

Rubbing noses, Angel interrupted, "In case you show up?"

"Now you're catching on!"

Jennilee came back in a trice with potted meat, Saltines, Vienna sausages, and fruit cups.

"No beanie weenies? I'm disappointed, Jennilee. You know how much I love them!" Pulling her in for a hug, Jeff snickered and snagged a sleeve of crackers and several cans.

Jennilee shot back, "I'll buy you a case when the store opens back up."

Slipping up beside Jennilee, drawing her close, Charlie groused, "Buy your own damn beanie weenies, ingrate."

Snorting a laugh, Jeff retorted, "You owe me for the flash-bang, Charlie Brown. Eat some monkey peters and hush."

Rolling her eyes, Angel shot Jennilee a look and mouthed, *monkey peters?*

Smirking, offering some of the bounty to Charlie, Jennilee shook her head. "Enough, children. Finish your snacks so we can go check on Mose."

Popping open a can of Vienna sausages, alternating those with crackers, Charlie polished off several cans and then some tins of potted meat and a whole sleeve of crackers and washed it down with a can of peaches.

Jewel scampered back and forth between her humans, making sure she got her share.

Getting from A to B required a lot of tacking and side roads and chainsawing, but they eventually made it to Garner House.

Mose was nowhere to be found until Jewel started barking her head off. Following her noise around behind his shop, the crowd came to a standstill.

Looking like an old time bargeman, Mose stood atop a stack of lumber, slowly poling it across what used to be his side yard and was currently his side *lake*. Lifting a hand in acknowledgement, he went back to what he was doing, each shove bringing him closer.

"What is he... Why is he moving those boards that way?" Angel looked from Mose to Jeff. Getting no answer, she switched her gaze to Charlie and then Jennilee.

Indicating a couple upright poles in the water, Jennilee smiled serenely, like what Mose was doing was an everyday occurrence. "He's putting the stack back where it belongs."

"But...how? Those boards aren't even tied together or anything."

Draping an arm around Angel's shoulder, Jeff drawled, "Haven't you figured it out by now? This crowd is capable of doing stuff—magic stuff no one else would even attempt—and making it look easy-peasy."

Positioning the floating stack like he was berthing a barge, Mose drove the flounder gig he was poling with into the ground, pinning the boards in place between that and the poles already there.

Jumping down, splashing toward them, white teeth flashed, a quick smile lighting his dark face. "Feel like I should be singing *O Solo Mio* like one of those fancy gondoliers in Venice."

Spinning in place, yipping at his low rumble, Jewel bolted toward him and threw herself into the air, secure in the knowledge he'd catch her.

Curving his arm around her, tucking the little mutt against his chest like a furry football with legs, Mose grinned. "Guess if you're here that means everything's okay at your place and my folk's and Grandy's. How bad is it in town?"

All of them turning toward Mose's cottage, Charlie grimaced. "Took us better than six, no seven, hours to get here. Saw a lot of trees on roofs. Sent Collins to the Mill Pond with some sawhorses and dynamite."

"Runnin' over?"

"Lappin' the white line."

"Huh. D.O.T.'s not gonna like that."

Charlie squared his shoulders and shot Mose a saucy grin. "Gonna like it a whole lot less if that road washes out and takes some innocent with it. Blowin' the bridge is gonna cost a lot less than replacing the berm and the roadway *and* the bridge."

Mose snickered. "B'sides. How would you get to and from your place if the road washes out? Build a ramp and play Evil Knievel?" Throwing his head back, Mose laughed loud and long.

Jeff gleefully chipped in, "Probably a runway. Or a rocket launch pad. Or…"

Ignoring their jibes, Charlie continued. "Saw a few people startin' cleanup. Most are gonna want to make sure the storm's over before they really hit it hard and heavy. Much damage here?"

"…a hot air balloon. No, I know! A helo pad!"

Mose talked over Jeff's head, ignoring him like he would a yapping puppy. Or a mosquito. "Tree down on the gazebo and lost a couple limbs from that huge old live oak on the south side. Think I can make some real purdy…"

Jennilee's laughter rang like chimes at Mose's speculative tone. "With all the storm damage, I'm sure you'll have all the wood even you can use and I'm equally sure everything you make with it will be absolutely gorgeous!"

"…a giant slingshot thingy like at the Circle! Course, then you'd have to have a landing pad. A giant trampoline! Or…"

Sharing a grin with Mose at Jennilee's exuberance and Jeff's shenanigans, Charlie shook his head. "Power's gonna be out awhile. Saw plenty of poles snapped off and lines down and the transformers are probably covered in salt."

"…what about…"

Mose harrumphed. "Better for cleanup. Hard enough without worryin' about gettin' electrocuted on top of it."

"Speaking of cleanup, I bought an old sawmill. Think we should set it up here or at the house? If we do it here, it could impact the renters. If we do it at the house, gonna have to transport the finished product a lot farther for you to use it."

Jeff kept expounding, rubbing his hands together like a little kid on Christmas morning. "...mud trucks? Like those huge ones on TV? The ones with tires as big as a regular size car? If the road washes out, it's gonna take a long time for the swamp to dry up. You could have a mud bog and charge admission!"

"Hmm." Mose shifted Jewel and considered. "House. I don't mind transporting. I know you're not doing this just for me so what all's goin' on in that busy brain of yours?"

Giving Mose a cheeky grin, Charlie evaded a direct answer. "Need some raw lumber. Got a couple projects in mind and with all the downed trees, it's a good time to collect logs."

Switching from gleeful to depressed in a heartbeat, Jeff moped like Eeyore. "Road's gonna be out forever, 'cause the State will have to do surveys and consult engineers and CAMA's gonna get in on it and they'll probably discover some rare and almost extinct five toed purple spotted newt that only lives in ten square feet of land right in the middle of where the new bridge needs to go and..."

Clapping a hand over his mouth, Angel laughed. "Where do you come up with all this stuff? How can you even think that fast and that far out of the box? You crack me up."

"Anything to make you smile, darlin'." Swooping in, Jeff pulled Angel tight against his chest and kissed her soundly.

Looking Heavenward, Mose heaved a long suffering sigh. "Not you two too. Isn't one lovey-dovey googley-eyed couple around here enough? Cut out your tomfoolery. We got a lot of work needs doin'."

Jeff grinned sappily. "Two-too. Or is that tutu? We can name our first..."

Angel grinned back. "Dog? 'Cause if you're namin' a dog Tutu, I'm gonna have to get my brothers to take you out back and beat some sense into you."

Jeff batted his eyes. "I was thinking...our first child. Two-too would certainly be...original."

Angel braced herself in the circle of Jeff's arms and smirked. "You're gonna name our son Two-too? Or you gonna spell it T-u-t-u? Better than Sue, I guess."

Mose shook his head. "Huh. Darla-girl, you fit in with their nonsense like you were born to it. Bein' around y'all is like living with the Little Rascals."

Rounding the corner of Garner House stopped all the teasing.

"Thought you said *a couple limbs*. Holy moly!"

Shrugging at Jeff's outburst, Mose' eyes glittered with plans and his fingers itched to get the curves and twists dried and milled and planed and…

Hooking her arm through his, Jennilee leaned her head on Mose's bicep. "You thinking jewelry boxes and stuff?"

"Yeah. Little projects. Hard to get any lengths of wood out of those but the grain is beautiful and with all the knots and burls… Bowls, maybe. It turns beautifully even if it is hard as a rock."

Jennilee smiled, knowing each piece Mose created would be a one of a kind masterpiece. "Saw some large cedars down and a couple cypress and that huge maple on the corner of Albright Lane. The guys know to be on the lookout."

"Thank you, Jennilee. I could launch my own furniture company with all the wood your crews salvage for me."

Charlie dragged his eyes off the destruction long enough to meet Mose's eyes. "Better than seeing it all go to waste. Which is exactly what'll happen to whatever we don't grab up." Added casually, "Bought a commercial log chipper when I bought the saw mill."

"Charlie-boy, I can see the wheels turning. What's that for?"

"Yeah, Charlie. Why'd you buy a chipper?" Jeff quirked a brow. "Plannin' on doin away with someone?"

"You, if you name your kid after a ruffly pink skirt."

Jeff snorted a laugh and Angel snickered.

Eyeing the man-high pile of cut wood, Jennilee chided, "Mose, you better not have done all this by yourself."

"Will and Josh did most of it. I just told them where to cut."

"Speaking of… Where…"

The sound of a chainsaw ripped through the thick air, turning Jennilee's head and sending Jewel into spaz mode, trying to get down. Well used to her tactics, Mose clamped down.

"Answers that question." Changing direction, they tromped around the house as a group.

The flattened gazebo came into view, as well as Josh and Will.

Working hard, they had the demolished gazebo unearthed from the giant loblolly that had smashed it flatter than a fritter.

A huge pile of sap and needle covered limbs rivaled the mountain of sawn off chunks.

Jeff quipped cheerfully, "Ha! Looks like we got here just in time! Won't have to worry about picking up those pinecones anymore."

Watching both Marines struggle to roll the last log out of the way, Jennilee mused, "They used to use those pines for masts on sailing ships. Took a lot of mules and men and rope and tackle to get one of those suckers cut down and aboard a ship."

Nearing them, Charlie spoke. "Lookin' good, guys."

One hand braced on the cant hook, breathing hard, Josh swiped his forearm across his face and blinked the sweat out of his eyes. "This is insane. Like boot camp in Hell."

Charlie nodded. "First hurricane?"

Will, just as sweaty, covered in sawdust from head to toe, shook off a work glove and reached over to scratch Jewel behind the ears. "Last one, too, If I have any say in the matter."

Hooking his thumbs in his belt loops, Jeff rocked on his heels and grinned like a lunatic. "Gotta love NC weather. 'Specially when it's like working out in a sauna while wearing long underwear. The old red kind, scratchy wool with the flap in the back."

Angel burst out laughing. "*Where* do you come up with this stuff?"

Charlie offered, "If you guys are up for more, along with any of your buddies who want to work, I'll pay good wages. Looks like you've got a handle on it here. We're gonna head back to town shortly. Holler if you need anything. Use Mose's CB. Otherwise, I'll see you and any bodies you can scrounge at the office tomorrow morning bright and early."

Josh shook his head. "Looks like it's gonna be just us for a bit. We were on the shortwave earlier and it's bad inland. Rain on top of rain. Not gonna be any outside help coming for days, maybe a week. Power might be out longer than that."

Charlie shrugged. "We'll deal. See you." Wrapping an arm around Jennilee, sharing a look with her and Mose, Charlie voiced their approval of all the guys' hard work. "We appreciate everything y'all've done here. No rent for six months."

Josh and Will shared their own look, nodded. "Not why we helped, but we accept. Thank you."

Walking back to the two-ton, Jennilee sandwiched between Charlie and Mose, Jennilee looked up at Mose. "We'll stop back by your parents' and let them know you're fine."

Mose gave her a smile and a solemn nod.

"Ooh! I know! A trebuchet!" Jeff danced energetically from foot to foot.

"Are you still on that kick?" Angel shook her head and grinned. "A catapult is all well and good, but what are you gonna do about the landing?"

Pretending to deflate, Jeff let his shoulders drop and kicked at the ground. "Where's Timmy when I need him? He'd back me up."

Charlie shot a smirking glance at Jeff. "Don't worry. They'll figure it out...on the way down."

Jeff snapped his fingers and looked smug. "Parachutes!"

The whole crowd burst into laughter.

～

TWO DAYS LATER, streets and yards mostly cleared and everyone accounted for except Mrs. Murdoch's orange tabby, the Fearsome Foursome dropped in the shade of a huge live oak.

Stared wearily at the sandwiches and sodas Grandy was handing out.

Flopping backward in the grass, one bite out of the PBJ resting on her belly, Angel took a deep breath. Blinked once, twice.

"Annnndddd, she's out." Sandwich in each hand, Jeff ran an adoring gaze over his lady love, currently emitting a chorus of soft snores, and munched contentedly.

Jennilee snorted a laugh. "She deserves it. Told you guys to leave." Took a bite of her own sandwich and a swig of her Pepsi, half-choked on the sweet carbonation and thumped her fist on her chest. Coughed. "Worse comin'."

Sharing a worried glance, not quite sure if they'd heard her right but certain they hadn't mistaken that same off kilter tone that scared the crap out of them every time, Charlie and Jeff came to attention like a couple bird dogs on point.

"Jennilee-baby? What'd you say?

Looking into Charlie's eyes, Jennilee flashed him a tired smile. "I said, Angel deserves to rest. She's worked like a dog."

Shooting a quick look at the still sleeping Angel, Jeff prodded, "No, baby. After that."

Blinking slowly at Charlie and Jeff, Jennilee cocked her head. "That y'all should've left?" Grinned tiredly at Jeff. "Then we could've just ribbed you about what a slacker you are, leaving us to all this cleanup by ourselves."

"After that, Jennilee-sweet."

"Nothing I remember. I choked on my Pepsi." Shooting worried glances back and forth between the two guys, Jennilee sat up straighter, narrowed her eyes, and tightened her lips.

Slipping an arm around her, Charlie pulled Jennilee close and dropped a kiss on her head. "Shh, Jennilee-honey. We thought you said something after you coughed. It's okay."

Doing his part, Jeff held out a chocolate chip cookie. "Here. Try not to choke again."

Sharing another look over Jennilee's head as she slumped against Charlie and closed her eyes, both of them scanned the visible yard, whatever was haunting Jennilee invisible to their searching gazes.

A sorely needed nap for all of them, and they were back at it.

Hauling logs, running chainsaws, pulling rakes, wheelbarrowing load after load of limbs and debris.

Taking advantage of the quiet as the chainsaw Charlie was using sputtered into blessed silence, Jeff let his hands drop and wiggled his gloves off, backhanded the sweat off his brow and pulled the neck of his shirt over his face to get the rest of it.

Not bothering to shake off his own gloves, Charlie used an arm to windshield wiper his own face, spitting out wood chips and sawdust and making a face. Snagging a milk jug full of water, uncapping it,

Charlie twisted his wrist in a moonshiner's move and sucked water till the sides caved in.

Offered the jug to Jeff, who repeated the gesture. Looking past Charlie as he lowered the jug, Jeff thrust his chin. "Hey, bro. Think we got a problem."

A quick glance over his shoulder in the indicated direction and Charlie spat, "Oh, hell." Grabbing the walkie-talkie hanging on his belt, Charlie started machine gunning orders.

Curling his lip, Jeff emitted an earsplitting whistle, waved the girls over when they looked up.

Reaching them first, Angel took the jug and drank gratefully.

Not too far behind, Jennilee stepped up and took her turn.

While she was drinking, Angel rubbed her arms in resignation of whatever the latest crisis was and demanded, "What now?"

Jeff swallowed and thrust his chin in the direction of the river.

Tipping her head down, looking up at Jeff with dramatically wide eyes, Angel huffed, "And? All I see is the river. Looks like the tide's risin.'"

Jennilee shivered and shook her head. "Should be going out."

Darting wary glances at her three best friends, Angel sighed. "I can tell that's a bad thing. Why?"

Eyes locked on Charlie, pacing and talking, Jennilee replied, "All that flooding inland? It's heading this way."

"Flood? On top of a hurricane and all this..." Eyes huge in her face, Angel waved a hand. "This place is flat as a fritter! Where are you supposed to go in a flood?"

Jennilee burst into laughter, Jeff hooked an arm around Angel and drew her close.

"You are *so* picking up our ways! You're even starting to talk like us!" Giving Angel a wink, Jennilee headed toward Charlie. Slipped a hand in Charlie's back pocket and leaned against him.

Jeff soothed, "Easy, girl. You're just tired. It's not that bad. We'll have to take a few precautions, and Charlie's..." Angel's head slewed around so fast as the fire siren cranked up Jeff had to jerk out of the way or risk a bloody nose. "...already on it. Flat is good, gives the water more room to spread out instead of getting deeper, and the tide's going out. It'll take a lot of the flood with it."

"But..."

"Charlie's already prepared for this contingency. He's got a network in place, everybody with a CB or a shortwave will know within minutes and they'll spread the word. The lower lying areas will be evacuated first, and we'll work our way out from there."

Angel half-sniffled, then sniped, "Evacuated to where? The top of the water tower?"

Giving her a squeeze and rubbing her arm, Jeff shook his head. "Good view from there. Wanna climb up with me?" Snickered at Angel's vehement head shake. "Charlie's got somebody stationed on the fire tower. You can see for miles up there. This won't be like a flash flood, it'll be more like...that Johnny Cash song. You know, the one where the kid keeps asking his dad how high the water's getting."

Angel blinked, and threw an elbow. "Yeah, well that didn't work out worth a damn."

Acting as if he didn't even notice, Jeff retorted confidently, "He didn't have Charlie and Jennilee."

"So where are they going to stash the inhabitants of the whole town? The entire area?"

"The Ridge, I'd expect."

"How high do you think..."

"The Ridge is? The ridge the town's named after? High enough."

"Well, how high..."

Throwing back his head, Jeff laughed, just before swooping in for a kiss. "Now you sound like that kid in the song."

CHAPTER 25

*A*ngel eyed—what seemed to her—the slight rise in front of them skeptically. "This? This is what you call a ridge? It's a... speed bump! No, I take that back. I've driven over higher speed bumps than this!"

Jeff grinned, unrepentant. "Hey, you take what you can get. You saw what this county looked like when we flew over it."

"Yeah, but I thought... It was an optical illusion or something. It can't be as flat as it looked!"

Jeff shot Angel another crooked grin. "Flat? You think this is flat? I'll take you up around Plymouth sometime. Mattamuskeet. That whole area's flat as a brand new Rand-McNally. Why, compared to them, we're positively mountainous."

Cupping her cheek, Jeff touched foreheads. Stroking his thumb along Angel's cheekbone, he murmured, "Stop worrying so much. Charlie always has a contingency plan. Always."

"You think everyone will come?"

Jeff shook his head. "Nah. Same's with the hurricane. Some people won't leave their homes, for whatever reason. Fear, arrogance, too old, too infirm, too stubborn, pets or critters they won't leave behind, you name it. Like any other place, there are those here who'll take advantage of this to help themselves to what doesn't belong to them, and most everyone around here learned to shoot when they were knee high to a grasshopper. No mercy for thieves."

Per Charlie's plan, people began trickling in, parking their vehicles as far up the slope as they could, some carrying tents and supplies, some with nothing more than the clothes on their backs.

Charlie directed some of those with FWD right on up to the top of the long ridge in case they were needed later, many more vehicles scattered out like confetti after a parade across the flatness of the town park.

Her back to his front, Jennilee watched from the security of Charlie's arms, Jeff and Angel right beside them, same pose. "I know this place doesn't look very high, Angel. It's the highest place in the county, believe it or not. Used to be covered in Chinquapin oaks. They all died, I think, from the same blight that killed all the Dutch Elms. Don't know that for sure, just a guess, but it seems like probable cause. They all disappeared before my time. Some of the older folks say…"

Charlie's walkie-talkie squawked. Listening for a moment, he clicked and began firing orders again. He came up for air to find Angel staring at him.

"How come you're in charge of this…mess, Charlie? Shouldn't there be someone…older…more…" Angel waved a hand.

Shooting Angel a movie star grin, Charlie shrugged. "Nobody else stepped up, and I've been talking about this for a long time with Chief Mac and the mayor. Everybody else is sitting around wringing their hands and waiting for someone to take charge. I did."

Angel frowned. "But what about stuff like…the Mill pond? You can't just…"

Jeff snorted a laugh. "Charlie's motto is, *Better to ask forgiveness than permission.* The State highway department can't do anything without fifteen letters of permission from the higher ups in Raleigh. By the time they get off their duffs and decided to make a move, we'll all be dust and long gone."

Putting his hands in his pockets and rocking on his heels, Jeff put on his best butter wouldn't melt in his mouth face. "Not that we know anything about it, but I heard someone dug the race out at the Mill pond, and the creek on the swamp side of the bridge so more water can escape. The road and the berm are safe and possibly no one will notice, or they'll think the water carved it out."

Angel squalled. "What about people like Miz Sadie and Mr. Jubal? They're already practically underwater."

Jennilee smiled. "There's underwater, and there's underwater."

Angel just shook her head.

"Can't get any wetter, Angel. Just deeper. Mr. Jubal and Miz Sadie live in a swampy area, so while they're squishy, it won't get much deeper where they are. The water just spreads out more. We won't be able to get to them except with a boat for a day or two, but they'll be fine. Their place didn't flood during Hazel. It'll be okay now."

Snuggling Angel, Jeff soothed. "Water's a funny thing. Especially in a flat area like this. It's not like in the foothills, or the mountains where the floods are defined by creek beds and valleys. Some places here that you think would be prime candidates won't be touched. Others that you think would never flood will be the first to go under and the last to dry out."

Charlie, walkie-talkie in hand and silent for the now, picked up Jeff's tale. "We've spent years talking to the older folks. Gathering their memories of Hazel and Camille and the unnamed storms before that. We've marked all the highest points the water reached and planned accordingly. See the white line painted on that pole over there?"

Waiting until Angel followed his pointing to the desired target, Charlie nodded. "That right there? Is as high as the water's ever gotten up this hill. We'll be fine."

"This...blip can in no way, shape, or form be construed as a *hill*. What about Grandy's? And your house? And.."

Charlie shrugged, unconcerned. "If we got a ten foot storm surge, I'd worry. This? Aggravation only, and we'll have to clean up again."

At Angel's defeated look, Jennilee moved close and enveloped her best friend in a tight hug. Charlie moved in behind Jennilee.

Her words muffled by Jennilee's shoulder, Angel muttered, "I feel like the filling in a sandwich."

Jeff made smacking noises and buried his face in Angel's neck. "Ummm. Liverwurst."

Angel shot an elbow into Jeff's side and made a Timmy-worthy gagging sound.

Patting Angel's shoulder, Jennilee assured, "Don't fret so, Angel. Think of this as an adventure."

Jeff left off his pretend eating. "Stories to tell your grandkids!"

Shooting an elbow back into his ribs again, Angel snickered. "Can we get past the kids first before you start worrying about grandkids?" Rounding on Charlie, Angel jabbed a finger in his direction to the tune of hearty laughter. "Just where did you get your hands on dynamite?"

Giving her an innocent look, Charlie just grinned.

Angel watched, and helped when she could, as a miniature tent city sprung up like toadstools. Heavy white canvas tents Charlie had commandeered from somewhere, along with port-a-potties.

Throwing out orders like a benign general herding recalcitrant civilians, Charlie got more accomplished in half an hour than anyone else could've in two days.

Tables and chairs, food tents, medic tent, you name it. Each area properly defined.

And through it all, Jennilee weaving her magic as she wove in and out and between, never getting more than a few steps from Charlie and yet seeming to be everywhere at once, showing absolutely no favoritism.

Treating the people who'd snubbed and derided her her whole life the same way she treated people who'd championed her.

Watching her calmly and efficiently settle yet another family with nothing but smiles and assurances—a family Angel knew for a fact had never had a kind word to speak about Jennilee— Angel shook her head.

Grumbled to Jeff, "How can she be so magnanimous? If that was me, I'd let them drown."

Trying to keep a straight face, Jeff lost the battle. "No you wouldn't, but you wouldn't be nice to them. Jennilee can't help it. They can be as ugly as they want. She won't say a word and she won't fight back. Let them say something against you or me or Heaven forbid, Charlie, and it's game over. Tiger unleashed."

~

THE FLOW OF PEOPLE, the last few showing up in boats, slowed and then trickled to a halt.

All of them gathered on the side of the hill, fearfully watching the steadily rising water.

Well before dark, Charlie and some of the bigger guys wrestled lights, like the huge drum ones on the side of the football field for after dark games, into place and pointed them down the hill.

The buzzing of hungry insects was drowned out by the surge of generators. Big generators. On trailers.

Jeff watched, and helped where he could. Marveled anew at Charlie's ability to organize.

Charlie'd obviously had all this in place, waiting for his word to go, go, go.

Had just plunked his weary ass in a lawn chair when strident tones caught his attention.

"Chief Mac, I demand…"

Heaving himself to his feet, Jeff muttered, "Here we go."

Reaching out and snagging his hand Angel inquired tiredly, "Just where are you going? Thought we were gonna sit for a bit."

"Gotta go play backup. Be back as soon as I can."

Insinuating himself into the knot of people crowded around Charlie and Chief Mac, prepared to take action if necessary, Jeff listened and decided.

Decided that for the most part, people were just plain stupidly ungrateful. Not to mention clueless. Had to wonder why Charlie and Jennilee spent so much time and effort trying to help these unappreciative sots.

Had his faith in humanity utterly restored and knew exactly why Charlie and Jennilee behaved as they did when little ol' Miz Eudora Whitley toddled over. Ninety if she was a day, and probably closer to a hundred, she looked like the love child of a woods sprite and a pencil troll.

Frail as a figurine made of spun sugar, her birdlike body was topped with a shock of wispy white hair that stood out around her head like a halo of dandelion fluff.

For all her fragile looks, she was a tough old bird.

Her cultured Southern drawl wrapped around them, warm as the humid night, as redolent with sultry sounds as magnolia blossoms perfuming the air. "Charlie, Jennilee, Ah just wanted to say think you for all your hard work. Why, Ah just don't know what Ah'd've done if you all hadn't come along when you did! And such a nice tent! With an air mattress! Have you evah?! Ah haven't camped out since Ah was a little girl, and this is evah so much better. Our tent was a moldy, mildewy leftover from WWI that leaked like a sieve and our mattress was a couple Army surplus blankets. The dark green wool ones with a black stripe on the end. Itched worse than a bad case of bedbugs. Those nice boys...confound it! What are their names? Bill and Ted? No, George and..."

Holding one of her birdlike claws in his hand, Charlie inserted gently, "Will and Josh?"

Bobbing her head like a dunking bird on the rim of a glass, Miz Eudora agreed. "That's it! Will and Josh! Such fine young gentlemen. They helped me into the boat—so exciting! Why Ah haven't had a heart flutter like that since my Harold, rest his soul, proposed. We had the nicest ride over here and then when we got here that tall handsome one—Will—let me talk on his radio. We used to do that during the second war to report planes and such. It was so scary and exciting at the same time. The blackouts were horrible, you couldn't let a light shine at night for anything. Germans, don't you know, and submarines off the coast and torpedoes and all manner of terrible things. Bodies washing up on the beach, and rationing, and substitutes for every-thing. That's where my recipe for mayonnaise cake came from. Mayon-naise is just eggs and oil, and unless you had chickens you could only get a few eggs now and then. And Ah'm rambling. Ah truly just wanted to say thank you."

Face wreathed in smiles, Jennilee shook her head. "No need for thank yous. It's our pleasure. And we'd love to listen to more of your ramblings, any time." Hooking her arm through Miz Eudora's and guiding the elder to a prime seat in a cushy chair, Jennilee knelt down beside her.

"In fact, Charlie and I were just talking about having a story telling night at Del's Diner. We'd love to hear your tales, and with your permission, record them. History is so important, and we're losing more and more every day. Maybe we could gather some of your recipes and have a cookbook made up."

Satisfied that the world was once again righted—with a lot of help from Charlie and Jennilee—Jeff headed back to his chair beside Angel. Dropped into it gratefully.

Rolling her head to look at him, almost asleep herself, Angel smiled. "Everything okay?"

Leaning over her and planting a big wet one on her lips, almost tipping his chair over, Jeff grinned. "Right as rain. Thank you."

Licking her lips like she was trying to decide if she wanted more right this instant, Angel asked, "Thank you for what?"

"For being you. For not being an ungrateful you know what. For loving me. For…"

Laughing, Angel held up a hand to slow his spiel. "Are you buttering me up for some adventure? 'Cause I'm exhausted. Can it wait?"

"No further adventures are scheduled at this time. I just wanted to say thank you. I don't want to be one of *those* people."

"The ones who take every single thing for granted and complain about everything?"

Giving Angel another kiss, even longer than the first one, Jeff pulled back a smidge. "You get me. I love that about you. I've watched Charlie and Jennilee for so long, I kinda despaired of ever finding someone who understood me like they do, and like they do each other. But you… You get me."

Coming out of her chair and plopping in Jeff's lap, Angel wrapped her arms around his neck. "I've got you, alright. Thank you, as well. You're such a good man, Jeff."

A coldly snobby voice rang out from somewhere in the crowd. "Will you two behave? There are kids here, for goodness sake!"

Staying right where she was, Angel threw back her head and laughed.

Jeff's hollered, "Thank you for reminding us!" had Angel nearly going into convulsions she was laughing so hard.

Still gasping, Angel snorted, "If we're the worst example the kids around here have, then they'll be fine."

Kissing the tip of her nose, Jeff nodded. "Much better to see two people in love than an old sourpuss with a stick up their...butt."

Not budging in the least, Angel settled more comfortably. "Timmy on his way?"

"Yep. With our dearly beloved in tow."

"Think he'll ever learn?"

"We'll see. Doubt if Charlie will ever forgive him."

"What about Jennilee? Never mind. Stupid question."

Timmy appeared beside them, bouncing like Tigger, BOF looking decidedly worse for wear.

"Can you please watch Timmy for a minute? I have to go to the bathroom and..." BOF shot a desperate look in Charlie's direction. "I have orders not to let the little twerp out of my sight."

When Jeff didn't say anything, Angel nodded. "Sure. Timmy, hop up in this chair and we'll see what we can spot in the water. Maybe an alligator? What do you think?"

Watching Timmy clamber over the side and into the lawn chair like it was a new type of jungle gym, extremely glad Jeff's hold was keeping the chair from tipping, Angel smiled sweetly at BOF. "I have six brothers."

Message received, BOF blanched and headed for the latrines at a run.

"Now why did you go and ruin all my fun, love?" Jeff nuzzled a giggle out of Angel and garnered another reprimanding holler for his trouble.

"You're here and my brothers aren't. Just letting BOF know I won't put up with any of his shenanigans."

Squirming in his chair like the seat was full of fireants and sand-spurs, Timmy pointed out at the steadily rising and roiling water. "Look! I think that's an alligator! Or maybe a crocodile!"

"Hey, Timmy-boy. Know how you tell the difference?" Jeff grinned wickedly at Angel.

Leaning perilously close, thoroughly intent on the answer, Timmy paid no attention as Jeff once more caught the boy's chair before it crashed. "How? How can you tell them apart?"

Angel shook her head and covered her face with her hand, trying to hold the laughter in and not ruin Jeff's joke.

Totally serious, putting a hand to the side of his mouth like he was trying to keep anyone else from horning in on their conversation, Jeff divulged in a mock whisper, "Well, Timmy, it's like this. Alligators say see you later and crocodiles say after while."

Timmy blinked, and lit up like a lightbulb.

Infectious laughter trailed behind the little monkey as he took off, looking for his next unsuspecting victim.

Hot on Timmy's heels, BOF tore by, throwing out a thank you as he streaked past Jeff and Angel.

Jeff watched them out of sight. "Huh. Whaddya know. Might be hope for BOF after all."

THE KIDS PLAYED as children are wont to do, running and screaming between and around the tents and gear, the adults sat around grim-faced and watched the water creeping up the slope.

Watched things bobbing in the water.

Alligators would've been a good thing.

A quick assembly line style sandwich and chip meal, and they all went back to watching, broken only by the arrival of various skiffs and johnboats bringing a last few rescues to dry land, all carrying harrowing tales of daring rescues from homes that had suddenly become islands or ponds and more than a few from rooftops.

Charlie ordered the lights turned on and they continued to watch as darkness fell. Some of the cars, the ones parked furthest out, disappeared a bit at a time, the way a chocolate chip cookie dunked in milk dissolves. A little around the edges, and then more, and more and then... Gone.

Played out, the younger kids finally gave out and gave up, most of them dropping in the grass close to their parents or in their parents' laps.

Plunked securely in their respective men's laps, Jennilee and Angel watched along with the other adults.

Half asleep, Angel bolted upright as something bobbed into the light and was gone. "Was that a…"

Jennilee answered sleepily, "A coffin? Yep."

"But…"

"That's why in so many of the older cemeteries around here the graves have cement comforters over them. Flood like this and coffins pop right out of the ground like it's Judgement Day."

Jeff snorted a laugh. "Cement comforter. Never heard 'em called that, but it makes sense. All those dead folks are tucked in, all warm and snuggled beneath their cement comforters."

Angel aimed a half-hearted swat in Jeff's direction. "I wondered, and now I know. Wish I didn't."

Eye shine had Charlie directing his handheld Q-Beam away from the water to the water's edge.

Angel gasped, "Is that a…"

Leaning around her, Jeff affirmed, "Looks like a black bear and a couple deer and…"

Angel squeaked quietly, not wanting to spook everyone, "A bear?!"

Charlie assured her, "They won't bother us unless we bother them. They're just trying to get out of the water, same as we are."

"Hey, Charlie."

All four looked over their shoulders as Josh called out.

Crouching beside Charlie, Josh nodded a greeting. "We've been on the shortwave nonstop. Got a call you might be interested in. Fella name of Marty Robbins. Says he'd like to speak with you."

Giving an obviously exhausted—and quite comfortable right where she was—Jennilee a quick kiss, eyeing the tent a few feet away and in a direct line of sight, Charlie nodded. Stood in a smooth move and deposited Jennilee in the chair he'd just vacated. "Be right back, Jennilee-love."

Crowding into the tent where Josh and Will had set up the short-wave equipment, Charlie took Will's seat and toggled the mic.

"Mr. Marty! Good to hear from you! You fare alright?"

"Hello, Charlie my lad! Fine, just fine. Y'all?"

"Let you know more in the light of day. Sittin' on the remains of an ancient sand dune watching the water rise right now."

"Give me the word and I'll have choppers in there to evac you pronto."

"Water seems to've stopped rising but we appreciate the offer. We're well set for supplies and shelter. Got everyone out of town that we thought was in danger and moved everything we could to higher ground. Worst problem right now is boredom and trying to keep some of these fools from killing themselves with stupid stunts."

Marty chuckled, "Always gotta be one macho lunkhead in every squad."

Charlie snorted a laugh. "What do you get when you mix a bunch of rednecks with a hurricane?"

"Exactly. Won't keep you. Just wanted to check and happened to come across your Marine buddy while I was scanning the dial. Stay safe, and call me if you need to. Tell that pretty little wife of yours hello for me."

"Will do. We'll keep you posted, Mr. Marty. Thanks again."

"Over and out."

Dancing in place like he was the one that'd taught Timmy everything he knew, Jeff jabbed Charlie. "Told you! For every bad thing…"

A LONG NIGHT became a longer day as the water receded by slow increments, and the clouds of mosquitoes multiplied exponentially until they sounded as loud as the chainsaws that'd been running nonstop the last few days.

Jeff muttered long and loud to anyone who'd listen about Minnesota, stupid idiot, mosquitoes only come out at dawn and dusk, like to stake him out here at high noon, teach him a thing or two about snakes and insects.

Having recruited the johnboats and tied them off to one side of the hill, Charlie and Jeff and a few select others made scheduled runs about town until the water became too shallow to do so, bringing back a few more bedraggled stragglers.

Second verse, same as the first, disaster and then cleanup.

The water level kept dropping until it was low enough most of the crowd dispersed.

The ones who could.

Those whose vehicles had gone underwater hung around at loose ends, along with those who'd been flooded out of their homes.

Jeff watched Charlie talking with each remaining family, knew he was extending more than sympathy as the tent city folded up and disappeared with all the efficacy of Ringling Brothers dismantling and heading for the next show.

Angel nudged Jeff. "What's he doing?"

Jeff snorted a laugh. "Probably setting them up with long term, low or no interest housing loans in exchange for cleaning the moat or scrubbing the tower walls. He won't give the money to them, 'cause when you hand out too much stuff for free, people take it for granted. Get greedy and demand more. Make them work for it and they appreciate it a whole lot."

"What moat?"

Jeff cracked up at Timmy's question. "The one around Charlie's castle, squirt."

Timmy's eyes lit and his face scrunched up, hopeful but not sure if Jeff was pulling his leg or not. "Charlie owns a castle? Where? I wanna go see it."

Angel rolled her eyes and remarked dryly, "The same one where he keeps his trebuchet."

"A trebu...what?"

Jeff's whole body lit up and he slung an arm around Timmy's shoulders. "You and I need to talk, Dennis. I've got an idea you're gonna love."

Timmy's lip poked out. "I don't know why y'all keep calling me Dennis. I don't get in *that* much trouble."

Giving the pouting boy a conspiratorial squeeze, Jeff confided, "It's not how much trouble you get in, it's how much mayhem you cause."

Timmy perked up. "Mayhem? What's that?"

Angel stifled a giggle, barely, as Jeff twined his fingers with hers and the three of them strolled in Charlie's and Jennilee's direction.

CHAPTER 26

*I*nside the tractor trailer parked in the hardware store's gravel lot, tossing crates of water and bleach and other staples, amongst the noise and heat and harsh breathing of the crew launching and receiving and launching the heavy items again and again, conga line style, they could hear the caterwauling.

"I deserve my fair share! Just because Charlie and that tramp he's married to think they're in charge... They're not gonna short me! I *demand* my fair share! I'll call the governor if I have to. The President!"

Straightening slowly, Charlie exchanged a grim look with Jeff. As one they moved to the opening, everyone else scattering out of their way, the barely cooler than Hades air outside the confined space a welcome relief after the stifling hell of being inside.

Bare chested, sweat running in rivers from the tops of their sweat-matted heads, down their torsos and soaking their jeans all the way to their tighty-whities, Charlie and Jeff stood side by side looking out. Not that they didn't already know who was doing the screech owl imitation.

Jabbing a finger at Charlie, Bertha kept right on squealing like a stuck pig.

Surveying the otherwise peaceful and suddenly utterly silent crowd, Charlie turned frigid eyes on Bertha. She never changed. Not her attitude, nor her manner of dress. Charlie had to wonder if the old bat had looked at a fashion magazine in the last...hundred years. Or even a mirror.

Still wearing the same cat-eye glasses and beehive bouffant she'd been sporting for the last couple-three decades, Bertha's expression never changed any more than her hairstyle. Looking like a piranha sucking on a lemon, her pruned up mouth and buck teeth didn't know how to say anything unless it was ugly.

"What is it you think you deserve, Bertha?"

"The same thing everyone else here is getting!"

Charlie swept an arm out. "You mean all these people standing politely in line and waiting their turns? The ones helping load stuff? The ones sharing like reasoning, *reasonable* adult human beings?"

Looking around smugly, trying to garner righteous support, Bertha spouted, "You can't keep all this for yourself! It's not right!"

"Bertha, what the hell are you talking about?"

"You! You and that Jezebel..."

The rest of her words were lost as a sharp lift of Charlie's chin sent Jeff and Tim scrambling.

Jeff to jump down and Tim scrounging for a clipboard.

Charlie's blazing eyes swept over the unwitting audience like a beam from Cape Lookout lighthouse on a dark and stormy night. Promising not safety, but retribution.

Completely on board, without a word spoken the crowd parted like the Red Sea, leaving a clear path from the tractor trailer to Bertha.

Framed in the open doorway like a portrait of a vengeful god, the carefully haphazard tumbles of supplies behind him the epitome of chaos, feet braced wide and arms crossed, sweat slick muscles gleaming, Charlie watched Bertha heading toward him like a tidal wave in a flowered housecoat.

"I want that generator, and water, and enough food... And I need..."

Jeff loaded each item onto a handcart as she pointed them out, Tim scribbling furiously all the while.

Watching Jeff like a vulture eyeing fresh roadkill, Bertha ordered,

"Load them in my car." Giving Charlie one last withering glare and a haughty sniff, Bertha turned to leave, completely oblivious to the angry murmurs coming from the crowd.

"Bertha."

A sudden, arctic silence as Charlie's voice rang out, loud and clear.

Hands on her hips, Bertha gathered herself to lambaste him.

The look on Charlie's face froze her words in her throat.

"You're forgetting something."

Bertha looked around, completely puzzled. Everyone there could see her ticking through items in her head, trying to decide what else she wanted. Not needed. Coveted.

Her house wasn't missing so much as a single shingle tab, and it had been well away from the flooding. Didn't even have a tree down in her yard.

Snapping out a hand to Tim in what was practically a sideways salute, Charlie took what Tim handed him without taking his eyes off Bertha.

Nose in the air, Bertha huffed, "Why, no. I don't believe I've forgotten a thing. Unless you want to send one of your minions to my house to unload it." Beady eyes shifting to Jeff, already planning what else she could coerce his well-muscled frame into doing while he was at her house, Bertha shook her head.

Not asking Bertha at all, Charlie voiced, "Tim?"

"No, I don't want a cripple..."

Answering Charlie, Tim's reply cut Bertha off mid-whine. "Upwards of nine hundred dollars."

Incensed, face turning red as everyone stared at her, Bertha stammered, "Nine hundred dollars? For unloading a few supplies? That's outrageous!"

Charlie shook his head like the slow tolling of a bell. "My guys are too valuable for such a menial task."

"Then what? What are you talking about?"

Perusing the paper he held, Charlie's eyes, cold as any shark's, fastened back on Bertha's. "That's how much it's gonna cost you if you want all the stuff Jeff's already loaded up for you."

Face going red, then white, then a nasty shade of green, Bertha screeched, "You can't charge me! That's illegal! You can't..."

Chief Mac stepped up to bat. "That's where you'd be wrong, Bertha."

"You! I should've known you'd stick up for this thief! You always have, no matter what crime he and that...witch commit."

Uniform shirt filthy and torn, sweat rings under his pits and arrowing down his chest, deep circles under his eyes, one hand resting on his cuffs, Mac huffed a laugh. A cold and weary sound. "You and your kind never give up, do you."

"Give up? What are you talking about? I'm trying to get some justice here, justice you obviously aren't going to see served."

Swiping a hand through his sweat-soaked hair, Mac heaved a sigh. Before he could answer, a voice in the crowd called out, "Injustice is more like it, Bertha."

As oblivious to the blatant sarcasm as she'd been to the previous mutterings, nodding her head, Bertha crowed, "See! Other people want what they deserve as well. I'm not the only one."

Snapping his cuffs free of his belt loop, way more in tune with the crowd's sentiments, Mac grinned. "Be more than happy to oblige. Charlie, you got any rope?"

Nodding again, Bertha looked around smugly just before a frown flitted across her piscine features.

Twirling the cuffs, Mac informed Charlie, "Only got the one set with me and they've got Bertha's name all over them."

"'Bout time," came from more than one throat.

Bertha's smugness turned to furious indignation. "Me? Why would you need to arrest me?"

"Too many charges to count. Bertha, you have the right..."

Her screeches rang like the cries of angry gulls. "It's against the law to hoard supplies in a disaster situation! You can't pick and choose who to dispense them to. It's..."

Charlie's quiet rebuttal cut her off in mid-screech. "I can if I bought them."

"Liar! The Red Cross or the National Guard brought those here. You're just being..."

Mac strolled a few steps closer, still twirling the cuffs. "Bertha. Do you see any Red Cross vans? Or National Guard uniforms?"

Looking around, mouth gaping like a front end loader with the bucket down, Bertha took in the jeans and shorts and T shirts, the young and old and middle aged. Civilians one and all.

Stopping in front of her, Mac informed her, "We can do this one of two ways. You leave right now, and we'll call it temporary insanity caused by heat and the hurricane."

Closing her mouth with a snap, Bertha drew herself up indignantly.

Another twirl of the cuffs and Mac added, "Or we can do this the hard way. You open your yap one more time—just once more—and I will cuff you and haul you off and lock you up for the duration. Your choice."

Bertha's eyes swept the crowd, a touch of fear showing through as she finally took in the fact they were not on her side.

"Not a dime, Bertha. Charlie hasn't charged anyone a single dime. Until you, and anything he charges you would never be enough."

"He..."

Bertha's yelp was drowned out by clapping and whistling as Mac spun her, snapped the cuffs on, and read Bertha her rights.

"Simon! Take our friend here to the hoosegow."

Mac's chief deputy, materializing at Mac's elbow like he'd popped out of a bottle and grinning fit to be tied, Simon led a dumbfounded Bertha through the crowd to the tune of *about time* and *finally* and *throw away the key.*

Striding amid a lot of backslapping and congratulatory remarks to where Charlie stood, arms crossed and face like a thundercloud, Mac clasped Charlie's proffered hand. Hefting himself up with Charlie's help and taking a stance beside Charlie, Chief Mac peered into the trailer, cast a glance over the milling crowd.

"Where's Jennilee?"

Charlie made a rude sound. "You actually think I'd let her..." Shaking his head, giving a full body shake like a wet dog, Charlie made a renewed attempt at being civil. "Let me start over, first by thanking you. That was well done and I—we—certainly appreciate it."

Slanting Charlie a grin, Mac nodded. "Way overdue, but you're welcome. She's pushed my last button."

Taking a deep breath, and then another and another, Charlie tucked his temper away. Mac didn't deserve to be lambasted, just because he was close and available. "Jennilee and Grandy and Miz Sadie are busting their asses preparing meals. They're all at the Diner, and I'm glad of it. Had Jennilee been here..." Charlie swallowed hard.

Mac clapped him on the shoulder.

Struggling for words, Charlie blew out a breath.

Agilely hopping up beside them, Jeff interjected cheerfully, "You'd probably have been arresting Charlie Bear instead of Bertha-cow. She pushed his last button and got on his last nerve a looonnnnggg time ago."

MORE THAN A FEW days and a lotta back breaking work later, major roads semi-open once again, Jeff looked from Charlie to Jennilee. Gave a regretful glance around their superb kitchen. "I gotta go, guys. Duty calls." Jeff fidgeted, miserable. Torn.

Jennilee agreed instantly, with no trace of censure or sarcasm, only admiration. "Of course you do. Shoo."

Ribbing Jeff, Charlie mocked, "Sure. Leave us with all this mess. You'll do anything to get out of work." Eyes locking with Jeff's, silent communication flowed between the guys. Whatever was drawing Jeff away had to do with Charlie's and Jennilee's mom's.

Automatically opening her mouth to defend Jeff, Angel caught the look that rocketed between the two men and bit her lip.

"Jennilee, I hate to leave you with all this cleanup. I promised to help..."

Cupping Jeff's face tenderly, Jennilee smiled. Shook her head. "Don't be silly. You have helped, tremendously, and you didn't win all those accolades and awards and sweat your way through two years of specialized schooling to help us clean up storm debris. You go help whomever needs you more. That's what you're going to school for. It's what you were born to do."

Clasping her shoulders, Jeff pulled Jennilee close for a smacking kiss on the cheek and hugged her tight. Resting his forehead against hers, Jeff murmured, "Thanks for always being my best cheerleader. For always believing in me."

"Forever and always, Jeff. You know that."

Holding Jennilee tight with one arm, Jeff opened the other for Charlie. Stepping close, Charlie thumped Jeff on the back, slipped his other arm around Jennilee. Throat tight, Charlie growled, "Forever and always tryin' to move in on my girl, more like."

Laughter burst from the three of them and Charlie moved closer to Jennilee, leaving a space open.

Angel was right there to fill it as the foursome gave each other what comfort they could.

They could all pretend, shelter Jennilee as much as possible, but she knew as well as they did exactly why Jeff had to leave.

Heaving a sigh, Angel hugged them tight. "I gotta get going as well, guys. Hate to leave you to this mess."

"You're better off leaving at the same time as Jeff, and we won't worry about you so much that way. Roads are likely to still be in bad shape. Leave your little car here and take one of ours. Take the jeep. In fact, best thing you can do is ride to Virginia with Jeff on his Harley and then head home from there. 70 Highway's likely to be closed around Kinston. The Neuse river is probably still over the banks all along that stretch."

Snickering, Angel shook her head. "There you go again with the strange words."

Jennilee laughed back. "Yep. Mr. Donnie's always said 70 Highway. Picked it up from him. Stay safe and hurry back, y'all."

Arms around each other, Angel kept pace with Jeff as he headed upstairs to pack Jeff's duffel with the bare necessities.

Pausing as they reached her doorway, Angel muttered, "Now I know what life is like in a war zone."

Pulling her close and pressing his lips to the top of her head, Jeff agreed. "Yeah. Not so much the fighting, but the sense of... Being out of time. You get so used to the war zone, you forget there's a real world out there that's concerned with far more than getting trees off roofs and no power and..."

Tightening her arm around his waist, Angel smirked. "No regular meal times?"

A snicker of his own followed by a shout of laughter and Jeff replied, "Well, with your background in catering and restaurant-ing, you shouldn't have any trouble keeping up with my eating habits."

Sobering, Angel wondered aloud, "If we're both gone, who's gonna watch Jennilee while Charlie's working his ass off?"

Jeff shrugged nonchalantly, as certain sure as if he'd borrowed Jennilee's future-duper ViewMaster. "Someone will turn up."

CHAPTER 27

"*B*en Adair."

Staring at the calloused palm being held out to her, Jennilee followed the burly arm up to the sturdy face. A vague memory stirred murkily, tried to assert itself, but between her exhaustion from grueling post hurricane cleanup and just plain life, she couldn't pin it down.

"Do I know you?" A sneaking suspicion that she did in fact know him, and that Charlie had a huge hand in whatever this military-ish/guard-ish man wanted from her, flared into being.

Charlie interrupted a little too cheerfully, "You may not remember, Jennilee, but we met Ben at the Kinston Bluejays game. I told him if he ever needed a job to look us up. He did, and here he is."

Jennilee crossed her arms and cocked her head, not buying it for a minute. There was only one reason she wouldn't remember the stranger and that reason had a lot to do with her meltdown after the confrontation with BOF. "Un huh. What's the going rate for babysitters nowadays?"

Ben had the good grace to look sheepish.

Charlie just grinned. "What? Ben needs a job and we had an opening."

Drumming her fingers on her bicep, Jennilee regarded the two co-conspirators with equal aggravation. "Mr…"

"Adair. Ben, please." Charlie'd said Jennilee was sharp as a tack, and that she'd balk at having him around. His new boss hadn't been lying. *Think, Ben!* He needed to come up with something brilliant or he was going to lose this job before he started.

"I hardly think…"

"Ma'am, please." Jennilee's eyebrows shot up and Ben immediately switched directions. "Miz Myers, I need this job." *Brilliant, Ben. Just brilliant.*

Jennilee sighed. "Jennilee, Ben. I don't suppose there's any way I can talk the two of you out of this."

Draping an arm around her shoulders, Charlie sobered. "Nope. It's this or we leave. Go to the mountains for awhile. Or the Grand Canyon. We've always wanted to see that. Take a world tour by hot air balloon. Your decision."

"Fine."

Ben eased back a couple steps at her tone. He recognized a pissed off female when he heard one. The two of them were going to have to work this out. Besides, Charlie'd said if Jennilee pitched too much of a hell-spell, there was plenty of other work available.

Turning so he faced her, Charlie said softly, "Jennilee-honey. No need to get pissy. I'm worried about you and I want to take care of you. I can't do the work I need to right now if I'm worried to death about letting you out of my sight."

Jennilee snapped, "Don't make me sound like a two year old who needs a nap."

Adding a sexy undertone to his answer, Charlie enthused, "Ooh. A nap. We could so do that."

"Don't make me laugh. I'm trying to be mad at you."

"You can be mad all you want as long as you're safe."

"Charlie…" Dropping her head on his chest, Jennilee melted into his hard frame as Charlie's arms came round her. "What set you off this time?"

He considered lying, for just a heartbeat. "A couple times…" Took a deep breath, considered not saying anything. Nope, Jennilee needed to know. To be on her guard. "I know how much you hate being protected. A couple times, and Jeff and Angel were right there, you... Went somewhere. Said something in a scary tone and had no memory of it afterward. Warnings. Warnings I'm hellbent on heeding. I can't lose you, Jennilee-love. I can't."

Pulling back, Jennilee searched Charlie's beloved face, stared into his eyes. A face she knew better than her own, eyes dearer to her than anything. "What? You're saying I... What? Had a seizure or something?"

Charlie shook his head. "Not a...seizure. More like...an out of body experience. You told us it was going to get bad. Then you said really bad, and then worse. We thought—hoped—it was the hurricane, and then the flood. But I've got this feeling of dread hanging over me and I can't shake it. Please don't fuss about Ben. I've been going out of my mind, and with Jeff and Angel leaving this morning... Please, Jennilee."

Throwing her arms around his waist and squeezing tight, Jennilee conceded defeat. She couldn't bear for Charlie to be so upset.

"I want you to start carrying a weapon with you. Everywhere. I'm serious, Jennilee."

Lifting her head, looking around at all the people suddenly overly interested in their work and not the spectacle the two of them were making, Jennilee made a face. "How many others know about my protection plan?"

Cupping her face, Charlie tried and failed to hide his wince. "Everyone in town knows how much I obsess about you. Just... promise me you won't go anywhere alone. Stay in sight of people you know you can trust. If something feels off to you, holler bloody murder."

Looking around him to Ben, pointedly ignoring the spatting couple, Jennilee called out, "You can come back now, Ben. I promise not to bite your head off." Watching him stride back, bearing precise, eyes sweeping constantly, Jennilee blew out a breath. "How long were you in the military?"

"Just a short stint, ma'am. Figured out quick that wasn't the life for me."

"The ma'am stuff needs to go, right now, or we're going to have a major problem."

"Charlie!" The urgent call came from the other side of the street, making all their heads turn. Jennilee waved to Chief Mac, not her usual exuberant wave but a more subtle chop that let him know she knew about his part in this fiasco.

"Go, Charlie. My babysitter and I are headed to the Diner with a load of…"

Kissing her fiercely, Charlie admonished, "Stay close to Ben. There's a handgun in the truck. And a holster."

Jennilee grumbled, "Brave man trusting me with a gun right now."

Already crossing the street, Charlie threw over his shoulder, "Guns. Shotgun in the back window rack."

Shooting a look at Ben, Jennilee got a nod in return. "Just so you know, Ben, I am capable of defending myself."

"So I've been told. You do what you've gotta do, and let me worry about defending you."

Sighing resolutely, Jennilee headed for the truck. Slanting a look at Ben, she winged a brow.

He made a go ahead motion. "You drive. I don't have a clue where we're going."

Stopping mid-word, Charlie turned at the sound of Jennilee's laughter.

"So you guys have been feeding how many people since the hurricane?" Staying out of the way, Ben watched in amazement as women-folk bustled here and there in the hot, crowded kitchen.

Shrugging, Jennilee looked around distractedly. "I have no idea. We kept the coolers at the Red and White going with one of our big generators. Mr. Ralph donated all the food in them to Grandy and we've been feeding whoever shows up. The generators here kept all our food cold, but even with what Mr. Ralph gave us we ran out pretty quick. Charlie had a semi truck trailer full of canned stuff and staples. Not steaks and baked potatoes, but we've kept all the workers fed and a great many of the displaced. The Salvation Army took care of the ones sheltering at the school."

"Charlie had…" Shaking his head, Ben tried again. "Why?"

Jennilee looked at Ben as if the answer should be self evident. "Because he's Charlie."

What seemed days later, Ben corralled Jennilee in a corner of the kitchen, big body in the way, arms spread wide.

Looking up, blinking like a stupefied bovine confronted with a determined cowboy seated on an expert cutting horse, Jennilee drew herself up. "Move, Ben. You're in my way."

"I am. Gonna stand right here until you sit down and eat."

Looking past him, Jennilee shook her head. "Got too much to do."

Seeming to follow Jennilee's train of thought, Ben answered in a patently false John Wayne accent. "Listen up, little lady. You are not getting me fired on my first day. Sit. Eat."

Narrowing her eyes at him, Jennilee drew in a breath that exploded out in a weary laugh. "Yessir, Mr. Babysitter. Five minutes."

"Half an hour."

"This is not a negotiation. I've got stuff to do."

"You're right." Pulling out a chair at the small table put there for the express use of the kitchen staff, Ben waited politely. Stubbornly.

Jennilee looked at him, looked at the chair. "You sound like you agree with me, but why do I get the feeling you're not?"

"There is no negotiating. You are going to sit, and you are going to eat." Ben jabbed a finger in the chair's direction. "You are going to sit here, while you're eating, for more than five minutes. At least half an hour." Ben smiled winsomely. Implacably.

Fisting her hands at her temples, Jennilee dropped into the proffered chair. Grimaced at the scarred table until a plate appeared in her vision, making her tummy growl. Stared. Tried to remember the last time she'd sat, much less eaten. Gave in and picked up her fork.

Sighed. She was just being stubborn. She was tired and she did need food. There was just so much to do… So much that needed doing…

Took a bite and chewed thoughtfully.

Keeping his feet, watching the woman in front of him as warily as if he thought she'd bolt at any second, Ben saw the instant she capitulated. Charlie'd said she was stubborn as a mule, and he hadn't lied.

Jennilee waved her fork at the empty seat across from her. "Sit, Ben. I'm getting a crick in my neck. Feel like you're a buzzard, waiting for me to keel over. Sit."

"Yes, ma..." Pulling out a chair, Ben craftily placed it in Jennilee's way, trapping her in the corner. She couldn't get out, couldn't get past him without slithering out of her chair and crawling under the table.

A couple more bites, a long draught of Miz Sadie's sweet tea that went down like blessed nectar, and Jennilee looked at Ben. Studied him until he wanted to squirm like he'd squirmed as a kid in the principal's office for some prank he—might or might not have—committed. Holding still, he waited her out.

Surprising the heck out of him, she cocked her head. "Thank you. For whatever you did at the ballgame. It's all kinda...muzzy."

Ben laughed out loud. That was so not what he'd been expecting to hear from her. "Charlie and Jeff did most all the work. I was just... cleanup. And referee."

"Well, whatever you think you did or didn't, you musta impressed Charlie. He only recruits the best." Another swallow of tea, and Jennilee finished smugly, "For babysitters."

Ben's laughter boomed out, and if he'd had any doubts about his job description, they evaporated. Whatever Charlie wanted him to do for this spitfire in front of him, he would. Figured that description fit all the men in this town he'd met and seen keeping an eye on Jennilee. The town doctor, the chief of police, a lawyer... Not to mention the man himself, and Mose. Tim. Will and Josh. No matter how hard they were working, no matter what they were doing, they watched her like Miss Prissy watching her lone chick with a whole den of foxes and another of weasels circling round.

Less than five minutes later, plate clean as a whistle, Ben watched as Jennilee finished her tea, took a deep breath, and leaned her head against the wall. Blinked once, twice, and...

Grandy sighed as she dropped her hand on Ben's shoulder and squeezed lightly. "She's out. Thank you for that, Ben. She'll stay that way for a bit. Let me get you something to eat."

Looking up at Miz Del, catching the look of love on her tired face, Ben nodded. "She always go out like that?"

Shaking her head, Grandy sighed. "If you can get her to sit, yes. She's like a little kid. She goes and goes and goes, protests she's not tired at all, and boom!"

~

SHADOWING Jennilee for the rest of that day and the next and the next, Ben had to agree. Shoot, just watching Jennilee buzz around like a hummingbird on speed wore him out, and he wasn't even working like she was. Kinda felt bad about not helping when there was so much that needed doing, but Charlie's orders had been explicit.

Ben was not to do anything except keep an eye on Jennilee. Period. Not to take his eyes off her for a second. Ben's job was…Jennilee.

Watching her flit from task to task, Ben mentally replayed his most important conversation with Charlie over and over.

When Charlie'd explained what he expected, Ben had looked at him, puzzled. "With all these eyes on her, why do you need me? If this is just a make-work job, give me something else to do. I'm not too proud to do manual labor."

Charlie had snickered, and sobered, almost in the same breath. "I don't need you right now for that. Got enough hands on deck to get the work done. What I need is someone to keep an eye on Jennilee. Someone she can't sweet-talk or bamboozle or circumvent. She's angelic and devious and determined, not to mention lethally quick. Anyone here will, at some point and through no fault of their own, let her distract them, and…poof! She's gone, doing something she's got no business doing. You're exactly the man I need for the job. You're used to keeping an eye out for trouble, and you've got enough experience to back it up. Even if I hadn't read your resume, you impressed me at the stadium and your talents were being wasted there. Kinda glad what's her name made you so miserable and you reached out to me."

Miserable wasn't the half of it, and Ben was more than glad Charlie had backed him and not the—self—esteemed Mrs. Smythe-Wharton.

Ben and Jennilee had quickly fallen into a routine. She drove wherever she needed to go and he rode shotgun. That way he could keep an eye out.

Not that he had any idea what he was supposed to be looking out for. Charlie had shown him pictures of Butch, and Sylvia, and Celie, and a few choice others, but Ben hadn't seen hide nor hair of any of them helping with the massive, ongoing amounts of hard labor. Not that he thought they would. Just from the sneer in Charlie's tone Ben could tell none of that crowd would be caught dead near anything resembling work.

Meanwhile, Jennilee buzzed about like a pollen-laden honeybee, picking up more here and there and leaving little bits of herself and the load she was carrying everywhere she touched down.

THE POWER FLICKERED, and everyone in the shadowy dining room instantly stopped what they were doing and stared up at the light fixtures…as if their concentrated vision would help it stay on.

It flickered on and off for a good forty-five minutes, before finally settling on *on*.

A tired cheer went up, and Jennilee's crew got right back to work, serving meals and refilling glasses.

Noticing quite a few of the menfolk—here for a quick lunch before they headed back out to the salt mines—conferring in one of the farthest corners, Ben's head came up and stayed up.

Seeing where his gaze was focused, Jennilee snickered. "Pay no attention to the men behind the curtain."

"I got that, Dorothy."

"She never said that, but whatever. They're just seeing who won the pool."

"What pool?"

Jennilee laughed outright. "Why, how long the power was gonna be off. Or when it was gonna come back on, whichever way you want to look at it."

Thrusting his chin in their direction, backs to the room and huddled up like a herd of cows at a feed station, Ben winged a brow.

"That?" Jennilee snorted and grinned. "Most of them are fine, upstanding men, with a lot of deacons and a few preachers thrown in for good measure, and their wives make up a great portion of the choirs and do-gooders and preacher's wives around here."

A matching grin spread across Ben's features. "Gotcha. How much you reckon it's worth to them?"

"They'll deny, deny, deny they ever placed ary a bet, but it's a good thing to keep in mind when you need something done."

"Why, Jennilee! Blackmail? I'd'a never expected that from you."

"I prefer to think of it as... A gentle nudge in the right direction."

"Meaning, the direction you want them to go in."

"Absolutely!"

"Speaking of which, you said we had somewhere to go?"

Sweeping the filled to capacity dining room with a practiced eye, Jennilee nodded. "Give it...half an hour and most of the crowd will be gone. Enough for the regular staff to handle it."

An hour later, after Ben had penned Jennilee in the kitchen corner long enough to sit down and eat, they were on their way.

Jennilee had given him the stink-eye the first few times he insisted on her taking a thirty minute break, insisting she had too much to do to stop for that long. Now, it was more the token protest of an exhausted little kid facing imminent nap-time, heavy-eyed and blankie in hand.

Watching several of the busboys carry loaded coolers of boxed meals to Jennilee's Crown Vic, trying to keep Jennilee from helping, Ben asked, "How come y'all had the lights on in the kitchen and not the rest of the restaurant?"

Jennilee shrugged. "The generators would handle it, but... With no idea how long the power was going to be off and how much longer the fuel would last, we'd rather supply power to the kitchen so we can see what we're doing and the fans are sorely needed. The stoves are gas, so no problem there. Consider the dining room...ambiance. Normally people pay considerable extra for that kind of atmosphere."

"I noticed there aren't many paying customers."

Another shrug and, "Doesn't matter. There's a basket by the door for donations, and we do ask that the customers leave a tip for the waitstaff if they can. Some of the crowd has been helping out here. Carrying in supplies, taking out the trash, washing dishes. Not really fair of us to charge when a great deal of the food was donated. Besides, a great many of these people are devastated. Homeless, for the most part and all of them are in a great deal of shock. Charlie and I have the means to help."

Getting in and buckling up, giving Jewel, already sprawled in the middle of the front seat, a belly rub, Ben shook his head. "I'll just be glad to get the AC back."

"You and me both!"

"So why don't you run it in your car when we're delivering meals?"

A wry look crossed Jennilee's face. "Better if we don't. You get used to the heat, and it doesn't bother you so much. Keep going in and out and it makes it worse."

"If you say so."

Jennilee scoffed, "City boy." Slanted Ben a look and burst into laughter. "Just picking. Crowd around here's gotten soft. We grew up without air, for the most part, and survived just fine. Wouldn't be without it now for love nor money. We've gotten spoiled. Especially at night. It's miserable trying to sleep around here with no AC. If you leave the windows open, the gnats and mosquitoes will eat you alive, no matter how good your screens are." Pausing thoughtfully for a moment, Jennilee mused, "I'm not convinced those dratted no-see-ums can't worm through glass. Not sure how anything so small can have such big teeth. If the nasty little suckers were any bigger, it'd be like being ravaged by a T-rex."

Jennilee laughed again, some memory obviously tickling her funny bone. "Charlie and I were in the last class at high school to pick our classes by which ones had AC."

"Seriously? No AC at school?"

"Nope. None on the buses either. We survived."

"Amazing what you learn to live with when you don't know any better."

Jennilee went quiet, like Ben had touched a nerve. "Yeah. Yeah it is."

Silence for awhile after that save for the hum of tires on pavement, not even a radio station to turn up since they were mostly all still out of commission.

On a long winding stretch of a narrow old two lane in the middle of nowhere, nearly to their last delivery, Jennilee rounded a blind curve. A huge oak lay astraddle the road.

Taking in the situation at a glance, she yanked the wheel hard to the right, stomped the brakes, and came to a sliding stop.

CHAPTER 28

*S*urveying the work they'd accomplished, noting what had yet to be done, Charlie called out, "That's it, guys. Same Bat time, same Bat channel tomorrow. Great job, y'all. We're getting there."

Taking in the lengthening shadows and the encroaching darkness, Charlie dusted his hands off. Placed them in the small of his back and stretched backwards, listened to his spine snap-crackle-pop. He was so looking forward to a cool shower and a meal and his wife.

Mostly his wife. He could live without the other two, but he needed Jennilee like he needed air.

Speaking of which…

Normally right there working beside him, since they'd been working separately, Jennilee had honed an uncanny sense for when he was going to call quitting time and usually showed up within moments, as if his call to dismiss summoned her out of thin air.

As the others called their goodnights and headed for their vehicles and their own versions of bliss, Charlie's head came up alertly when Mac pulled up. Everyone else stopped to see what the latest crisis was going to be.

Opening his door and stepping out, one arm braced on the door and one on the roof, Mac's face was grim. "Charlie. You seen Jennilee?"

The ball of dread, the same one Charlie'd gotten in his stomach every stinkin' time Jennilee'd gone back to her aunt's house through the gap in the hedge, grew teeth. The very same one that'd been roiling around for awhile now.

"Chief?" Charlie had gone pale beneath his tan, the one word he could get out sounding tinny and far away.

"Not trying to scare you, Charlie, but… Jennilee and Ben took off to make food deliveries. No one's seen them since and they're not answering the CB, just like you're not answering yours. Been trying to get ahold of you ever since the crowd alerted me. Figured you were just busy and didn't hear us. I'd'a been here sooner but I was all the way on the other side of the county checking on an elderly relative that hasn't been seen since…" Shook his head. "Simon and a couple other people already traced their route. No sign of them. Any chance she deviated?"

Charlie tried to swallow. Felt like there was a Chinese Chestnut seed-ball stuck in his throat, all those prickly parts digging in. He must've already swallowed a bushel of them, because his insides were shredding with every beat of his heart.

Without another word, Charlie turned away from Mac and strode toward the command tent pitched close by. A couple beats behind, Mac ducked inside in time to hear Charlie cursing roundly. Watched him twist a dial, flip a switch and throw out a command. "*Now*, Mr. Marty. Right now. She's gone missing and I need your friends yesterday."

Waiting till Charlie finished his terse conversation on the short-wave, Mac crossed his arms. "Charlie. What the hell have you called down on us?"

"Hell. You got that part right. You might not need to know. Go home, Mac. Scratch that, you don't need to know. Just stay out of the way."

"Not going anywhere until you answer me."

"Mr. Marty's ex military. He has…connections."

"To what? The A Team?"

Charlie snorted a humorless laugh. "Pretty much. I've had a bad feeling for awhile now. This has been building up, coming to a head. It stops now, and I'm giving you fair warning: Whatever Mr. Marty's friends need to do to rectify this, if anyone even thinks to prosecute, I will spend every penny I have on the best lawyers in the world."

"Charlie, you can't…"

"Oh, yes I can. And I will. I will get my Jennilee back, and the guilty parties will pay. If they suffer, so much the better."

"Charlie, you don't know…"

Charlie leveled an unapologetic look at a man he'd known and respected all his life, a man who might think a great deal less of Charlie after this. A man whose opinion mattered a great deal to Charlie. Normally. "Mac. I do know. Jennilee's my world, and we both know she'd never disappear without something being wrong. Why do you think I hired Ben? He's not just some security guard at the stadium. He might've taken that job because he was between jobs and needed the money, but his resume is impressive. Mr. Marty's friends will be here in a couple hours, maybe less. He said they're in Raleigh and they have air support."

"Not planning any bombing or strafing runs, are they?"

"If that's what they need to do." Charlie shrugged. "I couldn't care less if they change the geography of the whole county."

Mac considered. Charlie'd given him fair warning. Gave his tacit approval. "The crowd coming in on your airstrip?"

"Yeah. Mr. Marty knows about it and said he'd tell them. We discussed all this weeks ago."

"Do you want to know sort of where Jennilee disappeared? We've pinned down her last delivery and we know where she was heading next."

"If we know, so does anyone who wants to harm her. If you'd like to go…round up a few of the usual suspects, I can tell you where they most likely are."

Mac's eyebrows shot up.

"I've had people on Butch since… What?" As Mac's eyebrows got closer to his hairline, Charlie amended with a shrug, "Well, need to know, and all that. Celie's temporarily AWOL but I've got people on that. Sylvia's shacked up with Butch. That old single-wide out on Pine-tree Ridge Road with all the junkers on blocks in the yard. The one that looks like it should've been condemned a hundred years ago. The one that makes a roach motel look palatable."

"Charlie, you know that kind of surveillance is bordering on illegal. Hell, no kind of about it—it *is* illegal."

"Ask me if I care. Jennilee's…" Charlie choked on another one of those damn Chestnut balls. Wondered if hacking like a cat with a hairball would dislodge it. "Whatever's happened to my love more than justifies my unorthodox methods and my paranoia."

"Well. Let's make a couple passes around—just in case—before we head out to your place and shoo the cows off your runway."

Charlie and Mac stepped out of the tent.

A solid wall of coldly furious men met them, standing in a half circle, Mose and Tim in the forefront.

Mose growled, "What do you want us to do, Charlie?"

"I guess y'all heard. I've got help on the way, but until they get here…"

Floodlights on and lighting the grass runway, Charlie watched as several small twin engine planes, barely more than dark noises against the darker night sky, came in low over the pines and set down in a precision maneuver. Watched the men disembark and head his way with the bearing and demeanor of well seasoned soldiers.

The tallest man, one Mr. Marty had told Charlie was the leader of this band of merry men, made Charlie glad he wasn't the object being pursued. Even though Mr. Marty'd said Mason was about the same age as Charlie, that was one scary son of a bitch striding closer like he owned the world, like he'd burn you to ash if you thought to disagree. Flicking a knowing glance over the planes and the gear, Charlie figured maybe he did, was certain sure he not only could but would.

Mr. Marty had said Mason Salisbury was ugly.

Ugly didn't do the man justice.

Terrifying, more like.

And yet, right now, he was the most beautiful sight Charlie'd ever seen.

Wouldn't have cared if the whole crew stepped out of a spaceship with their ray guns and probes.

Noticing the man who took point—not Mason—Charlie made a spur of the moment decision.

Giving the front man a nod, holding his hand out, Charlie moved forward and introduced himself, *not* to the man in the forefront.

Keeping direct eye contact, Charlie said fervently, "Mr. Salisbury. I am so pleased to meet you, and your men. You come highly recommended. I can't thank you enough, and I'll pay whatever you ask. You have my word."

Nearly seven feet tall, Mason looked like a walking gargoyle. Lumpy, misshapen features, deep-set, almond shaped eyes like a jungle cat's, and enough muscle and weapons to put G.I. Joe to shame. Eyes that broadcast pain and retribution like twin beams from Cape Lookout lighthouse. Scary eyes.

Shaking off his uncomfortableness with Charlie's directness when he'd much rather have remained in the background, Mason rumbled, "Evenin'. We wouldn't be here if we hadn't wanted to come, no matter who recommended us. Or how much money you have." Mason's voice flowed around them like honeyed whiskey. "You need to brief myself and my team, and then go back to your home."

Eyes straying to the one anomaly, a boy-child, Charlie gave a curt nod. "I assumed as much. I'd like to introduce you to the Chief of Police for our town, Mac Williams. He's agreed to…your presence and whatever you have to do."

Giving Mac a nod, Mason rolled his shoulders, eager to get to it. "Charlie, I don't need, or want, your money. Marty's bragged about you to Tex till your ears should be burning. Keep it and use it for good, like you've been doing. Let us take care of exterminating the vermin. It's what we do."

"Whatever you need that I can supply, all you have to do is ask. Our home is at your disposal. We've got plenty of rooms ready for you."

Mason took a deep breath and nodded. He and his men didn't

always get such a warm welcome and he could be wrong, but Charlie didn't seem the type to change his mind once he'd made it. "Much appreciated."

Gesturing toward the barn and the vehicles parked around it, Charlie said, "Right this way. Just tell me what you need and I will make it happen. I've already got a fleet of vans and pickup trucks here. They're at your disposal for as long as you need them."

Inside the hangar, poring over maps a few moments later, Mac tapped a spot. "This is where it happened. There are two trees down here, ones that were deliberately cut and not ones the hurricane took down. There are tire squalls on the road, between where the trees were felled, and the trees have since been pulled off the road. If we hadn't been looking so hard, with all the downed trees along the roadsides around here, we'd never have noticed the anomaly. The perps and victims are long gone, so I forbid anyone from tromping around out there. It was full dark by the time we…"

"No sign of the bodyguard?"

Clenching his fists, Charlie shook his head. "No sign of anything. Not Jennilee, not Ben, not Jennilee's car, not her little dog, Jewel. Mason… You have to find her. She's my heart. Them. Find them." Took a deep breath, held it. "When you get her back, we need to talk about longterm bodyguards. Mr. Marty said you would know who. I want only the best. 24/7/365."

Mac chuckled, startling Mason and crew. "Jennilee's gonna hate that."

Sharing a long look, Charlie and Mason shrugged at the same time.

Charlie swallowed, hard. Stiffened his spine, more determined than ever. "We've eliminated a few suspects, but that doesn't mean they weren't involved. It just means…"

Mason finished, "…they had help and alibis."

Mac laughed outright and clapped Charlie on the shoulder as he surveyed the motley crew gathered around one of the scariest men he'd ever met, and not just on account of his looks. "Yep. Y'all are gonna fit in here just perfect."

"Mason. My mom disappeared years ago. A friend of ours recently found her body when he was out metal detecting. Jennilee's mom was brutally murdered about the same time my mom vanished. We think—in fact, I'm positive—there's a connection." Handing Mason a folder, Charlie locked eyes with Mason again. "Here's a picture of Jennilee, and the most viable suspects are in there."

Flipping through, handing the extensive bios to the man beside him, obviously Mason's second and almost as scary as Mason, Charlie watched their expressionless faces like Jewel watching her humans eat. Age-wise not much older than Charlie, the two in front of him had worlds more experience. And that wasn't even taking into consideration the boy lurking around the edges, fiddling non-stop with equipment.

The terror threatening to overwhelm Charlie reared its ugly head and battered mercilessly. "You don't think Jennilee has a chance, do you."

"Hey. Don't panic on us now. You've held it together. Let us do our job. Not belittling your fears, but at least she's still in-country."

Those few words held a world of bitter knowledge.

"Mason." Charlie took a deep breath. "I've got people everywhere keeping eyes on Jennilee, and CBs everywhere. We keep in touch, always. The one at the job site today… Someone changed the channel."

That nugget upped the stakes. Had the CB been turned off, it would've alerted them instantly to something wrong.

"Who had access?"

Charlie shook his head, furious at himself. "I dropped the ball. Didn't think about someone in our camp stabbing us in the back like that. Tons of people in and out all day. Could be upwards of a hundred or more." Stiffened and spat, "It won't happen again. I'll post a guard. No one will get close to our communication equipment without a presidential decree and the army to back it up."

Mac snorted a laugh. "Yep. Charlie's such a slacker. Can you believe he overlooked something? Not like he's been doing anything the last couple weeks except sitting around on his keister. Or his whole life for that matter."

Mason snickered at Mac's jibe. "Go get some sleep. That's an order. Jennilee's gonna need you bright eyed and bushy tailed."

Looking like he wanted to punch something or someone, Charlie protested, "I need to do...something."

"You did. You called us." Taking in Charlie's tense features, the rings under his eyes, and the cuts and calluses and blisters on his hands, giving Mac a pointed look, Mason tipped his head in a *get him out of here* gesture.

CHAPTER 29

*T*ires squalling, both sets of eyes followed the massive trunk to the side of the road and realized it had been deliberately felled.

Palming his weapon, Ben hissed, "Get us out of here, girl! Now!"

Jennilee put the car in reverse and floored it, just as a resounding thud from behind shook the Crown Vic and cued another downed tree. Jennilee cut the wheel again, sharply, to keep from running into the tree behind her.

"Get down! Arm yourself and stay in the car." With that, Ben opened his door and slithered out. Shots rang out instantly.

Skewed sideways across the road, bracketed by the downed trees, Jennilee's car was as trapped as a fly on flypaper. Not much wiggle room and more glue everywhere she turned. Woods crowding the road in front of them and behind them, there was no way to free the car.

Snatching the CB mic off its holder, Jennilee spoke quickly. "Base. Come in, base. Ben and I have a situation. At least two attackers, in the blind curve just past the old cow pasture on Harkness Farm Road. We're trapped. Shots fired. Send Chief Mac. Now!"

Shot after shot plinked and pinged into the passenger side of

Jennilee's Crown Vic, most peppering Ben's door, keeping him crouching behind it.

"Jennilee? Change of plans. I'm gonna draw their fire. I want you to run. Slide out, jump the tree trunk on your side and stay low beside it. Get into the woods and hide. Whoever downed that second tree is also on my side of the car."

"Ben... I'm a crack shot. I can..."

"No arguing. This is what I get the big bucks for. Go. On my count..."

Giving her a scant few seconds to set herself, Ben scanned the woods-line for the shooter. "Three. Two. Go!" Firing at the last place he'd spotted the sniper, perched high on the backside of a pine tree on what Ben catalogued as a portable deer stand, Ben prayed harder than he'd ever prayed in his life. Popped off a couple quick shots at the base of the biggest tree closest to the stump of the second downed tree. Worried about more than just failing at his job, he'd quickly come to adore Jennilee. How could anyone not?

Scratch that. Obviously someone didn't share his adoration of the boss' wife. Charlie didn't seem so over the top paranoid about Jennilee's safety now.

Doing as Ben commanded despite her misgivings, Jennilee escaped out her side and slipped-slithered over the trunk, Jewel on her heels, and disappeared into the woods on the opposite side of the road from the gunman. No gunfire accompanied her escape, so the intent was to take her alive.

The rumble of a big truck coming from Jennilee's side of the car lifted Ben's spirits. For less than half a second.

No calvary, only more bandidos.

An ancient pulpwood truck lumbered backwards around the bend. The kind with an attached log crane, its attendant pincer swinging and swaying like a hungry crab's.

Run, Jennilee, run!

A barrage of shots pinned Ben in place, and then, from the woods behind the scene, a triumphant bellow rent the air and poured ice water down Ben's spine, straight into his heart.

"We got 'er, boys! We got 'er!"

~

CHARLIE FINALLY GAVE up on the nightmare filled thrashing that was tonight's version of actual sleep. His mind kept supplying endless visions of Jennilee.

Imprisoned.

Tortured.

Beaten.

Raped.

Murdered.

Thrown in a hole like his mother, to be discovered—or not—at some far future date while Charlie quietly went insane and drank himself into oblivion the same way his father had for so many decades.

Loop.

Repeat.

Over and over again.

Choosing instead to pace their mansion, room by room, then the porches, then their workroom, Charlie wound up in the cemetery just as dawn was breaking. Standing in front of Amelia's headstone, kicking himself for not coming here first, Charlie choked out, "Amelia. Jennilee's been kidnapped, likely by the same scum who murdered both our moms. If you have any pull where you are, watch out for her. Please."

Dropping to his knees, hands over his face, Charlie rocked and keened.

Swore he felt fingers stroke through his hair and a soothing hand rest on his head for a long moment before sliding down his neck to pat-pat-pat between his shoulder blades, wasn't quite brave enough to open his eyes.

Taking the first deep breath he'd taken since Chief Mac pulled up yesterday, Charlie sank down with his back against the coolness of Amelia's headstone and watched the sun rise.

He'd take comfort where he could find it, even if it came from a ghost. Either that or have himself voluntarily committed.

CHAPTER 30

*I*n the kitchen mindlessly shoveling food in his maw when Mac walked in, Charlie barely paused.

Mac gave him a nod and claimed a seat at the table. Sliding a mug of coffee and a loaded plate in front of him, Suki spun away, back to what she was doing. Nodding his thanks, Mac addressed Charlie, "Good. Eat, Charlie. You're gonna need all the sustenance you can get. We both know this might be a long haul."

Chewing steadily, Charlie swigged his coffee, swallowed. Shook his head. "One way or the other, this will be over soon."

The quiet sounds of utensils and eating broken by the sound of vehicles arriving had both their heads coming up. Suki paused, similarly alert.

Slamming doors, and heavy footsteps.

Frozen in his seat, Charlie watched Mac get up and open the kitchen door to wave Mason's crew inside.

Taking her cue from Jennilee, Suki had the table set and the beautiful wood covered in filled to the brim platters and bowls and baskets in a trice.

Grimly blank faces answered the question Charlie couldn't ask.

Washing up at the kitchen sink, the silent men—and the boy—

ranged around the table. Picking up the thick white mug of blacker than black coffee, Mason drained it like it was iced. Blew out a breath. "We scouted out the woods around the scene. We did find... Scuff marks in the pinestraw where someone was standing in a couple different places, signs of a struggle, and some spent casings. Very little blood, so that's something."

Taking another long drink of the oversize mug of coffee Suki had refilled for him, Mason continued, "The downed trees have..." Mason made a pinching/hoisting/relocating motion with one of his deck plate hands. "...marks on them. We need to know who around here has a vehicle equipped with log moving equipment that fits that description."

Mac snorted a rude sound. "You're in prime pulpwood country. More than you can shake a stick at, but as huge as those trees were, I'm opting for a pulpwood truck with a built-in crane. I'll make note of the ones I know and start running queries at the DMV soon's I get back to the office, sooner if your phone lines are working. Could take awhile. And that's just the ones that are legal. Need some paper and a pencil and I'll get started."

"Use my office. Suki, will you walk him there and make sure he has everything he needs?" Waiting until Mac and Suki were out of sight, waiting a bit longer to make sure, Charlie stated, "I don't care if you do it or if you set it up so I can, I don't want these fuckers going to jail."

No one at the table, not even—especially not even—the boy with the ancient eyes—so much as blinked at Charlie's judge-jury-executioner pronouncement.

Mason nodded, in complete agreement. "We've got it. Jennilee won't have to worry about them ever again."

"How many?"

"At least three. One shooter, one lurker in the woods to capture Jennilee, and someone driving the truck?" Mason shrugged. "All we've got to go on right now."

"Possibly one more. They had to have an enclosed trailer to disappear Jennilee's Crown Vic. Everyone in three counties knows her vehicle and would've said something had they seen anyone else driving it. It's gotta be someone local. Strangers stick out way too much here."

Mouse chuffed, "No one stopped us, but we got plenty of sidewise looks, even as early as it is."

Charlie decreed in a steely tone, "If anyone asks, tell them you're working for me. If they have a problem with that, get their names and I'll take care of it."

A break, while they cleared the platters and bowls like starving locusts and Charlie stewed.

Spearing more sausage, Mason licked his lips. "Mighty fine vittles."

"Help yourselves. Jennilee loves to feed people, and insists on only the finest ingredients. That sausage came from Mr. Jubal's hogs. Eggs from our hens. Herbs from our garden. Fresh milk from…" Snapping his jaw shut, Charlie stopped his babbling.

"We checked out all the names you gave us." Swiping his fork across his plate, gathering the last crumbs and shaking his head at Charlie's silent offer of more, Mason leaned back in his chair like a king getting comfortable on his throne. "Got somethin' you might wanna see."

"Butch's head on a pike? Sylvia's right beside him? And…" Charlie rapped out a fast drum roll on the table. "…Celie in the dungeon on the rack?"

A beat of silence, and then the table erupted in laughter.

Mason gave Charlie a crooked little grin. "I like you, Charlie. I really do."

"Second!"

Nods all the way around the table.

"So what…"

Suki's fluting tones, and Mac's answering, deeper ones accompanying their footsteps as they came back down the hall had Mouse confiding quietly, "Gotta get rid of the official law first."

About the same time the twosome reentered the kitchen and just as Mac opened his mouth to start telling them what he'd found out, the sound of another car pulling up came in loud and clear through the open windows and still, humid air, momentarily halting any more revelations.

I.G., looking like he needed to be participating in show-and-tell instead of hanging with this crowd, pinned Charlie with a disbelieving glare. *"That's* your early warning system?"

Looking at I.G., noting—having already filed for future reference—the way Mason's men all deferred to the kid in all matters tech-geek, Charlie vowed, "Carte blanche."

Nodding approvingly, I.G. went back to being a locust.

A dapper older gentleman appeared at the screen door.

Between the food and the conversation and Amelia's reassurances, having recovered more of his usual self, Charlie got up and held the door. Taking in the tableau, Suki at the ready with an empty plate and a pot of coffee, Mr. Talton beamed. "No, thanks, Miss Suki, but I'm gratified to find so many here. Saves repeating myself."

Taking a long look around the table, Mr. Talton nodded to himself. "No need for introductions, and I never saw y'all." Sitting down, Mr. Talton folded his hands. "That matter you had me on, Charlie? I've found out what you wanted to know. I'm assuming you don't mind if these fine, upstanding, *invisible* gentlemen hear what I have to say?"

Charlie shook his head. "If I have anything to say in the matter, you better get used to seeing them around. Jennilee's gonna suck them right into the fold."

Eyeing Charlie thoughtfully, Mason made eye contact with his men. They each gave him a unanimous nod of approval.

Mr. Talton rubbed his hands together. "We were focused on Celie. Turns out she's…entertaining. Until she disappeared, she's barely been out of the motel room in…weeks. She's been entertaining…lots. Lots of men."

Charlie made a rude sound. "Guess that's an easy way to make money when you're too lazy to work at a real job, and we've known she was hooking since we had you follow her before. So if she's not the one who's been opening all those credit accounts in Jennilee's name, who is?"

Mr. Talton cleared his throat.

Catching on just a beat quicker than Mac, Charlie swore, "Like mother, like daughter."

Dipping his head in acknowledgement, Mr. Talton agreed. "Sylvia.

Not merely a page, she copied a whole chapter out of Celie's book of evil deeds. I've already forwarded the incriminating evidence to Tom, per your instructions, but I wanted to tell you in person. Especially in light of the recent developments."

Catching Mason up with a few succinct words, Charlie paced, furious countenance boding ill for the recipient of his fury.

Tipping his head, Mason winged a brow.

Stopping mid-step, Charlie blinked at Mason, swung his gaze to Mac and Mr. Talton. "Mac, what did you find out?"

"You're not gonna like it. I poked and prodded some of my buddies at the local DMV, as well as Raleigh DMV. Got through for just a moment before the phone lines crapped out again."

"Spit it out, Mac."

"Chad Atkins was issued a ticket for driving an unlicensed pulp-wood truck on the highway a week ago."

Charlie smacked a fist into his palm. "Knot's cousin, and one of his partners in crime."

"A partner who also happens to own a backhoe, a bulldozer, an excavator, and a large enclosed trailer. Has owned, for the last... Oh, twenty years or so."

Charlie sucked in a breath and locked his eyes on Mac's. "Just like Celie's house of cards, Knot's is coming down. Now all we have to do is figure out where he has Jennilee and how to get her back before he..." Choking, Charlie dropped into a chair, wheezed out another breath. Shot Mason a look of pure misery, tinged with hope.

The dominoes were lining up in an intricately interwoven pattern. The fall was going to be spectacular, one way or the other.

CHAPTER 31

Jennilee came to in a gloom-filled room. Bound and gagged, at least she wasn't blindfolded. A small warm body pressed close against her side, shivering and whimpering. They hadn't blindfolded her yesterday—last night, whenever—either. Knot wasn't planning on Jennilee getting out of this alive, so he didn't care if she saw him.

Same reason he'd left Jewel alive, same reason he'd let the little mutt stay with Jennilee. One more way to torture Jennilee, one more thing to hold over her head.

Just like Ben.

Jennilee had run, as he'd ordered, knowing it was futile and merely postponing the inevitable. She'd had her suspicions, confirmed when no one answered her desperate call on the CB. Charlie made sure it was always manned, no matter how busy he got.

Tearing through the thick underbrush on some barely there game trail, Jennilee'd bolted. Not like a scared rabbit, but like a hunted fox. All her senses on high alert, not taking the easy way, twisting and turning and changing direction often with no rhyme or reason.

Even knowing it was a set-up and despite being on her guard, even with Jewel right at Jennilee's heel, Jennilee hadn't been prepared for the sheer bad luck of Knot stepping out from behind one of the—nearly big enough to be old growth—loblollies. Even less prepared for the butt of his shotgun punching at her face and cracking her across the cheekbone as she turned her head to avoid the blow, not fast enough. The whole right side of her face was swollen and no doubt, blacker than the inside of a coal mine.

Taking advantage of her distraction, Knot stomped Jennilee's hand and kicked her gun off into the thick brush.

The blow hadn't rendered her unconscious. Dazed, knocked down, she'd been aware enough to watch Jewel launch herself at Knot and see her latch onto his forearm. Staggering to her feet, grabbing a thick branch off the ground while he was occupied with Jewel, Jennilee swung like she was in a batting cage going for a homer. Got in several good blows, bloodying his nose and splitting his lip, laying a fine bruise across his temple. A no holds barred backhand to her already bruised cheek sent her back to the ground, barely conscious this time. She watched, utterly helpless, as Knot grabbed the brave little dog by the throat. Watched him choke and shake her into submission then stuff her in a heavy canvas duffel. Jewel's sharp teeth had dished out plenty of damage, but not near as much as Knot had visited upon her.

The motionless lump that was Jewel had remained limp the entire time Knot was trussing Jennilee like a Christmas goose and getting her on her feet. Fading in and out, it was all she could do to stagger back out to the road, Knot alternately prodding her in the back with his shotgun and whacking the duffel with the barrel when he decreed Jennilee was taking too long.

She'd seen through blurry eyes, Ben still alive but on his knees, hands laced behind his neck. Another man, grinning and holding a gun to his head.

She'd seen too, the vicious blow to Ben's head that had knocked him out.

He wasn't in here with them. Said a prayer for the man she hadn't wanted as a bodyguard but didn't want, as an innocent and a friend, being tortured because of her.

Giving a whimper of her own, muffled through the gag, Jennilee was tickled to pieces when Jewel answered. The poor thing couldn't manage to get to her feet, but she dragged herself closer to Jennilee's head and ecstatically licked Jennilee's face.

Charlie would figure it out. They just had to hang on until he got here.

~

"Mac, I hate to even ask, but can you find something…anything…to arrest Butch for? Knot isn't going to…" Charlie swallowed painfully. "He's gonna want to keep Jennilee alive until Butch gets his shot at her."

Mac blinked, grinned, and came close to smacking his own forehead. "This whole thing has got me addled. Maybe it's time I let Simon or someone else take over. That's part of what I came out here to tell you. As soon as we figured out Jennilee was MIA, I sent Simon out to Butch's residence to check his whereabouts—eviction notice in hand—on the off chance Butch was there. Don't have to fake any charges. He's six months behind on rent. Our favorite asshole attacked Simon—with a loaded weapon—and he was drunk and high to boot. He's not getting out of jail any time soon."

Charlie grinned savagely. "That's gonna throw a wrench in their plans."

Mason drummed thick fingers on the table. All his men perked up instantly, knowing his sharp intelligence was working overtime. "That much big equipment is hard to hide. We need a list of all the empty barns and warehouse type buildings in the vicinity. They wouldn't risk going too far and maybe getting pulled. Especially if the Atkins guy is already on the radar with a ticket for moving his truck illegally. Where was he moving it from, and more important, to?"

Mac stood. "I'll get on that. At least the phone lines are working again. Somewhat. I'll keep you posted, even if I have to resign and let someone else take over."

Rising with him, Charlie shook his head. "Weren't you making fun of me last night? About sitting on my ass? You've been working every bit as hard the last couple weeks. Don't demean yourself or the work you do. This town needs you. If Ben survives this, and you need another deputy, he's a prime candidate. I doubt he'll allow himself to remain Jennilee's bodyguard. He'll see this as a failed mission and blame himself."

"No one's fault. Shit happens." Pushing back from the table, rising like one of the Easter Island monoliths come to life and ripping free of the earth, Mason tipped his head to Mac. "Want a couple of my guys to accompany you? We've got better communication gear. Less chasing ourselves in circles that way."

Mouse and I.G. were on their feet even as Mac was nodding.

"Wanna ride out to the hangar with us, Charlie? We've got more maps and…stuff that's gonna come in handy."

Mac nodded in agreement. "Go, Charlie. Do what you can, and I'll do the same. You don't need to stay by yourself right now anyway."

Charlie was about to follow the crowd out the door when Suki stretched up and gave him a hug. "I won't tell you not to worry 'cause I'd be wasting my breath. Have faith. That sounds better. Jennilee's a strong woman, and she loves you beyond reason, just like you love her. She'll come out of this okay."

Hugging her back, Charlie held on for a long moment. "Thanks, Suki. For breakfast, and for the lunch you've already started, and for everything you do. We're glad we've got you."

Blinking back the tears in her gorgeous eyes, Suki declared, "Wouldn't have it any other way. Scat. Go find Jennilee and bring her home. I've got loads of cleaning to see to, per Jennilee's instructions. The day crew'll be here shortly, and no way do we want to disappoint Jennilee when you get her home. Can't have her thinking we're slacking just 'cause she's not right here to keep an eye on us."

Lifting a hand to Mac as the officer took off, Charlie slid into a truck with Mason. "So, what is it you're so eager to show me that Mac doesn't need to know about?"

Starting the truck, Mason slanted Charlie a look.

Charlie listened as Mason drove down the dirt road to the airstrip. Felt his spirits rise unaccountably with each word that fell from Mason's lips.

"Did a little recon of our own last night. Checked on everyone you had on your watch list, set them up with protection. Your grandma, Mose's folks, Tim and his family, the whole list. After that..."

Listening to the end, Charlie asked about the most important person Mason hadn't mentioned. "What about Mose?"

Pulling up at the hangar, Mason turned the truck off. Thumb-tapped the steering wheel as he stared thoughtfully out the windshield. "Ran a background on all y'all, just as a precaution. That Mose of yours has more decorations than a twenty foot Christmas tree. He's gone under, and I almost pity whomever he catches up with."

Pondering that, knowing Mose could take care of himself and hoping this whole thing didn't throw him back into the funk that'd almost sucked him out of this world, Charlie got out of the truck.

Entering the enclosed end of the barn, Charlie stared at Sylvia. No pity in his gaze, he took in the smeared mascara, the wild eyes that proclaimed she was coming down off something, the high, high heels, too tight T and micro-mini hooker apparel.

The handcuff and gag accessories.

The deliberately uncomfortable chair she was bound to.

Crossing his tree trunk arms, Mason tipped his head. "Figured a little insurance wouldn't hurt."

Charlie's smile flashed, as evil as anything Celie had ever directed at Jennilee.

MEETING BACK at the house for the subs and chips and peanutbutter brownies Suki had ready and waiting, Mac caught them up.

Spreading a detailed map on the table, covered in red circles, Mac pointed out abandoned barns and sundry.

His hand dwarfing the footlong he held, Mason asserted, "They're gonna want to keep all the equipment close. Won't want to risk moving it now that they've sprung their trap."

Pushing his barely touched sub away, Charlie shuddered. "They murdered my mom and threw her in the trunk of her car. Buried car and all in an unused field. Jeff's on top of proving who murdered my mom like white on rice."

"So we're looking at at minimum, the trailer and the excavator, possibly the pulpwood truck. They'll need somewhere they own, or some place abandoned where no one will bother them."

Scrubbing both hands dejectedly across his face, Charlie asked the room at large, "Do you have any idea how many tobacco barns and pack-houses there are around here? Not to mention fish-houses."

Chewing slowly, Mason licked his lips. "Not even sure what you just said, but we'll divvy up the what-evers and check them one by one, starting with the ones closest to the scene."

Switching his amused gaze between Charlie and Mason, Mac inserted, "They'd've taken the backroads, so that'll eliminate a few. They wouldn't have chanced someone spotting them."

A beeping sound trilled, and Mason's crew all looked expectantly at I.G. Catching their interest, Charlie perked up and stared at the kid as well. While he might be the youngest of Mason's crew, he definitely had mad skills.

Without looking up from the monitor he held, something that looked to be some type of handheld game and something Charlie had heard Mason say was an invention of I.G.'s, I.G. asked, "What? You said carte blanche. You didn't say when."

Giving him a nod, Charlie asked, "Where's it located?"

"That one? At the paved road. Someone just turned into the driveway."

"Charlie."

All of them looked up at Suki's call.

"You need to hear this."

Charlie got slowly to his feet as Suki encouraged a white-faced teenager to step out of the hall and into the kitchen.

Hands clenched, the teenager lifted her chin. Quailed a bit as she took in the menacing amount of muscle seated around the table.

"Mr. Meyers, I..."

Stammering to a halt, she shook her head, straightened her spine, and started over.

"I lied to you on my job application."

Charlie's stomach bottomed out as he waited, certain sure the girl was terrified about admitting to more than lying on a job app. Suki wouldn't have bothered them otherwise.

"Everybody knows you wouldn't hire anyone who's kin to the Jones', and with good reason. He doesn't claim me, so I kinda figured it wouldn't count against me."

An ice shard stabbed Charlie in the gut. If he'd unknowingly invited a viper into his home, he'd...

Calm down, Charlie. She wouldn't be here admitting to a lie if that's all she was worried about.

"Everyone in town knows I ain't got no daddy. I mean, I do have one. Sperm donor, anyways." The girl swallowed. "My name's Evvie. Evelyn. Evelyn Adams."

Charlie stared, Mac said calmly, "Spit it out, girl."

"My daddy's Knot Jones' brother. Half brother, actually." Shrugged a thin shoulder. "Momma says he's my daddy, anyhow. Never been 'round much 'cept when he wants... Never mind. He's been sniffin' round momma a bunch lately. I just figured out a few minutes ago it's been ever since he found out I landed this job. I need this job, Mr. Meyers, and I'd never betray you or Mrs. Meyers. I think Miz Jennilee's the purtiest thing I ever laid eyes on. She's like an angel, all goodness and light. No matter what foulness the Jones' are always spoutin' about her."

Pinned like a struggling butterfly to a collector's board by all the eyes staring at her, Evvie doggedly kept going. "I didn't even know Miz Jennilee was missing until I got to work a little bit ago and then it started making sense."

"What? What started making sense?"

"Mr. Meyers, if I'd'a figured it out sooner, I'd'a sure come running to you. You gotta believe me."

Nodding jerkily, off balance and waiting for someone to finish snatching the rug out from under him, Charlie decided he better sit before he fell.

"I didn't pay 'em much mind at first. Mostly when Gear and Knot are around, I hide in my room, or out in the woods if it's real bad, and generally try to be invisible. They were drunk, as usual. They're mean drunks."

329

Evvie shivered, and none of the men there had any doubt why.

"I try to stay outta their way. The other night they were talkin' real loud, carryin' on while I was tryin' to sleep. Kept talkin' about some bitch and punishin' her. Half dreamin', at first I thought they meant one of their huntin' hounds, then I realized they were talkin' about a woman. Then they said somethin' about Grover—he's one of their sometime huntin' buddies—messin' with the CB. Said they'd told him to do it as a joke they were playin' on somebody and then they laughed extra loud…that's what made me wake up. I've heard that evil laughter plenty."

Charlie's eyes went frigid as he and Mason locked gazes. He'd worried and fretted about who'd changed the channel on the CB at work, fearing he had a viper in his midst. Grover was the answer to that question, and Mason had the solution.

Feeling sorry for the old but not old enough to be elderly man who'd lost everything in the hurricane and subsequent flood, Charlie'd given him a job. Not quite right, no family, he'd been the perfect Patsy for Knot's nefarious schemes.

Mason nodded. He wouldn't hurt the man, but he would remove him from Charlie's vicinity, find him gainful employment far, far away.

Evvie shuddered again. "They call him Gear, 'cause he's missin' teeth and 'cause his gears don't mesh quite right. What they were sayin'… Scared me. I musta made some kind of noise, 'cause they kicked my door open and dragged me out on the porch. Said if I told on 'em, they'd…" Gulped. "I didn't know what they thought I'd tell, or who I'd tell it to if I did. They didn't mention any names or anything."

Already pale, the freckles on her cheeks stood out like inkblots as Evvie ground to a halt.

"I didn't put two and two together until I got here today for work and found out Miz Jennilee had gone missing. They took her, Mr. Meyers. You have to get her back before they do something awful!" Evvie waved a hand at the crew seated around the table. "That's why they're all here, right? I didn't know people could love each other the way you two do until I met y'all. Please don't let them destroy her."

Indicating the empty chair he twirled out with one of his boat-sized combat boots, fully cognizant of what her admission had cost her, Mason said softly, "Sit."

Giving Mason a thorough once over, Evvie crossed the kitchen warily, like an animal approaching a known trap. Perched on the edge of the chair, ready to bolt if any of the men so much as raised their voice.

Keeping his voice low and soothing, Mason gave Evvie an encouraging nod. "Start from the beginning."

Evvie blurted, "You're scary." Cocked her head. "But I'm not scared of you. Much. More scared of them. You're one of the good guys."

Figuring her bullshit meter probably stayed pegged out, ready to flare into klaxons and warning strobes at the least hint of trouble, Mason nodded. "Yep. Did you hear them say where they were taking Jennilee?"

"Not for certain. They talked a bunch about making sure they had enough room and how no one could hear them." Slanting an apologetic glance at Charlie, Evvie made a face. "Do you want these guys to take me somewhere so's you don't have to hear this?"

Hands gripped tight on the arms of his chair to keep himself from lunging and shaking the halting confession out of the girl, Charlie shook his head. "Continue."

Sliding the map her way, Mason asked, "Any of these places we circled look familiar?"

Nervously chewing the end of her ponytail, studiously perusing the map, Charlie swore he saw Evvie's ears suddenly prick and swivel. Kid probably had hearing like a bat. Constant self defense would do that to a person. Jennilee'd been the same way while she lived at the Judge's.

Any anger Charlie held at Evvie's supposed duplicity drained away.

She wasn't complicit, and she'd obviously dared a great deal just to tell them what little she knew. Going by what she'd said, and what she hadn't, combined with her nervous mannerisms, she was probably expecting to be tenderized into jelly and thrown piece-meal to the crabs.

A few moments later they all heard another vehicle pull up, pickup by the sound. An old one. Evvie's bat-ears hadn't lied.

Without getting up, Charlie informed them, "Mr. Cyrus. He's an old friend of ours."

Fiddling with whatever had him so engrossed, I.G. told Charlie absently, "I'm gonna need a list of approved vehicles and tags."

Charlie rattled off a phone number. "That's Mr. Talton, the PI you met. We have him on retainer. I'll let him know he's to cooperate fully with y'all."

Too on edge to sit and wait, Charlie hustled out the door and down the long porch, meeting Mr. Cyrus before the older gentleman, wearing his habitual bib overalls, had gotten very far.

"'Fraid I got some disturbing news, Charlie."

"Come in, Mr. Cyrus. There's some people here who need to hear whatever it is."

Coming one step inside the kitchen door, eyeing the strangers, Mr. Cyrus came to a halt. He'd done a stint in the military, recognized mercenaries when he saw them. A wide grin lit his face. "Good! Jennilee's gonna need all of you and all the weapons you can scrounge. No offense, Mac. These boys'll be able to do things you're oath-bound not to."

Mac grimaced. "And with that, I'm outta here. Goin' back to town where I don't have to dither about stuff like this and I can pretend none of this is happening anywhere near my jurisdiction."

Taking Mac's seat, and the plate Suki handed him, Cyrus looked around the table. Grinned more. Hummed his approval as he took a bite of the perfectly done, thin sliced roast beef piled high on fresh rosemary bread.

Between bites, he elucidated, and got everyone's instant attention. "Saw an interesting procession go past my place yesterday. Didn't know it was important until I got to town today and heard Jennilee was missing."

Made a further sound of enjoyment as he took another bite. "Redneck parade. Pulpwood truck. Enclosed car trailer. Eighteen wheeler pulling a flatbed with a track-hoe on it."

Mason braced his forearms on the table. "You follow this...parade?"

"Nope."

All the men visibly wilted, none more than Charlie.

Smacking his lips, holding his sub at the ready, Cyrus' grin threatened to split his face. "Didn't need to. Only one place that road goes where you could hide any of that, much less all of it."

"Load up, men." Mason pointed a sausage sized digit at Charlie, flicked a glance at Evvie. "You stay here. Babysit."

Giving a terse nod, Charlie acquiesced. Pinning Evvie with a long stare, he told her, "Looks like you're bunking with Suki for the foreseeable future.

Evvie considered arguing. For a scant few seconds. Why? If she went home, Gear and Knot were likely to show up. More likely to beat the snot outta her, 'cause sure as shootin', they'd question her part in this misadventure just because she worked here. And because she was an available punching bag.

Not like she had any valuables to claim from her closet sized bedroom in their rundown to the point of falling around their ears trailer. The *comes with the job*, sorta uniform all the help wore—nice slacks and identical T shirts—was the nicest outfit she'd ever worn. Much less owned.

Evvie nodded back with no regrets whatsoever.

CHAPTER 32

*B*iting back a groan, Jennilee willed the tears away.

Not like she hadn't had plenty of practice at both.

It was a lot harder to do when someone else was on the receiving end of the pain.

And she was the cause.

Especially when she was the cause.

Knot and his brother Gear were working Ben over. Again.

Jewel lay in a limp heap in a dark corner of the gloomy old fish-house, against a pile of rotting net and odd pieces of lumber and broken coolers and corks. She hadn't moved since Knot punted her.

Jennilee'd vowed she'd kill Knot for that. He'd laughed and punched her in the temple. He did like his head shots. Tied to a massive beam in the center of the building as she was, the declaration had been flat out stupid, and probably added to her burgeoning concussion. It sure hadn't helped her remain upright. Jennilee'd sagged against the ropes holding her until the one around her neck threatened to cut off her air. Pushing upright on leaden legs, Jennilee dug deep.

Hurry up, Charlie! We can't hold on much longer!

Why are you waiting for Charlie? You've gotten out of plenty of jams by yourself, goober!

Jennilee's internal debate waffled back and forth like a badminton birdie missing half its feathers.

She'd been in some bad situations, just never tied up.

Think, Jennilee!

She at least knew where she was. She and Charlie had explored this old abandoned fish-house years ago on one of their many bike rides. The last viable remnant of a defunct fishing community, a big ware-house type building with an enclosed loading dock out front led to this back portion where the actual fish and shellfish had been processed. The long building stretched out over the water on pilings. Once there'd been a dock all along one side and across the end where the fishing trawlers tied up and offloaded their cargo. Now... It was a wonder it remained standing.

The supporting pilings leaned every which way like crooked teeth. The tin roof had peeled back in places and the wooden sides had rotted away here and there. All the windows had been boarded up and the floor was iffy at best.

Charlie and Jennilee had long since decided it was best left to the wasps and spiders and fiddler crabs.

Another plus, a huge one, Knot hadn't checked her pockets. Her knife was still there. If she could wiggle enough, she might be able to fish it out. Partly because of the width of the beam, her hands weren't tied tightly behind her. They'd counted more on the rope around her neck to hold her in place.

Knot's cousin Chad had stayed mostly outside the main fish-house in the loading area, although he'd stumble in occasionally to get a beer and gloat. The last time he'd gone back out—toting a full bottle of whiskey—the person-sized door inset in the huge sliding doors had swung shut but hadn't latched. Jennilee knew for a fact there were gaps everywhere in the walls surrounding the loading dock. Figuring that's where they'd stashed her car and the pulpwood truck and what-ever other heavy equipment—the smell of fresh diesel coated the air every time Chad came in and out—they'd used in their kidnapping endeavor, she knew there would be plenty of places a small dog could hide.

Jennilee watched intently as Jewel's paws twitched, like she was dreaming of chasing rabbits. Or coming around.

She had to get loose, had to get Jewel out of here. And Ben. Contorting like a circus performer, Jennilee hunched and twisted and finally slipped her arms one way and her hips the other enough to get her fingers in her pocket. Knot had taken her weapon and had—more felt her up than patted her down—missed the small pocket knife she always carried in her watch pocket. If she could just stretch a bit more…

There! She had it! Now…how was she going to…

Jennilee! Stop whining and just do it! This isn't near as bad as the outhouse full of snakes.

Catching her thumbnail in the groove, Jennilee carefully held the knife and worked it against her hip and her hand until the blade popped open. Wedged the knife until the blade met rope and began sawing despite the muscle tremors and screaming joints.

Slumping like she was close to losing consciousness, Jennilee played possum when Knot and Gear took a break from breaking Ben. Thank God they'd removed her gag when they'd brought her out here. A prisoner who couldn't beg and scream wasn't near as much fun.

As soon as they swaggered to the far side of the long room where they'd obviously set up camp, deep enough in their liquor she could smell it from here—and their snacks, not that they'd offer her any sustenance—that she hoped they couldn't hear her, she whispered, "Jewel. Jewel! Wanna go outside?"

Jewel's tail thumped weakly, once, twice. She lifted her head a fraction. Panted. Whined softly.

"Go on, girl. Go outside. The door's open. You can do it. Just like we taught you. Go find Charlie. Go!"

Jennilee held her breath as Jewel heaved painfully to her feet, got her bearings, and weeble-wobbled toward the door.

Nosing it open, she disappeared through the tiny gap.

Just in time as Knot and Gear, none the wiser, returned to torturing

Ben. Under one of the places in the roof where the tin had peeled back, Ben was spotlit like they'd done it on purpose. Maybe they had.

That meant Jennilee was more hidden, in a darker part of the fish-house where the roof remained intact. She could see the dust-spangled cobwebs festooning the rafters, the air full of dust motes. Amazing how a place that hadn't seen a fish scale in decades could still smell like it was in operation. Fish and salt water and algae and river mud mixed with diesel and motor oil overlaid with a faint trace of bleach.

Jennilee worked steadily at the tight cords wound around her wrists. Thin but super-strong, Knot had secured black net twine around Jennilee's wrists like he was a macrame expert going for the world title. Didn't help any that her hands were nearly numb.

A few more passes of her knife, and she felt the binds around her wrists give. Now, how to get the one around her neck without them noticing her hands were free.

That didn't even take into consideration her feet, also tied to the beam.

Taking a chance, hoping they couldn't see well with the contrast in light and dark, Jennilee brought her hands up and slipped her knife under the taut rope at her neck. A thick one this time, Knot's version of showing off. There, just there, a bit of wiggle room, and Jennilee's knife was little. Sharp as her knife was, it was taking forever to saw through this one without fatally jabbing herself.

Knot and Gear, having gleefully resumed their foul play, didn't even look up from their human pincushion/punching bag.

The rope around her neck gave with such suddenness Jennilee almost toppled over. Sliding her back slowly down the beam, gathering more than a few splinters as her shirt rucked up, Jennilee sank to her haunches and began working on the bindings around her ankles. Only the one rope to get through, twin to the one around her neck, and she could...

There.

Standing back up as slowly as she'd gone down, Jennilee was about to set the next part of her sketchy plan in motion. If she could just get to...

Froze as Knot, bloody to his elbows, glanced her way. Turned back to Ben.

In and out of consciousness, her acts of rebellion sapping what little energy she had, somehow managing to stay on her feet and hang on to her knife through the rolling waves, the next time the door opened, Jennilee stared blearily.

Blinked.

Knot appeared right in front of her and cut off her view of the door. Blinked.

She hadn't even seen him move.

Blinked.

Couldn't have seen what she thought she had. Wishful thinking.

"Well, what have we here? A little mouse turd trying to chew its way out of a trap. Not gonna happen. We're just waiting for my boy to show up before we start on you. Told him he could have first go. Can't have you getting loose before he pays you back some of what he owes you."

Blinked, blinked again. Her vision must be going. Shook her head and detonated a massive explosion of pain, followed by Knot getting in another blow to her head when he decided she was sassing him.

Still, no matter how she blinked, her eyes kept telling her the same thing: Mose had just slipped in the door. Both of him.

Darned if she was shaking her head again. She couldn't afford to pass out now. Sensing movement, thinking it was his cousin/lookout man and ignoring just *how* Jennilee had gotten free of the ropes— maybe he thought she'd chewed through, or magicked them gone— Knot turned his head to snarl something. Some order along the lines of *get back out there!* A frozen moment of disbelief in which he stared at Mose.

Swinging her arm, low and quick, Jennilee had the immense satisfaction of feeling her little knife sinking into Knot's stomach. Her pitiful inch and three quarters of steel wouldn't do much more damage than a thumbtack, probably couldn't even make it through Knot's spare tire to anything vital. To that end, Jennilee wrenched it sideways with all the strength she could muster.

A bellow from him, shots from Mose, and their cacophony added to the maelstrom already raging in Jennilee's head. Taking a few quick steps toward the only other viable door, a huge sliding affair that once upon a time had led to the now defunct dock, a door she doubted she had the strength to move right now but she had to if she wanted to live, and oh how she wanted to live. Eyes on freedom, Jennilee cried out as Knot wrapped his arms around her and body-slammed her to the floor.

Rolling *away* from the door with her in his arms, Knot dropped them both over the low lip and through the opening in the floor that had once been used to dispose of fish guts and heads.

While they were rolling and falling, Jennilee stabbed again and again, getting in blow after blow for Jewel and Ben. And Angel. Jeff. Charlie. Grandy. Their moms. Mr. Donny. Everyone who'd ever run afoul of Knot.

As hard and as much as she stabbed, Knot punched and kicked.

They hit the water and sank, still tangled together, Knot's hands going around Jennilee's throat.

Jennilee had a moment to think how glad she was it was high tide and there was more than a skim of water covering the oyster shells and sundry detritus, right before Knot's weight carried her under.

CHAPTER 33

*D*ropping Gear with a single shot between the eyes, Mose couldn't get a clear shot at Knot given the way he stood so close in front of Jennilee. His infuriated bellow rang until dust rained from the exposed rafters when Knot took them both to the floor and then the two of them dropped out of sight.

Leaving Ben—looking more dead than alive—where he was for the moment, Mose visually swept the rest of the fish-house. He'd already taken care of the watchman outside. Finding no other conspirators, Mose beelined for the darker square on the floor, weapon at the ready.

Nearly ten feet down, nothing but churned up mud was visible in the murky water.

About to jump in after them, Mose spun into a crouch at the sound of his name.

"Mose! Incoming friendlies! Don't shoot!"

Stepping over so most of his big body was behind the foot and a half-square beam Jennilee had been tied to, Mose waited and watched, all deadly intention.

"We're friends of Marty Robbins. Charlie sent us."

The door eased open, and several men filed in, going high, going low, sweeping with their weapons, the first one bigger even than Mose himself.

Hands out to his sides, the big guy stood still and kept talking while his men spread out to the left and right. "We spotted your truck down the road. Good work finding Jennilee."

Mose watched warily as one of the men went straight to Ben, firing orders about triage and bandages and too much blood—must be their medic—to another of the men who rapidly began cutting Ben loose.

"Mose! We're here to help. Where's Jennilee?"

A medic. Weapons. Camo. Search and destroy. A commanding officer barking orders.

The sounds of the jungle battered at Mose. A chopper flew low overhead. Monkeys screamed, then people, and the world erupted in flames and gunfire and bombs being dropped too close for comfort. The air smelled of grease-paint, nuoc mam, Napalm ravaged greenery, flames, and the stink of death all jumbled together into an unforgettable morass.

"Snap out of it, soldier! Jennilee needs you!"

Shaking his head dazedly as the sharp order reached him and the jungle receded as quickly as it'd come, Mose eased out from behind the beam. Didn't take his finger off the trigger.

The big guy repeated patiently but with just enough edge to get Mose's attention. "Mose. Jennilee?"

Jennilee!

Not fully back in the real world, not sure whether the camo-clad, weapons bedecked men he was seeing were real or extremely detailed figments, Mose gestured toward the hole in the floor.

Even if they weren't real, Jennilee was and she needed all the help he could muster.

CLAWING at Knot's face with her free hand, Jennilee kept stabbing at him with her knife. Knot grabbed her arm and gripped her wrist hard, squeezing until she lost her grip on her old friend, squeezing until her bones ground together. One hand still clamped around her throat,

Knot's greater weight forced her down until Jennilee's back touched bottom. A cloud of black mud instantly mushroomed, enveloping them, and still he kept his deadly grip on her throat.

Knowing better than to give in and try to futilely pry his hand loose, Jennilee felt around on the bottom, seining through the silky silt until her questing fingers touched an oyster shell, as empty and abandoned as the building above. Bringing it up, she slashed the razor sharp edge across where Knot's face should be, aiming blindly for his eyes.

He recoiled like a wounded squid, both hands grabbing at his face as blood filled the water like squid ink.

Quick and agile as a shrimp escaping a hungry trout, Jennilee drew her legs up, pushed off Knot with both feet, and eeled away.

Blind as a bat in the stirred up water, Jennilee swam mermaid style as hard as she could, arms protectively out in front of herself, trying not to run face first into any of the barnacle encrusted pilings. Knot's grasping fingers brushed at her ankle, slithered past and lost their chance. Jennilee undulated harder, propelling herself away to anywhere but where he was.

Bobbing to the surface, both to get a breath of air and to get her bearings, Jennilee heard Knot close behind her, doing the same. Foul curses blistered the air as Jennilee gulped a breath and dove, curving agilely around the piling directly in front of her like a dolphin pirouetting. Jinking and putting yet another piling between her and Knot's last known whereabouts, Jennilee came up for air again, sucked in a deep breath, held it. Gulping a few more shallow ones she dove again, careful to go parallel rather than down.

Only about three feet deep with deeper swirls around the pilings from the constant action of the water, Jennilee was ever so grateful it wasn't dead low tide. No way could she have slogged through the thigh deep and nearly quicksand muddy bottom to get away from Knot. Swimming, she had a decent chance.

Her body, as well trained to utilize her fight or flight as any professional soldier, ignored the pain and muzziness in her head as it sought sanctuary. Somewhere to regroup for a moment while she caught her breath and figured out her next move.

Had that really been Mose? Or had all her wishful thinking and the blows to her head addled her beyond reason?

She needed to get out in deeper water. Or at least less encumbered with debris water. If she could do that, she had a chance.

Breaking the surface like a frog scouting for danger, nothing but her eyes and nostrils showing, Jennilee got her bearings and another breath. That way!

She'd be alright as long as there weren't any surprises in the water she couldn't see—crab-pots, remnants of boat hulls, worn out motors —who knew what had fallen or been knocked off the dock, or people had thrown into the water as useless junk. No one who'd used the fish-house had worried about swimming under it.

If she could just get out to deeper water and swim-swim-swim, she could circle round and get back to shore and hide in the marsh grass. Or should she just swim out into the river? If Mose was here— IF, and she hadn't been happily hallucinating—he'd be on the lookout for her.

Swimming until she couldn't stay down any longer, Jennilee frogged again and sucked in air. A splash beside her had her disappearing under the water quick as a bullfrog detecting the stealthy tread of a determined gigger.

Changing direction, she darted off.

Next time she came up, same thing. Narrowly avoiding whatever Knot had thrown at her, Jennilee tried to go deeper.

How was Knot tracking her? It was gloomy under here, more shadow than light.

Kicking down too hard, Jennilee's foot struck the silty mud. Of course! Dummy. He didn't have to know where she was going. All he had to do was stand still and watch the water change color as Jennilee's passage stirred up clouds of mud and discolored the water, like watching the movements of a crab or a flounder and knowing exactly which direction it was headed.

Trying to remember the pattern of the pilings holding up the building, Jennilee thought—hoped—she had several between her and Knot. Coming up in the shadow of one for a breath, Jennilee let out a yowl of pain as something hard hit her barely exposed head. Going back under, Jennilee blinked in the murky water as a large chunk of cinderblock quickly sank out of sight.

Swim it was. She was going to have to go as far as she could, put as much distance between herself and Knot as possible. Mose would take care of him. All Jennilee had to do was stay alive.

~

Finding his words at last, Mose headed for the open trapdoor. "They're under the building. No one else here alive. Knot's a mean sumbitch and he'll stop at nothing."

As if to emphasize Mose's statements, a spate of curses turned the air blue.

Almost to himself, Mose voiced, "Jennilee's tougher and she's got me on her side. Us." With that, he stepped out into air and dropped out of sight.

~

The sound of gunshots rang clearly, even underwater as she was, stalling Jennilee's mad flight for just a beat before spurring her to greater efforts. With no way to know if that was Mose coming to her aid or Knot coming to his senses and using more than whatever he scrounged off the bottom, Jennilee wasn't about to give up now.

Swimming as far underwater as her starved lungs would allow and then driving herself even further, Jennilee scraped her forearm on the nasty barnacles covering a piling, automatically jerking her bloody limb back and hastily surfacing before she was ready.

A shot whizzed past her head and thunked into the pockmarked wooden surface—dark, wet wood liberally slathered in barnacles and accented by green slime—so close she felt the air move.

Gasping in a quick breath—not enough, not nearly enough, like partaking of a drop of water when you'd been parched for days—Jennilee sank back under, spots filling her vision, ears ringing with more than gunfire.

Not even attempting to marathon swim this time, she made sure she was on the other side of the piling and resurfaced. When had it gotten dark? Surely they couldn't have been down here that long? Sucking in breath after breath, Jennilee fought the rising tide of darkness.

◠

MOSE DIDN'T BOTHER CURSING. Wouldn't do any good.

Knot was—again—in a direct line between Mose and Jennilee with a checkerboard of pilings between Knot and Mose.

No matter.

More than one way to kill the bastard.

Slogging toward Knot, Mose planned and schemed, actively seeking an opportunity. Between the strange half-light and the distinct smell of pluff mud and brackish water and the scent of green and growing things amid the kill or be killed scenario so reminiscent of *there*, Mose was having a really hard time keeping himself in the here and now.

Didn't matter. All he had to do was keep the target in sight and eliminate it. Obliterate it.

Knot.

Bullseye.

Kept slogging.

He did curse when Knot chunked a piece of cinderblock, nothing but his arm visible as it arced out and he let fly, cursed more when it struck Jennilee's head and she sank back under the water. Mose had no doubt about where he was now. Jennilee needed him.

Let his weapon do his cursing when Knot took another shot at Jennilee, one that whizzed far too close to her precious head.

Finally realizing there was another person under the old building with them, one with a weapon, Knot spun and began firing at Mose around the piling he was hiding behind.

The sound of the shots galvanized Jennilee like a raccoon nosing the electric fence around a henhouse.

With a desperate leap, she dove and swam like Grandy was counting.

345

Have to stay under the water.

Swim.

A jagged stump of piling materialized out of the murky gloom, too close for Jennilee to entirely miss it. Like a boat running aground on an oyster rock, the barnacles gouged long welts into her side, deep enough to etch her ribs like scrimshaw.

Jennilee managed to stay underwater. More, managed somehow to hold in her scream and not lose precious air.

More shots, and the muffled sound of raised voices.

Jennilee swam.

The spots dancing in front of her eyes before were nothing compared to the strobes going off now amid the solar system space between worlds darkness.

Jennilee swam.

More muffled bangs and indistinguishable thumps, like sinking underwater while in a bubblebath. Normal noises took on all sorts of weird vibes, distorting until you couldn't make head nor tails of them, strange submarine plinks and pings.

Jennilee swam.

Faltering for a moment as she darted out from under the fish-house into bright sunlight—like a minnow fleeing from a Great Blue and not knowing which way to go—recovering, Jennilee swam. The water was still murky, but the sunlight drove away some of the cloudiness and spotlighted vague items.

An elongated skull appeared in front of her, canted in the mud, antlers still attached, eye sockets full of endless dark.

A blue crab, disturbed by her presence, zipped away and spidered over a plate, standing on edge, a bright orange crab painted on its half-obscured surface.

Rising out of the mud like a departing spaceship, a flounder fluttered its fins as it disappeared.

A school of fat butter minnows scattered every which way.

What was next? Wylie Coyote and Roadrunner?

Jennilee swam.

Had the sun gone behind a cloud? Had there been an eclipse? Whatever was wrong, it got darker and darker, and still Jennilee swam.

CHAPTER 34

*P*lowing determinedly toward his target, Mose saw shapes dropping on other side of him around the perimeter of the old fish-house, the other men coming to his aid. He didn't need them. Jennilee did.

To that end, Mose bellowed, "That way! Follow the trail of mud in the water."

The biggest one slogged away, out into the more open water.

Intent on his target, Mose ignored the bullets zinging around him like angry hornets. Just like he'd ignored them in Nam. If the sumbitches were intent on him, they weren't firing on his buddies.

Fruitless clicks as Knot ran out of ammo made Mose grin ferociously. Keeping the same steady pace, he didn't even duck as Knot threw the empty revolver at him and turned to run like the coward he was. Didn't get far. Between the sucking mud and the tractor trailer loads of cigarettes and the immeasurably vast quantities of liquor he'd consumed in his lifetime, Knot was in no shape for a real fight.

Catching up to his quarry, Mose spun Knot. The last thing Knot saw was Mose's grim smile, white teeth brilliant against all that midnight skin.

Glaring into Knot's hated face, claw marks everywhere and one eye a bloody mess, gel oozing out like a squished jellyfish, Mose growled, "Last time, Knot. Last time you or any of your crowd is gonna hurt my Jennilee. Go back to hell, where you belong." Letting Knot turn away like he had a real chance of escaping, Mose wrapped tree trunk arms around Knot's head and wrenched.

The extremely audible crack, like a cherry bomb going off, grounded Mose like nothing else could have. Jennilee was safe. This piece of scum would never bother her again, and there'd be no getting off on an appeal from some skanky lawyer.

Dropping the body like the waste of a human being it was, Mose began slogging again. Arms held high and out to the sides, balancing his twisting movements, he high-stepped his way toward the big man going after Jennilee.

Mason waded out, kept wading. Measured the distance with his eyes. He hadn't seen Jennilee surface. The mud trail was still going. He didn't see how. He'd never seen anyone who wasn't a SEAL go so long underwater.

Even with his long legs, he was having trouble catching up to Jennilee. His big body kept sinking nearly thigh deep into the silty mud with each step. Casting a look over his shoulder at the sound of a boat motor sputtering to life, Mason made sure it was one of his guys.

That same glance also showed Mose powering his way.

Not that he blamed the man.

Mose didn't know Mason and crew from Adam. Had only Mason's word that they were here to help Jennilee.

Turning back to the chase, Mason closed the distance.

Caught up with the end of the mud trail as it snailed to a stop.

Reaching down, feeling fabric, Mason locked on.

Thought he did.

Like a desperate fish on a hook approaching a boat and the fisherman therein, flip-flopping, making its last bid at escape, Jennilee wriggled and wormed and slid right out of his grasp.

Following the mud trail once more, Mason drove his hand into the water and snagged a limb this time. Hauled Jennilee's limp form out of the water.

Mose reached them about the same time the old wooden skiff did.

Pleas fell from his lips like rain from the sky as he snatched Jennilee from Mason and cradled her close. "Jennilee! *Jennilee!* Don't you give up now! Don't you dare! Not after that heroic fight. We won, baby. We won. Knot's dead and so's Gear. Charlie's waiting for you back at the house. Open those ocean eyes, girl."

Nothing. No twitch, no flicker, nothing resembling awareness. Mose wasn't even sure she was breathing. Giving her a shake, then a squeeze, he turned pleading eyes on Mason.

The big man jerked his head. "Get her in the boat. You need to get her to shore and to a hospital. Doc will check her over before you leave."

Easily lifting her slight weight over the side and placing her gently in another stranger's arms, Mose held his hands up and backed away. "I can't go with her."

"Sure you can. Take her in. Tell them you found Jewel wandering along the road and came out here to check this old place, since it's the only thing left around for miles. When you got here, those three lunkheads—no honor among thieves, and all that—were dead and Jennilee was adrift in the boat. We'll set it up and make sure there's no trace of you—or us—anywhere it shouldn't be before we ghost."

"How'd you know I found Jewel?"

"Saw her in your truck, figured that's what happened. Doc gave her a little something for the pain so you'll have to let the vet know she was acting drugged when you found her. Doc's bandaging up the worst of Ben's wounds. You've seen enough combat, tell them you carry a first aid kit in your truck."

Giving a terse nod at all of that, Mose clasped forearms with Mason, a warrior's promise.

"Mouse'll take you both to shore."

Hefting himself over the side of the skiff in a practiced move, Mose settled on the wooden bench seat and took Jennilee back from Mouse. Squeezed.

All three men stared in disbelief as a pod of dolphins came racing up to the skiff.

Their cries seeming to reach Jennilee where Mose's pleas had failed, Mose watched as one shallow breath came from Jennilee, then another, barely discernible. Hugging her to his chest, Mose breathed deep and rocked them both. Leaping high enough to peer into the boat, squeaking agitatedly, the pod escorted the skiff to shore.

CHAPTER 35

*D*oc Mason stood in the doorway of the hospital room—a room filled to overflowing with flowers. Thought of the waiting room he'd just left—a room just as full of people as this room was of blooms—people as well as blooms of every color and description. Only one person—a most important person—was missing to complete the circle of close family and friends—Jeff.

Pretty much everyone else had checked in at some point or other, or had a superb reason for not.

Doc's eyes met Del's and he eavesdropped shamelessly as she spoke to her grandson.

"Charlie Bear, Jeff just called. He's on his way."

Charlie didn't even take his eyes off the still form in front of him. "Thanks, Grandy. Did you hear that, Jennilee? Jeff will be here soon."

Doc's gaze focused on the couple inside, one in the bed and one beside it—Charlie and Jennilee. Impossible to think of one without the other, they were close, closer than any humans he'd ever seen, had been since they were born.

Charlie and Jennilee had finally reached their goal—they were married, they owned the house of their dreams, they were well on their way to having everything they'd ever wanted, and now this. Sometimes, life sucked.

Charlie sat in the same spot he'd been in the last couple of days. Beside Jennilee's bed, her hand in his, crooning softly, constantly. Doc shifted a bit nearer so he could catch Charlie's fervent whispers.

"Come on, Jennilee-love. Come back to me. Hear me. Hear me calling to you. You have to come back. Don't leave me here all alone. Come on Jennilee-baby. Don't let them win. We've beaten them before, we can do it again."

Charlie's pleas nearly broke Doc's heart. After all they'd been through, it just wasn't fair. If anyone deserved better it was the physically and emotionally battered angel lying in the bed and her stalwart defender.

"Open those ocean eyes of yours and look at me." Charlie commanded, pleaded, cajoled. "Come on Jennilee-honey. Wake up, and I'll brush your hair. Want me to sing to you some more? I can send Grandy for my guitar. I'll...light your way." Charlie's voice broke, just a bit and he bent his head over their clasped hands.

Doc cleared his throat softly. Charlie's head came up and he swiveled the least bit. Urged, "Let Del or Sadie or Angel or...someone else sit with her for awhile, Charlie. Get some rest. It won't do Jennilee any good if you make yourself sick tending her." Knew the offer was futile even as he made it.

"I'm not leaving her. In fact, I've just decided. I'm taking her home. There's nothing else you can do for her here. Sign the paperwork and do what you gotta and then we're outta here."

"Taking her..."

Charlie was right. There was nothing else the doctors or the hospital could do for her. Other than bruises, Jennilee just looked like she was sleeping. A sleeping princess under an evil spell—one that prevented her from waking. A kiss wasn't going to do it—Charlie had already tried numerous times. If any prince could, it was Charlie. Charlie, with his white blonde hair and dark chocolate eyes, eyes that saw only Jennilee. Charlie of the true heart with all the valor and courage, the chivalry, of a knight of old.

Even though Doc knew Charlie was talking about the antebellum mansion and grounds he and Jennilee had spent the better part of ten years lovingly restoring, he got an instant flashback to years earlier. When Charlie or Jennilee'd said *home* in that tone of voice, they'd meant Grandy's house.

Another flashback, and Doc knew exactly what part of *home* they craved. Like looking at a picture, he could clearly see the two of them as children. Charlie and Jennilee, ensconced in Grandy's handed-down-for-generations rocking chair, Jennilee in Charlie's lap, curled in a ball. Charlie, arms tight around her, rocking and singing to her in his wonderful baritone.

The rocking chair cure had worked time after time before, maybe it held one more miracle—for that's what it would take to bring Jennilee out of this and save both of them—a miracle.

That, and Jeff.

"Give it a little more time here, Charlie. At least until Jeff arrives."

Charlie didn't answer, and that was answer enough.

Doc left the room, head down and shoulders slumped, to fill out the paperwork and arrange for an ambulance to carry Jennilee home. Not that paperwork, or lack of, would stop Charlie from doing whatever he thought best for Jennilee.

People came and went. Charlie barely noticed anyone, at least until Jeff breezed in. Standing, listening to bones and joints snap-crackle-pop as he moved for the first time in ages, Charlie and Jeff came together in a hanging on and pounding backs everything's gonna be alright affirmation.

"She's gonna be okay, Charlie. She has to be."

Reluctantly breaking apart and taking seats on either side of the bed, Charlie announced, "I'm taking her home."

Jeff laughed. Laughed harder. Caught his breath. "What took you so long? Figured you'd already be at Grandy's."

A tiny grin quirked the corners of Charlie's lips, didn't come close to his eyes. "Doc wanted me to wait till you got here. Seems to think you can wave your magic wand or something."

"Maybe so, although I think you and Mose—where is the big lug—would be far more capable than l'il ole me."

"Mose won't come to the hospital. Said he didn't want Jennilee to wake up to a hangin' and he couldn't be here and not hold her hand or somethin'."

"Sure he's not just bein' a chickenshit about doctors and hospitals and such?"

"More like he's sufferin' flashbacks after what he did to get her back. Says he's not, but..." Charlie shrugged.

At Jeff's raised eyebrows, Charlie shook his head. "Got a lot to tell you."

"Same here, Charlie Brown. Same here. Sorry it took me so long to get here, but I was right in the middle of...things."

CHAPTER 36

*J*ennilee had no idea how long she'd been underwater, but she was pretty sure she'd not merely broken but had instead *shattered* all her previous records.

Those random things she'd glimpsed in the water were nothing compared to what revolved in front of her eyes now.

Nightmares of Butch—and Sylvia—tormenting her devolved into worse ones of Knot—and Celie—tormenting Charlie's mom and then her own.

Like reading a police report complete with pictures and detailed confessions, she *knew* all the things they'd done.

Had to do something about it.

She must've long since run out of oxygen. Her muscles were no longer responding to her commands. Jennilee floated, weightless. Maybe she'd died and was just too stubborn to acknowledge it. She didn't feel dead. What did dead feel like?

She couldn't be dead.

She couldn't just...leave Charlie.

He'd never survive.

More visions drifted in and swept around her like mud stirred up in a turbulent current.

Good gradually edging out bad as clean water swept the muddy away.

Mose and Suki and their kids.

Jeff and Angel and theirs.

Hers and Charlie's.

Endless couples and children she had no names for and absolutely no doubt she'd know them when the time was right.

Brothers and sisters of the heart, nieces and nephews and cousins, definitely of the heart. Babies and babies and more babies to add to her growing by leaps and bounds family.

How to get back so she could start the meet and greet? She had tons of things to do to get ready for them!

A distant flicker of light in the pitch black surrounding her. A will-o-the-wisp she couldn't seize no matter how hard she tried. Bobbing around and ahead of her like kids playing flashlight freeze tag while she remained frozen, awaiting someone to tag her and wake her up.

In some kind of crazy reverse game, Jennilee needed the touch of the light to unfreeze her instead of freezing her.

The light gradually slowed and came closer. Flickers that looked like cavorting dolphins solidified.

Into a beautiful woman, dressed to kill, 1950s style, all in shimmering gold today. Blonde hair, softly waved, sky blue eyes, and more love beaming out of her smile than Jennilee could comprehend.

"Amelia!"

As if Amelia's light-filled presence bore the longed for touch, as magical as the day Jennilee had swum with the dolphins, Jennilee suddenly found herself capable of movement and speech.

Stepping into Amelia's wide open arms, hugging back, Jennilee laughed and cried happy tears. Linking arms, the two women strolled and gabbed about everything in the world as if they were truly enjoying their garden on a brilliant, sunny day. Surrounded by trilling birds and a veritable rainbow of flowers in bloom, myriad scents perfuming the languid air, nothing but time well spent with a beloved friend.

A long, long while later, Amelia disengaged her arm from

Jennilee's. "It's time. I've so enjoyed our span together, but... It's time."

Backing away, holding a bright, flickering light in her cupped hands, more like a captured star than a firefly, the woman blew softly on her hands, sending the spark pinwheeling like dandelion fluff in Jennilee's direction, growing brighter with each rotation.

Amelia's words, as melodic as she was beautiful, chimed around Jennilee as Amelia slowly faded. "It's not your time, sweet girl. Charlie needs you. The world needs you. Go back, and be at peace. Charlie..."

The world turned to light, like an up close and personal solar flare.

Funny thing, the flare looked just like Charlie's beloved face.

CHAPTER 37

*J*ennilee's eyelids flickered the slightest bit.

A flicker that captured all Charlie's attention and drew him closer, like a drowning man sighting a possible rescue. A miner, caught in a cave-in, spotting a glimmer of light. Not sure if he was hallucinating, barely daring to hope.

Hand over hers, weaving their fingers together, Charlie waited breathlessly.

Scrambling out of his chair on the far side of her bed, Jeff stood and took Jennilee's other hand, mindful of the IV.

Eyes opening slowly, like they had lead weights affixed, Jennilee's eyes instinctively found Charlie's beloved face.

Licking dry lips, tongue thick amid a mouth full of foetid cotton, she tried to speak.

Instantly holding a straw to her lips, Charlie helped her sip some water.

Jennilee whispered, "Taylor Lee and Amelia Adele."

Waiting impatiently, especially since it looked like Charlie was too dumbstruck to respond, Jeff couldn't help himself. Frowning, Jeff asked for both of them. "Who's that, baby?" Unfamiliar names but it didn't sound like anyone who'd hurt Jennilee, and Jeff was all about paying back anyone and everyone who'd done this to her.

Face lighting from within, a slow smile creased Charlie's exhausted face right on up into his beautiful eyes as Jennilee's words sank in. "Our first two children."

Jeff blinked, blinked again. Looked from Charlie to Jennilee and back. "*First two*? How many are y'all plannin' on havin'?"

"A houseful." Charlie leaned closer and pressed his lips gently against Jennilee's.

Smacking a hand to his forehead, Jeff groaned. "A houseful? Y'alls house? That's gonna be…"

Jennilee rasped, "I saw them, Charlie. Plain as day. Talked to them. I can't wait to meet them in person."

Not doubting her for an instant, Charlie's voice cracked, the strain of the last few days breaking through. "You've been gone…awhile. Days."

Jennilee shivered and tightened her fingers on his. "Sorry. I came back as soon as I could."

Cracked more, brokenly. "Don't you ever apologize. Not to me. You came back. That's all that matters, Jennilee-love. I thought…"

Shaking her head, tears sparkling, Jennilee denied his unspoken words. "Oh, no. You're not getting rid of me that easily, my beloved."

Eyes locked, Charlie and Jennilee communed silently as Jeff heaved a silent, heartfelt sigh and quipped, "Not that any of us were worried or anything."

Taking her eyes off Charlie for the first time since she'd opened them, Jennilee briefly met Jeff's relieved gaze, looked around the flower-filled room, conspicuously devoid of any other people besides Jeff. "Where's Grandy?"

Charlie soothed, "She's fine. Finally gave in and fell asleep in the room next door. She's been right here the whole time."

"What about…Ben?"

"Easy, Jennilee-love. He's here, on another floor in ICU but he's recovering well. We'll go see him when you're ready."

Jeff gently squeezed the hand he held. "And I got here as soon as I could. Boy, oh boy, have I got news for you. It can wait till you're better, but you're not gonna believe who…"

Squeezing back, Jennilee stated, certain sure. "Knot Jones." At Jeff's shocked look, Jennilee's eyes went blank for a moment, as if looking inward at something the guys couldn't see. Vacant, like an abandoned house's windows. She nodded, shuddered—*shuttered*—and came back to them before they had time to panic. "He's the one."

Jeff's jaw dropped and Charlie stroked the hair back off Jennilee's face, not even blinking at her knowledge.

Focusing on Jeff, Jennilee smiled proudly, pursed her lips in an air kiss. "I knew you'd do it. I never doubted you."

Switching her gaze to Charlie, Jennilee's pain-filled ocean eyes sought his dark ones.

"Oh, no, Jennilee-sweet. None of this is your fault and you couldn't have known. None of us could have."

Jeff closed his jaw with a snap. "How'd you… Jennilee?"

"I don't know where I was but I saw…a lot of things, like… like watching a movie. I can't prove it, but Knot Jones killed both our moms. He and She Who Shall Not Be Named conspired together. They've been lovers for…forever and Sylvie's not… Not my uncle's child."

Stroking a hand lightly across the livid bruises on Jennilee's face, Charlie absorbed the implications. Rested his hand gently around the rope mark bruises circling her throat.

"If Sylvie's not…" Jeff turned greenish and gagged as the truth hit him. "Yuck. Gross. Dis…gusting. Sylvia and Butch are… That's just plain nasty. I think I'm gonna be sick."

Charlie murmured, "No wonder *she* didn't care if Sylvie had an abortion."

All professional now, Jeff declared in ringing tones, "You might not be able to prove it, but I damn sure can. That's what I was gonna tell you."

Jennilee's words came out short and choppy as she tried to explain what she'd somehow seen, the horror of it stealing her breath. "Charlie's mom—Iris—saw Knot with *her* in a compromising situation. They found out—she—Iris was going to New Bern and they left ahead of her. My mom's sister pretended to have car trouble. She lured Iris into stopping and they ambushed her. Knot killed her. Bashed the back of her head in. Just like he did my mom's. Knot did the deed but my aunt helped. She aided and abetted not only that murder but my mom's. How could she?" The last was nearly wailed.

"Easy, Jennilee." Hands on Jennilee's shoulders, Charlie gently held her battered form against the bed. "There's nothing any of us can do about it now. Settle. It's too late to get upset about stuff we had no control over, stuff that's over and done."

Jennilee subsided, but her tortured words were like broken glass, tearing jagged holes in Charlie's and Jeff's hearts.

"Same thing with my mom. After the Judge told...*her*...he was cutting her out of the will and leaving everything to my mom, they had a huge fight. The Judge had a terrible stroke and *she*...just left him. Just left her own father lying right there in his den and called her lover from her father's desk while she sat in the Judge's chair and watched her father writhing and gasping and fighting for his life. The two of them met up and had a picnic...*a picnic*...while they plotted. If my mom hadn't stumbled on their tryst, they were gonna do her in that night anyway. Knot did the deed while his lover cheered him on then they got back in his wooden skiff and left. Neither of our moms had a chance." Jennilee choked out, "Knot likes to hit women from behind, just hard enough to stun them so he can keep playing for awhile. Keep hitting. He lets them think they have a chance of getting away." Gave a half sob and spat, "Fooled him, didn't I?"

Biting his tongue to keep from cursing ripely, Jeff declared, "I don't even want to know how you know all this, Jennilee. What you just told us will never stand up in a court of law, but Knot's down and she's going down. I swear it."

Touching foreheads with Jennilee, calming her with his touch and his unshakeable faith in her, Charlie whispered, "Amelia."

Jeff shook his head and muttered, "You two and your ghost."

All of them fell silent as the room door opened.

"Jennilee! You're awake!"

Jeff moved aside as Grandy enfolded Jennilee in a hug. "Baby-girl, you scared all of us half to death!"

Face buried in Grandy's neck, Jennilee's incoherent reply had them all tearing up.

"Hush, now. Hush, child. Everything's gonna be just fine. We've got you back and everything's gonna be fine." Holding Jennilee, crooning, Grandy ordered, "Get Doc, right now. I just saw him in the hall."

Before Charlie could move, not that he intended to leave Jennilee's side anyway, Jeff shot for the door, hollering for Doc as soon as the door cracked open.

Looking like a Three Stooges skit, Doc and Mac tried to come through the doorway at the same time. Ran into each other, bounced off, looked at each other, and tried again. Taking a step back, Mac let Doc go first. Jumping agilely to one side so the twosome didn't run him over, Jeff held the door and got outta the way.

Jennilee looked up as they all crowded round the bed. Sniffled. "I feel like Dorothy. Right after she got back from Oz. I had the strangest, most terrifying, most wonderful dream, and you were there, and you, and you, and you and you. And all I wanted was to come home."

A babble of voices, and Jennilee's smile broke like the sun coming out from behind a storm cloud.

"Where's the big guy?"

When her soft words drew no answer, Jennilee demanded in a louder tone, "Where's the big guy? The scary looking one? He saved me and I need to thank him."

Everyone got quiet at once, all of them deliberately not answering.

"What? I know I didn't dream him. He looks really scary but he's not. Only to bad guys. He looks like...a gargoyle, but he's got a heart of gold."

"Another of your lost ones, Jennilee-love?" Questioning her gently, Charlie smiled his special-just-for-Jennilee smile.

Jennilee nodded, eyes getting heavy and words slurring. "Not just him. There's a bunch of guys, his men, I think, and some women. Brothers and sisters, Charlie. Everything's...foggy."

Charlie soothed, "Mason's already gone. But you're right. He's something else. He and his men. As soon as you feel better..."

Jennilee's eyes widened momentarily before trying to slam shut. "Mason! Yes! That's his name. Mason...Salisbury. He left because...he thought I'd be afraid of him. Charlie, you have to get him back here and..."

"All in good time, Jennilee-love. Rest. Rest now."

Fighting to stay conscious, Jennilee shook her head stubbornly. "Jeff."

"Right here, Jennilee." Moving back into her line of vision, Jeff verbally and visually assured her of his presence.

"Oh, Jeff. Where's Angel? I was right to be so worried about her. Knot said..."

"In the waiting room with about a million others." Giving Jennilee a lopsided grin, he teased, "Gonna give me the heads up on our life story?"

Without missing a beat, Jennilee replied, "And they lived happily ever after."

Wrapping a hand around her blanketed ankle, Jeff choked out, "You know I'm a sucker for beautiful princesses and happy endings."

"Kinda partial to love stories myself."

Charlie did a double take. "Hey! How'd you know about Mason?"

Any answer Jennilee might have given would have to wait. She was already asleep.

~

WOKE BACK up she didn't know how long later, and the first thing out of her mouth was a demand to see Mose, and on the heels of that, Jewel.

"Mose won't come to the hospital, Jennilee."

Struggling to sit up, Jennilee subsided when Charlie hit the up button on the bed. "He better not be feeling bad about his part in saving me or I'll..."

"Hush, Jennilee-sweet. He and Jewel are at our house, waiting for you. He didn't want to chance coming here, just in case someone thought he shouldn't be in your room or even showing so much concern over you. Hospital's not like Doc's office. He couldn't come here and keep his distance."

Jennilee's face darkened like a towering cumulonimbus about to rain down hellfire and retribution instead of merely golfball sized hail. "Nobody better say a word. Not after he risked his life to save mine. Not after what he did."

"Jennilee." Refusing to say anything else until she made eye contact, Charlie gave her a half-smile and a cut-eye toward the open door, urging caution. "He's at our house. Besides that, Mose didn't show up until everything had gone down and Knot and Gear and what's his name had killed each other fighting over you. Or the last bottle of liquor. Or whatever."

Jennilee blinked at that pronouncement. Not the way she remembered it, but maybe Knot had done serious damage with all those blows to her head. She'd worry about that later. She had more important fish to fry. Cocked her head, looking eerily like Jewel when she wasn't sure she was about to hear the *get the mouse* command but was hoping to. "At our house?"

"Suki's taking care of him. And Jewel."

A smug, satisfied smile lit Jennilee's face, highlighting the bruises. "When can I get out of here?"

"Now that you've come around, as soon as possible. I'd already told Doc I was takin' you home."

Jennilee met Charlie's eyes, held them. "Rockin' chair wouldn't't've worked this time."

Not sure how she could state that with such certainty, Charlie didn't doubt Jennilee and didn't argue. Just accepted, like he'd accepted everything else she'd told him and all she had yet to tell. "I was gonna give it my best shot, regardless."

"Thank you for not saying "irre"."

Charlie snorted a laugh. Waved a hand down Jennilee's body. "All this, and you're worried about my proper use of a word?"

Jennilee considered shrugging, thought better of it. Sitting up hurt more than enough. *Breathing* hurt. "Just what is *all this*?"

Charlie's face went dark. "Kidnapping. Torture. Abuse. Almost... dying. You scared me half to death, woman."

"Didn't mean to." Jennilee's turn, her face shuttered. "I did everything right. And still..."

"Don't even, Jennilee. The only reason you're here and breathing is because you fought like you did. I damn sure didn't..."

"Don't even go there, Charlie. You did everything you could to keep me safe and still... I didn't manage to kill Knot. Gave him a lot of grief, but he paid me back in spades."

Charlie ticked off things on his fingers, raising one with each reason. "Knot's dead, whether you did it or not. Ben is alive because of you. Jewel is alive because of you. We have a whole passel of new friends I can't wait for you to meet. We found you because of you." Splayed his fingers for emphasis. "Because. Of. You." Charlie sucked in a breath that felt like it'd come across hot coals laced with glass shards. "Most important, you're alive. Because of you. You could've given up at any point, but you didn't."

Falling silent, Charlie stared blindly out the window. "Someday, when you're better and this is far in the past, I'll take you out to that old fish-house and show you how far you swam underwater. Mason said you never came up for air once you broke out from under the building."

Ignoring Charlie's *what you did was impossible* tone, Jennilee deflected, "When do I get to meet Mason? I've got something important to tell him."

"Need to be careful what you blab about. Especially them. Most folks don't know about him and his crew, and that's the way they want it. They'll be back Friday week. That'll give you time to heal a bit and get your bearings back."

Jennilee frowned, then beamed. "The only time I lost my bearings was when I was swimming. Everything went totally dark there at the end, but I saw your light. All I had to do was move toward your light. You're like my own personal beacon, Charlie. Always. Brighter than Cape Lookout at the dark of the moon."

Standing up, turning his back to Jennilee, Charlie walked to the window. Braced his hands on the sill and tried not to pass out.

Jennilee threw that out so casually—*everything went dark at the end*—did she have any idea how close she'd come to dying? Charlie wasn't even sure she hadn't, that Amelia hadn't guided her back from...the other side.

Mason had told Charlie how far Jennilee'd swum. Being an expert marksman, Mason could judge distance pretty darn accurately, and he had no reason whatsoever to lie. Besides that, he was the one who'd waded out after her. An Olympic swimmer couldn't have gone that distance, not fresh off the starting block. And Jennilee had been anything but fresh.

Making fists, carefully, so Jennilee wouldn't see them, so she wouldn't notice the muscles in his back bunch up, Charlie vowed he'd take what he was given in the miracle department.

"Charlie?"

Spinning back to her, Charlie plastered a wide smile on his face. "Right here, Jennilee-love. Right here. Let's get you dressed and head home."

CHAPTER 38

*B*ringing back memories from when they'd invited Tim and
Rachel into their lives, Charlie had installed a temporary
wheelchair ramp. He refused to let Jennilee walk and she was too sore
to be carried.

Wheeling her up and in, Jennilee shot a dubious glance at the twin
staircases.

"Nothing doing, my lady. We're roosting down here for a bit." Fore-
stalling her disagreement at even temporarily abandoning their regular
rooms, rooms Jennilee'd infused with so much love merely entering
them was like walking into a warm, invisible cocoon, Charlie added,
"In the room right next to Mose."

"Thought you said he was alright."

"He is. Jewel's…"

Jennilee spat, "If Knot wasn't already dead, I'd kill him myself."

"So feisty. Love it. Don't ever change, Jennilee-love."

Stopping in the middle of the immense entryway, Charlie crouched
in front of Jennilee. Held out his closed hand. "Here. Mason and the
guys scoured the bottom till they found this."

Waiting till she lifted her hand, Charlie dropped something
smelling heavily of WD-40 into her open palm.

"My Old Timer! How… I dropped it in the silt when Knot was…"

"Gonna have to ask Mason and his guys. How about I get you another one?"

"What's wrong with this one, Charlie?"

"Nothing. I want to frame it. Blade open. Maybe with a little blood red paint dripping off the tip."

Still laughing softly when Charlie wheeled her down the hall, around the corner and into a comfortably appointed room, Jennilee quieted fast.

Mose stared at her, sober as a judge. Planted solidly in his lap, Jewel thumped her tail. Pricked her ears and whined but didn't get up. Probably *couldn't*.

Rolling her practically knee to knee with Mose, Charlie helped Jennilee stand, allowing it only because he knew she wasn't going far. Suki carefully took Jewel, pillow and all, from Mose's hands.

Twisting, Jennilee sank into Mose's lap. Holding her arms out for Jewel, Jennilee gently clasped Jewel to her heart and burrowed her face into Mose's neck as the tears began to stream down her face.

"Hush, girl. No cause to be cryin' now. We made it."

"Thanks to you."

Mose snorted rudely. "Me? All I did was cleanup. You got Jewel free. You got yourself free. You half-killed Knot before I ever got there. Poked him as full'a holes as a bald tire running over a nail spill."

Giving a push, Mose set the rocker in motion.

Jennilee's breath hitched and hiccuped like a little kid trying to stave off a crying jag. "I was so scared. Then I was furious. They kept hurting Ben, and Knot hurt Jewel so bad and all I could do was watch. He said they were gonna go after Angel and Suki and Jeff and you and…He said they were saving me for Butch. We gotta…"

Lifting her head, Jennilee sought Charlie. The fierce grin on his face said it all.

Dropping her head back down, she peered at Charlie beneath Mose's chin. "How?"

"He's in jail, Jennilee-baby. For the foreseeable future. So's Sylvia." *They'd spend the rest of their lives there, if Charlie had to buy a prison planet and ship them to it.* "Drugs, assault, extortion, credit card fraud, writing bad checks..." *Attempted murder.* "The list is endless. As endless as their sentences." *Celie would've been right there with them, with the added spice of prostitution and possession with intent to sell, courtesy of Knot the Pimp/Dealer. Enough drugs in her hotel room to put her away for life, even without Mr. Talton's surveillance and proof of deals. Knot had quite a racket going with his supposed woman. Too bad she'd...dropped off the map. For some reason, law enforcement thought Knot'd done away with her and they had yet to find the body.* "Oh, and Knot's family won't ever bother you again, Jennilee-sweet. Ever." *Thanks to Mason and crew paying the vast majority of them an extended visit and explaining the facts of life. Or death, as it were. And heartily recommending relocation. To another country. Preferably on another planet.* "Speaking of Knot's family, got someone you need to meet. When you're up to it. Told everyone no visitors for a bit, till you get rested up."

"I'm alright, Charlie. Despite looking like roadkill. I'm...alright." With those assurances, Jennilee was asleep. Just that fast.

Charlie paced, rigid and furious. How could Jennilee be reassuring him? Especially when she looked like...in her own words...roadkill? Bruised and battered, ligature marks around her neck and wrists and ankles, cuts and scrapes everywhere. How could she even think to blame herself? She'd gotten free—thank God for her penchant for sharp knives!—and basically saved them all. Not that Jennilee would ever see it that way, and there was no use arguing. She looked so bad, Mac had even put off officially taking her statement.

Head back, eyes closed, rocking Jennilee like she was a sick baby holding her favorite stuffed animal, Mose ordered, "Sit, Charlie Bear. Our girl says she's fine, then she's fine. She knows. Jennilee knows. She's stronger than most, and she survived this. Just like she survived her childhood. She might not ever talk about what happened, but she wasn't raped and she wasn't kilt. Sit. You're givin' me a crick in my neck."

Still pacing, Charlie spat, "No thanks to me."

The rocking chair stopped and Mose opened his eyes. "That what's crawled up your gizzard? You listen to me, and you listen good. Ever'-body's got talents. Mine is killin'. Mason's is... extraction, among other things. Yours... Yours is lovin' our Jennilee. You're the best person I know for findin' people you need with the talents to enhance and carry out whatever you've got planned. We did our part because you did yours. 'Nuff said."

Jennilee's breath hitched, and Mose put the chair back in motion. "Best you *sit*, and hush, afore you wake her up. Sleep's the best thing for her right now. When I've had my fill of settin' my mind at ease that she's alive and whole, then you take another turn and we'll anchor her to us."

Slipping up beside Charlie, Suki slid her arms around his waist and urged him to the couch. Sat beside him, eyes locked on Mose.

Draping an arm around Suki's shoulder, Charlie pulled her close, both of them needing the contact. For a long while, nothing was heard but soft breathing and the soothing, repetitive eenntt-ooo of the rocking chair.

"Finding the right people, huh? That's my talent?"

Mose snorted a laugh. "That, and lovin' our girl the way she oughtta be loved. Don't discount those so easily. You're exactly what she needs."

"Jeff told me the same thing a while back. Also told me everything that tries to harm Jennilee boomerangs back and deals out more friends and joy."

"Boy's got more sense 'n a bird dog. 'Bout time he used that head of his'n for somethin' besides a helmet rack." Rocking and chortling, grounding himself with Jennilee's slight form, Mose closed his eyes and smiled to himself.

Feeling Suki relax into his side, Charlie realized some inviolate turning point had been reached. Jennilee was back, safe, and Mose was on this side—the right side—of crazy.

Getting up after a bit, Suki slipped out silently, came back not too long after just as quietly. Mose rocked on, oblivious to anything except the gift he held. Suki noiselessly took picture after picture while Charlie grinned like a lunatic.

CHAPTER 39

A little over a week later, up and about, Jennilee once more held court. Bruises faded to mottled yellows and greens for the most part, barnacle gouges infection free and scabbed nicely, Jewel walking around on her own power and hardly limping at all.

The new and vastly improved warning system I.G. had installed pinged. Chimed immediately after to let them know it was an acceptable arrival. Didn't mean it wasn't someone in a vehicle they had no business being in, but there were plenty of cameras and a whole roomful of TV screens—in the recently converted space over the garage, therefore out of sight, out of mind to Jennilee—showing whoever was coming down the drive.

Charlie hadn't had to ask her opinion to know Jennilee would soundly veto a sky high wall surrounded by an alligator and piranha filled moat—with a locked gate complete with an armed guard in a secure gatehouse—but he'd insisted on the alarms. Not that someone couldn't come in through any part of the woods they owned, or buzz right up to their dock from the open river for that matter. Charlie hadn't bothered mentioning any of the multitude of other security alarms in place to Jennilee, but he sure rested easier knowing they were there. She couldn't fuss about what she didn't know about.

Standing up, anxious to meet Mason and crew, she flashed Charlie a look, so full of love he felt his heart swell until he thought it would burst.

He'd watched her like a momma hen with not one, but two—hell, a whole flock of—hungry hawks circling overhead and eyeing vulnerable chicks. He'd watched her insist on going to the ocean every day. Watched as she brooked no refusal, after the first few days of just wading or sinking down in the surf, on swimming in the healing salt water.

Heal she had. Jewel as well. Inside and out.

Faster than they should have.

Not that he was complaining.

Jennilee'd healed herself, and Jewel, and Mose, from soul-deep wounds that by rights should've taken months, if not lifetimes, to recover from.

Even Charlie himself was mostly recovered. Far more cautious, far more apt to be suspicious and far quicker to take action if his radar so much as thought about pinging, but... No more nightmares, and he could still breathe if Jennilee got out of his sight. No panic attacks when she did.

Not that he let her, much. He dogged her heels closer than Jewel, and that was saying something. Other than to use the bathroom in quick there and back trips, the little muttley hadn't gotten more than a breath away from Jennilee since they'd rocked with Mose.

Linking her fingers with Charlie's, Jennilee stepped out onto the porch and eagerly awaited the approaching guests.

Barefoot, wearing a gauzy, floaty summer dress of shimmering blue-green with tiny bright flowers embroidered all over and something airy that resembled baby's breath woven into the twist of hair haloing her head, the rest of her golden bright hair unbound, Jennilee looked every inch the triumphant fairy princess welcoming a returning warrior from a successful battle.

Mason crossed the yard slowly, letting her see him in the full light of day. Charlie'd told him Jennilee'd demanded an audience, but just because she thought she wanted to see him... The reality might change her mind.

Her eyes left Mason's face only long enough to take in the men and the slight boy flanking him like an honor guard. Right back to Mason's hedgerow mug.

Eyes alight, no trace of repugnance or fear visible, Jennilee held out both hands in welcome as Mason took his time climbing the steps.

Stopping himself, barely, from taking a knee, Mason gently clasped her small hands in his much larger paws.

"Welcome, Mason. And crew. Our home is yours, for as long as we all shall remain friends, in this world and the next unto infinity." Making her vow, Jennilee took a step forward and rose on tiptoe.

Leaning down to her, Mason accepted the face clasp, and the kiss she bestowed first on one high boned, misshapen cheek, then the other, and finally a long, gentle press of lips on his heavy forehead. Accepted too, the heartfelt hug and sigh that accompanied it.

"Come, sit. Talk a spell. Suki's on the way with refreshments." Leading them to the glider and porch swing and a cluster of comfortable chairs, Jennilee motioned Mason to an oversize seat obviously put there just for him. "First, you have my deepest gratitude, from the bottom of my heart."

Looking like he wanted to melt between the cracks in the porch boards, Mason took the proffered seat.

Giving a little laugh, Jennilee sat on the glider, waited until Charlie took his place beside her. "You think me too effusive, perhaps? Belittling my own part in our...adventure?"

Perching on the edge of his chair, patently uncomfortable with her acceptance and lavish praise, Mason shot a look at a silently laughing Mouse, and made an indecipherable choking sound. "You'd done all the hard part before we got there. We just managed cleanup."

Laughing again, a musical sound to rival the chimes singing softly further down the porch, Jennilee shook her head to a cherry blossom rain of miniature petals. Holding out her hands for Jewel when Charlie gently picked the little mutt up and offered her to Jennilee, she let the dog settle and petted her softly as Charlie draped his arm around Jennilee.

"Charlie has already expressed his thanks to you on our behalf, and now you have mine as well. My undying gratitude is not only on my part—and there is nothing I can do to thank you adequately for that—but for saving Mose."

A slight frown flickered across Mason's rugged, mismatched features. "Not sure if you remember anything about what happened, but Mose is the one who saved you. Took out all the bad guys before we ever got close."

Jennilee tipped her head. "Had you not been there, he would've been too late to pull me from the water, and that... That would have utterly destroyed him. You were both in the place you were supposed to be at exactly the time you were meant to be. Because you were, I get to stay with my beloved Charlie and our life proceeds as it was meant to, with no one being extirpated except the bad guys." Leaning into Charlie, fitting her body to his like they were human puzzle pieces, one hand stroking lightly down Jewel's back, Jennilee beamed.

Lemonade that tasted of nectar, sparkling sugar cookies dusted with fairy dust, a good deal of companionable banter between the men while Jennilee alternately beamed and catnapped.

Blinking and shaking herself awake from her latest mini-snooze, Jennilee turned her face up to Charlie. A quick brush of lips, taking Jewel and placing her on the porch, Charlie helped Jennilee stand, kept hold of her hands. A smile just for him, so brilliant with love it made Mason and crew look away, envy plain on their faces.

Holding out a hand to Mason, Jennilee met his eyes, peaceful ocean to solemn amber. "Come, walk with me."

Mason had no more power to deny her than a besotted knight had to disobey his beloved queen. Than a bug encased in amber had the power to change its position.

Grinning, Charlie seemed fully on board with whatever Jennilee had in mind. Privy, and complicit, no doubt. Sinking back down on the glider, Charlie waved them off.

Ambling around the vast yard, arm in arm, Jennilee slanted a look up at Mason, swept a hand out gracefully. "Are the flowers not beautiful? It takes much care, and judicious snipping and tending and fertilizing and weeding to keep the beds so. "When we found this place, it was a...jungle."

Mason looked, truly looked. He'd seen the damage from hurricanes before. That this place could be so...extraordinary after what it had recently been through said a lot for the love and dedication Charlie and Jennilee bestowed upon it.

Slanting another look at Mason, one that spoke volumes, Jennilee gave him a serene smile. "It took much work to bring it back to full glory, from the jungle and from the storm, but it has been more than worth the effort."

Knowing she was getting around to making a point, Mason waited to see what Jennilee would come up with next.

"The hurricane battered them to no end, stripped them almost entirely of leaf and flower and beat them into the ground, but as you can see, the plants responded with rampant growth and an excess of blooms in order to compensate. Human relationships are much the same. They must be tended in order to thrive. Sometimes they even benefit from a little of life's storms, becoming stronger in the process, and all the better for it."

They strolled for a bit, Mason letting the beauty surrounding him and the beauty on his arm soak into his soul. So much so that he stumbled when next Jennilee spoke.

"She weighs heavy on your heart."

Stumbling yet again, Mason quickly recovered. "She, who?"

A few more slow steps while Mason pondered how Jennilee knew he was missing a particular female. Jennilee didn't know him, they'd barely spoken a handful of words to each other, and yet... She treated him as a valued—*beloved*—member of her family. Stopped altogether as Jennilee turned to face him, putting her hands on his forearms and smiling up into his solemn eyes.

"It's time. Time for you to start working your way back to Willow. It's going to take years—long years—but you need each other. Life's storms have battered you both, and although you have both survived the storm, your garden is in sore need of tending so it may blossom and come to fruition."

Going up on tiptoe, hands on his shoulders, Jennilee whispered in his ear as Mason leaned down to her. "Promise me, Mason. Promise you'll at least eventually touch base with Willow. Just do that and see where it goes from there."

Blinking as stupidly as a pole-axed Minotaur, Mason shook his head. Wait... Jennilee guessing he had a woman somewhere wasn't that far out of the realm of possibility, given her talent for knowing things she couldn't have known, but... How had she known Willow's name?

Flummoxed, a nod was all he could manage. The thought of seeing Willow again, just the thought, tied him in knots. Having always kept tabs on her, he knew she had a life. A very good life. So did he, and he couldn't see any way the two were compatible. Even if, after all this time, she still held all his heart.

CHAPTER 40

*M*ason, usually content to stay silently in the background and let his men, especially Mouse, handle the conversations and interactions with others, finally gave up on his efforts to do so—despite all the emotions Jennilee's words had stirred up and all the things from his past clamoring for attention.

Since the moment Mason stepped onto the runway, Charlie wouldn't let him fade and now neither would Jennilee.

Jennilee wouldn't have let him even if he'd desired to do so, drawing him again and again into the quick banter flying back and forth. Jeff and Angel had joined them, and Mose.

Suki came out on the porch to stand behind Mose with her hand on his shoulder, his hand covering hers.

Hardly able to take his eyes off his hostess, Mason jerked back to awareness when he noticed everyone staring at him expectantly, like they were waiting for him to answer a question.

Mouse snickered and tipped his head. Held up a pinkie and wiggled it. "She's got you wrapped already."

Taking no offense, Charlie grinned at Mason.

Jennilee smiled beatifically. "We were discussing overlapping circles, and I said you completed one of ours and added to others, and still others."

At Mason's blank look, still grinning, Charlie offered, "Ever seen a Double Wedding Ring quilt?"

Jennilee's face glowed like the sun as she drew imaginary circles in the air and added, "Doesn't matter. You get the concept. Charlie and I form one circle, and we're friends with Mose and Jeff, who form more circles. Jeff and Angel are a circle unto themselves, Mose and Suki are another, all overlapping with pieces of their circle being important parts of our circle. Now we've added y'all to our circle."

Mason eyed them warily. "Just how big is this...circle?"

Laughing delightedly, Jennilee spread her arms wide. "Thiiissssss big. As big as it needs to be, with the infinite capacity to expand as needed."

"This matters because?"

Jennilee laughed again, a sweet, tinkling sound, as if the answer should be obvious to everyone. "Because you've become a part of our circle and you can't leave now without leaving a huge hole in ours, like a rent in the very fabric of space and time." Cocking her head, looking at Mason meaningfully, as if they were the only two people there, Jennilee smiled and added, "Besides, you have your own circle to add."

"Speaking of circles, Jennilee-love, I've got one to add to ours. Remember I told you I wanted to introduce you to someone? Suki?" Shooting a glance at the woman in question, Charlie gave her a nod.

Going inside, Suki returned in a blink with a teenager.

Taking Jennilee's hand in his, Charlie said, "Jennilee, meet Evvie. She had a great part in saving you."

Taking in the nervous girl, wringing her hands and shifting foot to foot, looking like she was about to bolt any second, Jennilee took a closer look. Tipped her head to the girl. "Thank you, for the part you played. You have my most sincere gratitude."

Evvie stood straighter and clenched her hands at her sides, face pinched. "You may not be so grateful after I tell you..." Deep breath. "I lied on my application. I'm...kinda-sorta kin to Knot. Not that I claim him."

Jennilee blinked, tilted her head as if listening to something—or someone—the others couldn't hear. Nodded as a slow smile worked its way across her face. "Welcome, and again, thank you. I'm kinda-sorta kin to my aunt, not that I claim her. Guess that makes you and I some kind of kin by default. I'd be more than happy to claim you, though."

Evvie came a step closer. "Why don't you hate me? My...sperm donor plotted with my uncle to kill you. My uncle killed your mom and Mr. Charlie's."

"Did you have anything to do with any of that?"

Evvie shook her head vehemently.

"Could you have stopped them?"

Evvie swallowed hard. "If I'd'a been smarter, or paid more attention, mebbe I coulda..."

Jennilee countered, "Maybe if you'd paid more attention, you'd be dead now. I'm alive, you're alive, and they're dead. Things worked out..." Pausing a moment, Jennilee shot Charlie a look brilliant with love, repeated her earlier words. "...as they were meant to."

"Aren't you...upset that you had a great part in killing Knot?"

Speaking to the girl—as she had to Mason—as if they were the only two there, Jennilee told her fiercely, "If you're waiting for me to say yes, to apologize for saving my own life, don't hold your breath. I don't regret one stab or blow I dealt Knot. I'd've done him more damage had I been able. I regret nothing, unless it's that my own mother didn't get the same chance to fight back."

Crossing her arms, Evvie gave Jennilee a conspiratorial smirk. "Good. 'Cause I'm not sorry they're dead. Sorry they hurt you, but not sorry at all you took them out."

Mason started clapping, slowly. The rest of the men joined them along with Angel and Suki, the only other females in attendance. All of them looked on, faces full of approval.

Jennilee beamed. "Now that we've decided we're on the same page, tell me about yourself. I need to know what kind of things you like. What you're good at. What you're passionate about."

Picking up on what Jennilee wasn't saying, Evvie glowered. "You're sending me away? Thought you didn't hate me?"

Jennilee kept right on smiling serenely. "You know you can't stay here. Here you'll never be more than Gear's by-blow. I'm not sending you away. I'm gifting you another chance at life. A fresh start."

"How do you know you can trust me? Maybe I'm just like…them."

"You think I'm like my aunt?"

"You're the polar opposite."

"And you're a very good fabricator. Well done."

Evvie blinked but didn't deny Jennilee's statement.

"You like to play like you're a stupid hick, but you've forgotten who you're talking to—to whom you are speaking. Forgotten yourself, more than once and dropped your dumb redneck act. Used proper grammar and words your so-called parents couldn't look up with both hands and a flashlight if someone else was holding the dictionary and pointed out the right spot on the page."

Clapping a hand over her mouth as the laugh Jennilee startled out of her burst free, Evvie shook her head. "If I'd ever had a sister, I'd want her to be you."

"Fair enough. Same here. No more acting with us. No one here wishes you anything but the best. Between our contacts, and Mason's, we'll see you well placed. Home and education-wise, not job-wise. That's entirely up to you. After you finish school. College too, if you're so inclined."

Giving a soft whistle, Mason pinned Jennilee with his amber eyes when she looked his way. "How do you know I have any contacts like that, little missy?"

Mose started laughing, a small chuckle followed by heartier and heartier laughs that morphed into full-out belly laughs. "Give it up, Mason. Jennilee sees all, knows all."

Smiling at something over Mose's shoulder—the same something Jewel was staring fixedly at—opposite the shoulder Suki was standing sentry behind, Jennilee laughed merrily. "Not everything, Mose. Just some."

"Huh. Think I can't see you confabbin' with your ghost again, don'cha."

Everyone else blinked in surprise, trading sizzling glances and looking from Mose to Jennilee and back as if both had lost their respective minds.

Mose's quiet rumble filled the air. "Thank you, Miz..." Cocked his head at Jennilee in a blatant smirk.

Jennilee gave a half-laugh.

"...Amelia. I'd'a been too late if you hadn't spoke up and pointed me in the right direction. Thank you."

Charlie sat up and snapped to attention like Jewel spotting a praying mantis. "Miz Amelia *spoke* to you?"

Mose drawled, "Unless the voice in my head—truck—wherever— has suddenly acquired the distinct tones of a well-bred Northern lady... Yeah. She...guided me. I was drivin' around aimlessly, praying for a sign. I heard her, clear as day. *Turn here.* Pret' near ran off the road lookin' for whoever'd spoken, but I did what she said and not too much farther on I spotted Jewel limping and staggering beside the road, and well..."

Rubbing his hands together, Jeff spouted, "The rest is history! Thank you, Miz Amelia!"

As on cue as if they'd rehearsed it for days, the rest of the crowd chorused, "Thank you, Miz Amelia!"

It might've been the chimes, or the breeze, or...

All of them, each and every one, heard a soft echo waft down the porch.

"You're welcome."

In the distinct tones of a well-bred Northern lady.

A REAL CHIME SOUNDED, and I.G. offered, "It's your chief of police." Threw out without looking up from the handheld monitor he was engrossed in, "Got somebody with him."

Just that quick, Mason and crew disappeared. Loaded into one of the pickups Charlie had provided and vamoosed toward the hangar.

By the time Mac and his passenger pulled up, there was no one left on the porch but Charlie and Jennilee and Jewel, and Jeff and Angel.

Rising, Charlie greeted Chief Mac, nodded to the man accompanying him. Waved a hand at the fresh set of refreshments Suki'd set out before she and Mose and Evvie also disappeared, inside.

Waving at Jennilee in a stay where you are gesture, Mac declined the eats. "Charlie, Jennilee. This is an old friend of mine, LaVerne Toler. He's with the State Bureau of Investigation."

Pulling a chair close to Jennilee, Mac sat and rested his elbows on his thighs, fingers laced. Spoke quietly, as if afraid any loud noise would spook Jennilee. Or shatter her, like a high pitched tone destroying crystal. "You're looking much better, sunshine. Gotta take your statement, and Mr. Toler—LaVerne—would like to speak with you."

Curled in Jennilee's lap, Jewel didn't even lift her head, merely flicked her ears and twitched the tip of her tail, a worried frown creasing her face at Mac's solemn tones.

Stroking her pup, leaning into Charlie as he resumed his seat beside her, Jennilee shook her head. "I can tell you what happened on the road, when they trapped us with the fallen trees and were shooting at us. After that... Everything gets muzzy, out of time sequence. Not sure I can make sense of it."

Mac encouraged, "Just tell me what you remember, in your own words."

Jennilee shivered, garnering a sympathetic whimper from Jewel and a squeeze from Charlie's arm, draped around her shoulder. "We— Ben and Jewel and myself—were delivering meals. We rounded a sharp curve and there was a tree across the road. I slammed on the brakes and threw it in reverse just as another tree crashed down behind us. Trying not to get us squished, I cranked the wheel hard and we ended up slewed sideways across the road. Someone started firing shots from the woods in front of us, all aimed at Ben's side of the car. I tried to call Charlie on the CB but I couldn't reach him. That's when I knew we were really in trouble. Ben told me to get out and run. I wanted to stay and help but he insisted. Ben covered me while I high-tailed it for the woods behind the car."

"Is that when Ben got shot?"

Jewel whimpered, Jennilee shook her head and whispered, "That was...later. At the fish-house. When I wouldn't..."

"It's okay, Jennilee. Knot can't hurt you now. Keep going."

"I did. Keep going. At first I was trying to get away so Ben's sacrifice wouldn't be in vain." Reaching her hands up, Jennilee grimaced and lightly traced both sides of her face. "Knot jumped out from behind a tree—I should've been paying more attention but by then I was intent on circling back to the road so I could help Ben—and clobbered me with the butt of his shotgun. I went down and he kicked my weapon out of my hand before I could recover enough to shoot him. Jewel attacked him and I got up and walloped him three or four times with a big branch, something sturdy that'd just come down in the hurricane. He backhanded me and..." Voice beginning to escalate with remembered pain, Jennilee trailed off.

Took a deep breath and continued. "Stupid me, stunned on the ground like a bird that's just flown into a window, and there's poor Jewel, fighting for all she's worth. She wouldn't let go of his arm so he choked her unconscious with his other hand. Then he stuffed her in a duffle and made me get on my feet, marched me back to the road. Every time I staggered, he whacked the duffle with his shotgun. I thought sure Jewel was dead."

Getting to her feet, Jewel placed her paws on Jennilee's chest and licked her mistress' face, whining in distress the whole time.

Burying her face in Jewel's soft fur, Jennilee fought for composure.

"Jennilee!" Charlie's heartfelt cry tore at all their heartstrings. "Jennilee! Stop! You're breaking my heart. You are so brave, so...amazing! You survived—not only your early life, but recent events that would've crushed anyone else! Stop beating yourself up for not being able to single-handedly stop three armed killers."

Mac added, "Charlie's right, Jennilee. You are amazing. Can you answer a few more questions?"

Thoroughly riled, Charlie insisted, "Enough. Jennilee's been through enough, Mac."

Jennilee's hand on his arm calmed Charlie. "No, my dearest love. I need to tell this. If it's too much for you to bear, go inside for a bit. You and Jeff and Angel go do...something."

"I'm not leaving you."

"Neither are we, Jennilee."

Blowing a kiss in Jeff's and Angel's direction, Jennilee sighed and rolled her head toward Charlie. "The thought of you is what gave me enough strength to get through all this. I'm sorry I caused you so much pain. Sorry I'm causing you pain now."

Foreheads touching, in a reiteration of his earlier words, Charlie hissed, "Don't you ever apologize to me, Jennilee-love. Ever. Not for any of this. You came back to me. That's all that matters."

Jennilee whispered, "I almost gave up. When Knot had me tied to that beam in the fish-house and he and Gear were torturing Jewel and Ben… Almost."

Jeff growled at the same time Jewel did.

Mac intervened, "Tell us about the fish-house, Jennilee."

Jennilee shrugged. "I have no memory of getting there. The last thing I remember from the kidnapping is… Making it back to the road. Ben on his knees. Gear holding a gun to his head. I thought they were gonna execute him right there. Knot's the one who made Gear back off so they could use Ben to make me fall in line."

"If they had you tied up at the fish-house, how'd you get loose?"

Jennilee laughed, a beautiful sound that dispelled the clouds of gloom hanging around like a steady wind dispels the stench of a rotten carcass. "Knot assumed my gun was my only weapon. Didn't even search. I had my little pocketknife in my watch pocket." Winked at Jeff as he fist-pumped. "While they were drinking and carousing and gloating, I urged Jewel to her feet—told her to go find Charlie—and she slipped out the door. They'd already hurt her so much, I knew she couldn't take any more. I was terrified it was already too late for her, but she came through like a champ. When they went back to torturing Ben…" Jennilee sucked in a breath. Bumping Jennilee under the chin with her head, Jewel commiserated. Charlie tangled his fingers in Jennilee's hair.

Taking comfort from her dog and her husband, Jennilee let it out in a rush. "They were so busy with Ben they didn't see me worming around and getting my knife out. Didn't see me cutting the ropes around my wrists and neck. They were so absorbed in their entertainment, they didn't even see me slide down the beam and cut the rope around my feet, then slide back up. Catching my breath, getting ready to make a run for the side door, I was wondering if I had enough strength left to force that huge old rusted thing open when Knot saw me. He tackled me to the floor and rolled me through the hatch and into the water. I don't remember anything after that, except trying to fight Knot off when he was attempting to drown me. Then I woke up in the hospital."

Mr. Toler spoke for the first time. "You don't remember anything else? Not how they died or how you ended up in that boat?"

"I would ask *what boat*, but that sounds redundant, as well as stupid. I told you everything I remember. There's a lot about that whole escapade I don't remember, and never want to. As for how they died, I'd venture to guess they had a falling out after I got away from them. They were white trash, mean drunk white trash, and I wouldn't put anything vile past them. They were all three obviously criminals, and mentally unstable to boot. If you want me to say I'm sorry they're dead and not going to spend the rest of their lives in jail on the public's dime, keep waiting. That entire family has had it in for me since I was little. I have nothing but the utmost contempt for the whole crowd."

Holding both hands up in a make-peace gesture, Mr. Toler tipped his head to Jennilee. "Nothing of the sort. I had to ask. To tell the truth, I'm glad it fell out the way it did. I didn't actually come out here to question you, merely came with the Chief here to pass on some good news. If they hadn't taken each other out, they'd have spent the next several lifetimes in prison. The crime perpetrated against you was merely the tip of the iceberg. Myself and several other organizations were close to closing an investigation against them—Knot Jones, especially—with charges of prostitution, human trafficking, prescription drug laundering, money laundering, you name it. You'll probably be getting visits from some other agencies as well."

"I don't know anything about their nefarious activities."

"Seems your aunt was Knot's girlfriend."

Jennilee shrugged. "We parted ways a long time ago. Her doings are none of my concern. I don't claim her and she's never claimed me."

Mr. Toler conceded with a nod. "Mac told me the same. Might interest you to know… We got an anonymous tip. Actually, the FBI received the brunt of it, along with a few other agencies who got tipped off, thanks to a friend of yours." Waved a hand at Jeff, who squirmed like Jewel when someone mentioned the word *vet*. Tickled about the ride, not so much with the destination.

Looking from one to the other, Jennilee asked, "Jeff? What do you have to do with an anonymous tip?"

Sucking in a breath, Jeff admitted, "Someone sent it to me with instructions to relay it to the nearest FBI office. Said they knew I'd been interested in catching your moms' murderers for forever, and this was pertinent information."

Finally relaxing a tad, Charlie bragged on his best bud, even though Mr. Toler was the only one who didn't already know. "Jeff's intent on joining them. Been working his way that way since high school. FBI'll be lucky to get him."

Jennilee asked slowly, almost dreading the answer. "What tip?"

"Well, then. Glad you asked. Mr. Rivenbark here received a letter with a safe deposit box key in it and a bank name and address."

Beaming like Jeff was his own firstborn and not merely his protege, Mac expounded. "Boy's got more sense'n a bird dog."

Charlie and Jennilee squeezed hands but didn't dare look at each other at this high praise, coming from people they valued for the second time in a matter of days.

"He took that letter straight to the authorities. Crowd took one look at his grades and accolades and aspirations and conceded he needed to be at the opening. You'll never guess what that box contained."

Jennilee cocked her head expectantly, a move uncannily mimicked by Jewel.

"Charlie, Jennilee..." Mac took a deep breath. "Knot kept a journal. Didn't know the sumbitch knew how to read, much less write. He detailed every murder, and there have been...a bunch. Way too many. Decades worth. Not just murders, kidnappings. He kept...souvenirs." Mac nodded at Jeff, who scooted closer. "Speaking of which, seeing's how Knot's dead and there won't be a trial..."

Digging in his pocket, Jeff held out a closed hand to Jennilee, as he'd once held his hand out to Mr. Donny. "Crowd awarded me the honor of doing this 'cause we've been friends so long."

Meeting his eyes, seeing nothing but love, Jennilee held out her cupped hand.

Dropping what he held, they all watched as Jennilee burst into tears, Angel hot on her heels.

Holding her shaking hand out to Charlie, Jennilee cried harder as he slipped her engagement and wedding rings back on her finger, right where they belonged.

A satisfied smile on his face, Mac nodded. "Since those are custom made and one of a kind, they were easy to identify. Found them in the fish-house with Knot's gear. Figured you'd rather have them now than later. I'd've gotten them to you sooner but I had to go through proper channels and a couple reams of paperwork all gussied up with a big ol' red tape bow."

Turning to Charlie, Jennilee sobbed. "I thought these were gone forever." Buried her face against his chest and wept. Finally lifting her head, tears slowing, Jennilee admitted, "I've felt...naked ever since he took them."

Brushing her hair back off her tear-wet face, Charlie smiled tenderly. "I already commissioned another set, rush order. Now you'll have a spare."

Jeff's wry observation made them all laugh. "If you have a spare set made for all the sparkles you've already given her... You're gonna have to build not just another jewelry box, but another house, Charlie Brown."

Tears still shining on her cheeks and in her eyes, Jennilee added, "I've felt so...adrift without my rings. I know they're just symbols, but... It broke my heart to come back to you without them, Charlie. Like I'd somehow...let you down."

Tangling his fingers in her hair, Charlie shook his head and admonished lovingly, "Silly woman. You back safe is all that matters."

Clearing his throat, Mr. Toler interjected, "You don't know how fortunate you are to have escaped him. You are the only woman who did. The *only* one. Since he killed your mothers, he's...escalated quite a bit. Refined his methods. Perfected his techniques. Very fortunate indeed. The man is...was... a complete and utter psychopath."

Jennilee's face hardened. "I clenched my fist and resisted as long as I could, but... He stomped Ben's fingers when I wouldn't give up my rings. When that didn't work... He and Gear started breaking Ben's fingers until I gave in. And then they..." Jennilee's breath hitched. "I still wouldn't take my rings off and give them to him but I unclenched my fist. Ben paid for my defiance. I should've just given in. I... couldn't. Something in me...just wouldn't cave without a fight."

Lifting her hand to his lips, Charlie kissed each finger in turn, more glad than he could say that her digits were unbroken. And still attached. More glad her shining spirit remained intact.

"While he was tormenting me with that, he talked about what he was going to do to..." Jennilee lifted anguished eyes to Angel. "When I told you to leave because it was about to be a bad time, I thought it was because of the hurricane. He said... He said..." Biting back a sound of abject pain, Jennilee blurted, "He was coming after you here. Said he was going to make me watch while they tortured you, and since you'd never clashed with Butch, they weren't going to wait to..."

Gulping a ragged breath, Jennilee bared her teeth. "He thought you were still here because your car was."

Charlie ground out, "Only way he could know that is if he had a spy here, or more likely, he's been spying on us from the river."

Jeff met Charlie's eyes as their thoughts ran the same path. "That skiff... The one that ended up on y'alls porch after the hurricane."

"No registration numbers."

"Just like the one Jennilee was found in."

Exchanging a significant glance with Jeff, unspoken words flowed as Charlie silently promised that avenue would be taken care of. Pronto.

If Mason and I.G. hadn't already. Charlie had merely told them to do whatever they needed to keep Jennilee safe. He'd been thinking more of an attack from the land side, but having vast quantities of experience, Mason and crew had probably considered all the angles— air, water, and land.

Unable to keep silent any longer, Jeff sat at attention with all the focus of Jewel about to pounce and deliver the killing blow to some small varmint. "Know what else was in that journal, Jennilee? You won't have to worry about you know who any more. Seems like Knot finally got as fed up with her whining as everyone else. She was only valuable to him as long as she was a cash cow. Seems her hooking and dealing have been funding his…pursuits for a long time. All he had to do was supply her some bad heroin and the problem took care of itself. Evidently they fancied themselves a modern day Bonnie and Clyde with a murderous bent and a heapin' side of psycho. Until Clyde got tired of Bonnie."

Mr. Toler frowned at Jeff's declaration, then gave in. It would soon be common knowledge anyway. "Your relative…was found yesterday at the end of a long dirt road to nowhere. Deceased. I'd offer my condolences, but given the nature of the problem, I don't see how they're appropriate."

Touching Jennilee's knee gently, Mac nodded. "Jennilee, your story jibes with Ben's. Mose stated when he got there, the other two were already dead inside and Knot was floating under the fish-house, also dead. Said he pulled you out of the skiff, cut Ben loose and staunched his wounds, then hightailed it for the hospital with the two of you and Jewel. Think we'll wrap this one up and close the case. Don't think anyone's gonna dig too deep into this cluster. It's just what it seems… Some white trash took it into their mealy heads to murder and pillage and they got their just desserts. Good thing Mose happened to drive out that way and find Jewel when he did. Any sooner and he'd've been caught in the middle of their little turf war. Any later and he'd've been too late to save you and Ben."

Mac's eyes said a lot more than his words.

Jennilee blinked. So Mac knew sorta what had gone down, just not all the details. She wasn't gonna say anything to the contrary, for sure and for certain. As far as she was concerned, that was exactly what happened.

CHAPTER 41

*E*xtremely battered but not entirely broken, Ben smiled up at Jennilee from his wheelchair. Going to her knees, Jennilee gently cradled his bandaged digits. Laid her cheek tenderly on his mangled hand and let her tears rain.

"Hey. Hey, pretty lady. None of that."

"I'm so sorry, Ben. I wouldn't have had this happen to you for the world. I should've just…"

"Hush that. Hush right now. You did exactly right. They were gonna hurt me whether you gave in or not, and watching you resist helped me stay strong. You are one brave, amazing lady, Jennilee. I'm honored to know you. I'm the one who should be apologizing to you. I was supposed to take care of you and I failed. Miserably."

Mason, Charlie, and Jeff simultaneously made the exact same rude sound.

Jeff beat the other two to it. "Now that the mutual pity party is over, can we just accept that everyone fought as hard as they could and did what they had to to survive? Instead of whining and feeling sorry for each other, the two of you should be rejoicing. You are the only two —The. Only. Two.—who survived Knot's rampage. He's been torturing and murdering people for decades. The two of you not only survived, you took him out. That's an accomplishment no one else can boast. Think of it this way... Because of the two of you, Knot will never, *ever*, hurt anyone else. No one else will ever have to wonder what happened to a loved one. Or spend the rest of their lives not knowing. Or find the body and have to live with the knowledge of the tortures he dispensed."

Sounding flippant, Jeff's eyes told another story. Privy to a lot of information about the investigation he hadn't shared with the rest of them, Jeff was closer than ever to his FBI goal.

Impressed with his drive and determination and his record, the FBI had sent several agents to speak with Jeff.

They'd met more than once, right here on the porch of Charlie's and Jennilee's house.

Here, because Jeff refused to leave. Not while Jennilee was still recovering.

Here, because he was savvy enough, determined enough, outstanding enough in his chosen field, that the FBI was willing to work with him in order to get him on board.

Besides, he hadn't been slacking while he'd been here. With power and internet restored, and with I.G.'s help and Mason's backing and the FBI's blessing, Jeff had dived deep into researching crimes and data bases. Working closely with the Feds and local LEOs he'd already contributed greatly to matching a spate of bodies and crime scenes to Knot's journal. Even caught a few the Feds had missed.

Why, Jeff and I. G. had already concocted a computer program to track like-crimes and correlate the data.

While Knot hadn't listed the names of his victims, he'd described them and the places he'd dumped the bodies—all up and down the East coast. Far too many aided and abetted by Jennilee's aunt, nearly twice as many without. Not always having the easy access to his cousin's heavy equipment, he'd had to be far more creative in disposing of the evidence.

A great many of the bodies had been found, but since there was no common denominator, no method to his madness—save an urge to cause pain and to destroy beautiful things—many of the crimes had never been linked.

Between Jeff's hard work prior to Jennilee's kidnapping and the evidence he'd produced to prove Knot had been instrumental in Iris' and Cynthia's deaths and the recent work he'd done...

Jeff was doing as much good as Knot had damage.

Speaking of doing good...

Mason shifted, and everyone's attention focused on him.

"Jennilee." Just that one word, and his whole mien softened. "I've seen how much you love the ocean, how much good being in and near it does you. I've got an island..."

Mason's benevolent offer got drowned out by Jeff's laughter. Holding his sides, Jeff sputtered, "I've...got...an...island." Jabbing a finger in Charlie's direction, he hooted and repeated, "I've got an island. Finally! Someone with more money than you! An island!"

A blink, and everyone on the porch joined in the merriment.

Waiting until he could be heard, Mason kept plugging. "In the Gulf. Private. Limited access. You're welcome, anytime. All of you. Except him." Jerking his massive head in Jeff's direction, Mason smirked evilly, making Jeff laugh so hard he slithered out of his chair.

Rolling on the porch floor, Jeff laughed some more. "If you think Jennilee will put up with you bullying me... Think again. She's always been my champion."

Blowing Jeff a kiss, Jennilee beamed. "Always will be."

MUCH LATER THAT SAME EVENING, thinking about Mason's offer and shooting a desultory once over at Jennilee's still healing bruises, Jeff looked glum. "If I'd been a little quicker, I coulda saved you a lotta grief. Sorry, Jennilee."

Jennilee's joyful laughter rang out, backed up by the different, *distant*, echo of another woman's jubilant accompaniment. "Jeff. Our dearest Jeff. Don't you dare. All this happened because it brought you one step closer to coming home. You're more than halfway through school and getting your degree, the FBI is seriously interested in recruiting you—and don't you dare let them undervalue you and your mad set of skills—and most important, you found our mothers' killers. Just like you promised so long ago."

"Yeah, but…"

Rising, clasping his face between her hands, Jennilee shook her head. "No buts. Everything happened just as it was supposed to. It's like you told me; You can't look at the bad. You have to see the good in all this. Look at all the new friends—brothers and sisters—we've gained from this experience. Mason and all his crew. Mr. Marty. You and Angel finally finding each other. Mose finally waking up to the reality of Suki. Ben. Even BOF, who, thanks to Charlie's sense of justice, just might actually turn out to be a decent human being instead of a worthless parasite. His family, which intersects in so many ways with ours. All the bad people that ended up gone or in jail. They won't ever hurt any one again."

Jeff stared moodily down into Jennilee's eyes. The goodness she radiated practically shone out like the full moon across the ocean.

"Even more, we're adding to our family. I figure in about six months or so, Rachel and Tim are gonna give their kids a new sibling. Another cousin for our kids to grow up with. And…" Dropping a hand to splay over her flat stomach, Jennilee beamed like the sun. "… in closer to nine months…"

Moving up behind her, Charlie covered her hand with his own and smirked at Jeff. "Better get busy, slowpoke. How else are our kids gonna be lifelong best buds and play on the same football team?"

Jeff blinked, blinked again, and whooped with delight. Picked Jennilee up and spun her in dizzying circles, laughing like a loon. Set her on her feet and backed her up against a mock-glaring Charlie with a stricken look on his face. Cupping her shoulders, he stammered, "Oops. Sorry. Are you okay? I didn't mean to…"

Throwing her arms around his neck, Jennilee buried her face and muffled her laughter. Pulled back and enthused, "I'm fine. We're fine. We can never thank you enough. Finish what you're doing and get back here as fast as you can. Let us know when you're ready and we'll pull some of our crews and get started on your house."

"Well…" Shooting Angel a moonstruck calf look, Jeff held out a hand. Waiting till she stepped close and took it, Jeff drew Angel even closer. "We were gonna wait, but… That weekend Angel went home with me… Let's just say—it took some doing but we've worked out our school and work schedules so we can be together—we're giving you fair warning not to plan anything for the third weekend in September."

Letting out a squeal, Jennilee hugged Jeff again, left him to Charlie's grinning back thumping to throw her arms around Angel.

"We were going to tell you, but then…all this happened. I need help… But you're…"

"Oh, sister! If you weren't a sister of my heart already, this would clinch it! And being pregnant doesn't mean I can't help with anything you need help with."

Hands over her face, Angel made a muffled sound, halfway between a laugh and a sob. Peeked at Jennilee through spread fingers. "Does anything ever disturb your…Zen? I love you so much and I'm so glad you're you!" Reaching out for Jeff's hand, Angel shared a look with him. "We want to… We'd like to… If it's alright with y'all…"

Somehow making sense of all that, Jennilee threw her arms around Angel again and squeezed tight. "Yes, to all of that! Do you want to have the wedding in the same place in our yard that we did, or… Ooh! Would y'all rather do it at the site of your future…"

Angel's turn to squeal, she turned puppy dog eyes on Jeff.

While Charlie was snickering and making string wrapped around his finger motions, Jeff was nodding enthusiastically.

"That would be…amazingly awesome!" Eyes locked with Angel's, everyone else invisible for all intents and purposes, Jeff let a slow grin cover his face.

He and Angel spoke simultaneously, "Under the big live oak."

Fist pumping, Charlie danced in a circle, snagged Jennilee and drew her into his exuberant movements. "We did it! We got Jeff a permanent woman…"

Jennilee chimed in, "…got him to move back home, and we've…"

He and Jennilee grinned and finished together, "…thoroughly corrupted both of you!"

Neither Jeff nor Angel looked up from the kiss they were totally immersed in, not even when Jewel added her high pitched yapping to the merriment.

CHAPTER 42

The third weekend in September rolled around all too quickly. Working methodically and—with a great deal of help from Angel's family and Grandy and Miz Sadie—waving her magic wand every which way with abandon, Jennilee beamed proudly as she watched the goings on. Handling the dress and tux part herself, she'd outdone herself with Angel's wedding dress and Jeff's tux.

In a repeat/reverse of hers and Charlie's wedding, now the maid of honor and best man were the bride and groom while she and Charlie were the matron of honor and best man. Getting a bird's eye view of Jeff striding purposefully down the aisle to take his place, and then eagerly anticipating Angel's arrival, Jennilee glimpsed a morsel of the joy their friends had felt watching hers and Charlie's nuptials.

All of their dreams were coming true, the pieces of their lives falling seamlessly into place.

On a beautiful, perfect fall day, with the afternoon sun beaming down out of the azure bowl of a cloudless sky, beneath the huge old live oak beribboned with streamers and twinkle lights, surrounded by an immense crowd of family and friends, Jeff and Angel said their I do's.

On the very spot where they'd unearthed material treasures.

On the very spot where they'd brought treasures worth far more to light.

Wearing a stunning—not that Jeff expected anything less—white dress with teal and gold accents, the teal the exact shade of Jeff's bedroom in Jennilee's and Charlie's house—and the color he and Angel'd agreed on for their bedroom in the house they were about to start building—Angel was radiant.

A dress Jennilee had lovingly sewn, complemented underneath by the same sexy blue garter Jennilee had worn and loaned to Angel.

The silver penannular clasp had been repurposed to hold Angel's curls back in a flower bedecked twist. Around her neck, strung on a new chain, was the golden locket they'd found on this very spot.

Slipping a hand in the pocket of his tux—charcoal with teal and gold accents—also sewn by Jennilee, Jeff fingered the mermaid keychain Jennilee'd given him. A talisman he'd carried with him every day since he picked it up off his bathroom counter and unwrapped it. A silver and jeweled replica to remind him of the real mermaid in his life. The one who could work miracles.

The one who conversed with ghosts and dolphins.

The one who'd given him his lady-love.

The brave, loving, beyond wonderful mermaid who was not only his sister of the heart, and his best friend's/brother of the heart's wife, but the one who would be sister-in-law to his own wife and aunt to their children.

Together, the four of them were...magical.

As their lives would be. Living near to each other, watching their kids grow up together, growing old together.

Standing under the live oak later as the brilliant day was turning to dusk, just the four of them, colored twinkle lights glowing as if they were real fairies, surrounded by family and music and the delicious scent of one of Mr. Jubal's perfectly barbecued pigs, a slight breezed wafted past.

And with it, in the tones of a well bred Northern lady, they all four heard Amelia's dulcet tones echo quietly above the sounds of music and merriment, "Well done, my friends. Well done."

ABOUT THE AUTHOR

As H S Skinner—and sometimes Heidi Skinner—I'm finally introducing my imaginary friends to my real friends! I write everything from sweet to spicy with some intrigue and fantasy thrown in!

I love cooking for my huge family, and gardening, and dogs and dragons and...

Welcome to my worlds and I hope you enjoy my imaginary friends as much as I do!

ALSO BY H S SKINNER

Jennilee's Light

My first book baby! And…precursor to Amelia's Echoes. Set in coastal NC, Jennilee's Light begins with a murder mystery and follows the boy and girl left behind through their tumultuous early lives into adulthood and a happily ever after.

Willow's Green Man

A spicy stand alone romance novel between unlikely protagonists and also a bridge between stories. The characters in Willow and Jennilee meet in Amelia's Echoes.

Jilly's Mural

A Young Adult fantasy with all the requisite epic fantasy elements. A young girl is sucked into an alternate world full of dragons and elves and magic in a good versus evil battle. Published under **Heidi Skinner** so there's a degree of separation in my adult and non-adult books.

Made in the USA
Middletown, DE
06 October 2023